A Storm
In From The Sea

A Storm In From The Sea

A Morgan Crew Mystery

Arthur Lee

Leeward Publishers, LLC
Winter Garden, Florida

A Storm In From The Sea

A Morgan Crew Mystery
By
Arthur A. Lee

This is a work of fiction. Names, characters, places and incidents are either the product of the author's imagination or are used fictionally, and resemblance to actual persons living or dead, business establishments, events or locales is entirely coincidental.

Copyright © 2009 & 2010 by Arthur A. Lee &

LEEWARD PUBLISHERS, LLC.

ISBN: 978-0615807188

Leeward Publishers
An Imprint of Leeward Publishers, LLC

To Jackie

**Thank you for your encouragement.
Thank you for pushing me to finish.**

Other Books by the Author

The Morgan Crew Mystery Series

The Las Vegas Murders
A Deadly London Fog
The Four Seasons Murders
The Hawaiian Sunset Murders
The Spy Who Would Not Speak
The West Texas Murders

A Storm In From The Sea
By
Arthur A. Lee

Contents

ONE - The Killers

A dozen sea gulls circled loudly above the nearly empty streets under black clouds outlined in silver by a full moon. A flock of wet, dirty pigeons gathered around a pool of dark rainwater in a trash lined gutter, picking at garbage that had been flushed to the side of the street by the rain. The storm that had wracked the northern California coastal town of San Marcos had blown itself out an hour before midnight. A damp, cold breath of ocean air drifted through the sad streets and past the derelict buildings of North Harbor, carrying with it an icy drizzle.

People seldom walked the streets of North Harbor at that time of night. Fear is a thing quickly learned, and those who called North Harbor home learned to fear the dirty streets and dark places. There were those people who lived in the darkness of North Harbor streets; the night people who preyed on those setting aside their fear just long enough to walk swiftly from building to building or from tavern to car.

Every third telephone pole lining the streets of North Harbor held a street lamp. Few of them worked however, and the one or two which were working threw a faint, eerie yellow tint across the low, thin fog which hugged the streets and broken curbs.

The barely perceptible rhythm of a base drum cut through the silence, coming from one of the taverns which would not close before the sun rose. The thump-thump . . . thump-thump . . . thump-thump-thump beat seemed to go on without ending. The older of the two men sitting in the black Cadillac parked at the curb, as far from any light as possible,

1

became irritated at the pounding, and wished it would end. The younger man picked up the rhythm with the fingertips of his left hand, drumming against the leather-covered dashboard. After a few seconds of this the older man, sitting behind the steering wheel, turned and looked at his partner.

"Cut that shit out," he said.

"Hey man," the younger one said, smiling and not stopping his tapping. "It's just music."

"No it isn't. It's annoying shit. Cut it out and keep your mind on business." The young man shrugged his shoulders, stopped tapping the dashboard, and leaned back in the leather seat and smiled. He said, "OK, man."

They had driven into North Harbor a few minutes before midnight, through the remnants of the storm. At first they could not find the address they had been given, many of the streets were unnamed and the heavy rain limited their vision, but finally they had found the house they wanted. It was a sad looking, beat up, forty-year-old, two-storied house that needed to be painted too many years ago. The broken front porch was filled with rusted crab traps, piles of useless rope, fishing nets, and weather-beaten cardboard boxes holding trash.

They had parked at the curb across the street from the house and studied it for a few minutes. To the right of the house was a vacant lot, filled with weeds and garbage, hiding the remnants of a building's crumbling foundation. To the left was another house, as run down and squalid as the house they were paid to find. There was a pale yellow glow coming from the front window of that house; the house they were looking for was dark. Across the street was a burned out building with darkened, derelict houses on either side.

The street in front of the Cadillac and to the rear was empty. A few drops of rain, pushed around by the wind, were hitting the windshield so that the wipers on the Cadillac had to be set at a slow interval. The night was cutting cold.

They left the engine running to keep the heater on. A black Cadillac, in that neighborhood, would attract the attention of anyone passing, but the two men knew beforehand that it would be unusual for anyone to be outside, walking, at that time of night.

They had walked slowly and cautiously to the front door of the house, their tan trench coats pulled tightly around them. The younger man had walked to the front window and tried to peer inside the house. Years of unwashed grime on the window and the darkness inside the house kept him from seeing anything inside.

The older man searched for a doorbell. He knocked loudly on the door, the sound reverberating through the cold night air. He looked around quickly to see if anyone had heard. The street remained empty and no lights came on in any of the houses nearby. No one answered the knock and both men agreed without speaking that the people they were looking for were not there.

They had worked together for nearly two years, a long time in their line of work. They had gotten to know each other and how each other thought. The jobs became routine for them. They had learned to move as with one unspoken thought. They could react together as either one would react alone.

They returned to the shelter of the Cadillac; the interior light bulbs had been removed so that when they opened the doors the street remained in darkness. They understood without having to discuss it that they would wait until the men returned home, as long as that took.

Starting the engine, the car was slowly backed up to the parking lot of a deserted convenience store at the corner. They parked close to the side of the building, in a deep shadow, the front end of the car extending beyond the walls just enough for them to see the house the three men they hunted would return to.

They sat quietly, only an occasional gust of wind from the ocean and the base thumping from the unknown bar broke the stillness of the night. The older man sat behind the wheel of the car, thinking. He thought of retirement once again.

He would be fifty-nine years old in a few months, an unusually long life for someone in his line of work where his peers seldom lived beyond forty. He thought of the house he owned down in the Florida Keys and of the time he wished he could spend there with Clare, if Clare would still have him after all these years. He had lived with Clare outside Chicago for almost four years, before she discovered what he did for a living. Then she left; no tears, no angry words, no yelling, and no incriminations. She just packed a bag and left. Of course he was able to find her; his connections were everywhere. But that was more than a year ago and he had not contacted her yet.

He arranged a good job for her with a good salary. He received monthly reports. One man she met, who was getting too close, dropped out of sight. He just disappeared without saying goodbye. He could arrange that sort of thing, too.

He thought of whether he had enough money put aside to retire. He added up in his mind all the cash drops all over the world; the safe deposit boxes stuffed with cash, the self-store rental units holding suitcases of more cash, the bags of money hidden in walls. It added up again, as it had the last time, to a few thousand less than three million. But to some people there is never enough. He needed more. He wasn't sure exactly how much more, but he did need more.

He thought of the man sitting next to him. He was hardly a man, really just a boy of 22 years. He had found him in New York, breaking into an Upper Eastside apartment.

****

When the boy had crawled through the bedroom window he had no idea what was happening inside. It was just a fairly easy burglary, something he did regularly. He stood unseen in the shadows of the doorway, calmly taking in the execution of the couple who lived there. It was a professional job; the boy could see that. The couple had been bound hand and foot with duct tape, more tape across their mouths. They lay on the bed, face down. Two muffled shots from a .22 revolver behind the right ear of each and the job had been over, except for the cleanup, he assumed.

The young man had stepped out of the shadows; the killer turned and leveled the revolver at the boy's chest. "You gonna leave them here?" the boy asked. A thin smile crossed his lips but he didn't show any fear.

"Who are you?" the killer asked.

"I just stopped by for the gold and jewelry and maybe for some cash if they leave it lying around. The stereo and TV are too damn heavy," he said looking around the expensively furnished apartment. "I take what I came for. You give me a hunnert'. I'll help you dump the bodies. I mean, you ain't gonna leave them here. And it'll be quicker if we work t'gether."

He was dressed in tight fitting, faded blue jeans and a new, black-leather, waist length, jacket. His hair was long and greased back, looking like a throwback to the fifties. But the killer also saw that the young man was solidly built and carried an easy, natural smirk. He had a confident grin that suggested he was not new to scenes of violence, that he had long since accepted and lived comfortably inside a world of brutality.

While the killer was considering his first impression of

the boy, he was being sized up carefully by the young burglar. The man was tall, maybe 6'2", and in good physical condition, considering what the boy saw as old age, perhaps 45 years. In fact the killer was well into his fifties but a daily routine that included a heavy workout and a five mile run, kept him looking ten years younger than he was. His hair was dark gray, thick, and cut short. There was something to the man's steel blue eyes that was unusual and almost frightening, a coldness, a hardness, the boy had never seen before. The man's eyelids hung casually, they reminded the boy of a Robert Mitchum movie he had watched on TV a few nights before.

Then the killer saw something that surprised him. Here was a young stranger who had just witnessed the execution of two people, a boy who looked like a street thug. Yet, he was wearing surgical gloves, just as the killer was wearing, and had worn for years. Maybe there was something to this boy? Something that belied the first impression the killer had of him.

He lowered the revolver but held it ready just in case. He relaxed his shoulders slightly and saw the boy relax his tightly wound body ever so slightly. They were a long way from trust, but testing a careful half-trust seemed to be warranted.

"What's your name, boy?"

The killer phrased the question carefully. If he were too unstrung, calling him a boy would bring a quick reaction: "I ain't no boy!" or something like that. If he were as immature as he appeared, he would reply with a street name.

"James Leonard," he answered without hesitating. "What's your name?" he paused and grinned, then said, "Old man?" he chuckled.

Ha! A sense of humor. Not a bad thing if the boy could control it. And the way he answered was just enough of a challenge to suggest he wasn't afraid. James, not Jim or Jimbo, or some such foolish street name. Shows some pride. Not bad, not bad at all.

"Do you want to talk? Maybe have some coffee?" the killer asked the boy.

James looked across the room at the two bodies bleeding into the satin comforter and then down at the man's revolver.

"Sure," he said, looking up at the man. "You want I should make some here or should we go somewhere? There's a Starbucks down the street."

"Here's fine. The kitchen's behind you."

They sat at a small wrought iron table with a heavy, smoked glass top. James had found some good Italian roast in the freezer, a coffee grinder, and an espresso machine. He made two double cups of strong espresso, pouring them into a couple of ceramic cups, and then steamed some milk, which he carefully floated onto the black coffee. The killer sat and watched James work. The boy knew how to make good coffee, and he worked efficiently, which had to come from experiencing some of the good things life offered.

James sat at the table across from the killer and sipped some of the rich foam from his cup. Looking over the rim at the older man, he said, "So, anyway. You never did tell me your name."

"Later," the man replied. "What makes you think I'd pay you to help me dispose of the bodies instead of killing you?"

"Because you're a pro. You don't kill unless you get paid or unless you got to," he said. "Maybe you'll kill me, if you think you have to. Or maybe you'll figure out that you maybe can use me, that I ain't no threat to you. I don't give a fuck about those two people in there," the boy said, pausing to sip some more foam from the coffee and then wiping a bit of it from his lips with the back of his hand.

"They could'a lived or died for all I care. I was gonna take what I could from them and if I had to kill them to do it, I would'a. I mean, I would of preferred to find no one at home. They usually out on'a Friday night, which is why I'm here now. So you killed'em instead of me havin' to do it. Now you got two bodies to get rid of. You alone might have a hard time, I mean, carrying them downstairs and all, without being seen. Maybe I can help . . .. For a hunnert bucks. Like you, I don't do nothin' for nothin'. And dead bodies don't bother me. I dumped a couple of my own in the East River over the years."

The killer stirred through the thick foam with a small spoon to get at the strong coffee underneath. He was considering what James had said. Maybe the boy could be useful. And he was right, killing was something he got paid to do, he took no pleasure in it. He had never killed anyone before without good reason or good pay, he was not about to start now. If he had to kill this boy, he would think it though first, consider all the possibilities, and weigh all the reasons for and against.

The biggest reason for killing the boy was, of course, that he had witnessed the killings. Never before, in a more than thirty year career, had anyone witnessed an execution by this man. He planned carefully, spending days, often weeks, working out every contingency. But he also knew that there were random occurrences, which could not be planned for. He had played the odds and had never been caught nor seen in all those years of work. This kid, this James Leonard, was one of those impossible to plan for random happenings that had to be taken care of one way or another.

"Suppose I do pay you to help me," he said to James. "Just what do you have in mind for getting rid of the bodies?"

"Depends," he answered. "Whoever paid you either wanted them dead for revenge or as an example. For revenge, they gotta be put somewhere where they ain't gonna be found. If they was an example, they gotta be found quick so as to tell others not to fuck up like they did. Which way is it?"

"OK, assume it was for revenge. How would you dispose of the bodies? Dump them in the East River?"

"No, man. That's stupid. They gonna float and be found in the morning. I once dumped a nigger drug dealer in a meat grinder in this dog and cat food processing plant down in Jersey. Now that's how you dump some fucker so they won't never be found."

James put his empty cup down and leaned back in the soft leather dinette chair. He pressed his left arm against his side, feeling for the weight of the Glock semi-auto tucked into his belt. It would be any minute now; the killer would either go for his revolver or go for his wallet. James felt he had only a fifty - fifty chance of taking the man, but that was all he ever expected. Life was like that; you only could expect a fifty - fifty chance at best.

"You know," he said to the man. "You haven't answered even one of my questions. . . But you sure do ask a lot of questions. Now, I been good enough to answer you all your questions. It's time you started answering some of mine."

"James," the killer said sighing. "In some ways you're a smart young man, you've even impressed me somewhat. If you aren't bullshiting me, you have some experience, and you make very good coffee. Yet, you are, in other ways, very tiring. My gun is lying on the table about four inches from my hand. I have two rounds left and, as you can see, the hammer is still cocked. Your gun is tightly wedged under your belt and safely zipped under your jacket. Oh yes, I'm good enough to recognize that you're carrying. Considering that, I don't have to answer any of your questions. At this moment, unless things change, you're dead. So for me to answer a dead man's questions is kind of . . . Well silly, isn't it?

"I figure," he went on after drinking from the cup once again. "You might be thinking you have some kind of chance against me, I mean if I decide I need to put you away. Don't fool yourself. I have probably twenty years experience on you. You'd have to think about it and I wouldn't."

"OK, mister man," James said, still grinning. "So you got me. Now, do I get my hunnert' bucks and help you, or what?"

"You don't get anything. I don't need to dispose of the bodies. They need to be found as they are. All I need to do is decide if you get left with them or not."

James, still smiling, offered to make another cup of coffee. He knew then that the man wasn't going to kill him. If he was going to, it would have been done long before then. He was being studied, his reaction to everything the killer said and did was being carefully considered, weighed, and filed away.

"So, like I said, this is some kind of example killing," he said to the killer. "Probably not sex or something like that. Someone that close wouldn't want the bodies found. I don't think you're the type to get involved in anything that stupid and risky anyway. So it's probably money and maybe the mob. That's ok; you don't need to tell me I'm right. So you don't need help this time, but maybe next time you do. All you gotta do is trust me," he said.

"Pull out your wallet," the man said. "Slowly. Toss it, easy, across the table, away from my gun."

James did as the man said, moving very slowly but still smiling and looking directly into the killer's eyes. The man picked up the wallet with his left hand, leaving his right hand on the table very near the gun. He flipped it open and risked taking his eyes off of James to look inside. He pried out a driver's license and without looking at it slipped it into his shirt pocket.

"With that," he said, "I can find you, I can find your mother if you have one, I can find your sister if you have one, I can find your girlfriend if you have one. You don't know who I am or who hired me. Go to the police and you incriminate yourself, a cheap burglar trying to cover up for killing two people. Go to the police and they will never find me. But I will find you."

He paused for a minute, staring deeply into the boy's eyes.

"Keep your mouth shut and maybe . . . just maybe . . . I might have work for you that will pay a lot more than a hundred dollars to dump some bodies, or some cheap B&E. In the meantime, put the cups and the spoons in the dishwasher. Use a lot of soap and turn it on full cycle. We both wore surgical gloves; with the cups washed there will be nothing left to put either of us here."

"Hell, man," James said. "Why not leave the fucking cups for someone else to wash?"

"You can get DNA from the saliva we left on the rims of the cups. Now wash them as I said. And if we ever meet in the future, don't . . . DON'T! . . . ever question what I say again."

****

They did meet again and James was taken on as a full-time apprentice to Robert Cordessco. All of that Robert thought about as he sat behind the wheel of the Cadillac, beside the vacant store, in the cold night of North Harbor, waiting for the three people they would kill to return.

Then headlights appeared in the street in front of them, interrupting Cordessco's thoughts. The lights went off as the beat up '79 Ford pick-up pulled into the driveway of the house they were watching. Shadows moved from the truck to the porch and into the house. It appeared, from the parking lot a block away, that here were three of them, maybe two holding onto the third and all but carrying him into the house.

Dim lights were turned on inside. Cordessco and Leonard waited a few moments then drove slowly, without headlights, to the curb in front of the house. They glanced to the front and rear, and then both climbed out of the Cadillac.

They each carried short barreled Winchester pump shotguns, the stocks removed and pistol grips installed. They walked quickly to the front door and James, in one motion, not breaking his stride, kicked open the flimsy door. The three men Cordessco and Leonard were looking for were in the living room of the house. One of them was slumped on a battered couch; the other two were standing nearby, looking at him.

James fired at the one on the right, cutting the man in half. Robert fired at the other as he started to run up the stairs, opening the man's back. The one on the couch jumped up and was running to the rear of the house. He ran into the wall separating the front room from what should have been a dining room and bounced off. He was staggering but he was young and quick and made a difficult target. Leonard fired at him, the blast ripping into the wall next to the man.

Cordessco pulled a 9mm Smith & Wesson from under his jacket and fired once as the man ran through a rear door of the house. He fired twice more but the man was gone into the darkness of the night.

They would find him, their job would not be called done until this man, too, was dead. They were paid for three, they would deliver three. But the noise would attract someone and that meant they could not chase him, they would have to find the man later. They walked slowly back to their car and drove off into the low fog and out of North Harbor.

TWO - Frederick Mark

Downtown is what the locals call the few square blocks of office buildings and small shops. Visitors to San Marcos from San Francisco and L.A. laugh when locals call it Downtown, but they don't laugh at the money held, controlled, and used in San Marcos' Downtown.

Although the Spanish first settled San Marcos in 1783, the oldest building in Downtown dates back to only 1981. Everything older than that has been ripped away to make way for the new buildings of steel and glass.

San Marcos is in a pleasant, small valley, which was once thickly wooded and green. Now, most of the native trees are gone. Office buildings and a shopping mall had been poured into the middle of town by those with money enough to do the pouring. Sculptured nursery stock now sits in pots and carefully planned little parks. The tallest and newest of the towers is the Mark Building, twenty-five floors of black glass, concrete, and steel overlooking San Marcos Harbor.

The bank owned by the Mark Corporation occupies the ground floor and the next two stories. The floors above are occupied by law firms, developers, investment brokerages, and overly expensive doctors, specializing in treating the illnesses of old, wealthy retired men who come to live their life out in San Marcos and in trying to keep rich women looking younger than they are.

The twenty-fifth floor penthouse of the Mark building is one suite of offices. In this suite Frederick Mark sat that day in the air-condition darkness of his marble floored office, behind the eight-foot long, hand carved mahogany desk he had brought from Spain several years ago. As he spoke into the phone, his carefully manicured fingernails tapped a military cadence on the in-laid leather of the desktop.

He spoke coldly and calculatingly into the phone, in a soft, whispered, deep voice intended to make the person listen intently or miss what was said.   "You don't understand", he said slowly, methodically, as he liked to do when hurting people, pronouncing each word, each syllable · with knife-edge perfection. "The girl came to me of her own free will. She's not a child. She wants to stay. And I am enjoying her. It will cost you if you want me to kick her out."

He listened to the pleading, the groveling on the line for a moment then interrupted, speaking a little louder, a little firmer, but equally as slow. "I don't give a damn. I don't give a damn what happens to you. I don't give a damn about your work, your business; I don't give a damn about the girl except that she's a really good fuck. Look, I don't have the time for this. I get the money, you get the girl. Until that time, as long as she wants to stay where she is, she'll stay."

He listened again. A smile crossed his lips. The same kind of smile that arose from some dark inner cavern when hearing a woman cry out in pain under his grasp. The kind of pleading cries that brought so much pleasure.

He paused and let the line hang in silence a moment or two as he sipped from the delicate china cup, filled with the strong, dark coffee he enjoyed. His secretary had carefully placed the silver tray on his desk, hoping with shaking hands to find the correct spot, the place where her boss insisted the tray be placed every day. The silver tray's feet were softly padded in velvet so as not to mar the polished surface of his prized desk.

Then he said into the phone, this time forcefully and quickly, his short patience having already been used up,

"You're wasting my time. There's nothing more to say. The girl wants to fuck for drugs. My doctor has prescribed certain medications for her which seems to satisfy her. I am doing nothing illegal. I haven't kidnapped her and she's free to go anytime that she wants. Until you pay me I won't force her to leave."

Frederick Mark did not wait for an answer before he placed the phone carefully and gently on its cradle. He leaned back in the soft, black leather chair, the fingers of his left hand again tapping a cadence on the desk as he looked out the dark, smoked glass windows of his office, onto the harbor below. He turned his chair slowly and once again admired what he owned, his prized possessions.

An original Monet hung lonely on the darkened left wall, illuminated by a spotlight hidden above in the ceiling. Pre-Columbian statuary lined a series of glass and chrome shelves, lit by fluorescent tubes. Frederick knew little of works of art and less about history, but experts had told him that the ugly little clay figurines were genuine. They had been smuggled out of Central America, and were worth three times what the thief would sell them for. That was enough for Frederick to make another cash purchase.

There was a small collection, five pieces in all, of jewel encrusted, gold and silver boxes with delicately hinged lids, smuggled out of Southeast Asia. Frederick had no idea of their use or purpose, but he knew a good purchase when he saw one.

Next to these was an eighteen-inch tall, black-wood, carved figurine from Africa. It was the ugliest thing Frederick had ever seen, with its swollen stomach and fat, sagging breasts that hung nearly to the top of the fat, bent legs. Its head appeared swollen, the eyes bulging, the lips puffed out to outrageous proportions. But the dealer had told him, with her usual accuracy that the figure had been "removed" from a museum in Cameroon and was very valuable.

The one thing Frederick regretted was that his things were merely a collection of inanimate objects. Too bad, he would often think, that people could not be in his permanent collection also. Carla, the antiques dealer who had directed Frederick toward the purchases of much of his collection, should be there.

Frederick closed his eyes and pictured this woman who seemed to need pain as much as he enjoyed inflicting it. Heat rose in him and he found himself roughly massaging the swelling mass between his legs. He heard once again the echoes of her screams of lust under his fingers as he moved them across her body, tightening here on the soft flesh, pushing slowly but inevitably there, almost to the point of puncturing the woman's skin. And she kept coming back; he never had to ask. Sometimes he would turn her away, roughly and caustically, telling her to leave. And she kept coming back. Frederick enjoyed that.

And of course he could not forget his wife of too many long years. He would have loved to have her bronzed in some position befitting the bitch. She never understood him, he thought once again. Suzanne never understood what sex should be. She lived in some dream world of meaningless soft touches and caresses, he thought. His fist came down hard on the desktop, rattling the china cups. Sex, like everything else in life, is dominance, he thought. "Twist people until they break or let them twist you," he said out loud, softly, to himself.

He turned his attention from women once again to the view of the harbor below, framed by the dark glass wall of his office. He had built his tower, carefully. He selected the site and bought the necessary variances from city employees cheaply. He had done all that so that whenever he finished a business deal, he would be able to sit back, as he was then, and look out over the bay with its small mouth opening out onto the Pacific.

He felt good, pleased with himself when wrapping up a business deal. He was certain that the meaningless, small person who wanted the girl back would come up with the money. A piddling sum to Frederick Mark, meaningless to someone who had acquired hundreds of millions, he laughed out loud. But the little man would have to sell everything he had, including maybe his soul. Frederick felt good. It was a feeling similar to seeing a woman cry out in pain, very satisfying. Very sexual.

Business to Frederick Mark had little to do with the making of money. Money was always there at the end. It wasn't the money, he told himself, it was the power. The power to destroy, to control, to see people hurt, to hear people plead. There lay the pleasure of business. As well as the pleasure of sex.

He laughed at the sad state of the person who would bring him the money in less than twenty-four hours. He was sure the money would be there in that time. He was seldom wrong when it came to people. Twenty-four hours for the small person to gather together more money than many people from the lower classes had ever seen before.

How could anyone subject themselves to that, he wondered? "Pigs", he said softly, aloud again without realizing it, his words echoing off the walls of the cold, empty office. "Slime, that's all they are. I'll teach them all a God damn good lesson."

Never again would he be laughed at, he assured himself, as they had done when he was a child. Never again would he be dressed in hand-me-downs. Never again would he go hungry.

The image of his parents flashed across his mind. He didn't like to think about them, he fought the images away, but now and then, without warning, they would return. Bright flashes that blacked out his sight and turned his stomach until he tasted the bile he had swallowed back so many times in his youth.

Images of their attempts at meaningless happiness raced before him. Their miserable blue-collar existence. The way they accepted filthy poverty rather than acquiring money, all the time wallowing in simplicity and calling it happiness. They left him to all those years of humiliation, believing he was merely average, when he wanted to scream out to them that he was special. But he could never find the words. He had tried many times but was never able to say anything, to do anything. Until that night when they slept holding each other in their arms.

Why did they do it to him? Why hadn't they acquired wealth for him? Why hadn't they been able to buy him what he wanted? He had waited patiently for all those years. He had wanted to communicate to them that he was not like the other boys who ran and played ball. His mind played life as if it were a chess game. He felt he could calculate all the possible moves of any situation well into the future, when others could not see what was happening in the immediate present. All they had to do was see that and acquire wealth for him so that his special talents could be used.

But they didn't, he had to acquire the beginnings of wealth himself. The paltry life insurance they carried was the start for Frederick Mark. Watching the flames lick at their bed before he left the burning house was the first step toward the life that should have been his from birth.

And when these memories danced around inside his head, despite his attempts at fighting them away, he knew what the last remembrance would be, as it always was. He saw the sudden explosion of flames as he walked slowly from the house. He could feel the heat on his face and hands as he stood at the curb, a man at seventeen, watching the embarrassingly small and ordinary house burn down around his parents. Then the fireman put his arm around Frederick's shoulder to comfort the newly orphaned boy. He had shrugged the unwelcome, dirty sleeve away.

The one token of his childhood taken with him and kept close by all these years felt heavy in his vest pocket. From the pocket he took out the scratched and dented old Zippo cigarette lighter, the one he had bought from a boy at school for a single dollar when a dollar meant so much. He had used the lighter to start the fire that night. He moved it between his fingers, feeling the stark coldness of the cheap metal. He ran his fingers over the familiar scratches and dents that he could find without looking.   He carefully replaced it in his vest pocket, as safe a place where it had remained all those years, and patted the full pocket lovingly.

The ringing of his phone brought him back from his wanderings.   The afternoon was barely half over and Frederick Mark had hours left in the day to make money and to see people squirm.

THREE – Murder

At eight PM, Monday through Saturday, Frederick Mark would check his gold Rolex against the time shown on the face of the elaborately carved 17th century grandfather clock that stood against the wall opposite the lavish white marble fireplace.

He would take a moment to finish whatever he was working on, then, satisfied with the day's work, he would leave his office and drive his Rolls Royce to the Country Club for dinner and his usual three martinis.

It was about time, he thought, to check once again on the progress his people were making on buying the Country Club outright. He scribbled a note to himself and carefully laid the paper near his telephone. As soon as the purchase was complete he would change its name to "The Mark Country Club". He laughed again. It had a ring to it, a good sound, and he would be able to derive years of pleasure in deciding who would be a member and who would be excluded.

By eleven P.M. every day, he was home. His children would be asleep or at least in their rooms so as not to bother him. He would see them briefly at breakfast. Any more than that and they would become pests. They would sit at the foot of the large table in the dining room while Frederick sat at his usual place at the head. The older girl at his left, the younger at his right, far enough away not to be heard, but close enough to be seen and watched in case they made a mess.

His wife of sixteen years would be in her room when he arrived home each evening, snoring deeply, with an empty bottle of vodka on the bedside table, as usual. Suzanne would inevitably sleep well past his 7 AM departure each morning, Monday through Saturday. Sunday he would sleep until 9 AM, enjoy a light breakfast alone, and leave at precisely 10 AM for the club and a day of golf. The routine never changed. Routine was a good thing, he was sure of that. When a routine was kept, people knew what was expected of them and there could not be any excuse for falling short of what Frederick expected.

Nothing was different that night, as routine demanded. As the resonant chimes of the grandfather clock slowly rang out the hour, Frederick Mark checked the time with his Rolex. He finished reading the memo report from his real estate broker, closed the cover of the file, and placed it carefully on the far right corner of his desk, adjusting it to be exactly equidistant to the desk's edges.

A glance at the desk and around the room told him everything was in place, neat and clean, as he required his office to be. Filth had no place near Frederick Mark. A clean, neat, orderly world was the sign of a successful world. The pigs and slime of the other world were filthy, that's why they lived in poverty, he reminded himself, and that's why they should suffer. Frederick Mark was successful, rich, powerful, and he owed much of what he had to his ability to be clean, he told himself proudly as he adjusted to his perfection the diamond ring on the left little finger of his perfectly manicured hand.

One more glance around the room to make sure nothing was out of place and he left.

Stepping out of his private elevator into the lobby of his building, he walked slowly toward the front door. The security guard at the door stood when he saw Mr. Mark approach, as was usual. He prepared to open the door for his employer. The guard had spent the last thirty minutes walking nervously around the lobby, checking and then re-checking, everything. He looked for dirt, smudges, cigarette butts, gum wrappers, anything that was out of place. As he did this, the janitor-supervisor did the same, wiping a clean rag here and there, checking the ashtrays, looking for any sign of microscopic dust in the front windows.

As Frederick walked through the lobby he glanced at the tall gray marble ashtrays next to the elevators holding pure white sand with a large 'M' pressed into the surface. He had to fire a janitor just the week before for allowing a cigarette butt to remain in one of them, a late leaving accountant having crushed it out just moments before Frederick walked by. Frederick Mark does not tolerate dirt; everyone had better understand that.

The guard saluted and smiled uneasily. Frederick Mark stepped by him without acknowledging his presence or looking directly at him. But he had surveyed the man's uniform, in one quick, experienced glance, to make sure it was clean, pressed, and presentable. He examined his hair, to make sure it was neatly trimmed, his hands, to make sure they were clean, and the man's shoes, to make sure they were polished and free of dust. The guard was clean, as one should be if in Frederick's employ.

He had often lectured to ungrateful people at the club, that one had to be sure people in subservient roles understand their place. Too much casualness with them is a bad thing, he insisted. It was enough that the man who held the door open for him, smiled nervously, and bowed his head as Frederick passed, had a job. For Frederick Mark to admit the guard existed, to actually speak with him or to thank him for doing what was expected of him would have been too much. One disciplines one's employees, one teaches one's servants, other than that they are not spoken to. If everyone, he often said, would raise their children as he raised his, when they grew into employees and servants, they would naturally know their place.

Outside there was a chilly dampness coming in from the sea; a storm would be settling in soon, Frederick thought. A slight breadth of a salty breeze blew across him. He buttoned his coat up around his neck.

He took a deep breadth of the clean, exhilarating sea air and began to walk the few steps to his car, which waited at the curb. The first bullet hit him squarely in the middle of his chest as he began to turn towards the car. The breadth of fresh, salty air he had started to take in exploded from him as he was picked up off the ground and pushed roughly back against the glass at the front of his building.

The second bullet hit him a fraction below his heart, the third in his abdomen. The bullets seemed to explode as they hit, tearing his torso open, from the neck to below the crotch.

The police reported so much damaged to Frederick Mark's body that the eventual loss of blood the corpse suffered was nearly total. The three bullets that hit him could not be found, save for tiny chards riddled throughout pieces of the body. The police speculated with good cause that they were explosive bullets, designed to fragment on impact.

No one would mark calendars, no one cried. Several people would celebrate the death, however. Life in San Marcos would go on.

FOUR - I Am Morgan Crew

 I had wanted to eat dinner alone at the country club. After two weeks in L.A., dealing with the family lawyers, accountants, and the people who ran the various family businesses, I felt I needed to get away from the world, from reality, from life and death. I needed to retreat to a quiet corner where I would be sheltered from the intrusions of life and reality. So I quickly returned to San Marcos.

 I had my Wall Street Journal to finish. I wanted to sip my usual two Wild Turkeys with a splash of club soda. I wanted to enjoy the crab stuffed sole which Chef Paulo knew I loved, and which he prepared especially for me whenever I wanted it, even when it was not on the menu.

 The San Marcos Country Club offered a rare shelter from a hypertensive world that, in my opinion, is spinning too fast. A world that would be better for everyone if slowed to the rpm's enjoyed a hundred years ago. I mean, wouldn't a leisurely ride in a horse drawn carriage be nice?

 Before I was born the architect and interior designer of the club had created a tasteful, relaxed atmosphere of tall ceilings and soft colors, reminiscent of a bygone era. I liked that about the club. It was the calming part of the now expanded building. The more modern additions to this retreat, added since my first days of membership, included those annoying, over-sized phones which took credit cards and sported two, sometimes three jacks for your modem and your fax and your printer, bringing the world of money-chasing into my environ of quiet yesterdays.

I loved it at the Club, not for its pretensions and shallowness, but because I could usually find a secluded, quiet corner, and with my newspaper held in front of me, few people who knew me would intrude into my solitude.

It had been a long two weeks in L.A.   Now that's a town I could easily live without ever seeing again even though I had been born in Los Angeles. I had spent the first seventeen years of my life there without ever seeing anything outside of Bel Air and occasional trips into Beverly Hills. I started attending private schools when I was twelve so I was sheltered from those non-rich kids who were seldom mentioned in our house. On the day I was born, the family CPAs and tax attorneys all phoned one another to spread the word that the wealthiest day-old boy in the United States, and first in line to the second largest family fortune in the U.S., had been born. I was named Morgan Ellington Crew. Morgan after my great grandfather. Ellington being my mother's family name. And crew because I am a Crew, of course.

I had, as a boy, a fanciful mental picture of the City of Angels: a place of grand houses, horses, and swimming pools; of lawn parties and limousines; of school chums who spoke with the finest of accents. And of Mexicans who were there to keep everything clean and neat for my family and my friend's families. It was not until I had finished college and taken my first tentative steps into the family industries that I saw the real L.A. - the poverty, the crime, the plastic, the garbage lined streets, and the chemical air. It took only a few months in business to realize that life in Los Angeles, outside of Bel Air, was not for me.

Socially, because of my family's fortune, I was accepted at the best homes in the world, and I was able to fit in well. Because of my acquired "social graces", I was welcome in society. I was considered very handsome, even if I do say so myself, as well as very eligible. And for you ladies out there, let me describe myself. I am just over six foot, two inches tall. My hair is dark and I like to leave it slightly long. My blue eyes are considered by the ladies to be very sexy.

OK, so you want the truth! I am about six foot two but on that frame I carry about twenty extra pounds I don't need, all under my belt. My hair is dark, but I had twice as much of it a few years ago. My eyes are blue but they are hidden behind glasses I wear when I read and when I drive. But when you got money, as they say, the little flaws are easily overlooked.

Although I had begun to feel uncomfortable in L.A. society, I felt there was something else out there, something beyond the wealth of L.A., the beaches of the South Pacific, and the ski slopes of Europe. I felt there had to be something real and I began to search for it.

I left that world and moved to San Marcos ten years ago, before my thirtieth birthday. San Marcos had been where my family had their country home, a place I had spent my summers in glorious childhood abandon amongst the quiet hills and sunny beaches, and I began a new life. A life that was grudgingly accepted by my family, discounted by the family accountants, and joked about behind my back by family friends. I am now known as a lazy layabout.

But I was in a search, a search for something that I knew existed, but I was unsure where to find it. My new life was centered on doing as little as possible, staying as far away from wealthy society as I could manage, and searching for what must be real in the world. Plus, I play a lot of golf, of course.

That night, as I sat in the Country Club's restaurant, the cool, clean night air drifted over the 18th green, through the tall, screened French doors and across my table. A faint, pleasant perfume of some flowers I could not identify rode on the breeze. I was enjoying the last few morsels of my dinner and squeezing the last drops out of a moderately good bottle of Chardonnay when Mitch Krueger sat at my table, across from me, unannounced and uninvited. He slid his chair around the table until he was uncomfortably next to me. He said in a whispered voice somewhere between frightened and secretive, "Sorry to bother you, Morgan. But I need to talk to you."

"Sure Mitch," I said, holding the fork inches from my mouth. "But how about letting me finish my dinner first?"

"Oh God! I am sorry," he said and inched away, for the first time noticing that I was eating. He hesitated at first then moved some more, scratching the chair across the polished oak floors. I had known Mitch for many years. Mitch had been a year ahead of me in school and we had played football together at Yale. We played golf together occasionally at the country club. I thought of him as a friend. He was obviously in trouble and I was never one to turn a friend away.

"No," I said. "That's OK. I'm done anyway." I gave up that last wonderful morsel of fish, laid the fork on the plate and pushed it away. "How about a brandy and we can talk?"

He accepted gratefully and when the two snifters were brought Mitch drank his hungrily and too quickly. When his glass was empty he pushed it away, folded his hands tightly in front of him and while looking down at the tabletop he said, "You know my daughter Barbara? Of course you know her, that's a stupid question."

"What's the matter Mitch?" I asked. "Is Barbara in some kind of trouble?"

"That's just it . . . I don't know . . . I mean . . . God this is hard . . . I mean, I don't know if she is or not." He was having difficulty breathing. He was taking short, shallow breaths and I was afraid he was going to hyperventilate and fall into my uneaten fish. I don't have a good bedside manner with sick people. I never know what to say and when I do say something, it's usually the wrong thing to say. So I reached out, touched his arm lightly, and said in as caring a voice as I could manage, "I don't understand, Mitch. Take a deep breath and tell me what's wrong."

Mitch had two children, a daughter Barbara and a son Mitch, Jr. The boy was what every father dreamed of. He is smart, athletic, handsome, a real gentleman, and back then about to enter the Naval Academy. Barbara, on the other hand, had been nothing but trouble since she learned that she could get what she wanted from her parents by either smiling temptingly and being overly cute, or by throwing a temper tantrum.

Mitch's wife, Loretta, was the youngest of six children of a wealthy family who had raised her to believe she was a "princess". Loretta was a stately beauty, elegant in her manner. She was also a snob, a bad tempered and self-centered bitch, like her mother before her. And she had spoiled her own daughter terribly, leaving Mitch to raise the boy while she instilled all her mis-beliefs, pride, and arrogance in Barbara.

Even though she had ignored Mitch, Jr. his whole life, the boy had grown into a fine young man as a result of his father's time and influence. Barbara, four years older than Mitch, Jr., had been in trouble starting at an age when other girls were still going to Brownie meetings and playing with Barbie dolls.

Mitch looked longingly at the empty snifter in front of him. I waived to a waiter to bring another, which Mitch finished, in one long swallow.

"Barbara's been fooling around with this damn kid gardener we took on a few months ago," he said. "I knew the kid was trouble, but . . . Well you know."

I knew that Mitch was a good provider and a nice guy, too nice to tell his bitchy wife to take Barbara and screw off.

He ran his business well but he didn't have much of a say at home.

"Anyway," he continued as he spun the empty snifter between his fingers. "The kid's tanned, looks like he stuffs a sock in his jeans, and likes to flex his biceps. I guess girls can be easily attracted to guys like that. Anyway, Barbara's been gone now for over a week. With the kid probably since he hasn't shown up at work either. I'm just scared. I don't know what to do."

"Mitch, the girl's over twenty-one," I said, trying to calm my friend. "I suppose if she wants to run off with some guy, well the law says she's allowed to."

"I know," he said. "And it's not the first time she's taken off . . . With some guy, I mean. But this one's different. He's not some local. I don't know anything about him except that he's got a wise mouth, and I've seen the two of them smoking dope. Right in my own front yard, the son of a bitch. I just think he's trouble, more than Barbara can handle maybe. She's never been exposed to anything, well . . . outside, you know? I guess I'm just plain scared this time. I just know things aren't right."

"Why me?" I asked. "Why tell me?"

"I want you to find her, Morgan. Find her and bring her home." I could hear the breath leave Mitch in a deep sigh, the sound of a man who has recognized and accepted defeat.

I didn't say anything. I sipped at my brandy and twirled it in its snifter, watching it gently and smoothly glide down the sides of the crystal. Mitch finally looked up at me, tears welling up in his eyes.

"You're the only friend I've got, Morgan. You're the only person I can trust. You know people. You can get things done. The Police won't do anything until it's too late. Please help me."

FIVE - It's All About Barbara

When Mitch Krueger came to me and asked that I find his daughter, my first thought was "Oh, man. Why me?" I am, you see, a soft touch. There's no other way to describe me and I admit it. I have the scent about me, the aura of one who would help anyone with anything. Panhandlers can see me coming from two blocks away. A door to door salesman can sell me anything. Lost and hungry dogs and cats always seem to find their way to my back door, where a good meal and a bowl of water can always be found.

So when Mitch asked for help, I had no choice but to agree to do what I could. At the time I had no idea what I could do for my friend. After all, if a young woman wants to run off with the gardener for a couple weeks of sex and fun in the sun, who's going to stop her? Maybe daddy might object, but it was the 21st Century and Barbara was over 21. Despite all that, I made up my mind to at least try.

The morning after speaking with Mitch at the club, I met him at his office on the eleventh floor of The Mark Building. Mitch owned a big construction company called InterPac Construction, Inc. His grandfather had started a small home-construction business; his father made it profitable; Mitch had made it big.

"Good to see you again, Morgan. Thank you for coming," Mitch said and waived me to a tall leather chair on the other side of his desk, which was cluttered with papers and blue prints. "How about some coffee?" he offered.

I gratefully accepted, secretly hoping a sweet pecan-

Danish or even a donut would arrive with the coffee. Nancy, Mitch's secretary, left to bring a tray of company mugs filled with steaming, strong, fresh coffee back to the office for us. Unfortunately, she didn't bring anything to eat. Oh well.

"I brought what records I had on the kid," Mitch said, handing photocopies of three papers to me. "I'm afraid I don't know very much about him. Like I said, it wasn't my decision to hire or keep the kid."

The first two photocopies were of a standard two page job application, the kind sold at any stationery store. The spaces were filled in with a series of sloppily hand-written, and for the most part, misspelled words. The kid's name was Hector Morales. It gave his home address as an apartment down at North Harbor. The street was one of many two and three story homes. Most are more than fifty years old and had been converted into run down apartments.

There was little else of any use on the form. Neither Mitch nor I could read what the kid had written for a social security number, but I figured it probably wasn't his real number anyway, if he had one at all. Chances were better than even the kid was an illegal alien.

The second photocopy was the back page of the application form, which listed his last two jobs although there was space for four. They were both gardening jobs and both down in L. A. The third page was a typewritten letter of reference from what was supposed to be his last employer, someone who gave an address in Beverly Hills.

It was addressed: "TO WHO IT MAY CONCENR". It was either typed very quickly and badly, or it was a phony. People who could afford a prestigious address in the Hills of Beverly would probably use WHOM instead of WHO and they wouldn't have misspelled 'concern".

There were other misspelled words. The type was obviously from an old manual machine, not from a new word processor or even a newer electric typewriter. But the paper it was written on was a good quality, not the kind of thing a poor, illegal, kid-gardener would have at hand.

It said simply that Hector was a good worker and knew how to garden. A scribbled signature at the bottom, under the typed name "Steven Rush", was purportedly his last employer.

"Did you contact his references?" I asked Mitch.

"No. We spoke to half a dozen people who advertised locally. This kid just walked up to our door one day. Loretta insisted we hire the kid even though I thought he wasn't qualified. You know how it is." He was embarrassed admitting this. I didn't press the subject.

"How did he get paid?"

"Once a week, on Fridays."

"No, I mean by check?"

"Oh, I'm sorry. No, he wanted cash, said he didn't have a bank account, and Loretta took care of that anyway. She always gave him cash to buy the materials he wanted, too. The damn kid never brought back a receipt. I told her she was getting ripped off, but, well you know how it is," he said again, lowering his eyes.

"Have you tried contacting Hector? Have you gone to his house?" I asked.

"No," he paused and said, "I guess I should have. I just couldn't face finding Barbara shacked up with that guy," he said.

"OK, I'll see what I can do," I said as I quickly finished my coffee and tried to remember if there was a Dunkin Donuts near Mitch's office. "But you'll have to remember that she is an adult and this is a big country. She could be anywhere."

"I know, just do the best you can," he said and started to get up.

"One last thing," I said as we walked to the door. "Money . . . Does she have any money of her own?

Anything she could get her hands on?"

"I was hoping you wouldn't ask that. I keep some money at home. In a safe in my den. It's gone," he said.

"How much?" I asked.

"A couple of thousand, maybe three, not much. She also has some jewelry. I guess she could have taken that. And she has a small checking account that Loretta deposits her allowance into. I don't know of anything else."

"A few thousand wouldn't keep them very long. It could be they'll be back soon looking for more," I said, trying to instill some hope in Mitch. "If I were you, I'd close out her bank account immediately. No sense giving them any more money than they have already."

I knew the chances were better than even that if Barbara had run off with Hector, they would blow her money fast and *she* wouldn't go to work to get more. Hector would not be able to earn enough as a gardener to keep them both in the fast lane. That left only Mitch as a source of cash. With no bank account to draw on, they would probably be back before I could get a good start finding them; at least I was hoping so.

"I think we should look through Barbara's room. Is that going to be O.K. with you?" I asked Mitch.

"Sure, it's alright with me. I don't know about Loretta, though."

"Maybe we could do it sometime when she's out. Do you know if she goes anywhere during the day?"

"Most afternoons she spends at the club. She's been taking tennis lessons from that new Pro they just hired. You know, the greasy guy with the pencil moustache who never quite made it as a pro?" he said and forced a smile.

"Ok," I said. "How about I meet you at your house this afternoon? Is two going to be alright for you?"

He said it would be all right without checking his schedule and shook my hand quickly and a little nervously. I left without another word spoken, closing the office door behind me.

I had known Mitch Krueger a long time. I had never seen him as uncomfortable and nervous as he was that day. It was cool in his office but he was sweating. His hands were shaking so badly that he spilt drops of coffee down his expensive silk tie when trying to bring the cup to his lips, without taking notice of it. I doubted that his spoiled, whore daughter running off once again, would get her father that upset. After all, she had done it so many times, with so many different local young studs, that he should be used to it by that time. Something else was bothering my friend, something Mitch didn't tell me. But was it any of my business?

SIX - Sandy D'Angelo

I knew that life could be complicated. I mean, I could care about the money, which I really don't. I did care about what I could do with the money. I know that's rationalizing, but I like to rationalize, it's something I do a lot of and I'm pretty damn good at it.

What good was it to feel guilty about being so rich? After all, if I gave all my money away, I rationalized whenever the thought arose, I would be poor and somebody else would be rich. Changing places didn't accomplish anything, I told myself. And of course, there was always the fact that I really like being rich and not having to work. I figure that playing golf and hanging out at the Country Club just had to be better than working for a living.

I could be married, which I am not. I could have some goals in life, which I do not. Well, maybe I would like to birdie the 623-yard, par five, dogleg left, over-the-lake, number 14 at the Country Club just once. And since I am day dreaming like that anyway, why not just one hole-in-one before I die. But no real goals, you know?

As for the money, there's a ton of it. I let Harper, Harper, Jascro & Nettles, Attorneys extraordinaire worry about it. They invest it and make it grow. They oversee the running of my many companies, which I feel just fine ignoring whenever I can.

But when important decisions are to be made, they call me in along with a few other prominent members of the Crew family. The attorneys and the family always turn to me and when absolutely necessary, I make the decision.

About the married part. Well I used to think that at forty I should be settled down to something resembling a normal life. But what the hell, I rationalize every time I think about it, I'm having a good time, and how many times had I heard about men well into their seventies fathering children? What difference would it make if I waited a few more years?

Oh, there are lots of women, all good looking and rich. They are generally the daughters and sometimes the wives of club members. They are tall, slim, tanned, athletic, well-educated, and cool. And, I can't forget nor ignore that they are pretentious, snobbish, phony and a few other things like cold and mechanical in bed. But they are so rich most men would put up with the chill for the money. They had made themselves available to me over the years, both the mothers and daughters, the married and the not married, but there came a time I did not have need of them.

Some time ago I started leaving the Country Club and going down the hill to Harborside where the commercial fishing fleet ties up. I found that an occasional day out in the Pacific on a sport fishing boat, with a line dropped in the water, the sun full, hot, and overhead, with a cooler full of beer, can be very relaxing after long days of doing nothing.

There was something about the comradery of unshaven men who smelt of fish and practiced grunting, swearing, and spitting, that brought some semblance of reality to my life. And reality was something I had been searching for, for many years.

The best part of a day of fishing came when the boat tied up, the catch was cleaned and bagged, and the "guys" headed off for a few final beers before staggering home. At the docks, down a side alley, there was a seedy little bar owned by a seedy old fella' named Captain Nicholas Bustacco, Cap'n Nick to his friends.

Cap'n Nick's Bar and Grill sits on an aged, creaking

pier out over the bay. There is a warehouse, unused for many years, on the shore side of Nick's, and a ripe old wooden building used to clean fish from the commercial trawlers, on the other side. The smells from the cleaning shed permeated through the cracked, thin walls and into Cap'n Nick's, but no one complained. It was all part of the atmosphere and Cap'n Nick's wouldn't have been the same without those special fragrances.

Nick's was a haven for the men of the San Marcos fishing fleet. The floors sported a sawdust covering, changed every month or so, whether it needed it or not! The walls were crowded with dusty black and white photos, turned yellow and brown with age, of old friends, boats, record size fish, and the odd newspaper clipping of one or another of Cap'n Nick's semi-disreputable friends, dressed in 1940's gangster flash.

There were torn fishing nets draped across one wall, heavy with cobwebs and bits and pieces of ship ornamentation, old glass floats, and odd pieces of ship's brass. Handmade ship models of 19th century, fully rigged schooners and steamers occupied positions of importance on small wooden shelves, encased in glass, and clouded with years of dust and grime. Of course, that is all gone now.

I was proud to call myself a friend of Cap'n Nick, and some of his friends could be found there most afternoons and evenings. But the one person who made Cap'n Nick's so very special was a young lady named Sandra D'Angelo.

She was a waitress at Cap'n Nick's and one of the main reasons that kept me going there, day after day, back in those days, before all hell broke loose in San Marcos.

Sandy was what all the woman at the Club weren't. She wasn't rich. She wasn't consumed with herself. Her hair was soft, thick, brown, the color being the only thing ordinary about it. It had never seen another color. It hung in delicately smooth waves across her shoulders and in the morning I would luxuriate as I lay in bed watching her brush it quickly, just a few strokes of the silver handled brush I had given her on our one-month anniversary together, until each hair fell into its natural place.

She wasn't as tall as most of the women who are on display at the Country Club. Her face wasn't as delicate but had a beauty to it unseen at the club. Her body was fuller, more sensual, and it moved with the ease and confidence of a cat rather than the practiced stiffness of a plastic model.

When she smiled, her eyes smiled first. They were dark blue, almost black, sometimes green, depending on how the light struck them. And what set her apart most from the women at the Club is that she has a brain and she uses it.

And I knew after first meeting her that when the time came for me to settle down, it would be with Sandy D'Angelo, I was sure of that. We would sail off into some sunset onboard a fish smelling scow, and be very happy. Something real, I would say to myself, trying to visualize the time in the sun, the happiness, the love we would share.

SEVEN - The Morelli Family

I first met Sandy a year before all hell broke out in my quiet hometown. I was walking back to my pride and joy, my best "grown-up" toy, a completely restored, British Green, 1967 MGB. It was after a day of sport fishing beyond the reef at the harbor's mouth, on a calm Pacific Ocean. I had booked a day on a group charter boat, the trawler "Santa Maria", the same boat I went out on many times each year. The owners, a leather-skinned old man and his two sons, kept a full locker of cold beer and they seemed to know right where the fish were.

The two sons of the boat's owner, who were also the boat's entire crew, walked with me and suggested we stop in Nick's Bar for one more beer, they would buy. I had never been inside the ratty looking bar; it wasn't the kind of place I was used to. But I followed them inside anyway because I never turned down a free beer.

"Cap'n!" Jeremy, the older of the brothers, called out as we walked into the musty, dark tavern. Years of weathering had toughened and wrinkled the skin of the man they called Cap'n. His ash-gray hair was thickly curled and hung almost to his shoulders. It continued in one line into a full, fluffy beard of slightly darker grays flecked with streaks of yellow. His nose, which had been broken a forgotten number of years before, stood sort of looking east when he was facing north. His face could fit nicely into any Pirate story you had ever read.

The rest of his six foot six-inch frame fit that mold

also. His tree trunk arms were covered with thickly matted gray hair and on each broad forearm he sported a tattoo, exposed by the rolled up sleeves of his worn and faded red plaid work shirt. On the left arm the letters U S M C carried over a wind curled red, white and blue banner; on the right a dolphin arched above the sea.

When Jeremy called to Cap'n Nick, the old man stepped from behind the bar with both bear-like arms held open to greet the two boys. I watched the old man step-clack-step-clack across the room on a real wooden peg leg right out of Treasure Island! I looked for a cutlass hanging from his belt and a parrot on his shoulder but there wasn't one.

He wore faded, heavy canvas denim jeans, the kind of work pants worn by most of the professional fishermen, only his were big enough for two or maybe even three of the normally lean, muscled crewman of the local fleet. His shirt looked as if it might second as pajamas.

"JESUS H CHRIST!" he boomed in a deep, bass voice that shook the very rafters of his tavern. He took both young men into his arms at the same time and hugged them out of breath. "You two boys ain't been in t'here f'months! I thought you might'a found a new place t'go! And where's that old man o'yours? Fishin' ain't so good and he haft'a give up boozin' or sumptin'?"

Jeremy pushed himself away from the giant and said, "He's coming. He's just finishing up some stuff. This here's one of our best customers", he said, slapping me on the shoulder.

"Morgan Crew, this is the famous Cap'n Nick who happens to make the best damn chowder on the whole damn West Coast."

"You watch that language, boy", the Cap'n said, feigning a serious scowl across his broad, red face. "You know God damn well your mother didn't like such talk."

Jeremy laughed and turned to me. "I've been told that if my mother hadn't been so smart as a young girl, she would have married Cap'n Nick instead of my father. He thinks he has to take care of me", he said.

"I've smacked your bare behind before, lad", he growled. "And I'll damn well do it agin' if you act up. I got that understandin' with your old man, you know."

Cap'n Nick laughed with a heavy growl. His words were salted with the constant movement of his big hands, which had the habit of jabbing, slapping, and punching whomever he was speaking to.

Jeremy's younger brother, Tony, was smiling but was his usually quiet self, standing off to the side, nervously wishing he could take part but not knowing what to say. He fidgeted; he laughed a little, and then jammed his hands deep into his pockets. He was smaller than his brother was, thinner, darker. His hair was jet black, thick, curly, and slicked back while Jeremy's was very blond, thin, cut short, and neatly combed. Tony had always been uncomfortable around people, but he smiled, and he agreed with what was said to him without saying much himself, while Jeremy enjoyed a calm of self confidence that allowed him to discuss, disagree, and joke intelligently. Tony lived his life in Jeremy's shadow. I used to wonder if Tony liked it there.

The Cap'n led Jeremy, Tony, and me to the end of the bar and drew three tall mugs of beer. Without turning from the taps, he yelled for someone named Sandy to bring three bowls of chowder for his friends.

"Morgan Crew?" the captain said. "Sounds like a good seafarin' name t'me. Seems I might'a heard the name before. You got fishermen in your family?"

I smiled at the joke of anybody thinking anyone in my family would have ever been a fisherman, but I managed to hold back the laughter. My family hadn't had dirt under their fingernails in over a hundred years. All my life I'd had to stifle a lot of laughs about my name and my family.

I had stopped trying to explain the name years before. In answer to Cap'n Nick's question about my name, I simply said, "I don't think so. None I've heard about anyway."

The door behind the bar swung open, kicked roughly by Cap'n Nick's waitress. She struggled with a large tray as she backed through the doorway and around the bar.

My eyes locked onto her. Old World Italians, like Cap'n Nick, would call it the 'thunderclap'. Although I was not aware of it at that moment, I was completely taken; my eyes, my heart, my mind were filled with the woman, and I would never be free of her. She was immediately beautiful, sexy, alluring. She was so completely different from the women I had grown up with and whom I knew at the Club.

There was something undeniably erotic about the woman, the way she walked, the way she frowned as she tried to balance the three large bowls of chowder on the tray, the way she yelled, "Oh shit!" as one of them slid off and crashed to the floor.

She was wearing tight fitting shorts, a loose sailor's middy blouse of well faded blue striped cotton, held tightly at her slim waist by elastic and old deck shoes. The blouse swelled wonderfully under her breasts. Her legs were trim and athletic, not skinny as is fashionable at the club, and there was a small crescent shaped mole on the outside of her right knee. Her hand glided down her tanned thigh, brushing off droplets of the spilt soup.

"Hey!" Cap'n Nick yelled. "What the hell! You O.K. Sandy? You hurt?"

"I'm O.K., Cap'n", she said, sliding the two remaining bowls onto the bar. "It's just the Goddamn heat. Can't you get the damn air conditioner fixed? You want me to cook and wait tables too, you gotta cool off that damn kitchen!"

"I tol' you the guy was coming. What you want me t'do?"

"Just get the damn thing fixed!" she yelled. She again brushed at her leg, tugged at the elastic waistband of her blouse, and then glanced at me. Her piercing eyes made a quick examination. There was no expression on her face and the glance probably took no more than a second or two, but I felt she liked what she saw, even though she gave no hint of that.

I had started to bring a frosty mug of beer to my lips when she had crashed through the doorway. I froze when I saw her and Jeremy saw the half-raised mug, my slack jaw, and the bedazzled look on my face.

"Hey, you O.K., Mr. Crew?" he said. "Mr. Crew," he repeated and touched my shoulder when I didn't answer. "Mr. Crew, you alright?"

Both the Cap'n and Tony Morelli looked at me. The smile washed quickly from Tony's face and was replaced by a sour scowl as he drained his glass and slammed it down onto the bar. The Cap'n thundered a laugh, shook his head, and walked away.

Every day for two weeks after that day I found myself in Cap'n Nick's. I made the excuse that the clam chowder was the best I'd ever had, but it didn't take much work on Sandy's part to figure out that nobody likes clam chowder that much. We both knew that Sandy was the reason I was there. And she didn't seem to mind. She encouraged me with her smiles and her time.

We spent a little time talking at first, I sat at the bar, and she stood behind it. After a few days she would sit with me at a table and I would buy her lunch. She happily accepted a dinner invitation and said she wanted to go to an Italian place nearby. It was one month to the day after she had spilt the chowder that she awoke next to me in my bed.

I had finally fallen asleep; it was after three in the morning. She had been curled like a dreaming child against me, breathing slowly, softly. Her silky hair cascaded across her face and onto my shoulder. Her head rested on my chest; her hand lay on my stomach.

I gave her the silver hairbrush set she had admired in the window of the antique shop the next day as we walked hand in hand around town after breakfast.

EIGHT - Go Find The Morellis

It was not quite a year after giving Sandy the silver brush set that my dinner at the club had been interrupted by Mitch Krueger. I had four hours to wait before meeting Mitch at his house, as we had arranged. The call of the sea and a new fishing rod was tugging at me once again. The months with Sandy had sped by before I had realized it, and during that time I had not thought of fishing.

While I waited for two o'clock to roll around, when I was supposed to meet Mitch at his home, I tried phoning to book a day with the Morelli's on their fishing boat. I thought Sandy might like a day fishing also. Although she had never given me a hint she might like a day in the hot sun on a smelly boat, I had hoped she would. I wasn't about to give her up for fishing. But could I give up fishing?

I found the Morelli's number disconnected. Directory Information did not have a new number. So I spent some of the time I had driving down to the docks and parked my beloved '67 MGB as close as I could to Cap'n Nick's, which turned out to be four blocks away.

Tourist season was at its height. It was a beautifully sunny and warm day, and the rickety old docks were crowded with city folk in town for the day. They strolled slowly, gawking in the windows of the gift shops that all carried the same postcards, coffee mugs, sea shell jewelry, plaster sea gulls, screen printed T-shirts, and cheap trinkets.

I elbowed my way as gently as possible through the crowd and continued to the far end of the docks. I passed

Cap'n Nick's and waved to Sandy through the grime-fogged window. She smiled, waived, and threw a kiss at me.

At the end of the dock, where the Santa Maria normally tied up, a different boat, a commercial trawler much larger than the Santa Maria, sat riding the swell. It had tons of fine mesh net coiled on a big reel at the aft that would be let out to trail behind the boat, and fill with fish and everything else that the ocean held.

There was a guy in tall rubber work boots hosing down the deck; bits of fish and flotsam picked up in the nets earlier that morning were being washed into the black water of the harbor. A few gulls circled frantically and very nosily just feet above the water, fighting over the bits of trash.

I cupped my hands around my mouth and called up to the man on the deck, "Have you seen the Santa Maria around anywhere?" I yelled.

The fisherman stopped his work, turned off the hose and looked down at me from the deck above. "Never heard of her!" he called above the screeching of the gulls. "Skipper just moved our moorage here. You best check with the Harbor Master, maybe she was moved somewhere's else."

At almost every slip along the pier, fishing boats, big and small, road the harbor's gentle swells, creaking and straining against the ropes that held them, making a sad, lonely sort of music in the near empty, late afternoon of the harbor. I stopped at the Cap'n's place before going to the Harbormaster's. What the hell, it was a chance to see Sandy, I rationalized once again.

"Hey, Morgan," she greeted me with a kiss and a big hug. "We still on for tonight?"

"Only if you bring me a cup of coffee," I answered.

Her eyes smiled. I had spent many years wondering what love was. I had seen too many arranged marriages. I had seen couples at the Country Club, married but unfaithful, who stayed together because it was easier than a divorce.

My parents, I believed, loved each other. I was still unsure, but I thought that love has got to be something close to seeing Sandy smile.

She brought a steaming mug of freshly brewed coffee to the bar where I sat. She leaned on her elbows against the old, smooth, dark wood, looking up at me, her hands cupped under her chin, her gray sweatshirt covered breasts resting on the counter top as if offered to me, knowingly tempting and teasing me.

"Are you really as rich as everybody says?" she asked playfully.

"Does it make any difference to you?"

"Sure. I mean if you're really rich it just makes you being a fantastic lover all the better," she said.

"Suppose I wasn't rich, maybe everybody just got the idea somewhere, and I'm really just a poor working stiff? And suppose I wasn't a fantastic lover, even though I know that couldn't *possibly* be true. Would you still be looking at me like that right now?" I asked.

"Hell, no!" she said with a sexy, deep laugh.

"So you can love me for my money or you can love me for my world-renowned expertise between the sheets or you can love me even better for both. But without either, you wouldn't know I even exist. Is that what you're saying?"

"Well, not exactly," she said, straightening up, tugging at the waistband of her sweatshirt, and looking very serious. "There's still that cute little kid's face of yours, and those adorable dimples on your butt, where nobody else had better see them or I'll punch your lights out. I guess I might still love you for those things."

We laughed and I sipped at the hot, strong coffee that was a far way from the usual stuff the Cap'n served. What Sandy had brought me was fresh, what the Cap'n usually served up was left cooking on the burner for a couple of hours until it reminded me of what a burnt rubber tire, flavored with asphalt, must taste like.

She was about to ask if I wanted anything to eat when Cap'n Nick step-clack- step-clacked by and I called to him. "Hey, Cap'n. Have you seen the Santa Maria around? I've got this urge for some fishing."

"No, as a matter 'fact, I ain't seen the boat, the boys, or their old man for couple months now. I don't know." He was standing less than four feet from me but his voice, as usual, roared like a deep-throated lion's. "Ya' know, there's something fishy there," the old man said. He stepped around behind the bar and topped up the mug for me with his really bad coffee, ruining what Sandy had gotten for me.

His voice lowered to a rare whisper as he leaned close to me and said, "The old man and the boys, they used t'come here all the time. Eat, drink, you know? Then they stopped but I still seen them walking by ever'day almost. Then for 'bout three, maybe four weeks now I don't see any of 'em and now the boat's clean gone for couple weeks. The old man, Franco, he and me, we used to fish together years ago when we was young. We the best kind of friends yet he don't even stop in and say good bye or nothin'. That ain't right, ya' know?"

"Well, Morgan honey," Sandy said. "You're supposed to know everybody and have all kinds of connections. You don't do a damn thing all day. Go find out what happened."

"Hey," the Captain said more closely to his normal canon of a voice. "That's right. You go find Franco and tell him I'm pissed off at him and he should come see me 'gain."

"I was on my way to the Harbormaster," I said. "I just wanted a cup of coffee"

Sandy grabbed the mug away, poured what coffee was left down the sink, rinsed the chipped mug at the bar's tap, and put it with a stack of almost clean mis-matched cups and mugs on a shelf behind her. She turned and glared at me, her hands on her hips.

"There," she said. "Now you're done." I shrugged, pushed myself off the stool, and walked out. Sometimes it's best to just do what you're told to do.

NINE - Find The Santa Maria

The Harbormaster's office shares a building with the Coast Guard and is at the south tip of the crescent shaped bay known as San Marcos Harbor, where Playa Del Flores Road ends. Playa Del Flores curves down from the hills and turns left in front of the harbor's Administration Building.

A small lawn of well tended, thick green grass holds two flagpoles, each based in a pyramid of cannon balls, painted black. One pole holds the Stars and Stripes, the other the California State flag. The building is a hundred and five years old. It is a two story, wood frame, structure, once the home of some sea captain relative of mine. It had been meticulously restored and painted a gleaming white trimmed in deep ocean blue. It is the pride of Harborside. It is the best-looking building in that area.

A walkway of concrete stepping stones, lined on both sides with football size, white painted rocks, separated the two flagpoles. I parked that day in one of the two spaces at the curb marked "Visitor" and walked into the building. I took the six steps up to the front door of the office two at a time and at the top regretted all those years of my youth I wasted smoking cigarettes.

Inside the Harbormaster's Office, at the reception desk, sat a young lady not too many years out of High School. She wore a bright red cashmere sweater with a deep V-neck. It was a deep enough cut so that there could be no mistake that it was all her under the soft fuzz of the sweater, and that no artificial ingredients had been added. She was about due for another trip to the beauty parlor to have the dark roots bleached to match the brass of the rest of her hair. Her lips, cheekbones, and fingernails matched the color of her sweater. All in all, she was a sight to been seen.

"Hi," she said sweetly. "What can I do for you?"

I was tempted to discuss the possibilities with her but I figured I had better find out where the Santa Maria was first. San Marcos is a small town and there weren't many secrets in Harborside. If I got carried away with this young thing, Sandy was sure to find out. So I stuck to business all the while remembering that I believe solidly in the age-old saying, "Look, but don't touch".

"I'm looking for a group charter boat, the Santa Maria. It used to tie up at pier 3, slip 23. Can you tell me where she moved to, please?"

"Oh sure," she said. "I can look that up for you."

She smiled sweetly again, seductively. She pushed herself away from the desk and stood up. Her skirt was dark blue, very tight, and she had to tug on it to bring it down to its full length, which wound up being about four or five inches above her knees.

Still smiling, showing two rows of very large, perfectly white teeth, she took a couple of steps toward three tan colored, metal filing cabinets lined up behind her desk to form a wall of sorts that separated her little reception area from the rest of the office. Lined across the tops of the cabinets were a few small plants, not in very good health, and five pictures of young men, either shirtless or in swim trunks. All of them were in very, very good health.

There was a desk-top computer sitting on top of her desk. I looked questioningly at it and she said, "Like, I don't get those things, ya' know? It's like quicker for me to use the books, ya' know?"

Each of the steps she took to get to the filing cabinets were taken with the fullest cooperation and physical help of her whole, overly developed young body, which worked against the restraint of the too-tight skirt and cashmere sweater. I could almost imagine the slow bump and grind beat of drums as she walked. It reminded me of the strip club I went to once with a bunch of fellow college friends.

She opened a drawer of one of the filing cabinets and started flipping through files. As she did she hummed a tune and kept time with a delicate sway of her ample hips. "Haven't I seen you around some place?" she asked, pausing to look over her shoulder, still smiling, her bedroom eyes drooping in a really good imitation of Marilyn Monroe.

"I don't think so."

"Seems like I might of seen you some place, ya' know. I mean like you're cute enough, ya' know, so like I might remember you, ya' know?"

The humming stopped but the hips kept going as she peered over her shoulder at me.

"It's not likely. I would certainly have remembered you," I said.

She giggled a little then said brightly, "Hmmm, I know, I'll bet you like to hang out up at Hobson Beach."

Hobson Beach is an isolated half-mile stretch of soft white sand accessible only by walking across a rocky field strewn with wild poppies and brown grass, and then down a well-worn and steep rocky dirt path that made the trip to the beach a real challenge. It was several miles north of San Marcos and was used by people who enjoy the beach, the sun, and the water without the restrictions of clothing. I had been there several times in my younger years. I would sneak out of the house and ride my bike to the beach. I was fascinated by the female anatomy when I was a boy.

"I don't think it was me . . . I mean, I haven't been there . . ." I wasn't about to tell her how many years it had been since I was down at Hobson Beach. Vanity was beginning to overtake me, and I felt myself sucking in my 40-year-old waist. "You must be mistaking me for someone else."

She turned slightly from the file cabinet and looked at me, smiling again, insolently, sexually daring me.

"Well, maybe it wasn't you. But I wouldn't mind if you like did sort of hang out there, if you know what I mean." She laughed at her joke. "I'm there like most Saturdays. If it isn't like raining, ya' know? Why not like join me sometime, ya' know?"

"Yeah," I said. "I might do that. How about the Santa Maria? Did you find anything yet?"

From the top drawer of the middle cabinet she pulled a two inch thick, blue bound book of computer printouts and carried it back to her desk, giving me a show of the front of her routine. She was peering deeply into my eyes and smiling in a wanton, knowing fashion. Laying the book on the desk she bent at the waist and began flipping through the pages. Bending over not only brought her closer to the pages but allowed me a clear, unobstructed view down inside her sweater and across her braless chest.

"Oh yes," she said, straightening up. "That's the Franco Morelli boat. We like don't know what happened. The slip fees were like five months behind, ya' know? And like the slip had been vacant for like over a month. We assigned it to someone else. If you see him, he needs to like come in and get the fees brought up to date." She smiled ever so sweetly again. I said I would tell him and said goodbye to her.

She called to me as I walked out the door, "Hey! If there's like ever anything I can do for you, like don't hesitate to come back!" There was too much emphasis on "anything" and she was far too young for me to even think of testing the limits of "anything". I ran to my car and sped away.

TEN - Franco Morelli

I drove too fast back to Cap'n Nick's and ran down the pier and inside where I asked Sandy for another coffee, the fresh stuff, not the thick paste that had been burning for a couple of hours. I sat at a table with Sandy and the Cap'n. I told them what I had found out at the Harbormaster's, but I didn't mention anything about the receptionist's ample proportions or her equally ample propositions. I figured keeping such things from Sandy was the smart thing to do. I didn't need to bail her out of jail from an assault charge.

"That don't make sense," the Cap'n said after I told them what I had found out. "Franco knows me and he knows if he got money trouble I gonna' help him out. And he wouldn't just up and leave San Marcos for nobody. Hell, he was born here and he learned t'fish here on his old man's boat with me."

"Cap'n's right," Sandy said. "Mr. Morelli's younger son, Anthony, has the hots for me. He wouldn't just leave without coming in to say good bye or nothing."

"He's got the hots for you?" I asked, feeling very territorial. Then I remembered that first day in Cap'n Nick's, the first time I had seen Sandy and she had spilled the bowl of chowder. And I remembered the dark scowl that crossed Tony's face when he saw how the thunderclap had struck me. I hadn't understood it back then. Now I did understand it.

"Oh come on, Morgan. He's just a kid," Sandy said, teasing me. "A great looking hunk of a kid alright," she said with a mischievous grin. "But just a kid all the same. And besides, he's too wild for me even if he wasn't so young."

"You got that right," the Cap'n said. "Tony, he's a wild kid. He been nothing but trouble to Franco since he was a little shit-pants. He always boozin', whorin', and running wild on that damn motorcycle he got. I tol' Franco he was too old to be having more kids, that he wouldn't be able to handle'em. But no, Franco ain't gonna listen to nobody. That Tony ain't like his brother Jeremy. Different mothers, ya' know?"

"I didn't know that," Sandy said, surprised at hearing this.

"Yeah, 'course. Franco married a back east Yank when he was young. They had two kids that done died at birth and then Jeremy. She was a beautiful girl, smart, and like a saint, even though she wasn't no Italian. But she was a small thing, lot'sa heart and passion but too frail like. She died giving birth to Jeremy. Franco was torn up over that, he wanted t'die, but he had the baby to think about. And Jeremy, he looks just like his mother, and Franco loves him like anything.

"Years later he meets this young Italian bitch. I tol' Franco she wasn't no good but he don't listen. He on fire for her. They get married and the old man wants 'nother kid. So they have and before he's a year old the bitch up and leaves. She takes a suitcase and his whole damn bank account, and leaves the kid. Can you beat that? Tony's been trouble ever since."

"Do you know where Franco lives?" I asked him.

"Sure. I write it down for you. You gonna go see what's up?"

"Yes, I thought maybe I would. I've had the best damn fishing from his boat, and I like him and his kids. They're good folks. If he's around and still fishing, I want to go out again. Sandy, I thought you might like a day out with them. What do you think?"

"I'd like that, but let's find out what happened to them first. I'm really worried."

The Cap'n went behind the bar and wrote out the Morelli's address on a scrap of greasy brown paper bag. I stayed at the table with Sandy and sipped at whatever was in the coffee mug Cap'n Nick had brought to me. Sandy had not made a fresh pot for me, as I hoped she would. I noticed Sandy never drank the coffee at the bar, even when she made a fresh pot for me. She seemed to like the coffee I made those mornings she woke up at my side, however. Smart lady, I thought.

About one fifteen I left to meet Mitch Krueger at his home. I decided not to mention my meeting with Mitch before I left. Sandy particularly disliked Loretta Krueger and I figured the less she knew of my trying to help people she didn't like, the better off I was.

I pushed the full cup of burnt coffee away, kissed Sandy, and walked out of Cap'n Nick's.

ELEVEN - Finding Barbara

Mitch Krueger's home was a newly built imitation of a stately mansion in a new development of similar homes located on the eastern border of the country club. It is two stories tall and too big. There is a lot of brick, big windows, and a few columns in the front. It would be almost impressive if it weren't so ostentatious.

Mitch's back yard is actually a view of the fifth tee and the pond behind the fourth green. An expensive landscaper had lots of trees and flowers carefully and professionally arranged and kept them manicured.

When I arrived at precisely 2 PM at Mitch's house, many of the yards in the neighborhood had their crews of workmen sweating over lawn mowers and clippers. Mitch's home had a decorative wall along the front sidewalk, made of simulated used brick. Big brass lamps stood at the entrance-way's wrought iron gate which opened onto the flagstone walk which snaked its way from the street to the gabled front door. I stopped at the front door but before I could press the big brass doorbell button, the door swung open and Mitch Krueger waived me in.

Mitch glanced outside, up and down the street, to see if any neighbors had seen me. He looked disapprovingly at my car parked at the curb, then looked towards me, apologetic for having been so obviously judgmental about the car. People seemed to think I should be driving a new and expensive BMW or Mercedes or Lexus or something like that. College kids drive MGB's.

"I'm sorry, Morgan." he said. "This whole thing has me shaken. Sometimes, I just don't know what I'm doing."

The interior of the home was like a photo layout in Better Homes and Gardens. Very professional and dramatic, but it left me with the feeling that I should be very careful, not touch anything, and maybe not sit anywhere either.

Mitch led me through the house, past a stone fireplace which separated the living room from the dining room, through a big pale oak kitchen with lots of professional stainless steel tables, stoves, and ovens, and into a small room.

It was a dark room compared to the rest of the house, probably because it sported only two small windows that looked out the west side of the house at a tall wooden fence separating Mitch's house from the neighbor's. The room was crowded with a desk, two chairs and three metal filing cabinets. Nothing else could have fit into the confined space. There was a thin veneer of dust on top of the cabinets, the chairs were well used and their legs heel-scuffed from use.

Mitch sat at the desk, squeezing himself into the chair, which was pushed against the back wall, and motioned for me to take the only other chair in the room.

"I thought we were going to look through Barbara's room?" I asked.

"Yes. That's what you suggested. I'm just . . . I guess I want to make sure I'm doing what's right," he stammered.

"Look, it's up to you. You came to me. You're the one asked me to help you find Barbara and I think it's probably important to look through her room to do that. I think we should see what clothes she's taken, what personal items she's left behind, that sort of thing. That's what they always do on TV, and it seems pretty logical to me."

Mitch fidgeted in his chair and nervously asked, "Look, suppose, I mean, she didn't run off. What if this kid took her and maybe hurt her. Or maybe he's gonna hurt her?"

"We don't know that, Mitch," I said, trying to sound reassuring. "Unless you know something you're not telling me. If that's the case, you should be talking to the police, not me. Barbara may be a lot of things but she's not dumb, and she's a strong person. Inside, I mean. She wouldn't just let some guy drag her off without putting up a fight. Someone would have heard. My God, you've got more than a dozen gardeners working in the neighborhood every day. Someone would have seen or heard something."

"I know, Morgan, I know. I've told myself that so many times."

"Is there something you're not telling me, Mitch?" I asked.

"No, Morgan. Of course not," he said without looking at me. But I felt I was being lied to.

"If there is something you know, I have to know it if you want my help," I said. "Eventually I'm going to call on people I know and see what they can do to help. If I do that, I need to tell them everything."

"You don't mean the police?" he said, obviously frightened at the thought of a police investigation.

"Yes, I do mean the police and several other people, too. If she is in trouble, the police will have to know."

"I don't want the police in on this, Morgan. I can't have them sticking their noses into my business."

"So tell me what you're not telling me. What am I not supposed to know?"

"No. No. There's nothing," he answered, got up and quickly left the room. He didn't ask me to follow him, but I hoped Mitch was going to take me to Barbara's room, so I followed. Mitch was walking fast, ahead of me, awkwardly looking around as we nearly ran through the house.

We returned by the same route we had taken through the big house a few moments before. We turned before reaching the front door and went up a staircase to the second floor. Mitch took the stairs two steps at a time, I took them slower, once again mentally blaming all those cigarettes, and fell behind.

At the top of the stairs was a long hallway that turned left twice. The hallway was lined with doors that were all closed. Mitch walked to the third door on the right, stood for a moment, then opened it quickly and took one brief step inside, blocking the doorway momentarily.

After a moment or two he did step aside and I could see the room was a girl's room, with lots of frills and pastels surrounding a white, four-poster bed. There was a vanity trimmed in lace cloth, with a large lighted mirror on top. Nearby was a tall chest of drawers on top of which were a half dozen bottles of perfume.

In the far corner sat an over-stuffed chair, which was covered with bright, flowery upholstery matching the floor length drapes on the room's four windows. The walls were papered in an expensive and simple floral print, which a designer chose to go with the print of the drapes and chair. The air of the room held traces of expensive scents and powders.

Playing this all by ear, I guessed I should see what clothes Barbara had taken with her. I went directly to a large double closet and slid one of the white louvered doors open. A light came on as the door swung open. Inside it was deep enough to walk into and it was lined on three walls with clothes, all appeared to be expensive and stylish. A quick right to left glance told me there were no empty hangers.

Shoes lined the floor, perhaps two dozen in all, all neatly arranged heal to back wall. Several shelves held assorted boxes, hats, and purses all again too neatly arranged to suggest that a somewhat flighty young lady lived there. I didn't have a whole lot of experience with teenage girls, at least not since I was a teenage boy. But that's another story. I was sure their rooms should not be as neat as that room was.

"Mitch," I asked as I looked again around the closet. "Has anyone been in here? To clean I mean?"

"Of course. We have a woman come in every day. Oh, I see," he said. "You mean we should have left the room the way Barbara left it. I'm sorry. She never did learn to keep her room clean. She just drops her stuff on the floor. If it weren't straightened up every day, you wouldn't be able to walk in here."

I turned and walked to the vanity. There were three small drawers on each side and one in the middle. I opened each and rifled through little piles of lace and silk. I remembered seeing a movie once where James Bond or somebody like him found some microfilm or something taped to the underside of a drawer. So I ran my hand behind and under each drawer and on the fourth I found some paper taped to the underside. I was surprised but tried not to show it. I kind of liked Mitch to think I knew what I was doing.

Mitch stepped next to me, trying to see what was written on the paper, but I turned as I opened the papers so that Mitch could not see anything that might be written on what I had found. There were two pieces of wrinkled papers, folded tightly together.

It was not exactly a letter. It was not addressed to anyone, but it was handwritten in the same sloppy hand and misspelled words as I had seen on Hector Morales' job application. It consisted of several paragraphs of filth describing in some detail what Hector had planned by way of a night of sex with some unnamed woman. I folded the papers and slid them into my inside jacket pocket.

"What was that?" Mitch asked.

"You don't need to see it," I answered and walked away towards the dresser.

"Wait a minute, Morgan, damn it! I have a right to know."

"But you don't have a need. Leave it with me," I said, interrupting him.

I went through the dresser as I had the vanity, without finding anything else of use. A quick check of the rest of the cleaned and straightened room told me that if Barbara had left with Hector, there was no way I could know if she had taken anything with her. Anything but the money from the safe.

"Did she have the combination to the safe?" I asked.

"Not exactly," Mitch answered. The question made him uneasy once again.

"What is it you're not telling me this time, Mitch?" I asked as we walked down the stairs.

He hesitated then admitted, "I usually leave the safe rolled."

"What the hell does that mean?" I was beginning to get angry with my friend. I wasn't there because I wanted to be. He had pled with me to help him and now he was being evasive and a real asshole.

"The safe has a six number combination," Mitch explained. "Most of the time I leave it rolled past the first five so all I have to do is turn it to the last number and it opens. Saves me a lot of time and I can never remember the damn numbers when I need to," he answered in an upbeat voice, trying to sound like what he did was a good idea. "I mean, I keep the combination written down in my office downstairs. But I can't remember the damn thing."

"Mitch," I said, stopping halfway down the staircase on our way back to the living room. I turned to face him. "The reason the safe has a six number combination is to make it as difficult as possible for a crook to get inside. By rolling it, as you say, you made it easy for anyone to get inside simply by turning the dial until the pin tumbles and the door opens. That's really smart."

"I know, Morgan. Please don't get on me. Things are so fucked up. I'm sorry," he said.

There was no need to search any other part of the house, I reasoned. It had been thoroughly cleaned several times since Barbara left; everything had been picked up and put away. And besides, Mitch was in no state to be of any help. He followed me to the front door, like a little puppy worried that he might be in trouble.

"OK, Mitch," I said as I opened the door and stepped outside. "I'll see what I can do."

"Remember," Mitch said, almost begging. "No police. I just couldn't stand for everyone to know."

I assured him I wouldn't go to the police. I began to step outside as a police patrol car pulled to the curb. Two uniformed officers got out, carefully adjusted their hats, and dusted off their uniforms. They slowly walked to the door and looked at me. "Mr. Mitchell Krueger?" one of them asked.

"No," I said. "This is Mitch," I said pointing behind me. "What's wrong?"

"May we speak with you, Mr. Krueger?" the officer asked. "May we come inside?"

"Oh my God! Oh my God!" Mitch said. His faced lost its color and for a minute I thought he was going to faint at our feet.

"Look," I said to the two cops. "I'm Morgan Crew. I'm a friend of Mr. Kruegers' and I'm trying to help him find his daughter. Does this have anything to do with her?"

"It would be better if we could talk inside," The other officer said. I held onto Mitch's arm, helping him walk into the house. Mitch fell into a chair, I stood next to him.

"Mr. Krueger, I'm afraid I have some very bad news

for you," the officer began. I waited for Mitch to say something but he remained slumped and silent. I'm not able to read minds, but I would have bet my last dollar that he and I were both thinking that Barbara was dead.

"It's your wife, Mr. Krueger. She's been killed."

Mitch did not react at all. He seemed to be frozen where he sat. I didn't like it at all. Any man would have collapsed or at least come near to it to hear that his wife was dead. But Mitch just sat there, as if waiting to be told something else. I didn't like it at all. And the two cops seemed to not like it either.

We were told that Loretta had been found in a cheap motel out on the highway. She had been found on the floor dressed in an inexpensive and very small nightgown, having been shot six times. The motel's maid had found her that morning. There were no suspects.

TWELVE – So Who Killed Loretta?

Mitch had a dazed and faraway look on his colorless face when I told him I had to go. He was like a kid who couldn't understand why he had to stay home with the baby-sitter; he wanted to go, too. I felt sorry for my friend, but there was nothing I could do for Mitch. All I really wanted to do right then was to get out of there.

But as I started for the door, the officer who was doing all the talking told me I had better stay for awhile, until they found out where Mitch and I had been the night before. It hadn't occurred to me that Mitch might be a suspect in his wife's death, and as for me, well, my gut suddenly started to turn when I realized that I might be a suspect also. I was Mitch's friend and I was with Mitch when the police got there. There were a whole string of reasons why the cops wanted me to stay; none of them were very pleasant to think about at the time.

"Look," I said to the officer. "Do you know who I am?"

I knew it sounded stupid as soon as I had said it. I regretted saying it as soon as the words had fallen from my lips. Both cops looked up at me, the younger one blushed and looked away, fighting to keep the grin off his face.

"No," the older of the two said. "Why don't you take a couple of minutes and you just tell me who the hell you are, Mr. Crew."

I had that coming, I knew it. "I'm sorry," I said. "I

sounded like a real asshole, didn't I?"

"As a matter of fact, you did," he answered. "Look, a woman has been murdered. Without meaning any particular disrespect, I know who you are and your money means nothing to me when a murder has been committed. Now sit down and wait until I get to you." He pointed to a chair.

I sat down, of course. I was beginning to feel like a suspect and the feeling didn't appeal to me very much. I debated whether or not I should be phoning Harper, Harper, Jascro & Nettles, Attorneys extraordinaire. But I figured if I said *anything* at that point, the two cops might divert their attention from Mitch to me. So I sat back and kept my mouth shut.

"Mr. Krueger," the officer said turning slowly to Mitch. "I'm sorry for your loss. I know how devastated you must be. But I have to have to ask you some questions. I hope you understand that it's necessary. Do you need a doctor? I can phone for one. Or is there anyone you should phone? A relative perhaps?"

"What do you mean? Do . . . Do . . . Do you suspect me?" Mitch's voice was trembling, his hands were shaking, and his face was as white as the proverbial sheet. Sweat beaded on his forehead, and little flecks of spit fell from his mouth as he spoke. "I'll sue you for false arrest."

"You're not under arrest, Mr. Krueger," the officer said in a soft voice. "Please calm down and let me ask you a few simple questions. You can be of great help to us in finding out what happened to Mrs. Krueger. Now, Mr. Krueger, when was the last time you saw your wife?"

"This morning . . . Yeah, this morning," Mitch answered, trying but not succeeding to sound calm, assured, and even a little defiant. Here was a guy who had just been told his wife had been murdered. There were no tears, no hysterics, and no emotions. I tried to imagine what I would do, how I would feel, if somebody just told me Sandy had been murdered. I would be over the edge, I told myself. I would be screaming, sobbing, running around like a crazy loon. The police would need to call for restraints and a doctor. I doubted I would ever return to sanity. Mitch just wasn't acting like he should.

"What time this morning?" the cop asked.

Mitch hesitated; his brow furrowed deeply, his hand quickly swiped at his forehead, catching some beads of sweat before they rolled into his eyes. "I don't know. About half past eight I guess. She went out. I don't know where. She didn't say. I didn't ask. She never told me what she was doing. Where she was going. I guess I really didn't care."

I squinted to see the nametag on the officer asking the questions. Vanity keeps me from wearing the glasses I need. The nametag read "Sgt. Tom Simpson". The other officer, much younger than Sgt. Simpson, had a bright shiny new name tag that read "Off. Matt Lowery". Lowery stood by quietly, shuffling from one foot to another, his hands clinched behind his back. I guessed this might be one of his first few days on the job

Sgt. Simpson on the other hand looked and sounded like he knew what he was doing. He was letting Mitch have as much rope as he wanted. I could see where this was going. Simpson would ask a simple question, then just stare at Mitch and let him ramble. Simpson hoped that Mitch would say something he shouldn't say.

I had the choice of sitting by and letting a friend get himself into trouble to protect myself. Or, I could say something and maybe take some of the heat off of Mitch. So, I swallowed hard, leaned forward in the chair, and said, "Look, Mitch, you're in no shape to be doing this right now. You're obviously in shock. Maybe I should call your doctor like the Sergeant suggested. What do you think?"

"Maybe you should call his attorney, Mr. Crew,"

Simpson suggested. "It looks like your friend here was the last one to see Mrs. Krueger alive. And it looks like he may have known she was having an affair with a tennis pro at the Country Club."

When he said that I looked across the room at Mitch. His mouth was hanging open and his eyes were very nearly bugged out of their sockets. But he didn't say anything, he didn't protest, he didn't defend, he didn't deny. It was like he was in a trance.

"Mrs. Krueger was wearing a tennis outfit when she left the house yesterday," Simpson said to me. "Neighbors tell me she went to the club almost every afternoon. For a lesson I'm told. Which is where she was yesterday afternoon at least. None of the neighbors saw her come home yesterday yet your friend saw her this morning." He turned back to look at Mitch and said, "I need to know where you and Mrs. Krueger were between about 3 PM yesterday and 9 AM this morning."

Mitch either couldn't or wouldn't answer. All color had drained from his face and sweat beaded across his forehead. Sgt. Simpson finally suggested that Mitch accompany him to Police Headquarters where they could get everything straightened out.

Simpson suggested that I come to the station as soon as possible and give them a statement. I, of course, agreed and walked out the front door with the three of them. Sgt. Simpson was holding onto Mitch's left arm, mostly to keep the dazed man from falling, but also to let him know he had to come with them.

Neighbors, mainly women at that time of day, were at their doors and in their yards, attracted by the unusual sight of a police car parked in their neighborhood. I stood at the curb and watched my friend as he got into the rear of the police car.

But why the hell would Mitch kill his wife? So she was

having an affair with a tennis pro? It was well known in San Marcos that Loretta would screw any hunk of muscle under 28 years of age, and a lot of not so hunks of muscle over that age. Mitch had to know that, too. So why now? Why get pissed off enough to kill her now? And why not suspect the tennis pro she was screwing? Maybe the cops knew something I didn't.

For the time being, I told myself that the best thing I could do for Mitch was to maybe try to find Mitch's daughter and the gardener she ran off with. If nothing else, Barbara should know of her mother's death, and doing that would keep my mind off my pending troubles with the police. I was rationalizing once again.

As I drove my MGB out of Mitch's gated and guarded community, I tried to think about Barbara and what I knew about her. Considering that she may have been planning to spend a lot of time between the sheets with Hector she probably wouldn't need many clothes. For whatever time the few thousand they took from the safe would last, she would be hard to find. There were a lot of cheap motels within a few hours' drive. But knowing Barbara and her avarice for expensive, material things, I couldn't picture her running off for a week, or even a couple of days of sex without first packing five or six suit cases.

The money they had taken, if they did get into the safe, could have taken them anywhere in the State. Maybe even out of State, but not for long. Checking local 'no-tell' motels might be a place to start, but I wondered if checking out Hector's address first might be smarter. Chances were better than even they were shacked up there anyway.

But before doing that I would stop at the Morelli's home since I had to pass there to get to North Harbor, anyway.

THIRTEEN - And More Dead Bodies

The address Cap'n Nick had given me for the Morelli family turned out to be an older but well maintained house in The Foothills, an area of San Marcos populated by middle class working families who, for the most part, took pride in their homes. The houses were small, but not too small. The yards were clean, but not professionally maintained. The cars were Chevys, Fords, a few foreign imports and a lot of pick-up trucks. The Stars and Stripes flew proudly in many of the yards.

I pulled to the curb and got out of the car. I saw from the street that the Morelli house was vacant, not even curtains remaining on the windows. I walked across the lawn, uncut for weeks, and peered through the large picture window at the front. I could see that the place had been emptied some time ago; dust was everywhere and only a few torn and empty cardboard boxes and wads of newspaper remained.

I went door to door in the neighborhood but no one could be of help. All they could tell me was that the Morelli family had lived there for many years. Franco had bought the house when it was newly built in the late 70's. People who lived nearby were concerned about Franco and Jeremy, some welcomed not having Tony around anymore. His reputation of being young and wild followed him.

From my car I phoned the electric company, the

garbage company, the water company, the telephone company. All services had been disconnected over three months before and no one had any addresses. At the Post Office I was able to get a forwarding address for Franco. The address surprised me; it was only blocks from Hector Morale's address in North Harbor.

I drove to the far north end of Harborside, to a decrepit area of seedy twenty dollar a night motels and stick wood buildings built forty and fifty years ago, which the natives of San Marcos call North Harbor.

Once, many years ago, North Harbor had been a fashionable vacation retreat. World War II was the killing blow for North Harbor. People were caught up in the home front battles. Gas tanks were empty and money was to be made in defense plants in the big cities. Battles on the other side of the ocean and too many dead sons and brothers and fathers occupied people's minds. There was little time for summer vacations when so many were being killed far from home. The vacationers did not come and San Marcos retreated into memories of better times, and like all memories, the reality faded.

Beer bars now draw patrons who want to see women dance naked on dark stages. The women, faces drawn in long masks of boredom and bodies scarred and tattooed, now share Front Street with vacant buildings and cheap flophouses. The once nice hotels and boarding houses, those that had not burned down or fallen under the weight of rot and age, quickly became dank and infested. Drunks sleep in the gutters. Hookers, pimps, drug dealers, and muggers roam the streets of North Harbor.

I found a place to park my beloved MGB and then pulled the canvass top up, wondering if my car would be there five minutes later. I was looking for number 803 Pacifica Street, which ran one block east and parallel to Front Street. The broken-down brown house I parked in front of had cracked and painted wooden numbers eight and three with an empty space between. I guessed from the numbers of the buildings to either side that the zero had long since fallen off and that I had found the house the Morelli's had moved to from their nice little place across town.

I walked slowly up the cracked, weed infested, walkway. The splintered and warped wooden steps at the front of the house were bare of paint or anything else that might protect them from the extremes of weather coming in from the Pacific. They creaked under foot but held me.

I wasn't so sure the porch would do the same. The floorboards were loose and rotten. The broken front porch was filled with rusted crab traps, piles of useless ropes, fishing nets and weather beaten cardboard boxes holding little more than trash. It was a tossup if the porch would accept the weight of anything else, like me for instance. Rags, piles of trash, empty cans of paint and marine varnish, lay across the patches of weeds which passed for lawn.

There was no button for a doorbell. There was a small hole next to the door where a doorbell had once resided. I knocked twice on the door and once on the cracked window next to it. No one answered.

Yellow-brown curtains that may have once been white and of good quality were hung across the grime encrusted window. The heavy layer of dirt and the clouded curtain kept me from seeing into the house. Dozens of dead flies clung to the tattered curtains and lined the sill. I watched a black and brown spider the size of a quarter ambled slowly across the carnage looking for a late lunch perhaps.

On the front porch of the house next door, an ancient fat black man sat on a torn, vinyl covered, auto's rear seat, propped up on several concrete blocks, now being used as a front porch lounge. His hair was solid gray, almost white, uncombed, and in desperate need of a barber. His puffy cheeks and heavy jowls held three or four days of equally gray stubble. Eyeglasses, taped at the bridge of his nose and on the left stem, covered rheumy, yellowed eyes. His huge girth was wrapped in multiple layers of torn, tattered sweaters of just about every color imaginable, all held around him by a belt of frayed hemp rope. He held on tightly to the neck of a bottle of Night Train in his right hand while the stub of a cigarette was about to burn the stained fat fingers of his left.

I stood on the sidewalk in front of the Morelli's house and called to him, "Excuse me. I'm looking for Franco Morelli. Have you seen him or his kids lately?"

"You talkin' t'me?" the man answered in a deep, rasping, phlegm filled voice.

"Yes, I am." I smiled and fought the urge to look around to make sure the old man and I were the only people nearby. "Have you seen Franco Morelli?" I asked.

"I done tol' you las' time an' I done tol' you time 'fo that I ain't the one keeps track of him."

"I've never been here before. You couldn't have told me."

"Well, you white folks all's looks 'like t'me."

He paused to cough a deep, racking cough, which doubled him over as far as his tremendous girth would allow, and then spit a ball of ugly red/yellow phlegm over the broken railing into the brown weeds of his front yard. "I ain't seen none of 'em fo' weeks. Don't care to, neither. You gots a cigarette or two you can spare?"

"Sorry, I don't smoke. Do the Morellis have any friends around?"

"How the hell I'm s'pposed to know? I look like a damn s'ciety sec'tary or sum'tin? You white folks keeps comin' 'round and axin' me this . . . axin' me that. How the hell I'm s'possed t'know?"

"Who's been coming around?"

"Mo' stupid fuckin' questions. I maybe should come

on down there and kick you lily-white ass so's you un'erstan'. Damn white folks in suits is jes' damn white folks in suits. Sometimes they gots shitty fuckin' cars like yours," he laughed at his joke. "An' sometimes they gots big damn black Cad'lacs. Still an' all, they's all the same. Ax'n stupid fuckin' questions, then ax'm agin'. Go on, ya'll leaves me 'lone now fo' I kicks yo' fuckin' ass."

I glanced around the neighborhood for someone else to ask. The building on the other side of 803 had been gutted by a fire some time ago and lay untouched since. Weeds grew four foot tall from inside the burnt frame and out the broken windows. Across the street there was a vacant lot, left to go wild. The nearest business was a seedy bar a block away on Front Street.

I returned to my car wondering why a successful fisherman like Franco Morelli would live in such a place. Why leave such a nice home vacant and move to this rat infested neighborhood?

I started the engine and backed up a few feet to the curb in front of where the fat guy sat on his makeshift couch.

"How long has Mr. Morelli lived here?" I called to him through the open window.

"Now you is axin' sump'tin' new and sump'tin I jes' might's be able t'help you with. Seems I might know jes' 'bout when they done move in. But my mem'ry ain't so good no more. I needs 'nother bottle or two to keeps the mem'ry fresh, ya' un'nerstan' whats I'm saying?"

I left the engine running as I stepped out of the MGB and pulled a ten-dollar bill out of my money clip. I walked to the man's front porch and took the first two of the four steps, then reached out and handed it to him. I really didn't want to get too close.

"Now, that's mo' like it. Why can't you white folks know what it takes t'know sump'tin? Them others pay 'stead of acting nasty, they might'a learned sum'tin, too."

He paused to take a long pull from the bottle of cheap wine, again wiped his mouth on his sleeve, and continued. "Them white folks done moved in 'bout three months 'go, 'bout three months it was. Fust' it was just the young-ass one. Like'n he wasn't 'nuff trouble, what with the loud music, an' them druggers comin' an' goin', an' him racin' that there damn mo'cycle all over all damn night. Then the old fart-ass man and t'other boy starts showin' up. Then nobody fo' quite some time now."

"When did you see them last?" I asked.

"Now you is axin' 'nother damn question, an' 'nother damn question d'serves 'nother bottle or two."

I carefully handed him another ten-dollar bill and stepped quickly back down onto the front walk as the old man smiled his yellow, broken tooth smile, and asked again for a cigarette. He took another long swallow from his bottle of wine, and said in a hoarse whisper, "Well, seems' like I might'a seen the old man and the bigga' kid 'round 'bout two, t'ree days 'go. Ain't seen'em 'round lately."

"How about the younger boy?

"Him I ain't seen fo' quite some time now. I ain't seen the young som'bitch fo' most a week or more."

Another fit of his hacking cough arose from deep inside him. I turned and walked away as the man was bent over, grasping the cigarette stub in one hand and the ever-present wine bottle in the other. I doubted there was anything else the old man could tell me that would be of any use to me.

I got back into the car. Before I drove away I used my cell phone to call the County Tax Assessor. It was a few minutes before five and if I was lucky I'd get them before the office closed. Bureaucrats close offices the very second the clock strikes five. However, I got them before they ran out the door that day.

The woman on the other end sounded angry that

anyone would make an enquiry that close to quitting time. She huffed and puffed but finally went to her computer, looked up the tax bill, and told me that number 803 was owned by Montgomery Properties, a local real estate company. I knew George Montgomery, the owner of Montgomery Properties. He was a member of the Country Club and one of my golf buddies.

He owned great numbers of properties in San Marcos including the new shopping mall near Downtown and several new housing developments, all done by George since his father passed away. There were rumors about them owning equally great numbers of slums in the North Harbor area, but neither George nor anyone else at Montgomery Properties ever spoke about properties there. If George owned 803 then I guessed they did own others, and if that's what George wanted, well it was his business and not mine. But he seemed to be doing well at Real Estate, especially in new developments.

I phoned George at his office and asked if it would be possible to get into the Morelli house. I told George the truth that nobody had seen the Morellis and his friends were beginning to worry.

"Oh, sure thing, Morgan," he said fumbling for words for a second or two. "Look, why don't I grab the key and meet you there."

"You don't have to do that yourself. I can come get the key."

"No, no. I'd just as soon do it myself. Look, let me be honest with you. We own several properties down there and, well damn it all, I'm just not proud of it. Dump them if I could, but there just isn't any market. I'd just as soon not publicize the fact."

"I understand and I appreciate you making the trip."

I turned the engine off and, rather than continue the bright conversation with the fat guy and his bottle, I turned on the radio and listened to some jazz while I waited for George.

It took George twenty minutes to make the ten-minute trip from his office. He apologized and said he had to take a phone call. He mumbled something about a problem closing a sale. We walked to the house as he fumbled with a big, round, brass key ring that held several dozen keys of assorted shapes and sizes.

"I think this is the one," he said. "I haven't figured out the new numbering system yet."

At the door he found out it wasn't the right key but the fifth one he tried worked. He pushed the battered wooden door open on its creaking, rusty hinges. The stench hit us like a ton of bricks. It nearly turned my stomach, and did the whole job on George. He ran for the edge of the porch and lost his lunch into the weeds.

The unmistakable fetor of days old human decay flooded into the street and kept me from going inside the house. From the front door I could see what once may have been Franco Morelli laying face down in the middle of the floor, a dried brown stain stretching out around him. Halfway up the stairs was another body, bent backward in an impossible contortion caused by the gaping hole in the small of his back. Probably one of the sons, I thought.

I closed the door, checked on George who was still emptying his stomach over the porch rail, and ran to my car. I phoned the San Marcos Police.

FOURTEEN - And The Storm Rolled In

Lt. Bob Sommers of the San Marcos Police Department arrived. He was driving his beat up, gray, 1998 unmarked Police Department issue Dodge. He put off replacing the wreck every year to put the money budgeted for a new car into something "more important" for the department.

He was followed by two new black and white police cruisers full of uniformed officers, sirens screaming, lights flashing, guns at the ready, cameras loaded, spools of yellow plastic ribbon to border off and isolate the area, spot lights to light it in when the sun set, radios blaring on loud speakers. Everything that was necessary to put on a show of force and expertise, as well as to show off the equipment they had.

I sat on the front fender of my MGB, watching the show and wishing I had not quit smoking. "Hi, Bob," I said, as I watched Sommers slowly pull his 230-pound frame from the battered, mud sprayed car, and start toward the house before seeing me. "They're dead!" I yelled to my friend. "And you don't have all that many taxpayers in this part of town that you need to put on such a show for."

He turned and waived then joined me in leaning against the fender of the MGB. He lit a cigarette and as usual let some of the smoke trail towards me. Bob is a good friend of mine and I had been pestering him for years to quit smoking, especially considering his weight problems, but he continued to smoke a pack a day and probably would continue to smoke a pack a day until the day it killed him.

He said, after exhaling a deep lungful, "Yeah, I know. But we don't get many murders around here and the guys like to make the most of every opportunity. All this crap," he said, waving one of his hands at the equipment the uniformed officers were working with, "costs a pretty penny and most of the time it just sits around gathering dust. Gives the boys something to do, you know? And it's cheaper than running practice drills."

Sitting on the MGB, a shiver of cold air struck me. I looked up to see the black clouds I had seen earlier that day were now directly over head and a strong breeze off the ocean was turning into the wind that typically fronted a storm coming in from the sea. I had seen it often enough to recognize it. A storm would hit in a few minutes. The breeze also blew Bob's cigarette smoke into my face again. I moved to the other side, up wind of the cigarette, and resumed leaning against the car.

"By the smell, I'd say they had be to dead at least four days, maybe five. It's pretty gross in there." I said.

"You a medical examiner now, Morgan?"

"No. I'm just spit balling, you know. They sure do smell bad though."

"Any ideas?" Bob asked. "Anything I should know?"

"If it is Franco Morelli and one of his sons, they dropped out of sight about a month ago. They've been acting strange for some time; you know, not associating with old friends and like that. I can't picture why a successful guy would want to live here. Joyous, over there," I said, pointing to the fat guy still on the porch next door. "He says the Morelli's moved in about three months ago, just about the time they started acting funny. That's all I know."

"And just why the hell are you looking for them?" he

asked. "What brought you here?"

"You're sitting on it."

"What the hell's that supposed to mean?" he said, flicking the stub of the cigarette into the gutter.

"You asked me what brought me here. My car ..... You know ..... The MGB?"

"OK, so you're a comedian. Now cut the shit and tell me why you're here."

"All I wanted was to spend a day fishing. The Santa Maria's the best-damned group charter around. You remember. I've been trying to get you to go with me but you're always to damn busy. I wanted to take Sandy out with me. When I couldn't phone Franco and couldn't find his boat, I started looking. I found out they left a pretty nice house some time ago and moved to this dump. I don't know why. George Montgomery over there owns the house and he opened the door."

George was sitting in the weeds of the front yard, his chin resting on his knees, his arms tightly locked around his folded legs. He was sickly pale and rocking back and forth, looking like he wasn't done vomiting yet. I heard the sirens of the ambulance behind me. "Maybe you had better radio for another ambulance for George. I don't think he's going to make it," I said to my detective friend.

I stayed for an hour and fifteen minutes. I watched a couple of people in surgical gowns, gloves, and masks carry two black plastic body bags from the house and drive them away. It was getting cold in the early evening; the black storm clouds had engulfed the entire sky overhead, turning it from gentle blue to a hard, cold grey. Drops of rain were beginning to fall.

The police did what they were supposed to do, and they put on a pretty good show doing it. They neatly strung up yellow plastic ribbon around the house. They took a massive amount of photos. One after another they each took a turn trying to talk to Joyous next door while he drank his cheap wine, smoked one cigarette after another, coughed, and spit at the front yard. No one could get anything of use out of him. I finally had to tell Bob to try a ten-dollar bill. That seemed to work but he didn't get anything I had not gotten.

The younger uniformed police officers, men and women, canvassed the neighborhood and spoke to the few people they could find sober enough to talk back.

Cold rain had begun to fall and the wind was really blowing when Bob walked back to my car. I had gotten George to sit in the front seat next to me, out of the weather. He was in no condition to drive so I insisted on taking him home.

"I guess that's it, Morgan," Bob said as he tried to lean into the MGB.

"Any idea how it happened? Who might have done it?" I asked.

"No. It's a real mess inside there. I'd say shotguns probably but as usual, no one heard anything. I guess I'll just wait for the coroner's report."

"Will you let me know, Bob? They were friends of mine," I asked.

Bob said he would and then ran for his car as the real storm hit in a blanket of blinding rain racing in from the sea. The crowds of spectators quickly disappeared in the darkness and rain. The police picked up all their expensive equipment, leaving the yellow ribbon ever so neatly strung around the property and a paper seal on the front door of the house.

I drove George home and told him I would arrange to have his car brought back the next day. George didn't seem to care. He just wanted to get into his house quickly. As I pulled to the curb in front of George's home, he pulled his suit coat over his head and ran up the walk and into the house without saying anything to me.

I then drove back to Harborside and ran through the rain to Cap'n Nick's. I had two large bourbons to warm myself up on the inside and to help me not care about being wet on the outside. I sat at the bar, the Cap'n and Sandy stood on the other side, and I began to tell them about what I had found.

Sandy's face turned suddenly ashen when she heard the story and she grabbed hold of the edge of the bar to keep from falling. "Were they men or women?" she asked.

"Both men, I think," I answered. I thought for a moment she was going to faint. But she ran off to the kitchen to cry. I wanted to comfort her, to hold her tightly, but I felt I should give her a few minutes to be alone first. Cap'n Nick slammed his fist on the bar and swore, "Goddamn! Why? Why Franco?"

"They aren't sure it is Franco yet. The shotguns did a hell of a lot of damage. We'll have to wait for positive ID."

"Bull shit! You know it's Franco! Somebody killed him and I want t'know who it was so I can kill'em myself."

"The police will take care of that," I said. "Bob Sommers is on it and he's good. If anybody can find who killed them, he will."

"Police be damned. I never trust cops. They no good. I gonna' find out myself. I got a gun, too. I gonna' find out an kill'em."

"No, you won't, Cap'n," I said trying to calm the old man down. "There's nothing you can do except get yourself in trouble."

"Who gonna stop me? I tell you I gonna find out who done it and I kill'em myself."

"I'm going to stop you if I have to. I won't let you do anything that stupid. Losing Franco is enough. I don't want to lose my other good friend. Bob Sommers is a friend of mine; we go back quite a few years. He's promised to keep

me up to date on what he finds. And I promise you that I will
see to it that he does everything possible to find out who
killed our friend. Use your head, Cap'n. You're angry,
you're all heated up. Stay here and let me take of it."

"O.K. You find out who killed Franco. You come tell
me and I kill'em myself with my bare hands. No guns, just
my hands." He held up his two meaty fists and curled the
powerful fingers around an imaginary neck. I didn't doubt for
one minute that the Captain could easily kill somebody with
those hands of his. And it probably wouldn't be the first time,
either.

"You won't kill anybody, Cap'n.   Let the cops do their
job."

"I tell you what I gonna do," he said, stepping back
and throwing his barrel chest out. "You go find out who
killed my friend. Do what y'a gotta do an' come back an' tell
me. You do that an' I leave it to the cops to put'em in jail."

"You want me to find out who killed the Morellis?
You've got to be out of your mind! How am I supposed to do
that?" I asked, incredulous at the idea.

"You know everybody. You keep saying that. You
just braggin' or what? You go do it an' I don't care what you
gotta do. You don't do it an' I will. You make the choice."

I had no choice to make. I had to do something to
keep the Cap'n out of trouble, until Bob Sommers made an
arrest. The Cap'n was an old world, hot tempered former
smuggler who believed in and lived his life according to that
old world's code of vengeance. I had no doubt that he would
actually kill someone to revenge his friends deaths.

"O.K.," I said. "You've got yourself a deal. But I want
your word that you'll stay out of this. No going off the deep
end. You don't hurt, talk to, or even look at anybody. OK?"

"Yeah, OK," he said. But could I believe him?

I poured a third bourbon from the bottle the Cap'n had
left in front of me and sipped it slowly as I debated with

myself to see if I could eat anything. I still had the smell of death from the house in my nostrils, and the picture of the torn apart bodies imprinted on my brain. Sandy finally came out of the kitchen, wiping the last of her tears from her eyes with a white kitchen towel. The Cap'n walked with her around the end of the bar to where I was sitting, his arm wrapped around her, holding her close to him, making her look small in comparison to his great bulk. She was given a bear hug by the huge peg legged seaman and then fell into my gentler arms.

"Everything's gonna be o.k. now," the Cap'n said, his hand on her shoulder. "Morgan, he gonna find out who killed Franco."

FIFTEEN – And Now Hector

If the two people I had found in the North Harbor slum were two of the Morelli family there was nothing I could do for them right then. I had to keep the Cap'n out of it, keep him under control, and keep him from doing something stupid. And I still had Mitch Krueger to think about. I was now trying to help two people when all I wanted to do was head out to the golf course. This whole thing of trying to be Mr. Nice-guy maybe wasn't panning out, I thought.

I still had to check out Hector Morales' place, I *had* promised to do that. So I drove back to North Harbor through the steady rain and found the address. After parking my car at the curb I waited behind the wheel, listening to a John Coltrane cut, knowing that the rain wasn't going to stop and that I was going to get soaked running up to the apartment door. So I turned off the radio and made a quick dash across the sidewalk and up the stairs and found shelter under the porch roof, sharing it with a burnt out light bulb, some trash, and some ugly bugs. The sun had set more than an hour before and the storm made it even darker that night.

The door was solid wood with a lead-glass oval insert, in remarkably good condition despite the peeling paint. It was a real antique, probably as old as they get in San Marcos. On the outside of the door hung a broken wooden screen door, supported by only the top one of what should have been three hinges. I pushed it aside, tried the door, and found it unlocked.

Inside the entryway the air was musty and old but better than I had expected for this part of town. A faded red oriental rug, with several holes worn in it, ran up the wooden staircase; a few pieces of old furniture sat in the thin hallway. A bare low-watt bulb hung from the ceiling above the first stair, casting a pale yellow light for about five feet around, leaving the rest of the stairway and hallway in darkness.

There were mailboxes just inside the doorway, six in all, built into the wall. The last one had 'H. MORALES' scribbled in pencil on a scrap of paper and taped under a letter slot. It was numbered apartment six.

Number six was the last door on the third floor. There was no light coming from under the door. I pressed my ear to the peeling paint on the thin door and heard nothing. I tried the knob but the door was locked. I knocked softly, three times, but there was no answer. If there were somebody in there - I rationalized once again - they'd surely come to the door or make some kind of noise.

I told myself that one-day I'd have to learn how to pick a lock, like Rockford did on T.V. The hallway was dimly lit by another single, low wattage, bulb, hung from the ceiling at the top of the stairs. The next nearest door was at the far end of the hall, near the stairs. I looked closely at the door. It was a not as solid looking as the front door had been. I guessed that the aged door was not very heavy, probably a hollow core, and that the lock was as old and flimsy as everything else. But it proved to be more solid than it looked when it held up under the two kicks that I gave it. The door jam, however, was not as sturdy and gave way, and the door to Hector's apartment swung open and crashed against the inside wall.

Anyplace else, the noise of the doorframe breaking would have stirred neighbors to at least look outside their doors. In that neighborhood, people learned to take care of themselves and the hell with what happened to anybody else.

Inside #6 I found what would have been a fairly nice place to live, were it not for the filth and mess everywhere. There was a fairly large living room, a modest kitchen, a bedroom, and a bath. Piles of clothes lay everywhere, bags of rotting garbage lay spilled, plates of molding food were scattered around, stacks of old newspapers lined the walls. The furniture, what there was of it, was a collection of Salvation Army rejects, torn, filthy and broken.

I imagined that the place was normally in the condition in which I had found it, which meant it would be impossible to tell when the last time was anyone had been there. I couldn't find the remains of any fresh food, although there were pots and pans and dishes growing various green and blue fuzzy things. Nothing else appeared to have been used recently.

The bed sheets were rumpled and in need of washing. I pawed carefully through the only closet in the place and found only what I would have expected to be there, that is a lot of dirty clothes

I left the apartment quietly. No one had seen me come in, and I walked down the stairs quickly but as softly as I could, hoping no one would see me leave. I really didn't want to answer a charge of breaking and entry into a filthy slum.

I got into my car as quickly as possible, trying to stay as dry as I could. My cell phone started ringing. "Yeah!" I said, by way of answering the phone, and was immediately sorry for sounding so grumpy.

"Hi, Morgan. This is Mitch . . . Mitch Krueger. I was hoping to get you. I need to talk to you."

"Mitch," I said, sounding quite exasperated. "Just tell me what you need."

"Well, look. You don't need to look for Barbara. I

mean, I want you to stop looking for her."

"Why?" I asked. I was curious at the sudden change of plans.

"Look, Morgan, please just stop looking for her, ok?"

"Are you at home?" I asked.

He didn't answer. I heard him breathing hard, in shallow gasps. I began to worry. The man might be sick, maybe having a heart attack or stroke. "I'm going to be at your house in ten minutes, Mitch," I said as I started the MGB's engine. "I want you to wait there, alright?"

I left some rubber on the driveway as I spun the car on the wet pavement. I regained control and sped away. Ignoring several stop signs, I ran a couple of red lights. I wasn't too worried about a cop stopping me in North Harbor. They were few and far between down there. When I approached Mitch's neighborhood I didn't slow down even while passing the guard's gatehouse, deciding the guard wouldn't want to get wet chasing me.

I slammed on the brakes, bringing the MGB to a skidding stop in front of Mitch's door. I ran to the door through the rain and punched the doorbell while I pounded on the door with my fist.

A too young lady holding a bright red-silk oriental robe tightly around her opened the door an inch or two and peered out at me. I thought I knew all of Mitch's relatives, but this sexy young thing, who was letting just enough of herself show from beneath the robe, was someone new.

"I need to see Mitch. Please let me in," I said. I tried to rationalize that I shouldn't really be surprised to see a woman in Mitch's house. I knew, as did most people in San Marcos, that Loretta had been whoring around town for years. Why shouldn't Mitch have a little something on the side, too? But tried as I might, I couldn't find justification for Mitch to have his little friend over hours after being told his wife had been murdered.

"Mitch doesn't want to see you." Her voice was slurred and I could smell booze, scotch I guessed, and a fair amount of it.

"Well, I need to see him. Please let me in."

"Go away or I'll call the police," she said, and she slammed the door as hard as she could, right in my face. I was torn between kicking the damn door down and going home. What the hell, it wasn't my kid. As I paced across the porch, getting soaked, I heard my cell phone ringing back in my car. I ran and made it to the car on the fifth ring, and picked it up.

"Morgan?" It was Mitch Krueger. "Morgan, is that you?"

"Of course it's me! Who the hell do you think it is!" I yelled into the phone. "What the hell's going on here?"

"Sorry, but it's best if you just forget all about this. See . . . Well . . . Everything's worked out. Everything's ok now."

"Is Barbara back?" I asked. "Have you heard from her?"

"Look, it's ok. You don't need to be concerned," he said.

"Who's your little friend, Mitch? Helping you plan your wife's funeral, is she?"

"That's none of your business, Morgan. You're a friend and you tried to help. But I don't need your help anymore. Just go away, will you."

"Mitch, are you O.K.? Are you in trouble? Are you sick?"

He didn't answer but I could hear his fast, short breaths over the line. "Did you hear me, Mitch?" I asked. "Are you O.K.? Do you need a doctor?"

"No. It's ok," he said in a whispered, muffled voice.

"OK, Mitch, have it your way. But it's possible your daughter could be in some trouble. Anytime you want, I'll go looking for her. Anytime you want. How did it go with the police?"

"Fine . . . fine. They just wanted to talk to me, get some facts, you know. It's O.K."

I waited, listened, but all I heard was the hyperventilated breathing on the other end of the line.

"Look, Mitch," I said. "If you need anything, anything at all, just call me. O.K.?"

Mitch didn't answer and a second later the line went dead. I sat in my MGB, turned on some jazz, and listened to the heavy rain pound on the car's canvass top. The rain blew so hard that I couldn't see out the windshield. San Marcos was blurred in front of me, and it was becoming blurred in my mind, too. In a matter of a couple of days, the pretty balloon that was San Marcos had been burst. Maybe it wasn't the ideal place after all, I thought. It, too, suffered from murder and depravity. I shivered, partly at the thought and partly from the cold, wet clothes I sat in.

I was wet, soaked to the skin, and cold. I was tired. I was feeling slightly sick and hoped I hadn't caught some flu or something from running around in the rain. I debated going home and getting drunk, or going to see Sandy. I decided I would feel better seeing Sandy, after I got into some dry clothes.

SIXTEEN – That Night At Home

I took the drive back to Cap'n Nick's slowly. I had time to think while I was at home, peeling the wet clothes off and then letting the hot water from the shower sooth me. And sometimes thinking long and hard on a subject isn't such a good thing. Looking back on all that happened from that point on, I wish now I had taken Sandy and run off to someplace, like maybe Santa Barbara, and spent a week or two on the beach. I mean, three people were dead, and as much as I might sympathize with their survivors, I should only have been concerned to the point of sympathy. I had no responsibility in any of it. If I had run away, what was to follow maybe would never have happened.

And then there was that nagging little voice. Even as a child, I had this thing that lived somewhere inside my head. Every time something just wasn't kosher, this thing, this little voice, whispered something in the back recesses of my mind. When it talks to me I can just barely hear it, and often I can't quite make out what it is saying. But I always knew, even as a child, it was trying to warn me of something that might wind up hurting me.

And right then, as I stood under the hot shower, it was saying quite clearly that something just didn't fit right and that something could mean trouble or danger for me. Over the years I had often brushed aside what the little voice was saying, and when I did I always wound up in some kind of trouble. As I had driven away from Mitch Krueger's house, I had heard the first faint whispers telling me to drive away from Mitch's problems, to not get myself involved at all. But that was one of those many times when I chose to disregard the little voice. But I would be very careful, and I promised myself to remember there was more coward in me than hero.

When I arrived at Cap'n Nick's, Sandy told me she didn't want to go out to dinner as we had planned. The news of finding the two bodies inside the Morelli home had upset her too much, she said. So I phoned to cancel our restaurant reservation and drove her to my home. Inside I started a fire in the big stone fireplace, poured two very large brandies, and as she sipped hers, curled on the floor in front of the flames, I went to the master bath and filled the tub with hot water for her.

Sandy liked my home; she was comfortable there and was beginning to feel as if it were her home, too. She had taken over half my closet and several of my dresser drawers, but I didn't complain.

I liked my house, too. After my father passed away, followed a few short months later by my broken hearted mother, I sold the old house on the hill that had been in the family since the mid-19th century. I bought a piece of land closer to Downtown, on the crest of a smaller hill and built my home. The Country Club's entire valley could be seen from the front of the house. There was a subdued view from large front windows, through the trees, of Indian Falls and part of the golf course across the valley, and on the rear deck I could sit and watch the fishing boats coming and going in San Marcos Harbor far below.

The road leading up the hill to the house ended at a small parking area where my friends left their cars. The house was on several levels, descending down the hillside on the rear. There were stone walls, lots of glass to let light in, tall ceilings, and a huge kitchen where I spent a lot of time cooking for Sandy and the many friends who were often there.

Sandy said she didn't want to, but I insisted she have a second brandy while she was soaking in the tub. After pouring it for her, I went to the kitchen and filled a pan with some of the beef soup I had made over the weekend. I enriched it with the top 20% of a bottle of deep red burgundy. I threw together a simple green salad and warmed a half loaf of crusty French bread. Cooking, I mean trying to cook well, has become a passion with me.

When the table near the glass doors leading out onto the back deck had been set, I called to her. She arrived feeling better, a little tipsy from the two large brandies, and wrapped in one of my thick cotton bathrobes. Her hair was a wonderful mess; damp curls framed her tear puffed, beautiful face. She pushed at her hair self-consciously but she had never looked more beautiful to me. She had washed all the tear-streaked makeup from her face, which was now colored by the second brandy and steamy bath. She kissed me quickly and sat at the table, one leg tucked under her as she often did, pulling the robe tightly around her.

I had been consumed in deep thought about Mitch Krueger, so deep in fact that I had failed to comprehend the depth of Sandy's emotional outpouring over the Morelli's. I hadn't fully appreciated it, that is, until I saw her sitting across the table from me, holding back her tears as she sipped small amounts of the soup's broth. Then it hit me; she should not be taking the deaths that hard. She just wasn't that close to them to be mourning at this depth. That little voice was saying something again. I kept hearing, amongst the whispered mumbling, "RUN AWAY, RUN AWAY".

We ate silently, watching the wind and rain come into the bay and swirl around the surrounding cliffs and through the bending trees. From the warm shelter of the house perched on top of the hill we could see the storm race in from the sea, be captured in the crescent hills of San Marcos, and whip around fiercely in an attempt to escape its confinement.

I opened a bottle of good, if not expensive, Pinot Noir, which went well with the beefy soup and bread. Sandy ate without thinking about what she was doing, her mind was somewhere else, but I let her eat all she could. When we were finished I filled the glasses with the last of the red wine and we sat back to watch the storm blow itself out.

Twenty minutes went by as we sat and watched the gale, before Sandy spoke a word. I had decided it was best to just be there, to be quiet, and to let her work it out inside herself. I didn't understand what was happening to her, so for the time being, I would keep quiet and listen.

I jumped slightly when she said suddenly, "I'm sorry I'm being such a lousy guest." She peered down into her wineglass and twirled the red liquid around into a tiny whirlpool. "I really wanted to invite you into that wonderful big tub of yours with me but I just feel so rotten. About Tony, I mean."

"They only found two bodies," I said, trying awkwardly to make her feel better, hoping I wasn't saying the wrong thing. "Maybe Tony wasn't one of them. We don't even know if they were the Morellis."

"The poor kid. Sometimes I thought he was just joking. Sometimes I thought he might be serious. You know, about wanting to date me? He was such a good-looking kid. Why'd he want to hang around with a broad ten years older than him when he could have any woman in town?"

"Hey, did you ever look at yourself in a mirror?" I asked. "Anybody would have to be stupid not to want to be with you."

"Thanks," she said. Her eyes smiled again. A good sign that she might be coming out of the blue funk that had enfolded her. "It's not that I worry about him or anything. I mean, I'm not in love with the kid or anything. I just feel so sorry for him and for his old man."

"Why?" I asked. I wanted to keep her talking. I wanted her to talk about what was really making her so emotional.

"Oh, you know. The kid was always trying to live up to his older brother, but Franco was really tough on the kid. Jeremy could do everything right. Jeremy could run the ship. Tony wasn't ready yet. Jeremy could fix the engines. Tony wasn't ready yet. You know." She sipped at her wine and stared blankly out the glass doors. "Jeremy never treated the kid badly, but Franco was always pushing him. He never let the kid do what kids were supposed to do. Sometimes I think Franco pushed so hard it caused Tony to hate his old man."

"Enough to kill him?" I asked without thinking about what I had said so suddenly.

"No," she said firmly, shaking her head, taking no offense. "Not Tony. Sure, he was as wild as everyone said, but kill his own father? No, I just know Tony could never do that. With all the bad things he was doing, I think he was really O.K. deep inside. I think maybe he was doing all those wild things to get back at Franco, or maybe just to get Franco to take notice of him."

"How wild was he?" I asked. "I only ever saw him on the boat and he seemed O.K. to me there. Maybe a little quite, but O.K."

"He was a kid, you know. Fast cars, motorcycles, lots of girls." She was peering deeply into her glass as if trying to see something in the swirling wine, and then she looked up at me quickly. "But that's because he was so damn cute. He got drunk once in awhile and got into a fight or two, but all kids do that. It's part of growing up. He told me once he had some marijuana and wanted me to smoke with him."

"Did you?" I asked.

"Of course not. That's not my thing. A little booze," she said raising her glass in a mock toast. "And you in bed. That's all I need to get me high."

She reached out and touched my hand lightly, smiling with those wonderful eyes of hers.

"I just know he wasn't a bad kid. I just know it. Do you think you can really find out who killed him?" she asked.

I didn't want to tell her that my whole plan on finding out who killed the Morellis was to sit patiently on the sidelines and let the police do their job. But I had to tell her something, something that would placate her for a time. I didn't want to disappoint her or have her angry with me.

"Let's find out if he's dead first," I said. "I'm sure Bob Sommers will let me know what's going on. We don't even know if the dead people are the Morellis. When there is something I can do, I will do it."

The storm blew itself out sometime during the night. Sandy slept deeply, curled against me, and hardly moved the night through. I watched her and thought about her, about how wonderful she was and how much I loved her. I brushed a strand of hair from her face shortly before falling asleep myself, about five in the morning.

We awoke to one of those beautiful days San Marcos enjoys. The ground outside was sodden and riddled with the remains of what had been stirred up during the night. The storm had been a loud one, most people would say violent, but not an uncommon one for San Marcos. After more than thirty years I had become used to these occasional breaks in the normally good weather, and I enjoyed watching them from the warmth, safety, and comfort of my home.

That morning greeted us with a clear blue sky, warm sun, and the promise of a good day. The occasional storm was enjoyed by most of the residents; they knew they needed it to keep the hillsides green and thick.   Whatever the reasons for the weather, I had the feeling that the weather that draws so many people to San Marcos would eventually be the cause of its demise from over-population. My quiet little town wasn't so quiet anymore and wasn't so little anymore.

Sandy put a pot of coffee on and put the dishes from the night before in the washer while I rode my bicycle down the hill to Sam Goldman's bakery.   I dodged the small branches and storm flotsam left in the street, riding both hand brakes down the paved curves to the fringe of Downtown.   The air smelled cool and clean after the rain which had left a bite of dampness behind.   The sun would soon take care of that.

When I finally reached the bakery that morning, I bought several raisin-bran muffins and a large loaf of the crusty bread I loved. I rode my bike to the bakery countless times when I was a kid.   Mr. Goldman would let me watch him make the wonderful cakes, rolls, and breads in the back of his shop, late into the night. We would talk baseball in the summer, football in the winter, and girls when I was a little older.   Two or three free cookies in a bag would always accompany my ride home.   He was old back then, yet he was still in the shop every day, now helping his two sons with the recipes.   Nowadays, I don't get the cookies anymore, damn it!

The ride down to Mr. Goldman's was easy.   The ride back was tough. I keep forgetting that the ride back home from Downtown is all uphill. I hardly worked up a sweat as a kid, now it about kills me.   But I made it, as I always do despite my complaining about it, without bothering to dodge the twigs and branches on the way home. Inside my house I fell into a chaise lounge on the deck where I lay for a few minutes trying to catch my breath.

Sandy brought the coffee outside from the kitchen and I managed to eat one of the rich muffins while she devoured two and started on a third. "Well," she asked. "Where do we start?"

"Well, if you really want to, how about we start in the living room. It's a bit cold out here to get naked. Or we could just go back to bed."

"I don't mean that."

"Where do we start what, then?" I asked.

"Where do we start looking for Tony's killer, of course?"

I sat up, put my coffee cup on the small glass topped table at my side, and turned to look at her. "First of all," I said. "*We* don't start doing anything, and second of all, the police are going to do just fine."

I was trying to sound authoritative, but I wasn't very good at that kind of thing. And I had the feeling I was starting one of those losing battles I had become used to getting into with Sandy.

"Cap'n Nick is counting on you. You promised. You have to find the killer."

"I said that so he wouldn't go off and get himself into trouble. Let the police do what they get paid to do."

This went on for a few minutes; I would tell her to butt out, she would insist on butting in. Like all women, she was holding an ace, and she played it with every intention of playing dirty and playing to win.

"There's no way I could have anything to do with a man who wouldn't do whatever he could to find the killer of a friend's best friend's son, and I certainly wouldn't let that man near enough to me to touch me if he couldn't and wouldn't find that killer . . ."

She went on and on without a break to take a breath. I didn't bother asking her to stop, she wouldn't anyway. Nor did I ask her to repeat what she had said, I knew she could have and would have. I simply slumped back into the chaise and set my mind to the fact that Sandy would be tagging along while I did what I could. That little voice in the back of my head began again. "RUN AWAY. RUN AWAY."

SEVENTEEN - Playing Detective

So Sandy D'Angelo and I were going to go off together to play detective. I had a deep, inside my gut, feeling that we were going to get ourselves into trouble. I hoped that trouble would just be with the police and not with a killer. But I also knew I could not stop Sandy.

I had no idea what I was going to do, but I felt I should tell Sandy about Mitch Krueger and his missing daughter, since she was going to be tagging along for a few days, poking her pretty little nose into what was obviously a police matter. I had already made up my mind that I would continue looking for Barbara, despite the little voice telling me not to.

And besides, it was a good excuse to not devote all my time to the Morellis, at least, that is, until I knew the two victims I had found were the Morellis. *And* when I was told they were the Morellis, well then it would be a police investigation and there was little I would be able to do anyway, which in my mind, brought me back to one worry, the Kruegers'. *And* fumbling around, trying to find a young slut, sounded like a safer way to spend time with Sandy than stumbling into the face of a murderer.

So we sat in the early morning sun and finished our coffee. Sandy finished the muffins. I took a deep breath and said, as nonchalantly as I could, "By the way. A friend from the country club asked me to look for his daughter. Seems she's run off with the gardener."

"Ummm, class conflict, huh?" she said with a sly look

101

on her face that said, 'Hey, this is going to be fun.'

"And just what is that supposed to mean?" I asked, already knowing the answer.

"Well," she said, setting aside the newspaper she had been reading. "We appear to have a country club girl, who in some people's minds means a very privileged person, involved with a gardener, who in those same people's minds means one of us lower class, working class, dregs of society. In short why not let the girl have a fling with what might well be the first real man she ever knew? After all, she can't have met very many real men at that snob warehouse you call a country club."

'That's cute," I said. "But in this case, the young lady might actually be in some trouble, of her own making probably, but still trouble."

"Oh, what kind? And if you say she married out of her station in life, I think I may kick you were you don't want to be kicked."

So I told her most of what I knew about Barbara Krueger, including the fact that her mother had been murdered the day after Barbara disappeared. I didn't tell her Mitch didn't want me going out looking for Barbara, I figured as long as we were going to play detective together, maybe I could interest her in something safer than the Morelli's murder.

Sandy had wanted to have some fun with me about class separation and all that until I mentioned the murder. Then the clever, mischievous smile disappeared and I saw a hint of fear quickly cross her face, which she did her best to camouflage.

"What's the matter?" I asked. "Did I say something wrong?"

She hesitated then said, "No. It's just . . . well, it's just that I hate to see a young girl get mixed up in dangerous stuff, you know. Some girls grow up too fast. I hate to see them used."

"Well, you're right of course," I agreed, trying to be supportive as, I imagined, a man is expected to be. "But in this case, I have a feeling Barbara Kruegers' not being used. I mean, her mother's been murdered. And I have a feeling that she's not involved in the murder. What that means is that Barbara may be using the gardener," I explained. "At least she's using Hector about as much as he's using her."

Sandy pushed herself out of her chair and paced across the deck, her arms folded tightly in front of her.

"I find that hard to believe," she said faintly. I barely heard her.

"What are we talking about here?" I asked as I pushed myself up to sit on the edge of the chaise. I blocked the sun from my eyes with my hand so that I could see her standing with her back to me, looking out across the hillside towards the bay. The slight morning breeze caught her long, soft hair and made it dance gently about her shoulders.

"Do you understand?" I asked. "The girl's mother has been murdered, the day after the girl disappeared? That's quite a coincidence and I don't believe in coincidences. I think that fact is slightly more important than a spoiled brat girl screwing some muscle bound punk."

"I know," she said, her back still turned to me and her arms crossed tightly in front of her.

"I just hate the thoughts of a young girl being used. I know her mother is dead, but I didn't know her mother."

"You've never met Barbara either."

"I know . . ."

"What's so hard to believe? A young girl who happens to like sex with a wide variety of guys?"

"That's just the point," she said, spinning around to face me. Tears were filling her eyes and spilling onto her cheeks. "She'll be dragged into really bad stuff eventually. Stuff like drugs and pain. That's all I'm saying."

The conversation was not going anywhere I wanted it to go and it was affecting Sandy too much, so I let it end there. I had too many other things to think about right then. I didn't want to think bad things about Sandy, but I couldn't stop myself from worrying. No matter what was happening, whatever I was not yet aware of, I would not stop loving her nor worrying about her.

EIGHTEEN - The Pretty Lady

Despite what was happening to my friends and my town, I had Sandy by my side. So not everything was bad. I both enjoyed having her with me, and I was grateful that I would be able to watch her closely, to talk with her. And most important of all to try to determine what, if anything, she was not telling me. And there was certainly something she was not telling me.

She was excited about playing detective, she dressed quickly that morning, hastily applying the minimal make-up she normally used, and rushed me out the door. Sandy had the idea that all you had to do was ask a few questions and someone was bound to confess, like they do on TV. At the end of all the Perry Mason movies the guilty person stands up and says, "Yes, I did it! Ha ha! I killed him and I'm glad of it!"

I had a strong suspicion that real life wasn't like that. Real crooks seldom confess. I had heard somewhere that ninety nine percent of everybody in prison was innocent if you were to listen to the prisoners and believe them. I knew it wasn't as easy as Sandy thought it would be, but what the hell, spending time with my girl was always fun, no matter what we were doing. If she wanted to play for a few days, I would play along with her.

She had also gotten the idea from somewhere that I owned a gun, which I do not.

"You mean to say," she said. "Here we are going after a bunch of killers, maybe psychos, and you aren't carrying a big gun!"

I, in fact, had fired a gun only once, at the police firing range. Bob Sommers had taken me, showed me how to handle and safely fire both a revolver and a semi-auto. I had never felt a fear of guns; I just never had felt a need to own one.

Sandy sat huddled in the far corner of my small car. Her arms were crossed tightly in front of her. She glared out the side window with a pouting face just because I wasn't carrying some kind of bazooka tucked under my arm in an uncomfortable shoulder rig, like she said real detectives always wear. I reminded her I wasn't a real detective, but that didn't make any difference to Sandy.

I knew that nothing could be done about the Morellis until the coroner made his report so I drove Sandy to the only place I could think of; North Harbor and the police-sealed Morelli home. I parked the MGB at the curb in front of the ramshackle house. Sandy jumped out quickly and all but ran up the front walk, jumping over the yellow crime scene tape, which by that time was hanging limp across the walk. I followed, trying to catch up to her. I reached her as she peered into the grime covered front window.

Not able to see anything inside, she suggested that we break the police seal on the front door and go inside to look for "clues". I explained that if she really wanted to find the killer it would be easier to do it outside of a jail cell, which is where we would certainly wind up if we broke the police crime scene seal on the door. She shrugged her shoulders, which was the closest thing I was going to get to an admission that I might be right.

The old man next door was on the torn automobile seat on his front porch. He held a newly lit cigarette between his fat, stained fingers, and drank from a new bottle of cheap wine, part of the twenty dollars I had given him probably. He coughed and spit, then drank some more wine. Sandy saw him, smiled broadly, waived and called out to him, "Hi! You must be the Morelli's neighbor. Can we talk to you for a minute?"

"Why, you certainly can, pretty lady. Not often 'nuff I gets to talk to pretty ladies, 'specially pretty as you. You come on up here." He waived his sweater wrapped, fat arm in a sweeping arc, spilling some of the wine from the bottle as a result, and grinned broadly, showing off his broken, yellow teeth.

I tried to grab her arm but she was too quick for me and shook out of my grip. She dodged and shrugged past me, and walked across the weed filled front yard to the old man's front steps. I followed her onto the garbage-strewn porch.

"Y'all sits ya'self down there, pretty lady," the old man said, motioning to a torn vinyl covered aluminum kitchen chair. She swept a few filthy rags off the chair with a quick movement of her hand and sat down, still managing to smile sweetly. She crossed her legs and expertly slid her skirt up showing a good four inches of well shaped leg above her knees, which was well appreciated by the old man.

Sandy smiled one of her big, bright smiles again, lighting up the dreary porch and the old man's face. "We're detectives," she began. I raised a hand and started to correct her, but before I could jump in to deny the assertion, both the old man and Sandy, in unison, told me to be quiet. There was no winning that one either.

"We're investigating the murders next door and we hope you can help us," she said.

"Anything I can do fo' you, little lady," he answered, smiling through the row of broken teeth and empty spaces, "I will most certainly do anything fo' you. Ax away." He tried to imitate a courtly bow but all he could manage was an unsteady sweep of his left arm and a nod of his head.

When he had finished and had straightened up, Sandy said, "That's great, I'm sure you'll be a great help. Mr. Crew here told me that other people have been asking about the Morellis. Do you know who they were?"

"Sure, I seen 'em 'round before. But don't know they names. They comes 'round now an' then t'collect the numbers. An' I seen 'em sellin' dope, too."

"How come you didn't tell me that yesterday?" I asked.

"'Cause you didn't ax, dummy!" he said, scowling up at me through blood shot eyes. He turned back to face Sandy and smiled quickly again, leaning forward and offering her the bottle. She smiled sweetly and said she couldn't drink while she was on her period. I almost burst out laughing, but managed to restrain myself.

"I done heard of women folk like that," he said taking a long swallow himself. "My sym'thies. What else you wanna know?"

"When was the last time they were around looking for the Morellis?"

"Let's see," he said thoughtfully, scratching a few days gray stubble on his several chins. "Roun' 'bout maybe a week ago, maybe that, maybe a day or two mo'."

"Did you hear any gunshots recently?" Sandy asked.

"'Course I did. Pretty lady, you lives 'round here, you hears' gunshots near every night. But I suspects you wants t'know 'bout the big ones. What I took t'be shotguns," he said knowingly, leaning forward, and whispering the words conspiratorially, with a wink of his rheumy eye. "Sure, I heard 'em. Four, maybe five of 'em. Real fast like. Like thunder. BOOM, BOOM, ya'know? Or big canons or sump'tin like, ya' unnerstan' what I'm sayin'?"

"When was that?" I asked quickly, now very interested in what I was hearing.

"Look, whitey," the old man said, looking up at me

slowly. "I is helpin' the little lady here, not you."

"When did you hear the shotguns?" Sandy asked.

He turned back to her and answered, "Five nights ago." He spoke sweetly, smiling again. "Would'a been Wednesday last week. Real early like. Woke me 'bout two, three in the morning."

"Did you see anything?"

"Looked out m'window. Saw the same damn ol' black Cad'lac that thems' dope an' numbers men drive. Parked right over there," he said pointing an unsteady, fat, bent finger at the curb across the street from the Morelli's house. "It was raining sump'tin fierce on an' off. Didn't go out, no I didn't. Too smart t'get myself in trouble knowin' nothin'. Best way is to know nothin', then nobody wants t'hurt ya'."

It seemed foolish to me to ask him anything directly so I asked Sandy to ask him if he had told this to the police the day before. She repeated my question.

"No! Why shoulds I?" He spit out the words along with a few drops of spittle. "White damn policeman never done nothin' fo' me 'cept put me in jail an' treat me like shit. The pretty lady here, she's too pretty not t'tell what I seen, though." He smiled again.

"Ask him if the men in the Cadillac have been back looking for the Morellis since the shooting," I said.

She repeated what I had said once again, and he answered, "Nope, I sits out here near ever' day t'watch the world go by and I ain't seen 'em since."

"Ask him . . ." this was getting ridiculous, I said to myself. "Ask him when they usually come back to collect the numbers." Sandy repeated my question.

"'Bout the first of every month, sometimes 'round the middle of the month too but not so often."

Sandy asked the next question on her own, "Did the Morellis have any friends in the neighborhood? Anybody that might know something?" I had to admit, she did have somewhat of a talent for this sort of thing.

"No," he answered. "Ain't nobody 'round here gots no friends to speak of. Kind of a bad place, unnerstan' what I'm sayin'? Lots of kids usin' drugs and shit. Once was a time this here ain't such a bad place t'live, back when's I was younger, ya' know. Not now . . . not now, no mo'."

He was leaning over, elbows resting on his fat knees, as far as his bulk of a waist would allow, and rocked softly back and forth, mumbling to himself. Then a hacking cough took hold that he tried to stem by taking a long swallow of the cheap wine.

I touched Sandy's shoulder and motioned that we should leave. She stood up and hesitated, wondering if there was anything she could do for the poor old fella. She decided there wasn't, but before we left she pulled a ten-dollar bill from her purse and left it on a grimy cardboard box next to the auto bench. He was still coughing and spitting phlegm as we drove away.

In the MGB, as we drove slowly through the streets of North Harbor, I explained to Sandy once again the importance of knowing what the Coroner's Report would say. The Morellis, I tried to explain, could still be alive for all we knew. She finally accepted this reasoning when I promised that as soon as I found out about the report, I would let her know. Since she had no idea what to do next in her "investigation", after talking to the old man, she decided that waiting to get the report might be a good idea.

It was nearly noon and Sandy was expected at work. I dropped her at the front of the pier and told her I would be back about seven or eight that evening. I explained that I had promised to have George Montgomery's car returned to him. She kissed me lightly and quickly, and walked down the pier.

I watched her gently swaying walk, a little slower perhaps than was usual, but she had a lot on her mind. I also had a lot on my mind. Like why was Sandy so upset just because a kid who had the hots for her might be dead? And where the hell was the Santa Maria? Big boats just don't vanish. Why were drug dealers and numbers runners in black Cadillacs looking for the Morellis? And if it were two of the Morellis in the house, why did drug dealers and numbers runners want them dead?

Too many questions, I thought. Too many answers that needed to be found and too many chances that Sandy just might be personally involved in this thing somehow and holding something back from me.

And more immediately, why wasn't George Montgomery's car where he had left it the night before? I had been expecting to see it parked in front of the old guy's slum, where it had been left, when I arrived with Sandy. But in that neighborhood it was very likely any car would be stripped down to its bones in just a few minutes, if not stolen within two minutes of them leaving it there. I realized he should have had someone pick it up the night before. I felt responsible for leaving it there over night. I hoped it hadn't been stolen, I would feel responsible for that, too, and I didn't want any more responsibility. I used the car cell phone to call George Montgomery.

"Hey, George. This is Morgan. I just came down to North Harbor to get your car and it's gone. I hope somebody didn't rip it off."

"No . . . No, it's o.k. I had somebody pick it up for me. Didn't want to leave it down there all night. You know," he said.

Maybe he was still shaken from the day before, but his voice was cracking uncharacteristically. We spoke for a few more minutes and I told George we needed to get out on the golf course again soon. He agreed and said he would call me the first minute he got some free time.

I started the engine of the MGB, but before I drove

away I made one more phone call. I wasn't one to be shy about using family influence and relatives to get done what I needed to have done. It was often easier than doing things myself. And, what the hell, I rationalized once again, my money supports a hell of a lot of people. If you have to be a part of the third richest family in the U.S., why not take advantage of it?

I had a poor relative on my mother's side of the family tree, (somewhere back in history, so I've been told, I was "unlucky" enough to have a relative who married badly, that is for love and not for money, and was cut off from the family wealth). He was a civilian official with the Coast Guard. Jack was a manager in the office responsible for registering and keeping track of commercial fishing boats anchored throughout Northern California. Like many of my relatives, he was more than happy to help his distinguished and rich relative.

I phoned Jack and asked him to have someone look for a boat. I described the Santa Maria and gave him the boat's registration number. Jack said he would, in fact he repeated that he would too many times and too enthusiastically.

I then drove up the hill and into San Marcos' Downtown district. I pulled to the curb in front of Police Headquarters. Inside, Bob Sommers saw me and called out, "I expected you four, five hours ago."

"Yeah, I was busy letting Sandy find out some things." I told him about the morning and what the old man had told Sandy, how she had manipulated the old guy with her smile and a little leg. I didn't tell Bob about my concern over what was bothering Sandy nor her reaction the night before when he told her about the bodies inside the Morelli's house.

Bob Sommers laughed and shook his head, he had tried to talk with the old guy, as had everyone else, and gotten only as far as a ten dollar bill would pay the fare. As it turned out, that ten dollars didn't take him as far as Sandy's smile and a great pair of legs took her.

"I'm not surprised he knew something," he said, sitting behind his desk and pointing at a chair for me to sit in. "Living right next door like that he had to know more than he told us. Maybe I should hire your girl. It would make things a lot easier around here."

"How about the Coroner's Report? Is it back yet?" I asked.

"No. They say I'll get it sometime tomorrow. Apparently they're having a hard time identifying one of the bodies. The one on the stairs they tentatively are saying is Jeremy Morelli. They got a fairly good match on fingerprints. The other they can't find any record of prints to match so they're waiting for dental records, if they can find any. They say he was an older man, so it wasn't Tony. I do know multiple shots from a 12 gauge using 00-buck magnum rounds killed them. Enough power there to take down a concrete wall, and they were hit at close range. Not much left to the one guy on the floor."

"Any ideas on who might have done it?" I asked. "Teddy Bear next door said he saw a car belonging to numbers bagmen," I reminded Lt. Sommers.

"Numbers bagmen! Were you been picking up the dialog? Been watching a lot of old Cagney movies?"

"Well, isn't that what they're called?" I asked.

"Could be. I've never actually met anybody in that business. But I'm not eliminating anybody right now. If you see Tony Morelli, tell him I want to talk with him. I *know* Tony. I *don't know* any bagmen." Bob said.

"You don't think he killed his own father and brother, do you?" I asked.

"I don't think anything yet," He answered truthfully. "The kid's a wild one, everyone knows that," Bob said. "And he's been busted on drug charges more than once. I don't trust anybody who's hooked on drugs. They do crazy things to get what they need."

I wasn't so surprised to hear that. Tony was probably a strange kid, and a wild one, as everyone said. Maybe the kid was strung out enough to kill his family. I made a mental note not to share that thought with Sandy, however.

"You didn't know that?" Bob asked, seeing my surprise. "His brother, Jeremy, too. That's how we got prints to I.D. him."

"Jeremy? Man, that's a surprise," I said. "I had heard stories about Tony, but Jeremy, too?"

"Jeremy only got busted once. I still believe he took the rap for his brother."

Bob told me of the incident that happened a little more than a year before. Jeremy and his brother were driving through town. Jeremy, driving the family's battered old pick-up truck, rolled through a stop sign and was pulled over by a uniformed officer. While the officer was looking over Jeremy's license and car registration he noticed a plastic baggy peeking out from under the front seat. It was empty except for the powdery remains of high quality cocaine.

Tony had been busted twice before for possession of small amounts of marijuana. A third arrest would come down hard on him. It was Bob's opinion that Jeremy took responsibility on that one, claiming it was his bag. Tony never protested, just watched his brother plead guilty and pay a small fine.

I let that sink in for a moment and then asked, "Can I get two favors from you, Bob?"

"I asked you once if you were going to get too deeply involved in this. You said no. Were you lying to me?"

"When you asked, I wasn't planning on getting into this thing. Since then Cap'n Nick insisted that I see what I could do in finding out who killed his friend. I have to at least make a show of doing something. The Cap'n's a friend of mine and yours too if I remember correctly."

I knew that if I was anybody else, if my name wasn't Morgan Crew, and if I wasn't a friend of Bob Sommers for so many years, and if I hadn't done so many big favors for him, I would have been kicked out of Bob's office right then and there.

"O.K., but no stupid independent stuff. You keep me up to date on every step you take. You keep that girlfriend of yours in line. And if you hold back one small thing, friend or no friend, I'll bust you hard for interfering in a police investigation. You may have a famous name, but you're only an ordinary civilian when it comes to murder. What are your two favors?"

I asked for names of drug dealers and numbers runners, both in North Harbor and the rest of San Marcos. I wrote down a half dozen names of suspects as Bob rattled them off.

I then asked for his permission to go into the Morelli's house. At first Bob said absolutely not, then, after enough pleading on my part, he reluctantly agreed, but only if he went with me, and only if I bought his lunch, which he specified had to be a very expensive lunch at the country club. I agreed.

NINETEEN - Missing Things

So I took Bob Sommers to the Country Club for a late, and very expensive, lunch. For Bob, it was a too rare pleasure to be inside that bastion of snobbery. He liked being inside the Country Club because he didn't get to go there very often. His bulk and cheap suits didn't fit in and he acted like a kid at the circus the few times I took him there.

Certainly the restaurant was a very good one. I like sitting on the patio when the sun was available and I enjoy good bourbon, almost as much as I enjoy the club's restaurant. And, my love of the golf course is well known. But I find it difficult to play the social games enjoyed at the club. I spend a lot of time at the club, enjoying the peace and quiet, loving the golf course, and ignoring most of my fellow club members.

But someone like Bob Sommers would have a hard time seeing past all the glitz. Bob enjoyed it because it was new and wonderful to him. And he ordered the most expensive item on the menu. It could have been boiled tripe and raw sea slugs for all he cared, just as long as it was the most expensive thing offered. And even though he was on duty he would order the most expensive bottle of wine he could locate on the menu. But he's a good friend. I didn't mind.

After lunch we rode in my MGB, with the top down, enjoying a warm afternoon, down to North Harbor and stopped in front of number 803. Bob stepped over the yellow plastic ribbon, which had been stretched across the front walk but now lay limp on the ground, and walked to the porch. I followed, unsure of why, exactly, I wanted to go inside the house, but feeling I should. The police and their lab people had been all over it and I assumed nothing of importance would be left. But I wanted to be able to tell Cap'n Nick I had actually done something.

At the broken door, Bob cut through the paper Police seal, opened the beat up door on squeaky hinges, and we stepped inside. The smell was only slightly less stomach turning than it had been the day George Montgomery and I had found the bodies. There was a slight breadth of cool air coming from the back of the house that made it just possible to stay inside.

To my left, as I stood in the doorway, was the staircase that led to the upper floor. Jeremy had been found lying on those stairs. The living room of the house was to the right. It held a few pieces of old, junk yard furniture. There were two dark, high back wooden chairs, one of which lay on its side. A cheap, low coffee table lay broken under the weight of what had probably been Franco Morelli falling on it. A brass floor lamp stood quietly in the far corner looking like a skinny, frightened, sentry over the death scene. Musty drapes hung across the windows keeping most of the light out but allowing a sickly yellow-brown haze to listlessly illuminate the room. Millions of flecks of dust danced in the haze.

We stepped around the dry brown stain in the middle of the bare wood floor and walked through an archway into what must once, in better days, have been a dining room. It was barren then save for several piles of old newspapers and a broken, empty orange crate. A hole in the middle of the ceiling above me testified to there once being a chandelier in the room.

I walked through a doorway that didn't have a door

hung in it, into a kitchen, Bob Sommers following me. Filth of untold time was everywhere. Brown water dripped from the green stem of a sink faucet. Something large and black ran from under a broken cabinet and out the back door of the house, which was standing open an inch or two. I hoped, because of the size of the dark thing, that it was a cat and not some ugly monster rodent. And if it was a monster rodent, I hoped it was a hermit.

Bob Sommers was in the living room. I called to him and asked, "Anything different than yesterday?"

"It's not as strong in here as it was, but everything else is the same. Why?"

"This back door is open."

"Yeah, it was open yesterday, too. We couldn't get it to close. The hinges must be broken or something."

I walked through the dining room and living room again, and noticed, without mentioning the fact to Bob, that every window was locked tightly and then barred with sections of broom handles. The front door, although old and tattered, had two dead bolt locks on the inside, neither of which had been in use at the time of the murders, and an iron bar stood in the corner next to the door. Obviously it was supposed to have been used to bar the door closed, perhaps against the foot of the stairs.

Everything had been locked tight - the front door by the police, the windows by the broom handles, everything except the back door, which was jammed open and wouldn't close. The Morelli's must have been security conscious, I assumed by the amount of locks available, and yet the back door was broken and jammed open. It didn't make sense.

I looked down as my left foot stepped on something small and crunchy. Whatever it was, the black insect was a pancake now. But I also saw some muddy footprints, just traces but unmistakable as footprints, lined up from the porch outside the broken back door into the house. I followed them as they gradually disappeared into nothingness in the dining room as the mud was worn from the wearer's shoes. The prints looked fairly fresh, as if they had been made the night before during the storm, perhaps even after the house had been sealed by the police. I bent down and touched some of the mud. It was still slightly damp.

I stepped over the piles of trash and walked up the stairs. The two bedrooms and small bath were empty, completely empty. Not even a sink in the bathroom. Even the pipes had been ripped out.

Some old cardboard boxes lay in the hallway, covered with dust. There were no fingerprints on the lids, the dust was undisturbed. The Police had obviously not looked inside. I did. They were each empty.

The windows upstairs had been covered with plywood and nailed shut. No light from outside came in at all. And only bare bulbs, hung from the ceiling by frayed wires, illuminated the rooms, one small bulb per room.

In the smaller of the two bedrooms I noticed that the dust covered floor had been disturbed by people walking across it, recently enough that the dust and dirt had not had a chance to cover the tracks. Probably just the cops, I thought. I saw a strange shadow on the floor in the far corner. I stepped carefully toward it and pulled the foul plastic window curtain back, away from the yellow grimy window, to let some light in. The shadow turned out to be a fairly clean, dirt and dust free area of bare wood floor, about a foot and a half square. I speculated that someone could have entered the house the night before, during the storm, by the broken back door.

They had left a few muddy footprints, and removed something, probably a dusty box, that had been there for awhile, leaving a clean area of floor exposed. Either the box had been removed before the cops arrived or, based on the untouched boxes in the hallway, the police had not opened the box and someone else had removed the box after the police left. It was obvious to me that this box had not been empty or it would not have been removed.

As good a cop as my friend was, his police force was still a small town police force. Big city cops would never have left cardboard boxes at a murder scene untouched. The San Marcos police probably assumed them to be like the trash that filled the rest of the house.

The small amount of daylight the clouded window let in revealed several other small spaces of dust free floor. I saw four spots left by the legs of what must have been a table about five feet by two feet and there were numerous fresh footprints disturbing the dust covered floor, too numerous to mean anything other than somebody had been in the room recently. But it did appear that besides the box, some smaller items, as well as a table had been removed.

Back in the dining room I opened a door I thought to be a closet but was in fact a stairway down to a basement. Dank musty dampness flooded out.

I tried the light switch near the door but nothing happened. I hesitated to walk down into the moldy darkness of the basement. I remembered the dark little thing that had scurried from under the cabinet and used it as an excuse not to go down into the basement. I would have bet money right then that the thing wasn't a hermit as I had hoped, and I didn't want to meet its family and friends.

Bob stepped beside me as I reconsidered the many reasons why going down there would be stupid and not worth the effort. He handed me a small flashlight, smirked broadly, waved me ahead of him, and followed me down the creaking wooden stairs. I am a coward, but why admit it?

The basement floor was bare earth, the walls stone and crumbling cement, the air still, cool, damp, and smelled of old age and mold. I took two steps onto the dirt and something crunched under my foot. It wasn't the same disgusting crunch as the insect in the kitchen that I had sent to the great beyond. Bob heard the sound also, so I didn't try to hide it from him. I instead bent over and pointed the light at my footprint in the loose dirt. Bits of broken glass reflected the light back at me. We both picked up fragments of the glass and examined them. Bob immediately identified it as a test tube, probably a five or six inch long test tube common to laboratories, he said. But not common to old dirt floored cellars, I thought.

We looked around for more of the same on the floor and on an old wooden table at the far end of the room. It was about six foot long, maybe longer. I mentally noted it was larger than the table which had been removed from the upstairs room. We could find nothing else except evidence of rats and other small living things neither of us wished to see.

Bob gathered all the glass we could find into a plastic bag and carefully wrote on it the date and place found. He then drew a deep circle in the dirt with the toe of his shoe, around my footprint, to show where we had found the glass.

Back upstairs, I took one more look at the rear door while Bob went outside to phone the police lab and told them to be ready for him in a few minutes. He wanted a priority identification of the glass and any remnants of what it had held. And I wanted a closer look at the door while Bob wasn't around.

The hinges on the door were in fact broken. The wood frame that was supposed to hold them had rotted into a soft, paper-like substance. I pulled at the door slightly, pulling it away from its frame, and it gave way at the top hinge. Dust and bits of rotten wood fell to the floor along with something metallic. I bent and picked up a spent bullet. It had lodged in the rotten wood of the frame so that it could not have been seen, unless one were to pull some of the wood frame away.

I wasn't exactly sure what the hell I was doing, but I slipped the bullet into my pocket and decided not to tell Bob about it nor about what I had seen in the upstairs bedroom just yet. I hadn't the faintest idea why I was doing what I was doing. The annoying little voice in the back of my head was advising me not to do it. But I felt a compelling urge, an overwhelming compulsion, to do something myself to find out who killed my friends.

I joined Bob Sommers outside and watched as he pulled the front door of the house closed and carefully sealed it with a fresh yellow and red Police crime scene seal.

I waived to the old man still sitting on his porch next door as we walked to the car. The old man spit over the railing. Well, I know who the hell my friends are.

"Think you'll want to talk to the old guy again?" I asked.

"Not really. He won't tell me anything. Not as much as he told Sandy, anyway. You're sure you told me everything he said?"

"Of course. I told you I wouldn't hold anything back." At least I wouldn't hold back anything the old guy said, rationalizing once again. I felt guilty about the bullet in my pocket and about what I had discovered upstairs. And I probably would tell Bob, eventually. But for now, I decided to keep a few things to myself.

As we drove away, to make conversation and to mask the guilt I was feeling, I told Bob about Barbara Krueger.

"So you think you can find her?" he asked.

"Hell, I don't know. But I feel like I have to try, and I have a favor to ask."

"Hey look, buddy. I'm not your private police records division. If Mitch Krueger wants to file a missing persons report, I'll see to it the department does what it can to find her."

"I'm not asking you to find her," I said. "I just want some background on Hector. Can you look up his criminal record for me?"

"You know I can't do that. Criminal records are confidential and only for law enforcement use. I can get in big trouble if I let you have an unauthorized rap sheet."

"You mean you really call them rap sheets? I thought that was just television stuff."

"No, we call them rap sheets," Bob said sarcastically. "And we consider civilians who interfere in a Police criminal investigation to be criminals themselves."

"Oh come on, Bob," I pleaded. "Who's going to know? I'm not going to tell anyone. And besides, you run that damn department. Who's going to get on you?"

"No," he said firmly.

"For dinner at the club?" I suggested.

"OK," he said quickly. "But I want one of those expensive bottles of French wine, understand? A real expensive bottle. And an expensive cigar after."

I dropped Bob off at Police Headquarters. There were a few things I had to do, a few questions I wanted to ask, and I didn't want a Police Detective around right then. Bob would phone me when he wanted to me about Hector's rap sheet. Until then, I needed to do some thinking and some running around alone.

TWENTY - Tony Morelli

I drove down the hill and parked at a meter on Front
Street near the piers. It was well into the afternoon, the sun
was low in the sky and approaching the sea. Front Street
was crowded with tourists who would be leaving in a few
hours. When I arrived most of the parking spaces were
taken, including the few in front of the Coast Guard Station
and Harbormaster's.

The air was very still and heavy. Only small ripples of
water washed up on the gravel shore beneath the wooden
wharf. There was a string of clouds above the sea, fiery red
against a deep blue sky. What's that saying? 'Red sky at
night, sailor's delight?' The fishing boats had long since
been tied up at their berths, their workday finished until three
or four the next morning, when they would again be out
beyond the sight of land, dropping their nets for the day's
catch.

The group charters were being scrubbed down and
the bait lockers refilled. Young boys, still in their school
clothes, sat and watched older men repair nets by hand.
They told the captivated boys stories of the sea and
made-up adventures of fighting pirates for treasure.

Some of the fishermen were still on the commercial
trawlers. They were the deckhands, the younger men who
were left to clean up the mess of a day's work. Some were
hosing down decks, some were repairing equipment; some
were simply standing around talking and smoking before

they went home.

I walked slowly down the wooden docks, toward the berth that used to be the home of the Santa Maria, stopping to talk with each of the fishermen I saw. Most knew the Santa Maria; none knew where she had disappeared to. The older men knew Franco Morelli and Jeremy. A few of the younger ones knew Tony Morelli. They were the young, wild ones, like Tony. They drank with him, chased women with him, probably got into trouble with him.

In talking with them I learned that Tony, in recent months, had become heavily involved in drug use, and had begun selling drugs in the harbor to finance his own needs. "Hell, man," one of them told me. "You want coke? Crack maybe? Ol' Tony M is the guy to see."

"Yeah," another said. "That guy's crazy. Got his hands on a ton of shit recently, and he'd sell it t'anybody, real cheap, too."

A skinny boy, with a terribly pock marked face and black and broken teeth told me, "Tony practically givin' the stuff away! Hellu'va lot cheaper than up in North Harbor. But I ain't seen him 'round recent like. Tell him to come see me," he laughed.

Others said, "He changed man. Used to be he was fun, but he got too deep into shit and it like warped his brain, man, ya' know?"

Still others said, "I ain't seen him and I don't want to, neither. He's trouble. Sellin' dope all over. One day somebody's gonna get himself killed with that stuff."

I found a young man I recognized from somewhere. At first I couldn't recall where I had seen him. He told me he had worked for the Morelli's for a few months a year before. He then recalled seeing me onboard the Santa Maria. He left to take a better paying job on a commercial trawler.

"Yeah, Mr. Crew," he said. "Me and Tony are the same age, we even went to school together. We was never that close but we did talk and it was him got me my first job. That was on the Santa Maria. Tony's an ok guy," he said, pausing to light a cigarette and letting the smoke blow towards me. But I didn't say anything about the smoke. I wanted to know what Tony's friend knew. So I suffered the stuff being blown in my face. "Lots of people wouldn't say so. He's just had a hard time growing up. I kind of think his old man wants him to be like that brother of his. And Tony ain't the type to be so . . . I wanna say square but that ain't the word."

"I know what you mean," I replied, trying to sound understanding and sympathetic. "Have you seen Tony lately?" I didn't tell anyone I spoke with about the bodies I had found. They would read about it in the papers or see it on TV. soon enough. I didn't feel it necessary to spread the bad news. And I figured that some people might not talk if they knew about the murders.

"No, him and me, we kind of . . . Well, we don't see eye to eye on a lot of things here lately."

"You mean the drugs?" I asked.

"Yeah, exactly. You heard, huh? Ya'know, I like Tony. I even envy him having the boat an' all. But he's got himself into something so bad. Well, I got a feeling he's not gonna be able to get out, ya'know?"

"I heard he was heavy into selling drugs lately. Is that what you mean?" I asked.

"Yeah. He must have come into a ton of the stuff. Been spreading it around right out in the open. Bound t'get busted soon. Ya'know, ordinarily, people don't talk openly about buyin' and usin' drugs. They keep it to themselves, ya'know? But people don't care about Tony. I hear'em talking about stuff Tony's selling right out in the open. Like maybe the law don't apply to him, ya'know? Like he can peddle stuff without worryin' about it."

"Is Jeremy involved, too?"

"Don't think so. I mean it sure would surprise me if he was. I know he got busted once but Tony told me it was his stuff and Jeremy was just protecting him. What surprises me is the old man. Why he don't beat the crap outta Tony, I don't know."

"Where does he get the drugs?"

"Ha! You got me. I mean I stay away from that stuff. Once in awhile I may go on up to North Harbor and have a few beers, pick up a woman, ya'know? I might even get drunk enough to get in a fight, ya' know? But that stuff Tony's into ain't my thing. I'm savin' pennies, nickels, dimes, anything, so's someday I can buy my own boat, ya'know. I ain't gonna throw it away like he's doing."

"How about girlfriends?" I asked. "I'm told Tony has a way with women."

"Ha! He must got something special tucked away in his jeans! Man, I never seen nothin' like it. When he wants, on a Saturday night f'instance, he might screw two, three broads. Once he did it to two sisters at the same time. Man, he's something else."

"Anybody special? I mean, anybody new or someone he's been seeing regularly?"

"Yeah, as a matter of fact. Now that you mention it. There is this cute little blond. I don't know her. Must be new in town. I only ever seen her with him and never talked to her. But what a fox! This great chest and the rest of her is mighty serious, too."

"Does she work around here? I sure would like to speak with her about Tony, maybe get him out of some of the trouble he's headed for."

"Don't know that, Mr. Crew. I know you and I'd like to help but like I said, I only seen her a couple times with Tony. But maybe Cap'n Nick might know. Tony had her there a couple times. I seen'em inside. I appreciate you wanting to help Tony. Like I said, he ain't so bad. Anything I can do just let me know."

I thanked him and watched him walk up the gangplank onto the trawler. It had been too easy to find out that Tony Morelli was selling drugs. Too many people knew it; too many freely admitted buying from him. How could it go on in such a small place for so long? Why didn't the police stop it? Was Tony really immune to the law, like the young guy had said?

All these thoughts were spinning around in my head. I had come to San Marcos for escape, and I found the world had followed me. Where could I go to find peace? What would I do? My first thought was to listen to that little voice and run from the trouble it said was coming my way. But then I would be running from my last hope for happiness in life. I made up my mind to stay, to do what I could do. I simply had no choice.

It was still too early to pick up Sandy, and I had to think about how I would approach Cap'n Nick about Tony's girlfriend. He had known about her, probably Sandy had known also, but neither had said anything to me. I had a feeling that I might be walking into a swamp. I felt like I was slowly sinking, the quicksand only above my ankles right then, but if I made a wrong move, if I twisted and turned too quickly, it might soon drown me. I had to think. I needed to get away long enough to reason out in my mind what I did not want to admit was happening.

So I drove to the Country Club, my ultimate sanctuary from reality. It was a warm late afternoon and a tall, cold beer sounded just right. I also needed time away from the harbor. I needed to get the salt air cleared from my lungs and disconnect my mind from the creaking of the Boats tied at the piers.

The Morellis, at least two of them that I knew about, had been killed. Maybe Tony was dead also since nobody had seen him recently. The Santa Maria had disappeared.

Drugs were poisoning the people in my town. And that little voice somewhere deep in the darkest caves of my brain began telling me that Sandy was somehow involved in all this. I needed time to think and the false Never-Never-Land of the club was about as far from reality as I could get in order to think clearly.

I sat in a half circle booth near a window overlooking the eighteenth green. It was a beautiful afternoon but I didn't have time for golf. Besides, my mind just wasn't on it. I turned around so as not to see the people on the green putt out, and tried to think clearly.

The more I thought of Sandy's reaction to what had happened, the more I was convinced it was more than just a deeply sensitive person with deep compassion for the deaths of friends. Added to the fact that Tony had a girlfriend she had not told me about, the more I realized that all was not as it should have been.

But was I just imagining monsters in the closet? Sandy was a very caring person, and very emotional. I remember the first time I took her fishing off the pier. I had to bait her hook because she felt sorry for the already dead and cut up mackerel. And she couldn't bear to see a fish hooked and landed. I had laughed then and asked why she ate fish. "That's different," she said, but didn't bother to explain the difference. Maybe, I hoped, I was just being stupidly jealous, over protective, and playing the idiot? I knew it was stupid to think that Sandy was involved with Tony. Maybe I was just looking for trouble where there wasn't any? I hoped so.

As I sat, sipping at the second beer, Mike Rahmsdorff came up from behind me and slapped me on the shoulder roughly, causing me to spill some of the beer from the tall glass onto my slacks. I brushed at the spilled beer and didn't try to restrain an annoyed scowl.

Mike is a prominent Insurance Broker in San Marcos.

He is a big, athletic looking, ruggedly handsome guy, with mounds of thick curly black hair, who has the Country Club women falling all over him all of the time. He has a glib, silver-tongued way about him that people are immediately attracted to. They are attracted, for some reason unknown to me because I had taken an immediate dislike to the man the first time I met him. Mike Rahmsdorff talks fast, often, and mainly about himself. In short, he is a jerk, a phony, and a male floozy if there is such a thing.

"Hey, Morgan. No golf today? It's a perfect day for it. What say? I'm really on my game. Thinking about turning pro," he said a little too loudly, as usual.

"No, I'm sorry Mike. I can't today. Maybe on Saturday."

"Sure thing. I'm going to keep trying until I beat you, and when I finally do beat you, we're going to start playing for money." He laughed boisterously, slapped me on the shoulder again, and looked at the empty space around the booth. I assumed that Mike expected me to move over so that he could sit in the booth, also. I didn't.

"Say, I didn't see you at the funeral the other day. What happened?"

"What funeral was that?" I asked, not wanting to get into a conversation, especially with Mike Rahmsdorff, but not able to be rude enough to get rid of the man quickly.

"Frederick Mark's! And what a turn out. Every society person from San Diego to San Fran showed up. Even a few from back East. I bet I handed out fifty cards. Man, I sure would like to sign up a couple of those big money people, you know? And I wouldn't mind putting it to a couple three of them back east dames, either."

"Oh, is that right?" I said. "And would you have your wife with you while you . . . how'd you say it? . . . Put it to them?"

He laughed and slapped me on the shoulder a third

time, but he didn't reply. I assumed I had made quite a joke. I sure do like to keep people happy.

"Speaking of wives. What a show his wife put on. Boy did you miss it," Mike said. He was leaning on the table now, trying to get as close to my face as he could. He kept looking at the seat next to me. I kept on not moving over.

"What do you mean, what did she do?"

I didn't really care what happened, but I also couldn't bring myself to tell Mike to screw off and not bother me. I had years of experience seeing through a phony front easily and readily. With all the business my family does and all the responsibility on my shoulders to manage that business, I meet phonies on a regular basis.

But I like to think I am a little better than people like Mike Rahmsdorff who was quick with an insult and a put-down. Until somebody was well past the point of being just normally obnoxious, I just let them be themselves. Mike was just being his normal self.

It was common knowledge that Mrs. Frederick Mark was a drunk. Since moving to San Marcos no one had ever seen her sober. She had been to the club many times. She arrived drunk and left, even more inebriated, with the help of several people.

Of course, I had heard about Frederick Mark's death. It had been in the headlines for days and the T.V. news carried little else. I was one of very few people not impressed with Frederick Mark and his business empire. Frankly, I thought the guy was a much bigger jerk than most of the other people at the Club, an even bigger jerk than Mike Rahmsdorff. And that's saying a lot, because there are a lot of jerks at the Club.

Frederick Mark expected people to be impressed with all his money, his businesses, and his power. I was fortunate enough to not have to be impressed by Frederick Mark. Frederick had nothing I wanted. I had more money than Frederick Mark would ever have had. Business bored me, and power is something I like to challenge.

I had heard all the stories about how Mark had beat his wife and brought whores home to his own bed while he had his wife watch. Hell, Mark had even bragged about it in the clubhouse bar. It was no wonder she hid inside a bottle.

I had met her and had spoken with her several times at the club. Although she was very drunk each time, she seemed to be a fairly nice person, at least when compared to her husband. I remembered her as quite thin and pale, with heavy eyes that were sunken behind deep, dark rings. Several times I had remarked to others that she may have been pretty at one time.

I had been told about the funeral, but it was easy enough for me to think of a thousand things I needed to do rather than go see Frederick Mark off to eternity in the hell he probably deserved. Whoever shot him, and my money was on the wife, may well have done the world a favor.

Mike Rahmsdorff remained standing at the edge of the booth, one hand on the seat back near my head now, the other on the tabletop. He leaned down, his face even closer to mine, as he always did when talking to someone.

He was telling me how Mrs. Mark had shown up in a black shroud of a dress, rumpled and muddy, with a long black veil hung from a wide brimmed hat crowned with a crumpled red paper rose on it. She was typically drunk and staggered into the hall, almost falling once. Someone had to grab her and help her to the empty front row of the funeral home chapel.

As one of Frederick's business associates was making up nice lies to say about Frederick for those gathered to mourn his death, Mrs. Mark began to laugh uncontrollably. She pushed herself to her feet and started screaming about what a bastard her husband had been, and what they would all say if they knew the truth about him. I would have bet that everyone there knew the truth about him. They were probably restrained from agreeing with her in hopes of hearing their names mentioned in the will.

Mike said her arms were flailing at the air, her fists striking out violently at something only she could see. She was finally helped out of the chapel and driven home in semi-consciousness. Mike was laughing but I was glad I hadn't been there to see it.

Mike finally moved to the other end of the booth, across the table from me, finally figuring out that I wasn't going to move for him to sit down. As he let himself slide into the booth he waived for the waitress but I told him I had to leave. I didn't need to profit at the expense of the poor woman and besides, I wasn't in any kind of mood to spend time with a loud mouth idiot. I imagined Mrs. Mark probably felt free for the first time in years and for that, I felt happy for her. I quickly slid out of the booth, ignoring Mike's feigned plea for me to stay.

As I walked past the bar to leave, the bartender, Charlie, called my name and held the phone out for me. "Phone call for you. It's Mrs. Frederick Mark."

TWENTY-ONE – Suzanne

I listened to the weak, bird like, quavering voice on the other end of the line.

"Mr. Crew, I hope you remember me?" she asked.

"Of course I remember you. My deepest sympathies on your husband's death."

"Thank you," she paused a few seconds then said, "I appreciate your thoughts, but your sympathies on Frederick's death are not necessary."

I decided not to pursue her comment any further. Whatever her feelings towards her husband and his death, they were not my business.

"What is it I can do for you, Mrs. Mark?"

"I'm afraid I need your help, Mr. Crew. I know of no one else I can turn to. It's very important. I can't talk on the phone. Can you come see me right away?"

Although I had seen her at the club several times, I had never spoken to her of anything but the weather and other meaninglessly light subjects. I was incredulous at receiving a phone call from her, especially a phone call asking for my help. I certainly didn't consider myself a friend, nor was I close enough an acquaintance to ask favors of. She couldn't need money. Frederick Mark was very rich. I had no idea what she wanted of me.

"Can you give me some idea what this is all about?" I asked. I wanted her to talk more so that I could find out if she were drunk or sober. So far she sounded sober.

"I told you I can't discuss it on the phone," she said, a little shortness of temper revealing itself. "I'm sorry. I need your help," she continued, more contrite. "It's vital I speak with you right away."

She sounded O.K., sober at least, if maybe a bit overwrought. There seemed to be a tinge of anxiety in her voice. And like the white knight who rides around trying to save fair maidens I said I would be at her home as soon as possible.

It was nearly half past six in the afternoon. I had an hour and a half before I would pick Sandy up from work. I drove across the hillsides to what is the second biggest home in San Marcos, second only to the old mansion I had grown up in. But this one was less than ten years old. It was commonly referred to as "The Mark Estate", without too much hyperbole.

It sat in a small valley among the foothills, surrounded by some twenty-three acres of land. There were horses in the white fenced pastures as I turned through the tall, red brick portals of the entry. The heavy, wrought iron gate was latched open which allowed me to drive onto the pea graveled drive without having to use the phone at the side of the entry. The drive wound among many tall, graceful willows for more than a hundred yards, to the house.

As I drove slowly up the winding, tree-lined drive I was reminded of the film, "Gone With The Wind". Frederick must have seen the movie, I thought, and tried to imitate Scarlet O'Hara's plantation house at Tara. There were tall white columns up the entire three stories of the house. Ivy-like vines, thick in pink and white blooms, clung to the columns and wound their way up to the roof. An emerald green lawn carpeted the front of the house, bordered in carefully groomed rose bushes. At the center of the lawn was a towering, aged, willow that swayed gently in the breeze. A white wrought iron bench girdled the trunk's base.

A long white porch ran the entire length of the front of the house and wrapped around both sides. The deep porch was lined with white wooden rocking chairs that moved in an empty, ghostly rhythm, each rocking back and forth in its own time in the cool breeze which blew across the front of the house.

On the other side of the driveway, running along the side of the house, was a pond a couple of hundred feet long and half that wide, with water lilies massed throughout. More stately willows and elms lined the far end of the pond. Beautifully exotic flowers grew along the edges. And in the water, which was fed by a small cascade tumbling over a curved line of big rocks, swam an even half dozen rare black swans.

I parked the old MGB near the pond, at the side of the porch and walked up the steps to the door. Before I could get within ten feet of the doors, they swung open and Suzanne Mark stood in the doorway to greet me.

Some years ago I would have been greeted by a tall, refined woman of classic beauty where now stood a thin female, older than her years. Clear, sexy blue eyes would have shined where now dull, sunken, pale eyes surrounded by tiny rivulets of red, covered by heavy, tired lids and dark surrounding shadows, starred at me through what might be a fog.

Her hair would have been soft and long years ago, it now hung in uncombed thinning strands showing streaks of grey. Her flesh had turned soft and limp, and hung loosely over her protruding bones. Her skin was dull, lifeless, with a sickly yellow-gray pallor laying behind the attempt at make-up. Her clothes, mis-matched in color and style, were obviously expensive but in need of a pressing, and looked as if she had not been out of them, day or night, for several days. She wrung her hands nervously around a small, delicate, lace trimmed lady's handkerchief, her face tense and drawn. It had only been minutes since she had stopped crying.

She stepped aside and, with a stiff, formal motion of her arm waived me in. She did not speak; her eyes did not meet mine, but peered downward in a mixture of tentativeness and awkward embarrassment.

The inside entryway was grand in an over-done, showy, carnival way. The ceiling reached up the entire three stories of the building. The hallways of the two upper floors were lined on either side with a railed walkway from which you could look down into the grandiose entry hall.

A large and gaudy, somehow cheap looking crystal chandelier hung on a heavy shiny brass chain from the ceiling high above, in the center of the entry way. The walls on either side of the wide hallway were lined with too many, not too well done, tall marble statues of naked men and women in classic Grecian poses. Paintings chosen obviously not for how they added to the room were hung everywhere. They bore no resemblance in style to anything else in the hallway nor to each other for that matter, but probably for their cost and investment value. Loudly colored furniture was crowded everywhere.

I did make note of how clean everything was, however. With all that was crammed into the hallway, not a fleck of dust appeared anywhere. The polished shine of everything was dazzling and was reflected off the highly polished marble of the hallway floor. The hallway was a poorly done gallery of showy ostentation.

She hadn't said a word yet but motioned to me in an uneasy, stiff, and unaccomplished attempt at sophistication to follow her into the first room to my left. I followed her as she stepped quickly, a little unsteadily, in front of me and into the room. Her hands were intertwined in front of her so tightly her protruding knuckles were turning white. The heels of her shoes echoed across the mirror-like marble floor. I found myself walking, self-consciously, as softly and silently as I could.

She wore an expensive pair of black high heels, but I noticed as I followed her, that the leather at the back of the two-inch heels was scuffed and torn. Her black skirt was of a very good wool but the hem at the back had unraveled and hung foolishly above her thin, but still nicely shaped calves and trim ankles. The skirt hung loosely on her, bought before she had lost what must have been ten or more pounds that she could not spare.

The room I followed her into turned out to be a library of sorts, lined on four walls with floor to ceiling cabinets of books. The cabinets had glass doors so that everyone could see the books inside. It was impressive, but I noticed that each of the cabinet doors was fastened closed with a tiny, bright brass padlock. I wondered if any of the books had ever been read, or were they locked away for pretentious safekeeping.

There were a few small tables throughout the room, each carefully surrounded by three chairs of identical design. They were dark cherry-wood carved in an elaborate oriental pattern, with bright red brocade upholstery. Each was an imitation of antique wing chairs.

At the table in the exact middle of the room a man was sitting on the edge of one of the chairs, uncomfortably fumbling with a manila folder, pretending to read the papers inside. I had seen him some place before, but I couldn't remember where. He was a short, chubby man, bald on top, with closely cropped black hair around the fringe of his very oval head. He wore inexpensive, plastic, tortoise shell glasses with a red hue to the frames. His suit was a good one but certainly not expensive, the fit off the rack. His shoes, although highly polished, were not new and not expensive.

He carefully closed the folder, placed it on the table

next to his chair with a precise, deliberate motion, and stood as I walked into the room. The entire movement was stiff and staged and perhaps a little nervous. He was a diminutive little guy, not more than five foot eight. He smiled a false, awkward, uneasy smile, and held out his hand as he said in a wavering voice, which attempted to be firm and formal, "Mr. Crew, so glad to meet you." He sounded as ill at ease as he looked.

Suzanne Mark stood next to him as I shook his hand. She said, "Mr. Crew, this is my personal attorney, Mr. Richard Bloome. We would like to speak with you, to enlist your help. Please be seated." She said in a very stiff, businesslike manner, but I continued to notice the trepidation in her voice. Behind her words was the unmistakable accent of an Ivy League education perfecting an East Coast, wealthy upbringing. She was trying to sound very sophisticated and proper but was having a very difficult time of it.

I sat where the wave of her hand indicated and said to the attorney, "Oh, yes. I remember hearing you in court. A couple of years ago. You were quite impressive the way you handled that jury. What was it, a slip and fall plaintiff case or something like that?" I remembered the case well since it was against a small company owned by my family, and involved a million dollar claim by an employee who had retired a week before. He said he hurt his back by slipping on a wet floor in the men's rest room after visiting some of his former workmates.

I was about to sell the place when the lawsuit was filed. I felt certain that the man had faked the accident to fund his retirement. I attended the first two days of the trial, saw he didn't have a very good case, and told my lawyers to settle with the employee for $75,000, which the man jumped at. Richard Bloome was given the impression he had scared my attorneys. He hadn't.

"You have a very good memory, Mr. Crew. Yes, it was a slip and fall, and we did win that one." I smiled but didn't say anything. What sense was there in tearing a person down for nothing? Bloome felt a little more comfortable now that I had recognized him.

Mrs. Mark interrupted, saying, "Yes, but this is much more important than some accident that happened a few years ago. I'm afraid someone is going to kill me and I want you to arrange something to protect me."

Bloome glanced at me apologetically over the rim of his glasses and went back to fumbling with the papers inside the folder he had laid on the table.

I swallowed hard, then said, "Wait a minute. What the hell do you think I can do to protect you?"

"Mr. Crew. I've lived here in San Marcos for many years. I have no friends. I receive no phone calls. Clerks in stores speak to me. Others pass me by on the street. At the Country Club, I drink too much. Members tend to avoid me. In all the years I have been here, you are the only person who has treated me with kindness. I know. We are far from being friends. But I am told you know people, you have a certain amount of influence, and you're known for helping people. Since you have been kind to me in the past, I would like you to be kind once again and arrange for my safety. I do not want to die."

"What makes you think someone is going to kill you, Mrs. Mark?" I asked.

"You know of course that my husband was murdered? The same people will try to kill me next. I know they will, don't ask me how. I just know they will try to kill me."

She was wringing the hell out of that poor little lace hanky she held. I waited a moment, both thinking and waiting for her to elaborate. When she didn't say anything I asked, "Why?"

"Because they will! Damn it, can't anyone see?" She

stood up abruptly and walked quickly across the room to a small bar where she hesitated for a moment, looking longingly at the crystal decanters lined up like little soldiers in shiny uniforms.

Bloome leaned towards me while her back was turned, and whispered, "I've been trying to explain to Mrs. Mark that it is quite unlikely someone would want to kill her. There just isn't any cause to believe someone would but she does believe it will happen. Please try to ease her mind, Mr. Crew."

Suzanne Mark turned quickly from the bar and walked back to us, still wringing her hands in front of her, her hanky being destroyed. I could see her eyes were filled with tears and I knew Bloome was right. I would try to ease her mind; I felt I had to at least try. It must have been a pretty rough time for her, I thought, having lost her husband in such a violent, sudden manner.

"Mrs. Mark," I said. "I think I can help you relocate, to a safer place that is. Some place where you can be safe until they catch your husband's killer."

"No," she answered, trying to sound firm, with a sideways movement of her head, I thought trying more to convince herself than me. "I can't leave here. I have no money of my own to speak of. Frederick died without leaving a will; he refused to allow my name to appear on anything, and the estate will be years in probate court according to Mr. Bloome. I must stay here and you must arrange something to protect me here."

"Money is not a problem," I said. "I can help in that regard. I have several houses you can use. Out of State." I reached out to touch her arm, trying to be comforting despite how uncomfortable I felt. But she pulled away, not allowing my touch.

"No!" she said. "I told you I must stay here."

"I'm not sure what I can do. Are you asking for a

bodyguard?"

"Yes, I suppose I am." Her eyes brightened at the suggestion. "I have phoned the police; they were polite enough but can do nothing. Until someone actually tries to kill me, they will do nothing. Then, of course, it will be too late. I want you . . . Please; I'm asking you . . . To intervene with the authorities. Get them to do something to help me before it's too late. I have two young children to think about."

"I suppose I can phone the police, but all I can do is ask. If they refuse, being a bodyguard is a little out of my line of work. I wouldn't know where to begin, or what to. I don't know . . . "

"I'll pay you whatever you want. Whatever you want. Although I have no money of my own right now, I can borrow a little, and if you want more I will see that the estate pays you."

"It's not a matter of money; it's a matter of responsibility."

Tears burst from her, her shoulders began to quake, her knees shook. I started to push myself out of the chair but Bloome was faster and reached her before she collapsed. He held her gently in his arms, she fell against him, and her head rested on his shoulder as she cried. That soft spot in my heart was being twisted until it began to hurt.

"Look," I said, wanting to say something to stop her from crying. "Suppose I arrange to have some uniformed security guards on the premises twenty four hours a day, and I'd check in several times each day just to see how things are going?"

She gently pushed herself away from Bloome and looked at me. I tried smiling again, and awkwardly, like a shy teenage kid, put my hand on her arm once again. This time she did not pull away.

"It sounds like a good idea to me, Suzanne," Bloome said softly. The familiarity with which he used her first name surprised me.

"Alright.   Do it.   But I will hold you personally responsible for anything that happens to me." She realized the foolishness of what she had said as soon as she said it. Her face colored and she looked away from both of us in embarrassment.

I told them I would like to make two personal phone calls and Bloome offered to show me across the hall to a telephone. I had hoped to get a few minutes alone with him and I hoped the phone calls would lead us to another room where we could talk without Suzanne Mark hearing.

After Bloome closed the library door behind us, as we walked slowly across the wide, marble, entryway hall, I asked, "O.K., now tell me what the hell is going on. Is she under a doctor's care?"

"No. She refuses. But she hasn't had a drink since the funeral and for her that's a miracle and a mile towards sanity. I honestly don't know why she thinks she is going to be killed."

"Any ideas why her husband was killed?" I asked as we walked into another overly large room directly across the hall from the library. It was heavily furnished in gaudy, modern, abstract trash. Lots of plastic furniture, chrome, and brightly-lit neon crap crowded everywhere.

Bloome walked straight to a small chrome and glass cart and asked if I wanted a drink. I felt like I needed one right then and said, "Bourbon, if there is any, straight and very large." Bloome poured a tall one over ice and an even taller scotch for himself.

"As to why Frederick was murdered, I hardly knew the man," he said in answer to my hallway question. "I've been Suzanne's attorney for years. I knew her before she married Frederick. What a mistake that was. I tried to warn her but she wouldn't listen."

"Tell me about the mistake," I said. I sat in a purple

appliance that I assumed was a chair but found that the human anatomy was not designed for the shape it forced my spine into. I pushed myself back onto my feet and decided to drink the bourbon standing up.

"Frederick Mark was evil and a bastard," Bloome began his story. "Not a bastard by birth mind you. He was a bastard by choice. He was born evil. He would screw and cheat his own mother out of her last fifty cents if he thought he could. In fact, there have been rumors for years that he might be responsible for the deaths of his own parents."

There was a sudden change in the man's voice. He spoke with some passion and I noticed the attorney's empty fist clinch and unfurl over and over. He paced the room as he spoke. He was taking this too personally to be just Suzanne Marks' personal attorney.

"Frederick Mark was obsessed with having things other people wanted. He hoped they would be envious of him. Just look around you," he said with a sudden sweep of his arm around the room. "Everything in this house was bought because someone else had said they liked it, or they wanted to buy it, or they thought it was art. It's all just stuff thrown together in a hodgepodge.

"Then he would invite the people in who said they liked the newest thing and laugh at them because he got it and they didn't. Pieces of ridiculously expensive artwork, bought for show. He couldn't name one artist if he tried.

"Then there were the women." His voice became louder, more strident and heated, his pacing quicker. "He didn't have affairs, he had conquests. He went after everyone else's women, married or not, and didn't stop until he had slept with them. He wasn't interested unless some other man was interested first.

"Some years ago he went to a party given by a business associate whose son had just graduated from Harvard Law School. The boy was the center of attraction at the party. The boy's father was beaming with unrestrained pride in his son. It drove Frederick crazy that he couldn't somehow get the boy for his own. The only thing left was to have a child of his own, a son who would go to Harvard Law and be better than this other man's boy.

"At the time he was involved in trying to get a beautiful, wonderful, young woman away from her lover. She came from a good family and the boy was a very promising medical student. She was at Wellesley, the young boy at Harvard. He was a very good friend of mine. I was an undergraduate there at the time. The two families had been planning the wedding for years." Bloome peered into his glass, swirling the scotch around, seeing the past in the whirlpool.

"Frederick Mark dazzled the child with money, jewelry, every expensive bauble that might blind her to who Frederick really was. When she finally went off with him, believing his lies despite what everyone told her, her family was furious and cut her off completely. The boy was devastated. He even attempted suicide. Thank goodness I found him and was able to help.

"Frederick married that woman and after she had given him two girl children and had lost the third . . . a boy by the way . . . he was told she could not have any further children.

"He was obsessed with having a son and hated her for not giving him one. The beatings had begun only months after they were married, she was drinking heavily during her third pregnancy. It was impossible to tell if the beatings or the drink caused her to lose the baby. Probably both.

"Shortly after she returned from the hospital, after a three-month stay, he started bringing home the other women. Oh, yes. What you've heard is all true. Sad but true. He slept with them I guess is how it is said. In their bed while forcing Suzanne to watch. Often he would force her to join them. It's all too terrible to talk about." With a closed fist wave of his arm he pushed aside a picture of Fredrick Mark, which sat in a stainless steel frame on a clear plastic table..

"I tried many times to get her to leave. I've contacted her family and they said they would help her if only she would leave this marriage. She never would. I believe she was afraid Frederick would kill her if she left. Perhaps he would have even killed the children. I believe he would have killed her eventually anyway. But I was never able to convince her of this."

He looked up at me, took a long drink, tried to smile again and continued.

"She never had anything to do with his business. Neither she nor I know much about what he did, except for the same stories you've probably heard. Real estate, investment banking, industries, buying and selling money on the world market. I wouldn't be surprised if most of what he did boarded on the illegal. I think we'll find a huge estate. But it all meant nothing to him or to anyone else.

"No. I don't know why she thinks she will be killed, but if helping her a little will keep her away from the bottle, please do what you can. I'm afraid she will certainly die if she goes back to drinking again. And don't worry about the money, I'll cover any expenses. When the estate closes she will be very wealthy and I can wait a few years to get my money back."

I told him I would do what I could. I assured Bloome that the money wasn't the problem, it was the responsibility that worried me, I repeated. I explained to the attorney that I wanted to make Suzanne feel better, to ease her pain if I could. But if someone was actually out there wanting to kill her, I doubted I could stop it, and I didn't want to feel even the slightest bit responsible for her death.

We shook hands. Bloome quickly downed the last

half-inch of scotch and left the room. He returned to the library while I made my phone calls. I first called Weedmarre Security Company, a large security guard outfit that supplied guards and security systems to many of the companies I owned. I also owned a 40% stake in the company.

I arranged to have three uniformed guards at the Mark Estate, on eight-hour shifts, twenty-four hours a day, seven days a week starting as soon as they could get there. I also told them that at least one woman had to be on the team at all times. They questioned who would pay for this. When I told them I would pay personally, they jumped at the chance of running up a large, guaranteed billing.

I then phoned Sandy and told her I would be a few minutes late getting there. I told her I would explain later. She wanted to know if it had anything to do with the Morellis. I said it didn't, kissed her over the phone and hung up.

Returning to the library I found Bloome and Suzanne Mark at the same little table. He was holding her right hand gently as she dabbed at her eyes with the overworked hanky in her left hand. A maid was just setting down a silver tray with a silver coffeepot and a delicate china plate covered with small sandwiches. Mrs. Mark invited me to sit with them and have something to eat. I told her I would but only if she joined me. Bloome smiled gratefully and the three of us each took one of the small sandwiches.

After she had eaten one of them, and at my insistence took a second, I told them about arranging for security guards, whom I would supervise I added, just to make her feel better. She touched my arm and I felt she was truly relieved and grateful when she thanked me. A veil seemed to be lifted from her and some small semblance of life returned to her eyes.

We talked about the weather and San Marcos, Bloome and I trying to keep the conversation away from what was worrying her, whether that was her husband's death or her fantasy of someone wanting to kill her. Less than an hour after my phone call to Weedmarre, the front doorbell chimed. The three of us walked to the door. Mrs. Mark opened it, and three husky, uniformed security guards walked in, one of them a woman whom I would not want to tangle with. I excused myself and walked further into the hall to speak with the guards away from Richard and Suzanne.

Each was experienced, one of the men and the burly woman were retired cops from San Francisco, none part time rent-a-cops. Each was licensed to carry a sidearm, which each had holstered at their side. I put one at the front door, one on the rear patio, and told the woman to wait inside, and to go wherever Mrs. Mark went. I emphasized that she was to be protected and no harm come to her.

When they were where I wanted them to be I gave each my cell phone number, my home phone number, and told them I could also be found at the Country Club or at Cap'n Nick's.

After assuring Mrs. Mark of her safety and seeing her go upstairs to her room, the female security guard a respectable five steps behind her, I said good night to Richard Bloome, expecting him to leave but not surprised when he didn't, and walked to my MGB.

TWENTY-TWO – So What Is She Hiding?

Sandy was sitting at a table in a far corner of Cap'n Nick's. She was leafing through the local newspaper, which is a rag with lots of advertising and little news, and humming a cheerful tune from some Disney movie I didn't immediately recognize. She was half through a mug of coffee. There were only a few old Sea Dogs in the bar that night. The place was fairly quiet. I sat across the table from her. She looked up and her eyes smiled once again.

"Well, hi big fella," she said happily. "You ready to take me out and spend lots of money on me?" She had spent a sleepless night engulfed in tears and worry, and now, after a few hours and a brief talk with a pitiful old drunk on his front porch, she was happy as a lark. It didn't make sense.

Sandy is a very stable, well-grounded person. She has a quick wit, a thirst for learning, a sharp tongue when needed, and a level of compassion unmatched by anyone I know. She did not have sudden or frequent mood swings nor sudden and frequent flights of emotion. I decided it was time to find out just what the hell was going on.

"They identified Jeremy Morelli," I told her bluntly. "They think the other one was Franco, they're waiting for dental records to make sure."

I reached across the table and took her hand in mine, expecting that she would need someone to hold onto. I watched her eyes closely. Our fingers intertwined and for the briefest moment I could feel some tension in her fingers as they grasped mine. But as quickly as I felt this, the tension was gone. And her eyes hid whatever it was she was feeling, very successfully. She gently pulled her hand away from mine.

Her eyes peered at something far away for the briefest of seconds, at something far away only she could see, in some deep recess of her mind. She continued to smile and brought the coffee cup to her lips with a steady hand.

As she sipped I saw the diamond sparkle of a small tear in the corner of her eye. The veil was being pierced but should I continue or stop? I had no desire to hurt her, to make her cry, but I had to know what was going on. I knew I loved this woman and the thought of her hiding something from me, of her being somehow involved with the Morelli family, was frightening to me.

Her emotions were tossing about like a skiff in a storm. It wasn't right; it wasn't what she should be feeling. She should be sad, of course. Sympathy for the death of friends, naturally, but not what I had seen.

She put the cup down, and with a quick motion of her hand she wiped the tear, trying to hide the motion by brushing at a lock of hair that had fallen across her forehead. Her hand took mine once again and she looked at me and tried to smile a happy, carefree smile. But behind the smile I sensed grief trying to burst through. She had tried to hold whatever it was inside of her, but she had failed. Whatever it was she was hiding from me was fighting its way to the surface. I still didn't know what the emotion was for and I had to find out.

"Why not tell me what the hell is going on," I said roughly as I pulled my fingers from her grasp. "One minute you're crying your eyes out like someone you love just died.

The next minute you're whistling and happy and ready to go out and party. It doesn't make sense. And you've got me worried."

It wasn't what I should have said, and certainly not in the tone of voice I would have chosen had not anger and jealousy overtaken me. But it was said and I let it ride.

"I don't know what you mean," she said defensively. She tried to fold the newspaper but her hands had begun shaking just enough to cause it to rustle. Then in frustration she tossed it aside onto the floor in a jumble and sat back stiffly in her chair. She tried to drink from the cup again but her hand had lost its steadiness and a stream of black coffee spilled across her chin. She quickly brushed it away, first with the back of her hand, then with a paper napkin, tossing the napkin angrily onto the floor next to the newspaper.

"I was upset because the kid might have been hurt, that's all," she said. "You always have to make a big thing out of nothing!"

She pushed herself away from the table, saying she was going to go to the ladies room and check on her face. She gave me a quick kiss on the cheek and walked away searching inside a purse that had been on the floor near her feet for some makeup. Cap'n Nick came from behind the bar with a beer for me and I asked the Cap'n to sit down for a minute.

"What's wrong with Sandy?" I asked.

"What you mean? She seems fine t'me. I guess she's a little shook up 'cause of Franco and Jeremy."

"Wait a minute. How did you know about Franco and Jeremy?" I asked.

As far as I knew, nothing had been released to the media yet. The police were still waiting positive I.D. Bob Sommers had told me, but he wouldn't have told anyone else, not yet.

"You tol' me. Yesterday. Don't you remember?"

"I told you they hadn't identified the bodies yet and not to jump to conclusions. What makes you think Franco and Jeremy are dead?"

The Cap'n frowned, thought for a few seconds, then said, "Sandy, she tol' me, I guess. Why? What's goin' on here?"

"Did she talk to anyone about that today? Any phone calls maybe?"

"Yeah, now that I think of it. She did get one 'bout three or so. Seemed real happy and she been real happy since. What you think?" he asked, frowning.

"Who was it? Did you answer the phone?"

"No, Sandy, she got it. What you worried 'bout?"

I didn't want to confide my worry about Sandy in anyone yet. I tried to smile and make light of his questions. "Oh, nothing probably," I said. "I guess I'm just worried about her, like you are. Forget it, as long as she's o.k."

He smiled, slapped me on the shoulder as hard as usual, and started to push himself away to return to the bar. I stopped him and said, "Tell me about Tony's girlfriend. I want to talk with her."

The Cap'n hesitated a moment then boomed in his usually loud voice, "What girlfriend? That boy, he got too many girls, too many for his own good, ya'know?"

"How about a blond with big tits? He had her in here a couple of times."

"Yeah, he had lots of blondes with big tits, an' he brought a couple here. I don' know, ya' know?"

He turned and walked back behind his bar. I was still worried but I hadn't yet figured out just what I was worried about. I had known Sandy for a year. In that time I had admitted to myself that I did love her, that I wanted her more than I had ever wanted anything or anybody.

Every time I was with her was the first day of love. Every time I lay next to her, watching her sleep, curled like a child, was a discovery of something wonderful. Every time I touched her, exploring the fascination of her, was the first time. For a year I had felt like a kid in love in spring. Suddenly, like a cold, hard, slap across the face, a wedge of doubt was slammed between the two of us.

I remember the day I admitted to loving her. It was a miserably cold, wet, winter day. We were on the floor in front of my fireplace. A roaring, warm blaze lit the midnight-darkened room. We were sipping an excellent cognac, talking about small things, laughing at silly jokes. The clock in the entryway struck twelve. She glanced at her wristwatch and said, "It's late. I have to go."

I touched her cheek, her head bent to caress my fingers between her white shoulder and her cheek. "It's early," I said.

"I have to be at work at ten in the morning."

"Call in sick."

"I can't. Cap'n Nick needs me there."

"I don't want you to go, damn it."

"My! Are we getting rough? I like it when you get rough. Order me around some more, big guy," she said, playfully searching for the ticklish spot she had found on my side.

"I'm serious," I said. "I don't want you to go."

"I'm serious, too," she answered, rolling away from me and pushing herself to her feet. She stood in front of me, looking down at me, the firelight dancing off her naked body, making her seem to move in surrealistically hypnotic rhythms that drew me into her.

"Please don't go," I said. I reached my hand up to her. "I love you, Sandy. Please don't go."

She took my hand in both of hers and knelt next to me. She was quiet for a few moments. She examined each finger of my hand closely, kneading the palm gently.

"That's pretty serious stuff," she said softly. "Is that

like a line you use on all the women when they want to leave and you're still horny?   Because if it is, it's a pretty rotten way to get another piece."

"It's not just a line," I said. "I've been thinking about it for a long time. I'm not sure I really know what love is supposed to feel like. I mean, are you supposed to jump up and down and shout? Does it make your toes curl? What's supposed to happen when you love someone?"

"I don't know how you're supposed to feel," she said. "Why not tell me how you feel?"

"If you want the truth, I feel pretty God damn scared. I feel confused. Like I want to run away one minute and run to you the next. I never considered the possibility I would one-day want to settle down with a woman. And the idea of having kids frightens me to death!

"I guess I'm pretty confused when I think of love; of what love is supposed to be. I've seen so many people . . . married people . . . out screwing around, unhappy with each other, looking for something they don't have at home. My folks had it all at home; love, happiness, satisfaction, and that's what I want someday."

"That's nice," she whispered as she kissed the tips of my fingers.

"It occurred to me," I continued, "I'm not exactly sure when the idea came to me, but I was thinking that it would be great to be like that with you. I tried picturing you in my mind sitting in front of the TV with a bunch of kids, years from now, you know? No matter how I tried to manipulate the picture, you were lovely and I was happy. No matter if we were in some mansion or a third floor walk up, I wanted to be there next to you on the couch, watching TV. I've tried and tried but I couldn't conjure up a situation where I wouldn't want to be next to you on that couch fifteen, twenty, seventy-five years from now. I also can't imagine not having you there next to me in the morning and every morning for seventy-five years and a lot longer than that."

"That's mighty serious stuff you're speaking there, Morgan Crew," she said. The flames from the logs caused her tears to shimmer like diamonds. "Unless I'm mistaken, what you're talking about is marriage and kids. The whole ball of wax."

"I guess you're right," I said. I touched her cheek and let a tear run onto the tip of my finger. She leaned closer to me and pressed her lips to mine.

She came back from the ladies room that evening at Cap'n Nick's with a restored face but with an uneasy, labored smile. We left a few minutes later. She asked again where we would have dinner and I suggested the Country Club. She laughed and said what she really wanted was pizza.

I had decided not to press the issue of the Morellis with her, partly out of fear for what I might learn, partly because pressing the issue with a person like Sandy would get me nowhere. She was too strong. I would have to be sure I maintained some semblance of patience. Time would be the best tool I could use to dig into what was going on. If anything was going on.

Somehow, Sandy had learned of the police identifying Franco and Jeremy. The only way she could have known that the two bodies I had found were Franco and his older son was by having some connection with the maze surrounding the deaths. The Police wouldn't have told her; perhaps the phone call had been from Tony?

So we went to a little place that specialized in thick crust pizza, the kind we like, and I watched her devour one half of a large pepperoni, sausage, mushroom, onion, and double cheese. One day, I told myself, I would have to find out where all the food she eats goes to. It never shows upon her as fat.

As we ate she asked, "So tell me. Why were you

late? You got a new girl on the side or something?" She mumbled the words through a mouthful of pizza and then washed it down with a quarter mug of dark beer.

I told her about Suzanne Mark and my meeting with her and that she had some hair-brained idea that someone was going to try to kill her. I told Sandy that I thought Mrs. Mark might be a little mentally off balance, what with the funeral and the years of booze. I didn't tell her about the details of her marriage to Frederick Mark, the violence, the whores. That kind of thing doesn't need to be discussed.

Sandy was happy that I would go out of my way to help Mrs. Mark. She told me I was a nice guy. I wondered if she would say that if she had known of the questions concerning her spinning around inside my brain.

We finished what we could of the pizza and I got a second pitcher of beer at the bar. Sandy plugged a few dollars into the jukebox and we spent an hour listening to music from the 50's and 60's, and sang along when the mood struck. Neither of us can sing worth a damn but after the second pitcher of beer we were harmonizing pretty damn well, at least we thought we were.

We left the pizza place a little after eleven. I was feeling pretty good about Sandy again. I had a nice little beer and pizza buzz going, and the little voice inside my head was too slurred for me to understand its warnings. I hugged her to me in the cool night air as we walked across the lot to my MGB. The questions remained spinning around the back of my mind, but I knew, or maybe I hoped, that there were reasonable answers to them.

As we pulled out of the lot she leaned against me, nibbled on my ear lobe and whispered, "Let's go try that big hot tub of yours. I've been dreaming about us in that obscene thing all day."

"Sounds like fun," I said. "But first, who phoned you today?" The words seemed to fall from my mouth without warning. I had not thought about saying it. I don't know why I said it. I regretted saying it immediately. Too much booze often loosens my tongue.

"Phoned me? I don't know," she said as she nibbled at my ear. "Let's talk about what nasty stuff we'll do in that hot tub."

I knew I was making a mistake. I knew I should keep my big mouth shut and not jump into this. All that beer was clouding my better judgment. I had convinced myself that patience and time would take care of everything and there I was, about to wildly push where I shouldn't be pushing. But I couldn't stop myself. Call it two pitchers of beer mixed with something small eating at my insides, some little demon inside my gut, straining to find out what the hell was going on.

"Someone phoned you at Cap'n Nick's earlier today. They told you Franco and Jeremy were dead, that it wasn't Tony I found in the house. You were completely distraught when you thought it was Tony who was dead. And too cool when I told you who was dead, that it wasn't Tony. If you're in some kind of trouble, if there's something I don't know about, tell me and I can help you. I can't help you if you don't confide in me. Tell me I'm crazy, that I'm in some childishly jealous rage. Convince me I'm just imagining all this. Convince me I'm completely bananas. Or tell me the truth."

She withdrew from me, pulled herself against the passenger door, crossed her arms in front of her, and stared blankly out the window.

"I don't know what you're talking about," she said. "If you plan on ruining this evening, tell me now and I'll go on home."

She spun suddenly to face me and said, "You told me it was the Morellis, remember?"

"I told you two unidentified bodies had been found.

You asked if they were male or female, which is another thing I'm wondering about. What difference would it make? Then you jumped to the conclusion that one of them was Tony Morelli and went into an emotional nosedive. This afternoon you get a telephone call and then you tell Cap'n Nick it was Franco and Jeremy in the house. Who phoned you?"

She sat close-lipped for a moment, arms hugging her chest tightly. She tapped her foot fast, nervously, on the floorboard, and scowled at me.

"Alright!" she shouted finally. "Nobody told me, I just knew it. Inside of me. Call it intuition. Can you understand that?"

She was lying. I finally accepted that. It might as well have been a hard punch in my soft stomach. Until I met Sandy, I had thought myself not capable of giving real love. I hoped I knew what love was supposed to be, at least what I thought it was supposed to be. I knew it was wanting to give everything you have inside yourself to that other person just because she is who she is, not for anything you can get or expect to get in return. I had done that with Sandy. And she had done it in return for me.

Until that moment, we had been one person. Our lives had been set on a course of making each other happy. There had been only truth, only giving, only caring about each other. Only love. With that one lie the mortality of the sandcastle that had been our love was washed away. Would we ever again be able to build that castle and hide away from the world inside it? Would I ever want to try to rebuild what we had?

In the worst of times, people live by hope alone, even when the very bread of life has been taken from them. I searched inside myself for that ray of hope. I knew that driving her away from me would gain nothing. If I could keep her near, talk with her slowly, over time, maybe I would find out the truth. If she left now, I would never know. But that meant I had to calm down, take hold of my feelings, and then suppress them. I had to allow the gut wrenching fear to be held in check.

So I forced a smile. A big, broad, toothy, High School play smile. I held out my arm to her and she leaned into it. I hugged her so tightly neither of us could breathe.

We drove to my house on the hill and we both admitted that we were too exhausted to jump into the hot tub. We undressed, uneasily, uncomfortably; our backs turned to each other, and crawled into bed. We both pretended to sleep as we lay awake next to each other long into the night.

TWENTY-THREE – The Santa Maria

The phone woke me at half past eight the next morning. Sandy groaned and rolled away from me, pulling the sheet with her over her head. Bright sunlight was flooding into the room through the big windows. I hadn't closed the drapes the night before. I wanted to stare at the stars and the pale moon well into the early morning.

"Who the hell is it and do you know what the hell time it is!" I growled for no particular reason except that I was pissed off at the world. I had been awake most of the night, and I had a stiff neck.

"This is Clayton and it's eight thirty in the morning. Did I wake you? Christ, I'm sorry."

It was Clayton Morgan, the distant cousin who worked for the Coast Guard. "Oh, sorry, Clay," I said. "Have you got something for me?"

"Yes, we've found the Santa Maria." Clayton told me that the Santa Maria was moored in a small private marina, about two miles north of the San Marcos city limits. He said it was just a matter of checking all the marina license reports on the Coast Guard District computer. He made it sound like an easy task, but I knew he had spent hours doing it. Clayton gave me the name of the marina, its address, and the slip number. I thanked my cousin and told him I owed him one.

"No problem," Clayton said. "Always glad to help a close relative." We weren't that close, but I let him get away with that one.

I knew he didn't do all that work because he liked me. Clay did it because of the money. I couldn't fault him for that. I know people respect the family assets and only tolerate me. What the hell. It gets me what I want.

I showered in the guest bathroom and dressed quietly without waking Sandy. She was still in a deep sleep when I left the house.

After stopping for coffee and one of Sam Goldman's wonderful cheese Danish, I drove to Harborside and pulled to the curb in front of the Harbormaster's office. Call it a wild shot in the dark, but it occurred to me the night before, as I lay awake thinking, that the description of Tony's blond girlfriend with big tits could well be the receptionist in the Harbor Master's office. I just couldn't believe that San Marcos was a big enough town to have two such well-endowed young ladies.

She was at her desk, bent over a desk-top computer, pecking slowly at the keys as she worked hard at searching out each letter. Speed typing was obviously not one of her skills. She probably had cut typing class in High School to be with the football team.

She looked up at me and smiled after I had stood at her desk for a moment or two.

"Well, I forget your name but I remember you," she said, smiling a big toothy smile. This time she was dressed in a garish tank top of purple, green, and red flowers with brightly colored parrots peeking out from behind them. A rainbow of red, green and yellow rhinestones arced from her shoulder across her breasts. In small black letters at her other shoulder was inscribed 'MAUI WOWIE'. Painted on black pants, an imitation gold chain belt, and gold colored, plastic sandals completed the outfit. As tastelessly loud as she was dressed, her thick, long, blond hair and well sculptured, Nordic featured face seemed to make everything somehow right.

"Well, thank you," I answered. "Actually I wanted to know if you know Tony Morelli."

"Sure," she said quickly, the smile unbroken. "Me and Tony go out now and then. He's a real pistol, if you know what I mean." She tried to wink suggestively but was not able to close one eye without the other following suit, no matter how hard she tried. I guessed coordination skills were not something she had been endowed with. She had been over-endowed with other skills, however.

"Have you seen him in the last week or so?" I asked.

"No, longer than that," she said, wrinkling her forehead in deep thought. "Me and him ain't . . . I mean haven't," she smiled innocently, "been out for almost two months. He got some girl he's supposed to have fallen hard for. Somebody new in town. I ain't . . . I mean I haven't seen her but I was told by some of my girlfriends, you know?"

"How come you didn't mention this when I came in asking about his boat?" I asked.

"You didn't ask," she said in a pleasant, empty-headed sort of way. She tilted her head to one side and smiled again, showing off all her big, white teeth.

"I don't suppose you know where I can find Tony, do you?"

"No, I sure don't. But if you see him, tell him I wouldn't mind getting together with him again."

"Where can I find his new girlfriend?"

"I sure don't know," she answered. She was leaning over her desk on her folded arms. A little more pressure and I was convinced whatever was holding her in her Maui Wowie tank top would burst and she would have that chest of hers all over the desk in front of me.

"How about your friends? Do they know her?"

"They sure don't. They just seen her, like me, I guess. Say, is this important or something?"

"Not really. I'm just trying to find the boat and the Morellis. But if you see Tony tell him Morgan Crew is looking for him."

She said she would do that, moistened her overly red lips with the tip of her tongue, smiled broadly again, and waved as I left the office.

So Tony had given up all his skirts for one steady piece of squeeze, as they say. And who was that one steady girl? Sandy's face kept appearing in front of me, but I forced myself to believe that was ridiculous.

I started north, out of my little town. Once I had gone over the last of the hills surrounding San Marcos the weather began to turn bad. I drove through fog and light rain across the flat, short highway to Route 1. Ten minutes later I took the first exit, a pock marked two lane road that allowed the MGB to bounce along at 20 miles an hour all the way back to the Pacific. A light rain was rapidly turning into a downpour.

I was dressed in a summer weight, tan sports jacket over a brown Izod golf shirt, and brown, lightweight cotton slacks. I had on a brand new pair of soft leather loafers that I knew would be ruined in the rain, seconds after I got out of the car. By the time I could see the ocean it was raining hard and I was planning on getting soaked.

After taking only two wrong turns I found a sign for the marina Clayton had told me about. I drove down a dead end road lined with run down beach cottages and over grown with tall beach grasses, and then onto a paved road that ended suddenly in unpaved, muddy goo that the old MGB got stuck in almost immediately. I managed to get it extricated by rocking the car back and forth. But the car was a muddy mess by the time I got it free.

I found the entrance to the marina I was looking for on

my left and turned into it. As I swung off the road into the
marina's parking lot, the Santa Maria stood out like a sore
thumb. There were about thirty or forty boats moored at the
marina, all expensive motor yachts or ocean going sailing
craft. The expensive toys of the rich. The work battered
Santa Maria was moored at the end of the last pier. It
looked rather sad and lonely tied up as far from the gleaming
yachts as could be managed.

I parked the MGB on a graveled patch as close to the
marina entrance as I could get. There was a tall chain link
fence running the length of the marina. The one gate that
allowed entrance to the docks was locked with a push button
series locking device. Without the proper code, I was locked
out.

I sounded the horn on the MGB five or six times but
no one responded. I got out of the car and wished once
again that I would one day remember to leave an umbrella in
the trunk. I couldn't see anyone on the docks, but a small
white clapboard building with a blue tile roof sat at the
bottom of a ramp that sloped down from the gate. A sign
swung in the wind from two hooks under the roof's eve which
read in neatly carved, blue painted letters, MANAGER'S
OFFICE. I called out to anyone who might be inside.

After the third yell a young, tanned, muscular, college
age guy stepped outside. He wore tight fitting white shorts
and brown boat shoes, no shirt or anything else to protect
him from the cold rain that was falling. His chest and arms
were made up of a lot of very showy muscles.

"What do you want?" he called back in an annoyed
voice.

"Hi, can you open the gate? I'd like to talk to
somebody about a boat and I'm getting drenched out here."

"The guy ain't here," he yelled back and started to
return to the office. "Well, how about you let me wait inside
for him! It's really wet out here!"

He hesitated a minute than stepped inside, and a buzzing sound at the gate told me he had unlocked it for me. I pushed it open and jogged down the ramp to the office. Inside I shook the rain off while the young guy leaned back against the wall on the two rear legs of a metal, armless side chair, an open Playboy magazine in one hand and a can of diet Pepsi in the other.

"It's nasty out there," I said.

"You should'a worn a coat or something," he answered without looking away from his magazine.

"It wasn't raining when I left this morning. I'm from San Marcos. I drove up to enquire about the Santa Maria over there."

"Yeah, well you'll have to wait 'till Mr. Burlington gets back. I just help out around here."

He wouldn't look at me as I spoke. He kept flipping through the pages of his magazine and stopping to look at the photos as he came to them. Every now and then he would take a drink from the can of pop. I was wet, tired, my new shoes were ruined, and I wasn't in a very good mood. This guy was really beginning to piss me off.

"Well, maybe you can help me out. Who's paying the moorage fees on the Santa Maria?" I asked.

"How the hell should I know? Wait 'till Burlington shows up, ok?"

"I suppose Mr. Burlington will have to look in his record book to find out who signed the Santa Maria in?" I suggested as I tried to get some of the water out of my shoes by stamping them on the floor. "And he'll probably have to look in that same book to see who is paying the fees?"

"Sure, I guess so. Just hang around and wait for him, Pops." He sneered and drank from the can again.

As he was drinking I hooked the toe of my shoe around one of the back legs of the chair the young man was lounging in and pulled it out from under him. He crashed to the floor, the can of Pepsi spilt down his chest and onto his shorts, the Playboy flew from his hands as he tried to catch himself.

He looked surprised for a second or two, then mad as hell. His face flamed and he started to get up. I kicked as hard as I could with the same foot I had flipped the chair, and caught him dead square on his right shin with the toe of my soggy shoe. He rolled over a couple of times, holding his leg and crying out in pain.

When he had stopped rolling and quieted a little, I said, "Now, instead of me waiting for your boss, why not just tell me where the record books are and I'll look it up myself."

He nodded his head toward the desk in the corner of the small office and said, "Bottom drawer." Inside the small drawer, I found two ledger size books, blue covered and dusty. One was labeled on the front in hand written block letters, 'REGISTRATION'; the other was labeled 'RECEIPTS'.

I put both on the desktop and opened the registration book first, flipping through it until I found the record for the Santa Maria. According to the record, Tony Morelli had registered the ship in, more than a month before. I tore out the registration page, folded it twice and slid it into my inside coat pocket.

The receipt book showed that the monthly fees had been paid six months in advance in cash, a total of $3090.00.

Muscles was sitting on the floor rubbing his shin, which was turning the most amazing shades of blue, black, purple and red I had ever seen. "Anybody living on board the Santa Maria?" I asked him.

"No, we don't allow live aboards for more than three days in a row."

"Anybody been coming to the boat, to take it out or

clean it up?" I asked.

"Yeah, the kid who checked her in. And some other guys, I don't know who."

Muscles was being very nice now. I pulled the chair he had been sitting on upright and straddled it, resting my arms on the chair back in front of me. Muscles stayed on the floor but pushed himself up against the wall, still rubbing his swollen leg.

"Describe these other guys."

"Hell, I don't know. They wear suits. Not like boat people, you know. Drive up in this big black Caddy. Two of 'em, they been here two maybe three times."

"What do they do when they come here?"

"They take the Goddamn boat out!" he snapped. "How am I supposed to know what the hell they do! They take the damn boat out and they bring it back! The kid was with them the first two times, not the last."

I thanked muscles for being so helpful and polite. As I left the office the young man pulled himself painfully up off the floor and hopped around the small office on one foot. He started swearing and yelling threats, warning me not to come back again. Apparently, if I ever did come back again I would be very sorry.

When I left the marina office it wasn't raining as hard as it had been when I had waited at the gate. I pulled the collar of my jacket up around my neck and ran down the wooden piers to the Santa Maria. On deck I found the door to the cabin closed and locked. But the hatch over the two big engines remained unlocked. I pulled it up and latched it open.

Reaching down I pulled a handful of wires off of each of the two big diesel engines. Not being a mechanic, I only hoped the engines wouldn't start without the wires. Maybe the two suits weren't mechanics. It was the best shot I had at keeping the Santa Maria where it was.

The rain was slowing into a light drizzle. I lowered the hatch covers and walked around the boat. Nothing seemed out of place, nothing was unusual. A few of the cabin's curtains were open. I looked inside. Again, nothing was out of place, except for one locker which was open and empty.

It had been quite awhile since I was onboard the Santa Maria. I tried to recall what the locker had been used for. I couldn't be positive, but I thought that the then open locker was where Franco had kept his shark rifle. The first thought that jumped into my head was, did Tony now have that gun? And if he did, what was he going to do with it?

Tony was still alive and now possibly armed. And Tony led back to Sandy. The connection was the important thing. The connection was what I had to delve out. And if possible, I had to keep the police from learning of that connection. Whatever it took to protect Sandy, I would do.

TWENTY-FOUR - Just Waiting

As I walked back to my car from the marina office, I tried to remember the phone number for Weedmarre Security. In the MGB, out of the rain, I punched up what I thought was the right number and found my memory to be pretty good. One day I'm going to learn how to use the memory on the cell phone. I told them I wanted another 24/7 guard added to my account and that I wanted the guard in plain clothes, outside the marina, to keep an eye on the Santa Maria but not to be seen by anybody. If anybody went aboard, I was to be notified immediately. I gave them all the phone numbers I could be reached at.

It was a long shot, but I had to admit that it was about the only shot I had at the time. It would take me about fifteen, maybe twenty minutes to get to the Santa Maria from San Marcos, depending on the weather and if I didn't care about speed limits and stop signs that is. In rush hour traffic, if I had to go through Downtown, that time could double.

But I was banking on the two suits in the big black Cadillac not being mechanics and not being able to quickly identify why the boat's engines wouldn't start. If they fooled around, maybe called their boss for instructions, maybe waited for a mechanic, whatever, I just might have enough time to get to them. A very long shot but the only shot I had. If Tony Morelli went to the boat, he would know what happened to the engines, and I stood no chance of getting to the boat in time. Maybe luck would be a lady, as The Chairman of the Board used to sing.

"That's not a problem," the Weedmarre clerk on the other end said. "But this is getting pretty expensive . . ."

Before he could finish I said, "I'll send my check for five thousand by special messenger before five today. But I want someone on this boat within one hour or I'll find a security company that can."

"I'll have someone there in less time than that," he said and hung up.

I then phoned Harper, Harper, Jascro and Nettles and told Harper, Jr., a nice young man but overly conservative in thought and dress, to send the check by special messenger that day. He asked for a reason, I told him because it was my money and I told him to do it. I hung up before the young attorney could reply.

Almost immediately upon hanging up, the cell phone rang. It was Bob Sommers.

"I've been trying to get you. Where've you been?" he asked.

"Out. Have you got something for me?"

"Yes. I ran a rap sheet on Hector Morales. It's so long it took a long time to print out. Tied up the printer. The guy's been into everything. Drugs, theft, you name it. He's got three arrests involving guns, took a shot at some guy over a drug deal gone bad. In short, he's a bad dude and you better watch your ass."

"Anything about him dealing? I mean selling in large quantities?" I asked.

"Small time. He's had two arrests for possession to sell. I think he sells to finance his own habits. Nothing big so far. Has he committed a crime that you know of?"

"He ran off with a friend's daughter. She's not a kid and probably not a virgin, either. And I doubt he had to force her. But, no. He didn't commit a crime that I know of, other than smoking dope in my friend's front yard."

"I can't put a want out on him for that. You keep me

up to date on Hector, hear me? He's dangerous."

I waited in the MGB on the road outside the marina parking lot for the Weedmarre man to show up. I spent the time listening to some good jazz on the radio. The rain had stopped completely and a rainbow crowned the Pacific to the northwest. A few birds circled overhead, the grey clouds breaking and disappearing above them. Despite the improving weather, I was soaked through, cold and uncomfortable.

After waiting a few minutes short of an hour, a dark brown Dodge Van drove down the street slowly, turned and drove back again, just as slowly. It made a left turn and disappeared. A moment later it drove by me again, pulled to the curb and stopped.

Before I could get out of the MGB and walk to the van, a woman jumped from the driver's side and walked casually toward me. She was heavy, but not really fat. More like a weight lifter is heavy. She crouched down at the side of the MGB to put our eyes at level.

"You must be Mr. Crew. I just got off the phone with the office. They said to check in with you."

I pointed out the Santa Marie to her, the locked gate, and the marina manager's office. I told her about 'muscles' in the office, and that the only thing I was interested in was anyone going on or near the Santa Maria. I made sure someone would be in the van twenty-four hours a day until someone showed up at the Santa Maria. She assured me there would not be a problem.

After briefing the woman on what I wanted, I made sure she had all my phone numbers, and I told her not to wait to phone me the second anyone touched the Santa Maria. She said she would be on a six-hour shift and told me again, I assumed trying to reassure me, that someone from Weedmarre would be there twenty-four hours a day to earn my money, until I told them to stop. She walked back to the van and I left the marina.

As I drove back to San Marcos, I decided to check in on Mrs. Mark. I phoned her home and a woman with a slight Spanish accent answered. I told her who I was and asked to speak to the inside security guard. In a few seconds the guard was on the phone.

"This is Morgan Crew. How are things going there?"

"Just fine. No problems," the man answered. "Mrs. Mark wants to go out this afternoon. Mr. Bloome suggested some shopping. We are arranging for a female employee to accompany her."

"I thought there was supposed to be one female inside the house all the time? That's what I asked for," I shouted into the cell phone.

"We had a mix up in assignments, sir. The woman who was supposed to be here today was called off to some kind of special assignment. Watching a boat or something weird like that. But a supervisor, Mary Tanner, is on her way here now to accompany Mrs. Mark." I felt bad that I had sounded off at the guard when I learned that the woman who was supposed to be there was called off because of me. I also planned on having a word with Weedmarre management. Were they that short of people? Maybe I needed to find a new security company.

"O.K. That's great. But you follow in a second car. It'll make Mrs. Mark feel important," I said. I liked the feeling of authority, even if I was telling the guard to do something he probably would have done anyway.

"Yeah, anything you say, Mr. Crew," the guard answered, a little frustration sounding in his voice. I hung up the phone, deciding there was no need to speak with Suzanne Mark.

I then punched in Mitch Krueger's phone number and listened to the phone ring seven times before Mitch answered.

"This is Morgan. How're you doing?"

"Just fine," he answered. He sounded annoyed, but I really didn't care anymore.

"Have you heard anything from your daughter, yet?"

"No."

I waited but Mitch didn't say anything else. He sounded like I was bothering him again.

"I had a criminal record check done on Hector Morales, Mitch. Thought you should know about it. He's a pretty bad fella."

"Morgan, I asked you to leave this alone," he said raising his voice to an angry level.

"I am, Mitch. I've got something more important to do but I wanted you to know that Hector has a long criminal record. Drugs and guns."

I said it not just to let him know what I had found out about Hector, but to perhaps scare him enough to worry about his daughter being involved with the boy.

"I know that," he answered quickly.

"What do you mean, you know that? Are you saying he told you all about his career in crime before you hired him?"

"Just leave it alone, Morgan. Please."

"I don't understand you, Mitch. Aren't you concerned about your kid?" I asked. "Is she home? Have you seen her?"

"Look. I'm sorry to put it to you like this, Morgan. You've always been a good friend. I know you just want to try to help. But it's none of your business now. Keep out of it, please."

"Then you've heard from her?" I asked hopefully.

He didn't answer right away. I heard him breathing heavily. "Yes, damn it. She's ok. Leave it alone," he said and slammed the phone down.

This whole thing was getting to be too much for me. It

seemed that everybody was hiding something from me. First Mitch, then Sandy, even Mrs. Mark wasn't being totally truthful with me. I felt like I was becoming a pawn for everybody, being pushed around the game board, not important enough to worry about or to confide in, only to be used for some end game which was unknown to me.

Well, I was getting sick and tired of feeling like that. I had reached that point where the more people tried to use me, the more I was determined to get the answers, no matter what it took. I was beginning to get angry, something rare for the easy going, run from your troubles, person I had learned to be. And I felt good getting angry.

I told myself I was going to find out what the hell was going on. I was going to find out why the Morelli's died. I was going to find out what the hell was going on with the Santa Maria. I would find Tony Morelli. I would find out what was going on with Mitch Krueger and his daughter. I would find out why Mrs. Mark was lying to me. And most important of all, I would find out what part Sandy D'Angelo had in the Morelli's deaths. Yes, damn it, I told myself. I would do it.

When I arrived back in San Marcos I drove to my house. Mrs. Olivera, my cleaning lady, was there and she opened the door for me, greeting me with her customary broad smile.

"Hi. Is Miss D'Angelo still here?" I asked.

"No sir. I been here since about ten this morning and she's not here," she answered in her softly flowing Mexican-Spanish accent.

Mrs. Olivera felt she was more than just a housekeeper. In her mind she was taking care of me, she was responsible for me. I would always be a young boy to her, a boy without a mother, so she would be there when a mother was needed. She did not at first approve of Sandy spending the night with me. But Sandy quickly became her friend and before I knew it, Mrs. Olivera was bringing fresh orange juice and coffee for us in the morning.

But Sandy had already left that morning. She must have called a cab to take her home so she could change for work. I went upstairs and peeled my wet clothes off, showered once again, and dressed. It was well past noon and I hadn't eaten since the Danish and coffee I had for breakfast. A large bowl of chowder and a couple of cold beers at Cap'n Nick's sounded great.

At Cap'n Nick's I took my usual table overlooking the dark water of the harbor and ordered a beer and the chowder, with a side of garlic-cheese bread. Nancy, Cap'n Nick's niece and his other waitress, smiled as she walked off to the kitchen to get my chowder. I didn't see Sandy. I figured the captain had her in the kitchen once again, sweating over a hot stove. I waived to the Cap'n and he step-clacked, step-clacked to the table.

"You got my girl slaving away in the kitchen again?" I asked.

"No. She call in sick today, said she must'a ate somethin' bad or somethin'. Maybe you should go see she needs anythin'."

That sounded a little strange. She was not sick the night before and had been sleeping peacefully when I left that morning, but I said I would check on her.

It was a short drive to Sandy's apartment. I arrived a little before two. I first tried the bell, and then knocked, but there was no answer. I punched up her number on the cell phone and let it ring twelve times with no answer.

There was nothing left to do but go home and wait. Wait for Sandy. Wait for someone to go to the Santa Maria. Wait to hear from Bob Sommers. Wait for Mrs. Mark to calm down so I could send the security guards home. Wait for Hector to show up, probably in trouble somewhere.

At home, I paced around the deck until the six o'clock news hour started on TV. I couldn't concentrate on it and finally turned it off. I tried Sandy's phone again and she answered on the second ring.

"Oh, hi, lover!" she said brightly. "You coming over to see me tonight?"

"Sure, I'd love to. But the Cap'n said you weren't feeling well. Are you O.K. now?"

She laughed a little kid's laugh and said, "I just needed a day off. Mental health day, you know? Last night was tough. I just needed a day to lie around and think about it. Don't you dare tell the Cap'n!"

"I was at your place this afternoon. Tried phoning you, too."

"Well . . . I guess that's when I was taking a nap. You know me when I fall sleep, dead to the world."

Her voice sounded normal, bright and cheerful. But there was that slight pause before telling me she had taken a nap. I heard it. I tried unsuccessfully to convince myself I was just seeing demons where none existed. And that damn little voice I kept hearing was warning me to keep my big mouth shut. But I couldn't.

"I think you're holding something back from me, Sandy," I said.

"What do you mean?" she said. "Look, don't start that again. Why are you upset with me?"

"I'm not upset. I'm worried. I love you, you know I do, and I worry about you. That's all. I just have the feeling there's something about this Morelli thing you're not telling me."

"Don't be silly. There is nothing wrong," she said firmly. "I love you and I want to make love to you again," she said each word slowly and emphatically. "Right now, so get that cute little behind of yours over here this instant."

She hung up before I could say anything more. My hand was not even off the phone before it rang again. It was the Weedmarre Security Guard at Mrs. Mark's. Someone had tried to kill her as she arrived home from her shopping trip.

TWENTY-FIVE – The Bullet

I broke every speed law on the books getting to the Mark Estate. I spun the old MGB to a loud stop at Suzanne Mark's front door. Just seconds behind me, the first of two police cars got there, their lights flashing and sirens blaring. They had followed me for the last mile but I hadn't pulled over to let them pass. I assumed they were both going to the same place I was, anyway.

At the front door I was greeted by one of the guards. He asked to see my driver's license to make sure I was who I said I was, and then stepped aside to let me into the house. Behind me the guard stepped aside for the two policemen who were running up the steps, still behind me but trying hard to catch up. The first cop grabbed me by the shoulder as we entered the house and spun me around.

"OK," he said, as he held me by my lapels and roughly pushed me against the nearest wall. "Who the hell are you?"

"Morgan Crew. I hired the guards," I said, shrugging from his grip.

"Oh . . . Sorry Mr. Crew. I didn't know it was you." He quickly pulled his hands away. "What the hell happened?"

"You know as much as I do," I answered. "Let's go find out."

In the hallway a middle-aged but very attractive woman who was dressed in a well-tailored, gray business suit met us. A gold badge was pinned to her jacket identifying her as a Weedmarre Security agent. Inscribed on the badge was *SENIOR SUPERVISOR*. I told her who I was and asked her what had happened. She looked at the two policemen then slowly turned to look at me. I guess she knew who was paying the bill.

She explained that she and the guard I had spoken with on the phone had taken Mrs. Mark shopping. Nothing had happened out of the ordinary, until they arrived back at the Mark estate. As they were getting out of the car a shot rang out.

She said she was at Mrs. Mark's side and reacted quickly. She pushed Mrs. Mark to the ground and dived on top of her. The guard at the door and the one who had followed the shopping spree in a separate car had both seen the muzzle flash and started firing at the bushes a hundred yards away where the shot had come from, but at that range their .38 revolvers did little more than scare the shooter off.

No one was hurt, but Suzanne Mark fell into hysterics. She had to be carried to her room. I was called first, then the police, then Mrs. Mark's doctor in that order. The doctor arrived as the police and I were being told what had happened.

The two police officers began taking statements from the guards. I went into the library to phone Sandy.

"Oh my God! Is she O.K.?" she said when I told her what had happened.

"Yes, shaken quite a bit, but o.k. I guess I just never figured anybody would really try to kill her. Look, do me a favor. Look up the number for an attorney, Richard Bloome. Try his office first, then his home. Tell him to get over here fast. I'll come to your place as soon as I can."

She said she would and told me not to worry about her; she would grab something to eat and wait up for me. "Don't worry about the time, just come over whenever you can," she said.

Outside I went to where the shot fired at Mrs. Mark had hit the house. A hole, big enough to put my fist into, glared at me from the frame to the left of the big doors. The white painted wood at the edge of the hole was burnt brown.

"That was no ordinary bullet", I said out loud to myself without realizing it. I am far from an expert at ballistics. The one time I had gone to the police firing range with Bob Summers the three San Marcos officers who passed for a SWAT Team were at the range. They were test firing a rifle using explosive bullets. I saw what they can do. They can cause a hell of a lot of damage even if they barely touched a victim. What would be a minor scratch on the arm with an ordinary bullet would rip a person's arm off with an explosive bullet.

Seeing the burnt wood and extensive damage to the doorframe triggered that little voice inside my head again. I couldn't make the connection right then, but I should have. There was something I should have known. But I just couldn't focus on it. Later, I told myself, sort it out later, when I had time to sit down and think calmly about it. Too much was happening too quickly.

Then I remembered reading in the newspapers that the same kind of deadly explosive bullet had killed Frederick Mark. I phoned Bob Sommers using my cell phone. I didn't want anyone inside the house to hear the call. Bob was at the Mark Estate fifteen minutes later.

"It's just plain crazy, Bob. I mean, why try to kill that poor old . . ." I was going to say 'that poor old drunk' but I caught myself before I could say it. I felt bad wanting to think of anyone that way. But she did have the reputation of being a messy drunk, regardless of the causes or the reasons.

"I don't know, Morgan. It doesn't make a damn bit of sense."

I showed Bob the hole near the door. He recognized

it as the remnants of an explosive bullet and confirmed that Frederick Mark had been killed by the same type of bullet.

After looking at it closely he turned to me and asked, "Is she involved with her husband's businesses?"

"I'm told she wasn't. Her attorney, Richard Bloome, filled me in. You can get it better from him when he shows up. I asked Sandy to phone him."

"How's she doing?" he asked.

"Fine, I guess," I answered. "The Morelli thing hit her pretty hard but she's getting over it."

"Anything I should know on the Morelli murders?" he asked, looking right into my eyes.

"When and if I find out something, I'll let you know," I lied right back into my good friend's eyes.

"O.K., Morgan. Have it your way. But you screw up and I'll come down on you so hard, all your family, all your friends won't be able to put Humpty back together again."

I laughed - nervously - because I knew Bob meant it and he knew I'd have to call in every favor owed to me, and every relative I ever had to get me out of the jam Bob would put me in.

"Anything more from the coroner?" I asked.

"Is this a one way street? Do I get something back?"

"You'll know what I find, if I find anything." I didn't tell him when I'd tell him, but I knew I would eventually have to tell him what I learned, if in fact I could learn anything. There goes that old rationalization again.

"O.K. They found minute traces of cocaine on Jeremy's clothing. He had nothing internally, just two or three microscopic flecks of some of the purest stuff to hit California in years. Not the kind of stuff you normally find on the streets. It's the kind of shit that gets cut before being retailed. Nothing on the other body. They're still waiting for dental records but I looked at the body closely, I'm sure it was Franco."

"How about that test tube we found in the basement?" I asked. I had a feeling I was pressing my luck with my friend, but I needed to know anyway.

"The lab says it had traces of chemicals that are used to process crack cocaine. We've been seeing a lot of that in North Harbor lately. Looks like the Morellis might have been in the drug trade and in it deeper than you could have imagined."

We walked into the pretentious entry hall of Suzanne Marks' home. Bob was astounded at the expensive gaudiness of the place. He went to the two uniformed officers and asked the guards a few more questions. I went upstairs where I met Suzanne's doctor leaving her room. In answer to my question he told me she would be all right. He had given her a strong sedative and she would sleep the night and most of the next day.

Back at the front door I quietly told the guards that they were to stay and not to let Mrs. Mark out of the house again, without first checking with me. They assured me they would do as I wanted.

TWENTY-SIX – Why Kill Suzanne?

After pulling out of the long graveled driveway, I stopped at the curb outside the entrance gate of the Mark Estate and got out of the MGB. The drive leading up to the house from the road was somewhat flat for about a hundred yards, with a few gently undulating dips and rises, and then began a long, slow, upward curve about halfway into the property.

Several tall willow trees lined the driveway and blocked my view of the house. I figured that anyone in the house would not be able to see me where I stood. And I could not see anything of the house but the roof from where I stood. A car or a person passing through the gate or on the level part of the drive would not be seen by anyone at the house until they reached the top of the slope and started down towards the house.

On either side of the graveled drive leading to the house were long, tall, white-wooden fences. Evenly spaced along the drive, similar fences struck off perpendicularly to form separate pastures of emerald green fields. Most of the fenced sections were empty of animals. On the left, three well-groomed thoroughbreds peacefully grazed in one section.

I climbed through the fence on the right and walked along the line of willows. The grass under foot was soft and quite deep. Bright orange poppies were massed everywhere a fence post sprung from the ground. Nothing had grazed in these sections of pastures for some time.

I continued walking and squeezed my way through two more section fences. The fields were sloping up and I began to watch the ground very closely as I walked. I came upon a break in the white fence. It appeared the rails had been broken rather than simply removed. At my feet lay the tracks of a motorcycle that had torn up the soft ground as it raced away from the house and driveway. About fifty yards from the house, just over the crest of the hill, I stopped.

Thickly grown junipers, about three feet tall, filled the ground between the willows near the house. This would be the spot the shot had been fired from, I guessed. I bent down and searched under the sharp juniper branches. It took some digging around and two scratched hands, but I found a shell casing from a rifle. It was a Winchester thirty-0-six.

Again I heard that strange, uneasy voice rumbling in the back of my head.

Something I should know, something that was important, but something that stood just out of my reach. It would have to wait. There was too much to think about, everything was getting confused and jumbled up.

The brass went into my jacket pocket with the 9-mm bullet I had taken from the Morelli's house in North Harbor. Again, Bob Sommers would have to wait on this one. I stepped out into the driveway, away from the willows, where I could easily be seen from the house. Two of the security guards and one uniformed cop were standing on the porch. I called and waived to them, and signaled as best I could that they should send the police officers down to me. They got the idea and a few minutes later Bob Sommers and a uniformed officer were climbing through the fence behind me.

"It looks like this is where the shooter might have been," I said to them. "Looks like he was on a motorcycle." I pointed to the muddy tracks leading away across the field. I said nothing about the rifle brass I had found.

Bob told the uniformed officer to search the area. He and I walked across the pasture, following the torn grass and soft dirt left by the motorcycle, to where the tracks entered the blacktop surfaced road.

We found the fence had been roughly broken from the outside, the rails having been pushed in, to allow access by whoever rode the bike. Since there were no deep tire tracks leading into the pasture from the road, Bob and I agreed that whoever broke the fence walked the bike in so as not to be heard or seen, and then rode it out, fast, leaving the tracks.

The tracks had deeply scared the soft pasture but disappeared onto the street. The surrounding homes were all horsey type places; big pieces of land with lots of trees, and houses set far back into the lots. The chance of anyone seeing a motorcyclist was slim but I knew without asking or suggesting that Bob would have the area canvassed anyway.

We walked back to the bushes and Bob asked the officer who had been left to search the area if he had found anything.

"No," he said. "The place is clean. A few jumbled footprints and the tire tracks. I've ordered casts to be made."

"Good. No spent shells around?" Bob asked.

"Couldn't find one."

Bob turned to me and asked, "I don't suppose you found one, did you?"

"Oh, come on Bob. If I had found anything and kept it from you, what motive would I have? Do you think I want to get raked over the coals?"

I left Bob there and drove directly to Sandy's apartment where she greeted me with a flying bear hug at the door.

"Oh! It's so good to see you again, lover!" she said

and kissed me hard. I held her off the ground and returned the kiss, then spun her around in the air and dropped her softly onto the couch.

Making love with Sandy D'Angelo was often wild, always wonderful, never boring, and each time I held her would forever be burnt into my memory.

I awoke the next morning to the smell of breakfast. She had cooked scrambled eggs and bacon, poured orange juice and burnt some toast, all of which I wolfed into my empty stomach, having missed dinner the night before. While starting on the second pot of coffee I asked her, "By the way, did you speak with Richard Bloome?"

"Yes finally. I called his office; he wasn't there. Called his home and couldn't get an answer. Then I called his office back and asked where he was, said it was very important. They said he was late getting back from court, they didn't know where he was. So I left a message and twenty minutes later he called me. I told him what happened and he said he would get right over there."

She pushed herself away from her small kitchen table and started clearing away the dirty dishes.

"What did he sound like?" I asked. "I mean, upset or what?"

"Kind of I guess," she said as she started to fill the sink with water. "I thought it was kind of strange at the time. He asked several questions really slow, like he was talking to a child or something, which I didn't appreciate by the way, about how Mrs. Mark was and all that. Finally I told him if he really wanted to know he should get his ass over there and find out for himself."

"Did he sound scared? Did you sense any fear in his voice?"

She turned to me, her hands dripping soapy water on the floor, and asked, "You don't think he had anything to do with it, do you?"

"At this point I don't know anything, except that anybody but me could have tried to kill her. Just like the Morellis. According to Bob Sommers, their murders didn't have anything to do with a burglary or robbery, so anybody involved with them could have killed them, except for me."

"Anybody?" she asked. She had turned back to the sink and was busy scrubbing egg off a dish. "That's a pretty big group of people. It even includes me, you know."

I looked at her across the rim of the coffee cup but I didn't answer. Sandy and I spent the next several days together without talking of either the Morellis or Suzanne Mark. This interlude with Sandy put the idea of being alone to think things out far from my mind. I did phone the Mark Estate several times a day to make sure everything was running without problems. Most of the time one of the guards would answer the phone, on occasion I spoke with Richard Bloome who seemed to be there more than I had expected him to be.

There was something about the little fat guy that I needed to know. Something about him that perhaps I didn't like. I had to find out what it was. He obviously had some involvement with the Mark's, perhaps money, perhaps jealousy, perhaps something else.

I had a strong suspicion that Bloome wanted Frederick Mark dead, for any one of several reasons. But no matter how many times I thought about it, no matter how many reasons Bloome might want Frederick Mark dead, I could not find a reason to believe he would have wanted Suzanne Mark dead.

It was obvious there was some feeling between the little guy and Suzanne. Then again, maybe he was jealous that he couldn't get into any of the real money Frederick controlled? Maybe he had gotten into that money without Suzanne knowing and there was a business reason to kill Frederick? Maybe he thought he would get into it now that

Suzanne would control Fredrick's wealth, either through her trust of him or maybe by having her himself?

But if any of those things were true, they each created a circle within a circle, bringing me back to the one as yet unanswered question. Why try to kill Suzanne? That part of it didn't make sense, no matter who the suspect was.

But that line of thought, suspecting Bloome, was all so stupid I thought finally. There must have been a hundred people who would have killed Frederick Mark given the chance. How many of those hundred could be connected with Suzanne as well as Frederick and ride a motorcycle? I'd bet not very many. And the motorcycle brought me back to the other names.

There were only two people I knew who rode a motorcycle. Tony Morelli was one. But connecting him with Suzanne Mark was even wilder than suspecting Bloome. I pushed the name from my mind's primary list of suspects, filing it off to the side.

Hector Morales also rode a motorcycle, and he had a police record involving drugs and attempted murder. But what in hell would connect him to the Marks'? Nothing that I could put my finger on. Hector had seen a chance to run off with a young babe and spend her money. Mitch Krueger was not connected with Suzanne Mark in any way I knew of, yet Loretta Krueger had been murdered about the same time Hector and Barbara ran off. Still no connection, but I knew that in real life coincidences seldom happened.

It was all becoming too confusing for me. The more I thought about everything surrounding the Morellis, the Kruegers, and now Suzanne Mark, the more jumbled up everything was becoming. I was mixing up names and crimes. I knew also that the police would not be making such wild guesses and suppositions. They would be carefully analyzing evidence and facts, meticulously moving towards the people responsible. I had to keep reminding myself that I wasn't exactly Dick Tracy.

But there were three things I had that the police didn't have: the Santa Maria, the spent bullet from the Morelli's house, and the rifle brass I had found at the Mark Estate. Unmistakable evidence and about the only real evidence I had. And it was evidence I was withholding from the police for some reason I was not yet sure of. Now that I had a tiger by the tail all I had to do was figure out what the hell to do with the damn tiger. Two phone calls brought me back to the world of reality.

The first was for Sandy. It was Cap'n Nick, telling her he needed her at the bar. She said she would be there as soon as she could. Our little vacation had ended.

As she dressed I said, "Look, you don't need to work. Why not just stay here with me."

"That sounds wonderful. But the idea of being a 'kept woman' doesn't appeal to me very much. I like for you to buy me stuff, it makes me feel good, like I'm worth something to you. But I need to pay my own rent, so that I feel I'm worth something to *me*, too."

"Do you mean Mrs. Morgan Crew would be a kept woman?"

She turned slowly to look at me, her face suddenly ashen, and asked in a shaky voice, "Do I hear a proposal of immediate marriage in that or are you talking about your mother?"

"I guess you hear a proposal of immediate marriage. I love you, Sandra D'Angelo. I want to be with you forever. I'm just not as happy when you're not around as I am with you."

"We've talked about this before," she said. "And I really want us to be married, you know that. I just want it to be the right time. What about all those babes at the country club, with all their bucks and humongous bongers?" she asked. I could see a few tears welling up in her gorgeous eyes once again.

"I don't need the bucks, and you've got the best humongous bongers around. Come on, how about quitting Cap'n Nick's and we get married next Saturday? We'll head down to Santa Barbara and spend a month or so on a honeymoon."

She ran to me and we held each other tightly so that I found that breathing anything but her wonderful scent was impossible. She was crying and sniffling as she pulled herself away and said, "You're amazing, Morgan Crew. I love you so much. Give me 'till tomorrow to think about. Not that I'm going to be stupid enough to let you get away, mind you. The answer will be a definite yes," she said, poking me hard in the ribs with her fingers. "I just need some time to lay back and luxuriate in this damn wonderful feeling."

It took her some time to fix her makeup and then re-fix it because she started crying again, but she finally left, driving her beat up 1970, smoke belching, VW Bug down the driveway towards the harbor.

The second call came minutes after she had left. Weedmarre Security was reporting two men boarding the Santa Maria.

TWENTY-SEVEN – They'll Come Back To Kill You

The black Cadillac pulled slowly into the paved parking lot at the marina where the Santa Maria had been tied up. Robert Cordessco was driving; James Leonard slouched in the front seat, his eyes closed under the dark sunglasses he wore. There were a few cars and trucks in the lot, as well as one beat up brown van.

The two men got out of the Cadillac and walked to the locked gate, punched in a code number, pushed the gate open and walked down the ramp to the small office building.

They were going to walk past the office, go directly to the Santa Maria, but were stopped by the young man inside whom I had spoken to.

"Hey, you guys are the ones from the Santa Maria, aren't you?"

Jim Leonard answered, "Yeah . . . Why?"

"There was some guy here the other day. Asking about your boat."

"Oh yeah?" Leonard said. The young man was talking to Robert Cordessco, but Cordessco said nothing, letting Leonard speak for them. "And just what did this guy want?"

"He was a real bastard, sucker punched me. Man, if he ever shows up here again I'll . . ."

"I'm sure you will," Leonard said, interrupting the boy's

191

bragging. "But just what was he interested in?"

"He wanted to know who brought the Santa Maria here. Asked all kinds of questions, but I didn't tell him nothing."

"So this guy left without finding out anything about the Santa Maria?" Leonard asked.

"Well, not exactly."

"And what do you mean, not exactly? Did this fella find out what he was looking for or not?" Leonard demanded.

"He took a look at the marina's registration books," the young man said. "The guy actually kicked me . . . Right in the shin . . . Man, in a fair fight I'd clean his clock, ya'know?"

"Yeah," Leonard said. "I know. You look like you're in good shape. Probably kick the shit outta this guy in a fair fight, right? Who was this guy? What's his name?"

"Don't know. Just some punk guy. If he ever comes back, I'll hold him here for you, if you want. Won't give him the chance to sucker punch me again, you know?"

They thanked the young guy and told him to go ahead and hold the guy, if he ever showed up again. They laughed at their joke as they walked quickly to the Santa Maria.

"I don't like this," Leonard said. "Who the hell could be looking for the Santa Maria?"

"I don't know," Cordessco answered with an exaggerated shrug of his shoulders.

"It wasn't the cops, they don't work like that. If it wasn't the cops, it doesn't make much difference. As far as I'm concerned, this guy can have the damn boat. I'm sick of stinking up my clothes taking that old barge out anyway."

"Hell, the money's good," Leonard said.

"Yeah, but any slug can steer a damn boat. This kind of work isn't what I do, and you shouldn't be happy about it either. Ruins a person's reputation."

"I suppose so. But I kind'a like getting out on the

water. Maybe we should tell the man to get some guys to work the boat and we go out as security only?"

They stopped at the Santa Maria and looked the fishing boat over carefully before climbing on board. They thought they might be able to tell if whoever had enquired about the Santa Maria had fooled with it. Robert Cordessco climbed on board first and carefully examined the working deck and the flying bridge. Jim Leonard unlocked the cabin door and climbed first into the weather bridge, and then down into the cabin. Nothing had been moved or disturbed. The locker door that had been broken into days before lay partially open, as usual. The cabin door, being locked securely and not showing signs of tampering, confirmed for both men that whoever it was, he had not gotten inside the boat.

"So, O.K.," Leonard said. "He wasn't smart enough to get onboard. What do we do? You think maybe we should call the man and let him know?"

Cordessco checked his watch, thought for a moment, then answered, "We got a schedule to keep. That ship isn't going to wait forever for us. Let's go get the shipment, then we can tell him later."

Leonard climbed up to the flying bridge, took of his suit jacket, hung it neatly and carefully over the back of the Captain's Bench, and then tried to start the motors. He had taken a liking to handling the boat. Having grown up in the inner city, he had seldom seen an ocean, more or less been out on it. He learned quickly and handled the boat well.

The two men had been taking the Santa Maria out onto the Pacific, beyond sight of land, several times a week. Cordessco would wait inside the cabin while Leonard kept the correct course. Robert Cordessco was not much of a seaman; in rough weather he would spend a good deal of time bent over the toilet in the ship's head. But the pay was good. And he didn't have to kill anyone.

Leonard turned the key and listened to the starter motor grind. He turned it again, then another time. The engines would not kick over. He switched fuel tanks, still nothing.

Cordessco climbed up onto the flying bridge. "What the hell's wrong," he asked.

"Don't know. Engines won't start."

Cordessco was as much of a mechanic as Jim Leonard was, and Leonard knew *nothing* of engines. "You got gas?" Cordessco asked, not knowing what else to suggest.

"Yeah. The gauges say both tanks are full. I tried both engines, neither wants to kick over. You think that guy fucked with'em?"

"Yeah, Jim. I think that guy fucked with them," he said sarcastically. "The question is what the hell do we do now?"

Leonard stopped turning the keys, punched the console, and followed Cordessco down the ladder onto the working deck. They saw the hatches and assuming there would be something under them, they lifted and latched them open. The two men stood looking down into the engine hold, not knowing what they were looking for.

"Go get that kid from the office," Cordessco told Leonard.

The young guy reluctantly went with Jim Leonard to the Santa Maria. "Look, I'm not a mechanic," he told them. "I can phone somebody if you want. There's a guy over at Harborside in San Marcos who comes out here. It won't take him long. Maybe an hour is all."

"O.K.," Cordessco said. "Go phone him and tell him to make it quick. Jim, you go with him and phone the man. Tell him we're having engine trouble."

I drove like hell out of San Marcos to the marina. I hoped it would take time for them to first figure out what was wrong with the boat. Then I hoped they wouldn't bolt when they found the wires had been removed. I hoped they would have to call someone and get told what to do. I hoped they would go looking for new wires or do something that would take more time, enough time for me to get there. I hoped a lot of things as I pushed the old MGB to its limits.

The car fish-tailed a couple of times around corners. Time was short, but I had to slow it down a little or risk not getting there at all. As it turned out, I had little to worry about. I pulled into the parking lot of the marina and was joined by the Weedmarre surveillance man. The woman who met me there the other day was not working that shift. There was a black Cadillac parked nearby in the marina lot. I used binoculars from the van to look down onto the Santa Maria.

The broad work deck was empty. The curtains were drawn inside the cabin. The Weedmarre man told me all that he had seen. Two men had walked through the gate, using a code to open the lock. They had stopped at the manager's office for a few minutes, when they left they were walking quickly, and appeared to be angry, to the Santa Maria.

He finished the story by saying the younger of the two men had returned to the manager's office, made a phone call, and then walked back to the boat. "That's their car," the Weedmarre agent said, pointing with his thumb over his shoulder at the big, black Cadillac. "I phoned the plate into the office and they're running it right now. We should have an answer in a couple of minutes."

The Weedmarre man was Harry Lund. He is an ex-San Francisco cop. He had taken a medical retirement after taking a bullet in the hip that left him mobile but with a limp too sever to continue on the force. He worked part-time, on-call for Weedmarre. He was a big guy, with thick salt and peppered hair, and about 50 years of age. But he had the body of someone who took care of himself. I asked him if he carried a gun and was shown a short barreled .38 special in a waist holster at Harry's side and a license that he pulled from his wallet to carry the concealed weapon.

"Are you up to a little excitement?" I asked.

"You're the one paying the bill," he answered without hesitation.

The marina registration I had taken from the manager's office had the code assigned to the Santa Maria to unlock the chain link gate. I gave the code to Harry and told him to follow me into the marina a few minutes after I had gone down the ramp and to walk casually as if he were a boat owner.

I walked to the gate, punched in the code, and walked quickly down the ramp, past the office, and toward the Santa Maria. As I walked past the Harbormaster's office I glanced in through the window. The young guy with all the muscles was still there, engrossed in his Playboy magazine. He didn't see me as I passed by.

I was on the third step of four on the ladder onto the Santa Maria's work deck when the cabin door opened and a big guy with a big gun waived me onto the deck and into the cabin. I quickly stepped onto the deck, raised my hands over my head, smiled uneasily, and gingerly walked through the open cabin door, as I was told to do. I also was hoping Harry Lund wouldn't let me down. It took several seconds for my eyes to adjust from the bright sunlight outside to the darkness inside. The smell of the fishing boat was strong in the closed cabin. The temperature inside was 15 or 20 degrees hotter than outside. When the shadows turned into figures, I saw two men, both carrying similar Walther 9mm semi-automatics and both were pointed directly at my chest.

The older one waved his gun slightly again, in the direction of a cushioned bench that ran along the right hand wall of the cabin. I didn't hesitate; I moved quickly and sat at the far end of the bench. As I started to put my hands down onto my lap, the younger one smiled and with a slight movement of his gun suggested that wouldn't be a very good idea. Not being one to piss off anybody holding a gun on me, my hands went right back up.

The one who had directed me to sit slid his gun into a holster slung under his arm, lit a cigarette, and sat on the tall bench behind the ship's wheel. I didn't bother complaining about the smoke. He blew out a slow cloud of smoke toward the ceiling, looked at me and said in a slow, soft, very menacing voice, "You don't look like a boat mechanic. Who are you and what's your interest in this boat?"

"Would you believe my name is John Smith and I was wondering if this boat was for sale? Always wanted a great ship like this."

Robert Cordessco let a cloud of smoke curl lazily towards the ceiling again, then said, "I suppose someone with a sense of humor would think that was funny. Unfortunately, I don't have a sense of humor. One more time; who are you and why are you interested in this boat?"

Before I could answer, we all heard loud, heavy steps coming down the wooden pier toward the Santa Maria. The steps stopped near the rear deck and the person called, "Excuse me! Anybody on board? You've got oil leaking from your engines and it's fouling my bow! Anybody on board?"

Cordessco drew his gun and motioned silently for his partner to go out and see what the problem was. Jim Leonard slid out of the shoulder harness that held his automatic. He loosened his red silk tie and walked out onto the deck. He still didn't look like a fisherman, but he felt casual was better than formal.

Harry Lund was standing one foot on the deck the other on the ladder from the pier. "Mind if I come on board? You've got one hell'uva oil leak down there. Christ, it's all over the bow of my boat over there."

Harry exaggerated his limp and walked to the rear railing next to where the fishing nets hung and looked over, pointing. Jim Leonard walked to the rail next to Harry and leaned over. Harry reached down, grabbed Jim's ankles and flipped him into the water.

Cordessco heard the splash and his partner's yell. He quickly backed to the cabin door, keeping the gun leveled at me, opened the door with his left hand and glanced out. He saw no one but he heard his partner splashing around in the murky harbor water and yelling for help. When he put his head out of the doorway Harry hit him hard with the butt end of his revolver. He slumped to the floor and rolled into the cabin.

By the time he came around he found himself tied nicely and sitting on the floor next to his dripping-wet partner, who was also tied, hands behind his back.

I had both of their guns tucked into my belt and was sitting on the bench again. Harry was standing at the door, his .38 held casually in their direction.

Cordessco said, "You cops? Let me see a badge."

"Sorry," I answered. "I'm not a cop. But I can get one if you want."

"If you aren't cops," Jim Leonard said, "Do you know what the hell you're doing? Do you know who you're screwing with?"

"Gosh, no. Harry, do you know?" I answered, feigning a look of wonderment. Harry answered with a shrug of his shoulders. "Why don't you two tough guys tell me?" I said.

The older of the two gunmen looked from me to Harry Lund and back to me again. "You're dead, you know that, don't you?" he said. "You won't live to see the sun come up again."

"Seems to me that I've got all the artillery and you guys are the ones who stand a chance of not seeing the sun," I said. "Now, who are you working for? You don't look smart enough to be self-employed. And my guess is you ain't a couple of fishermen."

Neither answered. I pulled one of their guns out, held it on them and spoke over my shoulder, not taking my eyes off of them. "Harry, you've already earned a $500 bonus. Do you mind earning another $500?"

"Not at all," he answered. "Which one do you want shot in the balls?" He pulled the hammer back on his gun and lowered the sights slightly.

"Oh, it doesn't make any difference to me. You choose one and if I don't find out their boss's name in ten seconds, castrate the son of a bitch."

I enjoyed talking tough like that. I felt like Bogart or Mitchum in some old black and white movie. It's something I hadn't had much practice at, but I found I was pretty good at it. My mind raced around all the tough guy movies I had seen. I didn't want to come off like a cheap PI impersonator, but I found it hard to stay out of that kind of character. I felt I might do better with a Dirt Harry imitation, but then decided not to push it.

"OK. WAIT A MINUTE!" Cordessco said, pushing himself backward, trying to climb the cabin wall.

"Shut your mouth, Bob, for Christ sake!" Leonard said. "They ain't gonna do nothin'."

But all Robert Cordessco could think about was retirement and a place in the sun somewhere. He had been killing people for over thirty years and had never spent a day in jail. He was too close. It had been too many years; he was too old to throw it all away.

"It isn't worth it," he said. "They can't get to Mr. Springer. They'll be dead soon anyway. I'm not going to get shot for nothing. I've got too much to lose."

"Smart move, Bob," I said. Springer. A new name and something to work on "Now tell me who this Mr.

Springer is."

"Marc Springer. That's all I can tell you."

The name was somewhat familiar, I had heard it somewhere, I couldn't remember where. But it would take me time to recall where and time was something I didn't have right then. Besides, I rationalized, it was fun playing the tough guy and I didn't know if I would ever have this chance again.

"You'll tell me more or my friend here will take target practice on you." I realized I was sounding like James Cagney now. I told myself I had better cut it out or they would be laughing at me.

Harry took a step forward and leveled his revolver between the man's legs. Bob Cordessco was kicking with his heels, trying to push himself through the cabin's wall. He was sweating; panic had gripped him tightly; his hands and feet struggled with the cords tying them. Jim Leonard sat quietly, a clear look of disgust on his face as he watched his partner fall apart.

He saw fear in Robert Cordessco's eyes. It was all over for Cordessco, Leonard knew that. If they survived, which Leonard was sure they would, Cordessco could no longer be trusted and would be out of the business. Leonard knew he would eventually have to kill his friend and teacher, just to keep him quiet. Fear would eventually loosen Cordessco's lips.

Jim Leonard knew he was alone then. He had lost the man who had taught him so much. Their eyes met and locked. Cordessco froze in mid-movement, his shoulders sank and an audible rush of air left him, as if the very life inside him had been expelled.

He turned and looked at me, a beaten man who knew he was finished. "Shit, I tell you and somebody kills me. I don't and you kill me. What difference does it make? I gave you a name, isn't that enough? I'm probably dead just telling you that."

What he said made excellent sense to me. I wasn't going to get anything more out of him. I had something to go on, a name that was somewhat familiar but meant nothing right then.

"You want me to call in the police now?" Harry Lund asked.

"No, they couldn't hold these guys anyway. They haven't done anything we can prove. Besides, I want them to go back to Mr. Marc Springer and tell him someone is looking for him."

"That's a mistake," Harry said. "These guys will be sent after you."

I wanted to say something like 'I'm hard to kill' but I thought that might be too theatrical. "They'll have to find me, first," I said, a whole lot too much confidence having been built up by acting like a movie tough guy.

I kept both of the guns. Harry untied both of them and we watched them shrug into their suit coats, the empty shoulder holsters not filling the gap of extra material under their arms. We walked the two suits to their big black Cadillac. We said goodbye and watched them speed away, leaving a cloud of dust and pebbles behind.

Back at my car, I gave Harry five $100 bills, which I peeled from my money clip. Before we left I asked Harry to check with his office to see if they had been able to run a make on the Cadillac's license plate. We walked to the van and he climbed inside to use the phone.

After some conversation I only half listened to, he stepped outside and told me, "There's some confusion on the plate. It seems DMV has the number registered to a 1986 Ford pickup truck that was totaled about a year ago. Belonged to some farmer up in the Sacramento Valley named Whitley."

Somehow, I wasn't all that surprised. I thanked Harry

anyway and wrote down the plate number in my address book for future use.

"You ever need me again, just call. I've got a feeling you made a mistake letting those two hoods go. As I said, they'll be back and they'll be looking for you," he said, as he handed me a Weedmarre business card with his home phone number written on it. I assured him I would keep the card handy.

TWENTY-EIGHT - The Lobster Traps

It was a beautifully warm afternoon. I put the top down on the old MGB and drove south into San Francisco. I drove across the bay to U. C. Berkeley and parked as close as I could to the Sciences Building on campus.

Dr. Peter Gruff had been teaching there since time immemorial. He had once worked for my father and had been the only person who had ever been able to get an understanding of chemistry into my brain. I had asked him for help one summer. I was flunking High School chemistry and needed to re-take and pass the class the following fall or be forced to leave the very private school I attended.

Dr. Gruff took a liking to me and tutored me so that I could just barely get passing grades. He and I had kept in touch over the years; he would send me a Christmas card, I would make a donation to some charity in the Doctor's name.

When I arrived on campus the Doctor was where I expected him to be, in his lab with a small group of students, intent on delving into the mysteries of the cadaver on the table. He held his students enraptured over the body they were cutting into. He was gifted with a talent to impart even the most difficult facts to the most difficult students so that they were able to understand and learn.

"Dr. Gruff," I called from the doorway.

"Don't bother me now, boy! Can't you see I'm busy!" he said without looking up from his work. His name suited him perfectly.

"Dr. Gruff. May I speak with you, please?"

He looked up, peering over the top of his heavy glasses which hung perilously close to the tip of his long, thin nose. His students, about twelve in this class, turned to see who had interrupted the lecture and demonstration. Dr. Gruff smiled when he recognized his former student.

"Morgan, my boy! Come in! Come in!" He waived an arm broadly causing his frayed, grey, drab and wrinkled lab coat to slip off his shoulder.

I really didn't want to get too near the cadaver. Dead people with open chest cavities were not my favorite thing. But I swallowed hard and walked in, about halfway to the table. The students surrounding the table smiled knowingly to each other, seeing the discomfort I felt at being near the body.

Dr. Gruff understood. He peeled his latex gloves off and told the students to continue whatever it was they were doing. He then led me to a small office at the far end of the lab room. It was the size of an overcrowded closet, made smaller by the numerous piles of books and paper and computer printouts stacked shoulder high everywhere.

After a few minutes of talk and good natured laughter about the old days when I was trying to pass chemistry and still find time to pick up a few girls at protest rallies, I showed the Doctor the 9mm bullet I had taken from the back door frame of the Morelli's house. I then pulled both of the 9mm Walthers from my belt and asked, "Can you see if this came from either of these guns?"

It was as if he had been asked to demonstrate a simple lab experiment to visiting High School students. He didn't hesitate a second before walking me back to the lab nor did he ask me why. The extent of his curiosity reached to the pending experiment in front of him and no further.

He told his students that they might be interested in what he was going to do. He introduced his former student to his class. One young lady with hair of an unnatural red-orange hue, said, "Oh, I know you! You're that rich guy I read about." The class laughed, I smiled.

The doctor walked us through the entire process of firing a bullet from each of the guns into a barrel filled with some kind of fibrous material. He carefully removed the first bullet with long tongs sheathed in soft plastic, fired the second pistol, removed that spent bullet and then the class and I followed him as he carried both to a nearby table on which a very strange looking computer stood.

He asked one of his students to fix the first of the spent bullets in a brass clamp, which would allow the spent bullet to be revolved and positioned it under a bright light on a small plastic table that looked something like a flatbed scanner.

Next to it, in a similar clamp, the Doctor fixed the bullet I had taken from the doorway of the Morelli's home.

Dr. Gruff slowly spun each clamp while he starred at a computer monitor, which showed a picture of both bullets, side by side on a split screen. He continued to spin the clamps slowly trying to match up rifling groove markings from the barrels of the guns on the bullets. After several minutes of huffing and hawing and mumbling to himself, the computer screen flashed the words "NOT A MATCH".

Dr. Gruff took the first bullet out and said it didn't match at all. He went through the same process for the bullet from the second Walther. He spun each slowly until the screen flashed "MATCH".

I saw the brightly lit, enlarged images of both bullets. But even my unpracticed eye I could see that the grooves imbedded in each by the rifling of the gun barrel matched exactly, just as the computer had figured out.

There could be no doubt. The two suits on the boat driving the black Cadillac were the same suits driving the black Caddy who had been looking for the Morellis. It seems they found them, killed at least two of them, and for some as yet unknown reason, stole their boat.

That left me in utter bewilderment. The bewilderment came from knowing that Tony Morelli had been on the Santa Maria at least once with the two men who had killed his father and brother. He had signed the mooring papers at the marina. He had paid a large chunk of cash to the marina for slip fees, when it was obvious his father was having financial problems. I started believing Tony Morelli may have taken an active part in the murders of his family. But why?

Dr. Gruff handed the two guns to me, placed the three bullets in separate, small plastic bags, sealed them carefully, and wrote an identifying note on each adding his initials and the date. He handed them to me and I slid them into my coat pocket.

The Doctor put his arm around my shoulder and walked me to the lab door in a fatherly sort of way, leaving his students behind. At the door he leaned close to my ear and whispered, "Be careful, Morgan. Don't get yourself killed." As it turned out, that was the best advice I had had in a very long time.

****

Bob Cordessco and Jim Leonard sat silently in chairs facing each other, between them was a large, glass topped coffee table holding an oversized, bright red ceramic ashtray and a stack of unread news magazines, all not quite a year old. The condo was on the top floor of the building. From the deck you could see out onto San Marcos harbor.

Neither man spoke. Jim glared at his partner, Cordessco's shoulders slumped, and his eyes had lost the glow of life. His breath came in short, shallow, rare, and forced movements of his chest. His skin had turned grey and lifeless. His fingers gripped the chair's arms tightly and twitched every few seconds.

From a room at the rear of the large living room, two men walked quickly towards them. Jim Leonard sat up a little straighter, Bob Cordessco remained slumped. They had gone directly to Marc Springer's condo in San Marcos from the Santa Maria. Leonard had seen the green and red MGB in the marina parking lot and had remembered the license plate number. He had told the whole story to Marc Springer, his employer, and had given him the plate number.

Marc Springer stood in front of the cold fireplace, Cordessco to his right, Leonard to his left. He rocked back and forth on his heals; his hands behind his back, a mean grin across his thin lips. He looked from one of the men to the other and back again. Finally, after what seemed an eternity, he said, "O.K., Jim. I checked that plate number. I believe you."

"Thank you, Mr. Springer," Leonard said, interrupting his boss and receiving an ugly glare of contempt for having done so.

"So I've got two jobs for you to clean up this mess. The guy with the college pansy car is Morgan Crew. He's some rich bastard who owns most everything around here. The guy has lots of friends and influence everywhere. At first I didn't believe you because I couldn't place him doing what he did. I mean he had no reason, right?

"Then I found out he was a friend to those Morelli assholes. I want him dead, and I want you to be careful. I don't want nobody to find him. Make him disappear, you understand?"

"Yeah," Jim Leonard said.   "Like that other guy. Dump him five miles out. I know how to do it."

"The second job I got for you is to kill that fucker sitting over there." He pointed harshly at Bob Cordessco. "I got no use for old fuckers who can't keep their mouth shut. You may have been somethin' in your day, old man. But you just used up whatever points you got comin'."

"I know what needs to be done, Mr. Springer," Leonard said. He looked across at his one time instructor. Cordessco looked up and they made eye contact. Leonard quickly looked away.   He would take Cordessco out somewhere and do what had to be done; he would get it over with quickly. His partner would feel no pain and then he would go on with his career.

In their Cadillac, Leonard drove as Bob Cordessco sat in the back seat, his arms uncomfortably behind him, held by the tightly clamped handcuffs.   As they drove toward the harbor, Cordessco said, "Can't you let me slide on this one, Jim? After all I've done for you? Can't you let me slide?"

"There's no way he wouldn't know.   Then what happens to me?"

"No, I swear, Jim. I'd disappear. You'd never hear from me again, no one would ever see me again."

"Can't do it, Bob. You fucked up. Accept it. Hell, you knew what would happen."

They were quiet for awhile, and then Bob asked, "Can I write something down?"

"What?"

"I guess like my will, you know. I want Clare to get my stuff. Help me, OK?"

Leonard pulled the Cadillac to the side of the road and reached into the glove box. He pulled a scrap of paper and a mechanical pencil from the glove box. As Cordessco related a list of where he had hidden the millions he had accumulated, Leonard wrote down numbers and places, and

Clare's name and address. "Get it to her, will you? You owe me that much."

Leonard slipped the scrap of paper into his coat pocket. "Yeah, you got, pal," he said.

After Bob Cordessco's body was dismembered and placed inside a dozen weighted crab traps, and dumped overboard many miles out to sea, Jim Leonard looked again at the scrap of paper and felt very pleased at just how much money he had inherited from his friend and teacher.

TWENTY-NINE - Playing Tennis

The name Marc Springer was not on the list of local drug dealers Bob Sommers had given me, yet the name was still somewhat familiar. I had to find out who this Marc Springer was before Marc Springer found out who I was. Then it occurred to me that Harry Lund had run the license plate on the black Cadillac easily enough. My MGB had been parked in the same lot at the marina as their Caddy. Fear shot up my spine as I realized that they had probably gotten my plates, too. That was not my first stupid mistake. I was certain it wouldn't be my last.

Harry Lund had warned me not to let the two of them just walk away. Harry was an ex-cop. He knew what he was doing. I was a rich nobody who was playing games and feeling good about making out to be a tough guy. What should I do, I wondered? Where should I go? I had no idea. I wound up driving to the Country Club without realizing it or even thinking about where I was going. I didn't stop at the gate but the guard knew me and just shrugged his shoulders as I sped by him.

I parked in the lot, and without thinking about it I left the MGB in the sun rather than looking for a shady spot as I usually did. I stumbled up the steps and into the Club's bar and sat on a stool. Charlie, the bartender, brought me a Wild Turkey and Club Soda without being asked.

I tossed down the drink and said, "Give me another." I said it roughly and pushed the empty glass across the bar. "I'm sorry, Charlie. I didn't mean to sound like that. Please, pour another one for me."

I drank the second bourbon slower than the first and felt engulfed in the artificial calmness that too much alcohol brings on. I had never been a heavy drinker. Two or three drinks got the better of me. With the second drink, I told myself I was feeling better. The thought of someone out there, looking for me, maybe wanting to kill me, was beginning to get lost in the light fog the bourbon brought with it. And the Country Club itself lent some semblance of protection. After all, it was members only, the gate guard wouldn't let strangers in, and I doubted any members were hired killers.

Feeling better, and since I was there anyway, I thought I might ask some questions about Barbara Krueger and her tennis pro boyfriend, to get my mind off of who might be out looking for me. I hoped the club would be a safe place to spend some time, get myself under control, and maybe figure out what I should do. I left the bar and walked to the Club Manager's office.

Jack Lawrence had started at the club as an assistant greens-keeper before I was born. Today he is a young looking, tanned, fit and trim, sixty eight year old with a six handicap, and ultimately became the manager of the San Marcos Country Club and its Golf Club, Tennis Club and Swim Club.

He stood and shook my hand as I walked into his office. "Well, Morgan," he said. "Good to see you. Please sit down. Can I get you anything? Coffee? A drink maybe?"

"No, nothing," I said and then paused. "On second thought, I could use a really stiff bourbon, straight." Jack could see and hear that I had already had a few, but he phoned the bar anyway and then sat back to hear what I had to say.

"I need to ask you a few questions. I hope I'm not interrupting something important."

"Nonsense. Anything I can do. Is there a problem with the club? Something needing repair?"

"No Jack. I need to talk with you about your tennis pro, Dean Crosslund."

"Oh that," he said. "Wait till I close the door."

As he stood and started for the door, a waiter entered the office carrying a silver tray that held a tall drink. He placed it on the desk and left without saying a word. By the time Jack had shut the door and returned to his desk, I had finished half of the four fingers of bourbon.

Jack frowned but didn't say anything about it. He did say, "The police have been phoning about him, too. They want to talk with him. Has he done something I should know about? The police wouldn't tell me why they wanted to talk to him."

"Apparently he was having an affair with a member's wife."

"Oh, hell. I do not condone affairs between wives and employees, Morgan. You know that. I don't want the club dragged into a messy divorce."

"There won't be a divorce," I said. "This wife was found dead."

"You mean Dean killed a member?" Jack said, starting out of his chair.

"I don't think anyone knows who killed her yet, but I'm sure the police would like to speak with Dean and so would I. Is he here?"

"No. Like I told the police, he hasn't shown up for the past couple of weeks. I thought he had just walked off the job. You know how these guys are, real flighty. He's the third pro I've had to hire in the past five years." He watched as I finished the drink in one long, quick, swallow. "Hey, are you all right? You better be careful drinking like that."

"Yeah, I'm O.K. Just a little worried and tired."

"Anything I can help with?"

"What can you tell me about him, Jack?" I asked.

"Not a whole lot, Morgan. He came from Scottsdale, Arizona. Good references. Used to be on the pro tour but never made it big. The members all tell me he teaches well and he's polite and good tempered. That's all I can hope for in these types of guys, you know? I don't know anything about his personal life. I've never had any complaints about him coming on to the women."

"I'd like to get his home address and if you don't mind, and I'd like to talk to some of the people he works with."

"No problem," he said. He turned in his swivel chair and pulled open the top of two drawers of a short, maplewood filing cabinet. He pulled a thin file from the drawer and opened it, then wrote down an address on a scrap of paper and handed it to me.

"I don't mind you talking to anybody you think you need to, Morgan. Just do me a favor and keep it as quite as you can. We don't want a lot of rumors floating around. At least no more than would float around anyway."

I assured Jack I would be as careful as possible, thanked him and left his office. I walked across the club grounds, through the rose garden, to the tennis facility. There is a strikingly modern wooden building that housed the tennis club's pro shop and four indoor courts. There are also six courts outside, but with San Marcos' rare but sudden weather changes and storms, the indoor courts were very necessary.

Besides Dean Crosslund, the head pro, the tennis club had a young assistant pro, an athletic, college age woman, and "Uncle Dan". Uncle is what everybody called him because he acted like everybody's Uncle. He is a nice guy who is always willing to help anybody in any way he can.

Uncle Dan was in his seventies, looked eighty, and told everybody he felt ninety, but he still ran the tennis pro shop, kept the locker room clean, did what repairs were necessary around the courts, and gave advice to tennis players, even though he no longer played the game himself. He was sitting on a tall stool behind the cash register in the pro shop, reading a newspaper.

"Uncle Dan," I said. "Hi, how are you doing?" I knew I was slurring my words slightly by that time and walking a little unsteadily. Uncle Dan saw this but said nothing. He was used to seeing the members after they had one too many, but he was surprised to see me in that condition. There really is a first for everything, he told himself.

"Why, Morgan! You finally giving up that silly golf and taking up a real man's sport?"

"Not on your life. Look, Uncle Dan. I need to ask you about Dean. I understand that he hasn't been around for awhile."

"Yes, and if you don't mind my saying so, thank God. I hope he's found somewhere else to work."

"Why do you say that?" I asked as I tried to lean my elbow against the counter and almost missed. Uncle Dan decided to ignore that, also.

He looked around the pro shop; no one was there except for the two of us. He sat forward to whisper conspiratorially. "Just between the two of us . . . and you know I don't like to talk bad about people . . . if he had stayed here I would have bet there would have been trouble. In fact I'd bet right now that some woman's husband has made a complaint about him and that's why he's not working here anymore."

"You mean he's a chase skirter . . . I mean skirt chaser?" I asked, the bourbon doing what it did best.

"Skirt chaser?" he said scoffing. "The man makes a pass at anything in a skirt, young or old. But he's real good at it; I've heard him. He's a real cool one, he is. And women seem to fall at his feet. I guess they're flattered that such a good-looking guy would be interested in them. Not one of them has complained, not one of them. But it's been good for the tennis club. I mean, membership sure has jumped since he's been here."

"Anybody special?" I asked. "Any particular woman that he's been spending a lot of time with?"

"Nah. There's always a couple of the wives around. You know. Just between you and me, I have a hunch his flirting has gone beyond flirting more than once. I mean, I think he may be involved with more than one of the wives. You know, I mean sleeping with them."

"How about Loretta Krueger?" I asked. "Have you ever seen her with Dean?"

"You bet. She was always around, hanging on to him. And her daughter, too."

"Barbara Krueger? She was having an affair with Dean, too?"

"An affair? I don't know about that," he said. "But she hangs around with him as much as the mother. I guess I don't blame the kid, but Mrs. Krueger is married, after all."

"But you don't know if Loretta Krueger was having an affair with him, do you? Maybe she was just hanging around, too?"

"Oh yes I do. I caught them once back in the stock room. She had her blouse and bra off and her hand right down his pants. I don't think they saw me though, they were kind of busy, you know? If it hadn't of been a member I would have raised hell."

I thanked Uncle Dan and told him he was a big help. I asked him to keep what he had told me between the two of us. He assured me he would, and then he said, "There is one other thing. I guess I should tell somebody now that Dean's left. Maybe I'm just old fashion, you know? But I just don't think this drug thing that's going around is right."

"You mean Dean was using some kind of drugs?"

"Yes, he was. I found a small plastic bag with some

kind of white powder in it once. I didn't know what it was and I asked Dean. He grabbed it from me and got really mad, swore at me and told me to mind my own business. And I've seen him selling whatever it was to members a couple of times."

"You didn't report this to anybody?"

"No. I guess I should have, but I don't like to cause trouble."

I thanked Uncle Dan once again and walked, still unsteadily, out to the courts. I wanted to speak with the assistant pro but she was in the middle of a lesson. It was a nice, warm afternoon so I sat on a bench courtside and watched. My head was starting to hurt and my stomach felt funny. But I felt safe at the Club, the sun felt good and I was willing to waste some time.

She had five teenagers on the court, patiently trying to teach them how to handle a smooth backhand. I watched for about ten minutes until the lesson ended, and she walked off the court, wiping her forehead with a towel, although she didn't appear to be sweating.

"Excuse me," I called to her. She stopped and looked at me curiously, recognizing a member who had just come from the bar, then smiled.

"Hi," she said. "Need a lesson?"

"Thanks, but I'm afraid I'm a golfer"

"Sssshhh. Don't let people hear you say that around here. You're in tennis-only country at this end of the club."

"OK," I said in an exaggerated, slurred, whisper. "You're not going to turn me in to the tennis police, are you?"

We both laughed as she walked to me and held out her hand. "Hi, I'm Stacey. What can I do for you?"

"Glad to meet you," I said taking her hand. She had a firm, masculine-like handshake. Although she had to look up at me from her 5'5" height, she was tanned, muscular, and fit.

"I'm Morgan Crew. I was hoping to talk with you about Dean. He hasn't been around lately. Have you seen him or spoken with him in the last couple of weeks?"

"Well, excuse me, Mr. Crew. But why do you want to know?"

"I'm trying to find him. I need to talk to him about a member who might be in trouble."

"Oh, is that right. Who's in trouble?" she asked. She took a small step backward, dabbed at her forehead again, and smiled up at me.

"I'm supposed to keep that confidential, you understand."

"No, I don't. I don't know you. You didn't show me a badge. You look like a member and not a cop. You've had a few drinks. And you start asking personal questions about my boss. I'm afraid I can't help you," she said and started to walk away.

"Wait a minute," I said and took hold of her arm.

"How'd you like to lose that hand? Let go of me," she shot back at me.

I let her go immediately. "I'm sorry," I said. "Please talk to Jack Lawrence. I'm trying to find the runaway daughter of a club member."

"And you think Dean ran off with her?" she asked.

"No. In fact I know he didn't. But I know he was having an affair with her."

"An affair! That's bullshit! You're either lying or you've got the wrong person."

"Why? What makes you say he wasn't having an affair with a member?"

"Because," she said and paused. "Because he and I are engaged and he wouldn't do that."

"You're engaged to Dean Crosslund?" I asked, astonished and not absolutely sure of what I had heard. "I guess I really do need to talk with you. Look, please just phone Jack Lawrence. He'll tell you it's ok to talk to me."

"Is this some kind of rip off?" she said. "What the hell is this all about? Are you trying to get Dean in some kind of trouble?"

"No," I said. "I need to talk with you. It's important and I'm not trying to get anyone in trouble. Actually, I'm trying to get myself out of trouble."

She finally agreed to talk with me and we started for the pro shop. I had to move quickly to keep up with her. She phoned Jack Lawrence and spoke with Uncle Dan. They both told her who I was and assured her it would be all right to talk with me. There was a small locker room and shower at the rear of the pro shop, meant for the pros use only. We went there to talk in private.

"First of all," I said as we sat on the single bench in the ten by ten room. "Have you seen or spoken with Dean in the past few days?"

"No, I haven't. And I'm really worried, too. It's not like him to just up and leave," she said. She was sitting on the edge of the wooden bench, twisting her towel tightly, then whipping it at nothing, then twisting it again, like a kid in a High School gym's locker room.

"How long have you known him?"

"Almost a year now. We met at a small tourney down in Carmel. It was like love at first sight, you know what I mean? We fell hard for each other, right off. He got me this job here. I mean, I wasn't doing too well on the tour; Dean made me realize that. There were young kids, fourteen and fifteen years old that could beat me. Dean explained to me that I could make a nice living teaching, and we could be together, too."

"Do you live with Dean?" I asked.

"No, not that we didn't want to," she said too quickly. "But Dean says it wouldn't look good, I mean if anyone at the club found out, you know? But he found me a nice apartment nearby and we spend a lot of time together, you know?"

"You must know that he's considered quite a lady's man around here. Doesn't that bother you?"

"Oh, I know what everybody thinks. But Dean explained that to me right off. He said he has to keep up that kind of front so we can keep our jobs here. You see, we're saving to buy our own tennis place after we get married. It takes a lot of money, so we bank almost everything we make. And Dean is just leading those old ladies on, to get them to take lessons so we can make more money quicker. He's explained it all to me, you see." She paused and looked up at me. "I suppose I shouldn't be telling you that. I mean, I don't want to get us in trouble. You won't tell anybody, will you?"

"I won't tell anybody. I promise," I said.

She seemed to accept my simple promise, smiled slightly and then went on telling me about Dean.

"He's got a great head for business. Better than I do. In another year or two, he says we're outta here and on our own." She laughed, nervously.

"You've got some good investments going then?" I asked.

"Oh, sure. Dean's doing a wonderful job. He says we have nearly $50,000 saved now. Isn't that great?"

"That is good. Where do you keep the money?"

"Oh, Dean takes care of that. You see, for tax reasons it's sheltered and stuff like that."

"I see. That's real good. I hope you make it."

I didn't want to tell her that she was being ripped off, not by some member of the Club, but by her boy friend.

"Look," she said as she stood up and tossed her towel into a corner. "I've got to take a shower, do you mind?"

"Well, I do have some more questions for you, but I guess I can come back."

"That's ok; you can ask me while I shower, if that's ok."

With one quick movement of her hands behind her back and a shrug of her shoulders, her tennis outfit was lying at her feet and she stood in front of me dressed only in a small, lacy bra and panties, ankle socks and tennis shoes.

"Dean tells me I shouldn't be ashamed of my body. He says it's the thing to be free and open like. Do you mind?"

"I guess not, if you don't," I said.

Faster than I could catch with my now blood shot eyes, she was out of the bra and panties and sitting on the bench next to me pulling off her shoes and socks. Her breasts were small, almost childlike, and the rest of her body was toned and youthfully athletic, almost like a young boy's. There was a small patch of pale pubic hair under her flat stomach, the same color as the short-cropped hair on her head. She stood for a moment, a little uncomfortably, letting me look her up and down, as if that's what she was supposed to do for homework that day. Then she turned suddenly and walked into the shower. I waited on the bench.

I heard the shower and heard her splashing around. "Do you have any idea where Dean is?" I called out to her.

"No, I really don't, but he'll be back soon. I know he will."

"Have you been to his place? I mean in the last week or so?"

"No, Dean doesn't like me to just drop in. You see, if anybody from the club was there, they might find out about us."

"Tell me, if you don't mind. How old are you? I mean you look awfully young."

"Yeah, that's what Dean says, too. He can't believe I'm almost twenty. He says I look too cute to be that old.

Isn't that great?"

THIRTY - Parnell Rigsby

OK, I admit it. I was afraid to leave the Country Club. Maybe the bourbon had something to do with it, but I wasn't about to leave. It had always been a sanctuary, now it felt like a fortress, protecting me from the invaders. Besides, I had no place else to go. At least until I could clear my head. So I returned to the club's private bar, but I asked Charlie for coffee and drank three cups of it, hot and strong and black. The ocean inside my head began to calm, the storm subsided, and I began to think reasonably of what I should do next.

The first thought was to run to Bob Sommers and tell him everything, give him the bullets and the two guns, let him take over, and then catch the first jet to someplace far away. But I wasn't ready to do that. Sandy was still the unexplained wild card in the jumbled deck. I had to make sure she was protected before anything else, even before protecting myself.

So, I decided I had to confront Marc Springer and that if I were to confront him and survive that confrontation I would have to know everything there was to know about the man. I quickly drank down the last of the coffee, stood, and decided my head was clear enough, my stomach settled enough, and my courage was ever so slightly built up. I drove to the San Marcos Public Library.

When the San Marcos library was a dark, dank, one room shack with only two windows, a little more than two hundred well used books, three beat up tables, and six wooden chairs, (long before I was a glimmer in my father's eyes) a little old lady known only as Mrs. Fields ran the place. More than forty years later Mrs. Fields is still a little old lady and she still works at the library every day. She no longer runs the expansive library, but she is an integral part of its workings.

After wasting about an hour in the upstairs racks and shelves of books, I took the elevator down to the basement, to Mrs. Fields' research area. I started by flipping through the old, dusty index cards that were filed by the multi-thousands in beat-up old drawers off in a corner. I was looking for cards referencing newspaper articles filed by the library.

All I needed to do was leaf through the cards until I found what I wanted; at least that's what I told myself. I started by looking in the Sh - Su drawer for SPRINGER. There were a few references to a doctor in the 1950s who had been working with Dr. Salk on the polio vaccine; one card about a local young lady who joined the Peace Corps in 1964; a series on champion spaniels being bred locally, but nothing on Marc Springer.

I next went to the D's and started looking through the sixty or so cards relating to stories on drugs in the last ten years. There were many stories that I had either missed or overlooked in the daily news, but none of the cards mentioned a Marc Springer.

The San Marcos Police Department publishes their daily blotter, their record of calls and dispatches, in the local newspaper. Mrs. Fields used to clip this from the paper daily and paste the record in the latest volume of a series of heavy and dusty scrapbooks. Now the newspaper is on-line and kept in some nether-world of computer chips. I went to the old ledgers and searched through four volumes encompassing the last two years of clippings. Still nothing.

I went to the back issues of telephone books the

library kept and started ten years back, flipping through each right up to the current volume. In the 1994 issue the name Marc Springer appeared for the first and last time. Only a phone number appeared, no address. Mr. Springer may well not have been a San Marcos resident now, but he once was.

There was nothing left for me to do but start looking up every article about drugs noted on the cards to see if Springer's name showed up. I was about a half-hour into this all day job when Mrs. Fields tapped me on the shoulder. She is a small, delicately thin woman, about five foot nothing, with a bun of wispy gray hair pulled tightly to the back of her head. She has worn the same wire framed glasses with the brightly colored beaded cord, which is the only surrender to color in her grey and brown apparel, as long as I could remember. She has a grandmotherly smile and I sometimes expect her to have a plate of chocolate chip cookies and a glass of milk to offer me even today.

"Morgan," she said, touching me lightly on the shoulder. "I have told you many times that you can't find what you are looking for in those old volumes. You are not looking in the right place. Now you've been here for over an hour. I just don't know what I will do with you. Come with me to the terminal."

I explained that I was doing research on a name and that all I had was the name. I sounded like and felt like a kid making an excuse to a reproving, but kindly old school teacher for not having a homework assignment in on time.

"You must know why you are looking up this name," she said as she sat in front of the desktop computer.

"Well, of course." I had to admit it, I was feeling really embarrassed. I had never taken the time to figure out computers. I didn't own one and whenever some business thing needed a computer for any reason, I sat back and let others punch the keyboard. Now here was an old lady, probably twice my age or maybe more, sitting at the keyboard because I was completely and totally computer illiterate. I really wanted Mrs. Fields to like me and be proud of me, the same way I felt thirty years ago but I felt that wasn't going to happen that afternoon.

"I think the guy may have something to do with selling drugs here in town," I said.

She tsk - tsked at me again and said in a reproving 'what am I ever going to do with you' voice, "Watch closely, Morgan. You should know better than this after all I've taught you."

She punched a few keys, faster than my eyes could follow. The screen flashed and different colored pages came and went too fast. Finally, she stopped at a screen where she would enter what she knew would be pertinent information.

She started with 'arrests', made a few notations, went to 'Police Investigations', made a few more notations, and sat back so I could see her notes. It was a list of dates and names of newspapers.

"Now we need to look up these articles. If his name doesn't appear in any of them I can safely say his name won't appear anywhere", she said looking up at me and wagging her finger like a schoolteacher talking to her most difficult student.

She was right of course. In less than ten minutes, from the list she had given me, she had pulled up an old newspaper on the computer and had found the name Marc Springer in an article in the old San Marcos Post, an afternoon daily that had been out of business since 1989.

The article, which had run just a few weeks before the paper closed its doors, was a lengthy investigative editorial about the sudden influx of illegal drugs into San Marcos. It filled one half a page of the paper and near the end, speculated on the names of people who might be bosses in the trade. Prominent among the names was Marc Springer.

The article, in what was a very broad leap, tried to tie these names in with Parnell Rigsby. That was a name I knew well.

In the late 70's Parnell Rigsby had been accused of some scandal on Wall Street involving some Washington D.C. political hacks. He wound up skipping the country with many millions of other people's dollars from an investment firm he ran. Every now and then over the years his name would appear in connection with some big money, questionably legal operation, but this was the first I recalled reading of any suspected connection with drugs.

In 1998 the San Marcos Post was bought by Frederick Mark, who shut it down so fast that city heads were spinning for months. He sold off the company assets and that was that. That happened shortly after this editorial article had come out. Another coincidence? I was convinced that Freud was right, coincidences don't happen.

The current phone book told me that the former owner of the Post was still in town. Brad Humphrey lived quietly in a small house south of town in one of the older housing developments of San Marcos. To satisfy my curiosity, I would talk with him to see if the editorial had anything to do with the buyout. Like the proverbial "Fool", I was about to rush in where Angels feared to go. I should have camped out at the Club for the next couple of weeks.

THIRTY-ONE – Hide Wherever You Can

I sat in my car in front of the library for a long time. Soft, cool jazz drifted from the speakers, what I liked to call 'smoky barroom jazz', but I wasn't listening. I knew that both Tony Morelli and Hector Morales had ties with the drug trade, and that Dean Crosslund was at least selling small time at the Country Club.

I mentally flipped a coin; should I bring Bob Sommers in now, or should I dig a little further? Despite that annoying, nagging little voice in the back recesses of my brain telling me again to run away and hide, I picked up the cell phone and punched in Mitch Krueger's number.

"Mitch," I said when he answered the phone. "This is Morgan. Don't say anything, just listen. This thing has gotten bigger than you can realize. I think you've heard from Barbara and Hector. I need to talk to Hector and I want to know where he is."

"Well, you can't. I told you . . ."

"Damn it, Mitch! God damn it! Don't screw with me! I'll put you out of business if you screw with me! You know I can and I goddamn will!" I let myself calm down a little and lowered my voice. "You know Sandy D'Angelo? She's in trouble and I think it may be connected somehow to Hector. I need to talk to him. Please," I begged.

He didn't answer right away. I could hear him breathing on the other end of the line and I could hear a female voice asking whom he was talking to. Then he said, "I'll see what I can do," and the line went dead, he had hung up.

Before going to Brad Humphrey's house I stopped at the harbor and walked to Cap'n Nick's. I had a creepy feeling that I was being watched but I wanted to see Sandy again, even if only for a minute, and I risked being seen by one of Marc Springer's people just to see her for that minute.

"She ain't here," Cap'n Nick said. He was behind the bar, a towel in his hands drying beer glasses and lining them up on a rubber drain at the edge of the bar.

"Did she go home?" I asked.

"Yeah, I guess so. She don't say. She actin' real strange, ya'know? She happy then she ain't. What's up?"

"How long ago did she leave?"

"I don' know. A hour. Maybe more. You hurt her, Morgan?" he said in his tough gravelly voice.

"No," I answered. "I asked her to marry me."

"Well, that explains it! I'm happy f'you both!" he said, almost as an afterthought. But he didn't seem happy and he didn't act happy as he should have. He continued wiping the glasses dry, one after the next. I sensed there was something the Cap'n knew, something I wasn't being told, something both Sandy and the Cap'n weren't telling me.

"Look, Nick," I said. I had never called the Cap'n anything but Cap'n before. It seemed like everything was changing, even my friendships. "I think there's something wrong. I think that maybe Sandy and you know more about this Morelli thing then you've told me. I think you know what that something is, what she knows, what I don't know. I can help Sandy if she's in some kind of trouble. But you have to help me first."

"I don't know what you talkin' 'bout," he said roughly. He tossed the towel onto the bar and started for the kitchen. I ran around the bar and caught him as he was pushing the swinging door open.

"Don't hand me that, Nick," I said, spinning him around.

The Cap'n's big right arm brushed my hand away as if it were an annoying insect that had landed on him. Then he grabbed my jacket in both his bear-paw hands and lifted me nearly off the saw dust covered floor.

"Don't touch me, Morgan! You a friend but I break you in half you ever touch me again. Sandy went home. Forget it and just go to her. Forget everything and everything'll be O.K."

I drove to her apartment and rang the bell, knocked on the door, rang the bell again, and peered into the window over her kitchen sink. She wasn't there and her beat up VW wasn't in sight. After debating the pros and cons of kicking down the front door, I left a note instead, asking her to phone me.

But where could I go now? I could hide out at the Country Club. I could leave town and be safe. But that wouldn't help Sandy. Despite my growing fear, I knew I had to stay out there, stay visible, keep asking questions, and help Sandy if I could.

So, I drove slowly, methodically, up the hills away from Harborside, and without realizing where I was driving to, I found myself at the curb in front of my home. When I walked into the house I found the letter on the entryway table. It was from Sandy.

My Love,

Yes! I want to marry you and nothing will ever change that. I want to be with you now and I want to spend the rest of my life and more with you, devoting myself to making you happy.

But first I have something that I must do. I hope you will understand and forgive me. I have a responsibility that must be fulfilled before we can be together. When I am done I will run back to you, as fast as I can, I promise.

Please don't be mad at me. You are the fulfillment of every dream I've ever had and I couldn't bear to be without you. Please wait for me and don't stop loving me.

I LOVE YOU!

Sandy

Uncontrollable anger and fear overtook everything else. It was a situation I knew I had to control, but I couldn't. Everything – life itself – was whirling away from me. The grief of reading her letter left a white-hot heat of rage and a silent cry for revenge inside of me. I hope one day I can be forgiven for the thoughts that filled my head that day.

I read the letter over and over again, and tried to convince myself that it was not as serious as I took it to be. After all, she never once mentioned the Morelli killing. Maybe I was just assuming things that couldn't be true. She must have meant something else, a family problem or illness, perhaps. But if that were the case, why was she so vague? Why leave a note and not speak to me directly? No, she was involved. Somehow she was involved in some or all of what was going on, I knew it.

I pulled myself together with two very large bourbons, and when the false calm and confidence enveloped me once again I felt I maybe could talk without letting my fear show. I phoned Bob Sommers at the San Marcos Police Department.

"I need to know who somebody is, Bob. And I'm afraid that as of about a half-hour ago things have changed radically. I won't be able to tell you why I need to know."

There was quiet on the line for a few moments, and then I heard him say, "You've been a long time friend of mine, Morgan. I can help you if you let me."

"It's suddenly become very personal, Bob. Who is Marc Springer?"

There was a pause again. I could hear Bob's breathing, short and shallow, on the other end of the line, with a rattle of keyboards and printers in the background mingling with a dozen voices.

"Marc Springer? You're in over your head, Morgan. You can't handle that one alone, you'll get killed."

"Who is he, Bob? I have to know. Tell me about Springer." I had hung around Bob's office often enough to know police routine and to know that Bob had gotten another cop on the line and from that point on our conversation was being monitored and recorded, and probably traced, too.

"I've got the file here, Morgan," he said, his voice careful and the words spoken slowly, softly and calmly. "I can't tell you much . . . It's still an open file, you understand?"

Bob waited for an answer from me that did not come. He gave me clips of facts but as he spoke I could hear the growing caution in his voice. There was not one shred of evidence that would put Springer in jail for even an hour, but so much suspicion and conjecture that a blind man would know Marc Springer was dirty.

"Springer has been in town since early 1994. He's taken over just about everything. Runs his own mini-Mafia," Bob said. "Before he got here there were a few hoods in town, mostly in North Harbor, who ran a little pot and smack, a few whores, some book making, that kind of thing. Since Springer arrived we can't find anybody who's independent. They either work for him or they don't work. And a couple of them have been found dead, too. The problem is we can't link him up directly to anything. Everybody's too scared.

"That should tell you enough to get you out of this. Morgan, I want you in my office in the next fifteen minutes. I want you to write down everything you know and then I want you out of whatever the hell it is you're into."

"Where's he from?" I asked.

"God damn it!" he shouted. "I told you to get out! I'll have your ass up on obstruction charges! I'll see you in jail! At least there you'll be safe!"

I hung up the phone and left the house running. I figured Bob had a job to do and although Bob might want to help me as much as he could, he would also have sent a patrol car to my home to pick me up. I drove to a Texaco station at the edge of town and used the phone booth there to call Bob Sommers again. Enough time had elapsed so that he would know I was not at my house. He would be alone at his desk, waiting there, I hoped, anticipating that I would phone him again.

"Can you talk?" I asked.

"Damn it all, Morgan! I suppose you want my ass in the sling with yours?" He spoke in a whisper, cupping his mouth over the phone in his crowded office.

"Where's he from?" I asked again.

"Back east somewhere. He has a record of sorts in

New York, a few arrests but no convictions. The Feds say he's connected with Parnell Rigsby."

"I already figured that one out," I told him. "He's the guy who took off with big bucks some years ago, isn't he?" I asked, knowing the answer.

"You haven't been reading the papers, maybe? The Feds are still after him for defrauding over a hundred million from investors in his scams. They suspect he's living in grand style somewhere in the Caribbean and running tons of cocaine into the States, possibly out of Cuba. Is Springer involved with the Morelli murders somehow?"

"Have you tied Rigsby directly to Springer?" I asked without answering Bob's question.

"You can't go off alone on this one, Morgan. If I have to I will have you busted for obstruction of justice, I mean it, damn it! I want you in my office in fifteen minutes and if you're not here I'm going to put an APB out on you."

"That means there isn't one out on me already?" I asked.

"I got you a reprieve. A very temporary reprieve. I convinced Captain Logan it wouldn't look good to arrest Morgan Crew. That damn family name you carry around with you, you know. But he wants you in here and off whatever the hell you're into."

"You've got to help me, Bob. I can't tell you why right now, but you have to help me."

"I don't have to do anything, Morgan. Friendship isn't going to sink an investigation that's years in the making. For your own good, come in now. The Feds aren't going to be as impressed with your family name as we are. They think we're just hicks out here now and they don't want us messing with Springer at all."

I hung the phone back in its cradle without another word. My MGB would stand out like brown shoes in a room full of tuxedos, so I drove it to the Greyhound Bus Station and parked it in the rear lot, behind several parked buses. From there I walked the six blocks, via side streets, to the Hertz Car Rental office and used the Amex Black Card with Harper, Harper, Jascro & Nettles name on it to rent a spanking new Ford Mustang, a very loud red color, but it would serve its purpose.

I put the 9mm auto that had fired the shot in the Morelli house into the car's glove box and adjusted the other in my belt so that it was more comfortable. I stopped at Curly's Sporting Goods where I bought a box of 9mm Winchester Silver Tips and two clips for the pistol. I hoped I wasn't going to need them, but I was prepared to use the gun if I had to.

THIRTY-TWO - Brad Humphrey's Story

I then drove to Brad Humphrey's house, the former owner of the Post newspaper. I needed to know more about the people I was up against. Although I knew quite a lot about Parnell Rigsby and Frederick Mark, I still knew next to nothing about Marc Springer. I had very few places to go for that information.

The neighborhood is vastly different from my neighborhood in the hills, from Mitch Krueger's, from the Country Club, and certainly from Suzanne Mark's estate. The homes there are modest ranch styles and small, not unlike the Morelli's former home. They are crowded together, and show signs of age and needed repairs. Older model cars and a few pick-up trucks lined the streets and driveways. Crabgrass and dandelions spotted the lawns, and kids toys were everywhere.

An old man in rumpled tan slacks, a soup-stained plaid flannel shirt, and frayed red suspenders came to the door. His face sagged around his eyes, and at his jowls he wore the stubble of several days gone without shaving. It was mostly grey to match the thinning, gray uncombed hair of his head. On his feet he wore cracked vinyl bedroom slippers, the kind without backs so that his bare feet slid around in them. In his hand he held a can of beer. His face was drawn and thin under its sadly drooping, colorless skin. Bushy salt and pepper eyebrows crowned half-closed eyes that had lost the warm spark of life some years before.

"Excuse me, I'm looking for Mr. Brad Humphrey," I said.

"That's me. Who're you?" He slurred the words, squinting intently like he had forgotten his eyeglasses.

"I'm Morgan Crew and I'd like to talk with you about the San Marcos Post."

He stared at me for a moment, blinking his eyes to bring them into focus and to give himself time for his brain to also focus. He stood, blocking the doorway, his left hand holding onto the door's edge to steady himself, and took a drink from the can.

"I know you," he said. "What I mean is I know your name. Folks like you seldom get out to my part of town. What'ya wanna talk about the Post about? She's dead now, you know."

"I know. I want to find out why she's dead. Why you sold the paper and the story you were running on Marc Springer."

"Marc Springer?" he said surprised, his eyes trying to open full under the heavy lids. "I don't know nothin'. Leave me 'lone."

He tried to close the door but I pushed back on it gently with one hand and almost sent him reeling backward onto the floor. He'd had a few too many and he wasn't very steady on his feet. I stepped inside, closed the door behind me and said, "Look, I can't stay outside for very long. Some people are looking for me. I'll pay you to talk to me. How much do you want?"

"Shit! How much you gonna pay when they come back an' kill me?"

"Who's going to kill you?"

"Springer, 'course. And that God damn Frederick Mark."

I was able to get Humphrey into a chair that bore his

outline and the stains of many years of spilled beer and food. He slumped into a corner of it and took another pull from the can, draining it. I looked over his shoulder and found the kitchen, went in, and took another can from the over-ripe refrigerator. There was little else inside it but several six packs of cheep beer.

The inside of the house was filthy. The carpet was stained and littered with molding food and cigarette butts. It was tattered, it smelled, and it hadn't been close to a vacuum cleaner in too long a time. Clothes lay strewn everywhere. Dishes were in piles and a thick odor of fetid uncleanness hung in the air. In every corner and on most of the old furniture throughout what I could see of the house, lay piles of newspapers. I figured that there were more than a few years of papers stacked inside Humphrey's home, bringing a sick, damp smell of mold to the old house.

Along the far wall, behind the chair in which Brad slumped, was a cabinet with glass doors, six shelves inside, holding a collection of books. They were neatly arranged and appeared clean. I guessed they were the last things of value Brad Humphrey owned.

I pulled a black vinyl footstool into the center of the room, a few feet in front of Brad's chair, and from it I moved a plate half full of several days old food onto the floor. I sat on the worn out stool and watched the man pry open the can of beer I had gotten for him. He took a long swallow and then looked at me with glassy eyes.

"Why do you wanna know?" he asked.

"I want to put Springer in jail for murder. And I want to protect someone I love, if I can."

Brad thought about this, his eyes half closed, his head swaying gently as he mumbled something to himself. Then he said, "I used to have someone I loved. Before all this of course." He waived his free hand in a wide arc to take in the whole room. "She left me after it all happened. Can't blame her, though. Have to be stupid to live scared like I do."

"Are you scared of Marc Springer?"

"And that God damn Frederick Mark, 'course! Who'd you think? Killed my dog, you know? Did you know they killed my little dog? My wife found the poor old mutt hanging by its neck from a tree in our front yard. Guts cut out. Damn cruel thing to do to a innocent little dog, ya'know."

"Why did they do that?"

"'Cause I asked for the money Mark promised me when he bought the Post," he said and took another swallow. Beer trickled from the corners of his mouth and hung on the stubble on his chin. He wiped it off with the cuff of his dirty shirt.

"You mean you were never paid for the paper?"

"Oh, I got some. 'Nuff to keep me in beer for the rest of my life. Lost the house, the car, the dog, the wife. But I can afford to drink all the beer I want." He bent forward and laughed a short, strangled laugh, spewing droplets of beer and saliva from his puffy lips.

"Ya'see, Mark signed papers saying I would get three point two million. That was about a million more than the whole damn paper would have ever been worth. I had to laugh at the time. Thought I was taking the son'bitch real good.

"He put up two hun'red thousand as down payment and told me to sign the sales agreement or my wife would end up just like the poor dog. Did you know he was that kind of bastard?"

"Frederick Mark is dead," I told him. "Did you know that?"

"Dead? That bastards' dead? Ha! That's rich. Somebody finally got up the guts to kill the bastard. What'ya know 'bout that. Ya'know," he said, leaning close to me and winking a bloodshot eye. "I never was much of a religious kinda' guy. The wife, she used to get me to church now and then, I mean, but I never believed in stuff like heaven or hell. But I sure hope I'm wrong so's that damn bastard can burn in hell."

"How did you know he was murdered? Did you kill him?" I asked.

He sank back into his chair, drank from the beer can again, and said, "No. Wanted to but I got no guts." His limp hand pointed at his swollen stomach and the stained shirt with two buttons missing which covered it. "Guess I just assumed the bastard wouldn't die an old man. Too many people hate him. He's destroyed too many people. Too many people would want to kill him."

I believed him. "So you sold the Post to Frederick Mark, he shut it down, sold off the assets for a couple of million, paid you two hundred thousand and pocketed the rest."

"You got it, sonny. Say, how 'bout you getting me another beer? My leg's been hurting here recently. Kind'a hard to walk," he said, rubbing his right thigh and dropping the empty can to the floor.

I went to the kitchen and brought another can to him, opened it, and handed it into his shaking left hand.

"This here's the leg they broke," he said, still rubbing his thigh.

"They broke your leg?"

"Sure. Roughed me up real good. Worse was the leg, though. That was after the wife left and they had no one else to beat up. Damn leg never did heal right. See, at first I wouldn't sign the papers 'till I got all the money. Said I'd take him to court and all that shit. Thought if I played it right I'd get the money and the wife would come back. But all's I got was a busted leg and a few weeks in the damn hospital."

"So you finally sold out to Mark?"

"'Course I did. I was scared and I don't mind admitting it. They scared me good. And I'm still scared. I'd like to die, but I'm too scared to die.　If I had any guts I'd publish the whole damn story 'bout Mark and Springer and let them kill me.　But I'm just too damn scared."

He drained the can of beer and let it slip from his fingers onto the floor.　He didn't ask for another and I didn't offer.　I needed to find out more about Frederick Mark and Marc Springer, and I needed Brad Humphrey awake to do that.

"Why did Mark want to buy the Post?" I asked.

"The story I was running on Springer.　You read any of it?"

"Just a little," I said.　I wanted to hear it from Brad, to get what was not in print.

"It was a good story," he said.　"Some damn good 'vestigative reporting, ya'know.　Did it all myself, too. Couldn't trust nobody.　'Member that, son.　Don't trust nobody, 'cause Springer's got ever'body by the damn nuts. Even the cops.　Would have liked to finish the story and seen that bastard in jail.　But . . ."

He let his words drift off and his eyes closed as his head slumped onto his chest.　I reached out and shook his knee gently.

"Brad," I whispered.　"Brad, wake up.　I need to talk to you."

"Huh?　Oh, 'course.　Sorry, I slip off now and then. Got in the habit.　There isn't anything else to do, ya' know?" He tried to sit up straight but his arms were too weak, so he settled back into the slouch the chair had become accustomed to.

"'Course, I read a lot," he said, waving towards the books lined up behind him.　"Haven't lost that yet.　Really enjoy reading good books."

I spent over an hour with Brad Humphrey that day.　I wanted to leave with everything I could.　I talked Brad into drinking a cup of coffee.　I found an open jar of instant coffee in the kitchen, washed out a cracked mug while the water was heating in a dented pan I had found at the bottom of the crowded sink.

Brad managed to finish most of the steaming mug of double strength coffee and asked for another can of beer. I poured another coffee instead, which he took without complaint. Halfway through the second mug he said, "I began that series when a young girl, just a high school kid, you know, was found dead up in North Harbor. Overdose of heroin they said. Just a poor fifteen year old girl. What a damn shame.

"Well, it didn't take much to learn that San Marcos High School was thick with drugs. You could buy whatever you wanted, right there in the hallways between classes. I put a couple of reporters on it, but they couldn't . . . Hell, truth is they wouldn't do the job.

"See, we got a lot of bad people here in our quiet little town." He laughed which started him coughing. His face turned scarlet and he gagged, but managed to control the cough finally. "I used t'hear lots of people call San Marcos that," he went on as if nothing had interrupted what he was saying. "Ain't that somethin'? A quiet little town."

I smiled at that. How often had I called San Marcos that same thing? I had heard it all my life. San Marcos used to be our quiet little town.

"Like hell!" Brad went on. "Oh, you'd never know it, 'course. On the surface, it's a beautiful place with lots'a nice folks like ya'self. But underneath, it's all just dirty money, drugs, killings, sex. My people were bought off. Those that wouldn't be bought were scared off.

"So I took it up myself. Found out that ol' San Marcos was a major import point for drugs. Bring it in through the harbor, see? Found out that Marc Springer was running things around here, at least he was fronting it. I lucked onto a meeting between him and Frederick Mark up there in North

Harbor.

"Got a phone call one afternoon, don't know who it was, somebody with a heavy accent anyway like a lot of fishermen down there. Says I should go to this bar out by the harbor. Can't remember the name now. Anyway, says I should go there and see who's there. So I did and I walked in on a party ol' Springer and Frederick Mark were having with a bunch of naked girls.

"They didn't see me, too busy I guess. I got out as fast as I could and I started researching connections between the two of them. Started implying in the series about a connection between drugs in San Marcos, Springer and some big business type people.

"After the first article like that, in fact the day it came out, Frederick Mark offered to buy the paper. I figured to lead him on, ya' know? Try to get some information out of him. But he killed my dog and the threats started coming in. After the wife got scared and left and I got outta the hospital, there wasn't much else to do but sell. So I did," he said with a resigned shrug of his thin shoulders.

"Now, understand," he said, his voice gradually becoming a little steadier after the coffee. "I have no proof, but look at it from my point of view. I see their sex party, start to run the story. Frederick Mark makes an offer to buy me out. Frederick Mark threatens me and my family. Marc Springer carries out the threats. I sell. Mark closes the paper and nothing more is ever heard about Marc Springer. Kind of looks like Springer and Mark care about each other. Maybe Frederick Mark was Springer's boss?"

I hadn't considered that. "Do you have any notes or files on the story?" I asked.

"No, they all went with the sale. A lot of the detail I've forgotten about. Time and booze has a way of doing that. Most of the stuff is gone forever. But I remember what I knew. I mean that Springer is dirty. But he'll never fall.

They own everything, did you know that? They own the city, the state. They own the cops, the government. For all I know, they own you, and you'll run back and tell them I'm still talking. You're not going to do that are you?"

There was a sudden rush of fear overwhelming his gaunt face. What little color there was in his thin, too old face drained quickly. He was considering that maybe he had said too much. Maybe he should have just kept his mouth shut, as he had all those past years. There wasn't much I could tell him except the truth.

"No," I said. "I want them out of the way as much as you do. Do you need any money?" I asked, reaching for my money clip.

"No, thanks. I got some left. Enough to last, anyway. Ya'see, I'm told I got a chest full of cancer. Oh, hell. Don't let that worry you," he said to my reaction. "Don't mean a damn thing. I got about six, maybe seven months still and enough money to last. I got nothing to live for. Lost it all. In fact, six months seems like a damn long time, ya'know? Although I do worry about after. Do you think we just die? Or is there really heaven and hell?" His eyes clouded and filled with tears that would not run. Too many tears over too many years, a man only has so much inside.

I left Brad with a fresh can of beer from the refrigerator. He was mumbling to himself, talking to some person only he could see. Maybe asking someone to make time go just a little faster for awhile.

THIRTY-THREE - Keep Out Of Sight

I was cautious when I left Brad Humphrey's house. I walked slowly and casually out to the Mustang parked at the curb. I took quick, darting glances both left and right, but if a police car had been on the street, I had absolutely no idea what I would have done, except run perhaps.

My next stop would have to be Mitch Krueger's. I had to get some straight answers from someone. I was fed up with everyone's evasiveness, and Mitch seemed like as good a person as any to start getting tough with. I was beginning to put together a picture of what was going on in San Marcos and I had to know if Hector Morales, Dean Crosslund, and any of the Krueger's were connected to that picture. If they were, it was a mighty big picture.

Driving carefully and being sure to obey every traffic sign and law, I tried to remember to neither speed nor drive too slowly, but my hands were shaking and sweat was beading on my forehead. I was scared but determined to go on.

As I drove through Downtown I passed several police cars without attracting attention. When I reached Mitch's neighborhood I circled the block twice before pulling to the curb. I knew, in that neighborhood, nosy women with little else to do would be at their windows, keeping track of what everyone else was doing, so they would have something to talk about over bridge that night. So I walked slowly, maybe a little stiffly, not being used to being on the run from the law, so to speak.

Mitch opened the door before I could ring the bell or knock. He stared incredulously at me for a second or two, and then tried to slam the door shut. Everybody wanted to slam doors in my face! I pushed back on the door, finding it more difficult than when I did the same thing at Brad Humphrey's, but still able to keep the door from closing.

Mitch tried to stop me and found he couldn't. He let the door swing open and I stepped inside, pushing Mitch out of my way. "What the hell do you think you're doing!" he yelled. "Get out before I phone the police!"

"You're not going to phone anybody, Mitch," I said as I walked into his living room.

"And you're going to stop me?" he said as he reached for the phone.

Before his hand could reach it, I pulled open my jacket and showed him the gun tucked in at my waist. Mitch stopped, stood up ramrod straight, and took a step backward.

"Are you crazy?" he said. "What are you doing? You're not going to shoot me, are you? I don't want you to hurt me." He slowly backed away from me, his hands held out in front of him.

"I just need some information, Mitch," I said and sat in a big, over-stuffed chair. It was very comfortable; I sank into it, and for the first time I realized just how tired he was. It had been a long day, starting by tangling with the two hoods on the Santa Maria, a lunch consisting of too much bourbon and nothing else, hours in the library, and ended with my talk with Brad Humphreys. Exhaustion had settled in and I realized how hungry I was. Sitting in the soft armchair started my head spinning. In short, I wasn't in any mood to take any crap from Mitch Krueger.

"Now sit down and pay attention," I said and he sat. "I want to know what the hell is going on and I want to know now. And I don't want any bullshit. I want the truth."

"I don't know what you're talking about," he said. He stood up straight very quickly and turned his back on me. He picked up a rumpled pack of cigarettes from a table and shook the last one out. He fumbled with it, dropped it on the floor, and picked it up with a shaking hand before lighting it. A cloud of smoke rose above him as he turned around to face me once again.

"I want you out of here, Morgan. You don't know what can happen to you. Just get out and go home," he said. His face was bright red and beads of sweat covered his forehead. His hand was shaking so badly I thought he might lose the cigarette.

"I want to know what happened to Barbara and Hector," I said emphatically.

"Barbara came home. She's ok. There's nothing more you need to do. I'm sorry I asked you to look for her. She's ok. Now get out."

"Is she here?"

He inhaled heavily and a length of ash dropped from the glowing tip of the cigarette. His face was drawn tight, his eyes closed, he looked as if he were in pain. But he said nothing.

"I said, is Barbara here?" I repeated

"No . . . No, she's not here."

"Where is she?"

"That's none of your damn business."

"How about Hector? I want to talk to him."

"So go talk to him. I don't give a damn," he said and flicked some ash towards an ashtray and missed.

"Where is he?"

"How the hell am I supposed to know? The son of a bitch doesn't check in with me!"

I was tired of his attitude and I was beginning to feel sick. The room was filling with acrid cigarette smoke and my eyes and nose were beginning to burn from it. Mitch stamped out the cigarette in an overflowing ashtray, reached into his shirt pocket and took out another pack. He lit another quickly and inhaled deeply once again. This time it choked him and he coughed violently. I thought he was about to puke when he fell into a chair, bent over, his head between his knees. The coughing subsided.

"You do know that both your wife and daughter were screwing Dean Crosslund at the club, don't you?" I asked. I figured that if I got him really angry he might tell me something he wouldn't otherwise say.

"You're a son of a bitch, you know that, Morgan?

"Yeah, I'm a son of a bitch and your wife and daughter are whores. Does that make you feel better? Or maybe you like knowing somebody else was screwing your wife? Is that why you killed her?"

He was leaning forward, his elbows on his knees, his hands locked tightly together so that he was crushing the cigarette between his fingers, and his knuckles were white. He looked up at me slowly and said in a soft voice, "I didn't kill her, Morgan. I didn't kill her."

"But you know who did, don't you?"

His eyes burned into mine. I could see the anger rising slowly in Mitch.

"Was it Barbara?" I asked. "Did Barbara kill her mother because she was jealous? She wanted Dean all to herself?"

"No you bastard. You're wrong."

"Then Hector killed her," I said. "Maybe he and Loretta were involved. Was it Hector?"

"No," he said. "If it were, I would have killed him myself."

"You know who killed Loretta. Tell me and maybe I

can help."

"You can't help. Nobody can help. It's all too late to help."

Tears were forming in Mitch's bloodshot eyes. But I needed to keep him going; I needed to force him into making a mistake.

"Dean Crosslund was using and selling drugs at the club. Did he have Barbara as a customer?" I asked.

"What the hell difference does it make?" Mitch answered despondently.

"How about Loretta? Was she using, too?"

"Of course she was! You know that, you bastard!"

"That makes you pretty mad, doesn't it, Mitch? I mean, to know your wife and daughter were going to bed with the guy who supplied them with drugs? Were they paying for it or just screwing for it?" I said as mean as I could manage.

"I ought'a kill you, Morgan. You know that? I ought'a kill you."

"You killed Dean Crosslund, didn't you, Mitch? That's why no one has seen him. You've killed Dean because of what he was doing to your wife and kid, haven't you?"

"And if I did, who's going to prove it?" he answered. "I mean, are you going to prove it? That's a laugh! If you weren't so Goddamn rich you'd be out driving a cab somewhere. Don't you know how silly you are? How really stupid you are? What are you trying to do, play some kind of TV hero or something? You couldn't prove the time of day if you had to. People around here would laugh their asses off! All you can do is play golf and strut around like some kind of rich asshole. People laugh at you behind your fucking back, you asshole! And besides, you're gonna be dead soon anyway."

"What the hell does that mean?"

"You'll find out," he said and laughed a mocking little

laugh.

Mitch was either trying to frighten me off, threaten me, or he knew something I didn't know. But I wasn't finished with him yet.

"How about Loretta? Did you kill her?" I asked, ignoring what Mitch had said for the time being.

"I'm going to be honest with you, Morgan," he said. He slouched back in his chair and tried to smile. "I was going to. I hated her. I truly hated her. And you're right, she was a cheap whore. Oh yes, she was out screwing more people than just Dean Crosslund. But I didn't have to kill her. She dug her own grave."

"What does that mean?"

"You're so god damn smart. You figure it out. I'm not going to get killed for her or for you," he said.

"So now not only will I be murdered, but you're going to be murdered, too?" I asked, trying to sound like it was a fantasy, even though I knew inside of me that Mitch just could be right.

"You're so stupid, Morgan. You're so damn stupid," he said laughing again and shaking his head at the joke only he could see. "You should thank God you were born rich. You'd be in a real pickle if you were normal, like everybody else. You have no idea what you're into, do you?"

"OK, so I'm stupid. Explain it all to me."

"I'm not gonna do shit for you, ol' buddy. I'm just going to keep my mouth shut and live to a ripe old age."

"Marc Springer's somehow involved in all this, isn't he?" I asked.

Mitch didn't have to answer. His face, suddenly pale white with fear told me Springer was at the center of it somehow. "I thought so," I said, satisfied that I was right. "Dean was selling drugs . . . For Springer, I'll bet. I imagine someone like Marc Springer saw a gold mine with all the money floating around at the country club. Dean was probably an obvious choice for a dealer. He's a popular party type, probably always in need of money. I'll bet he and Springer were pretty close buddies, too. Probably did some partying together."

I was making this all up as I went along but as I said it the connection hit me. I knew then who had killed Loretta Krueger.

"Loretta must have met Springer through Crosslund, right?" I suggested. Mitch didn't answer, but I knew I was right.

"Loretta was a good-looking woman. She was screwing Marc Springer, too, wasn't she?"

Mitch's eyes closed and his head and shoulders drooped sullenly. I felt I was right, of course. But I didn't have to tell Mitch I was right. Mitch knew I was right. Marc Springer had killed Loretta. Why? Sex, drugs, any number of slight wrongs she may have committed. Like not giving up Crosslund when she became involved with Springer, maybe. The why wasn't all that important, so long as I knew I was right.

And Mitch's fear was perfectly logical and understandable to me. Anybody in their right mind would be scared of someone like Marc Springer. I was scared. But the fear wasn't going to stop me.

I pushed myself out of the chair. I had to steady myself on the chair's overstuffed arm. Getting up so quickly caused my head to spin again, and for a minute I thought I was going to black out. Mitch saw this and lunged at me.

He caught me around the waist, his lowered head slammed into my chest, knocking the wind out of me. We fell backwards and rolled over the arm of the chair and onto the floor. Mitch was yelling, cursing. He was kicking and began flailing his arms wildly. He wasn't hurting me as much as surprising me.

I easily rolled over on top of him and managed to pin

his arms to the ground. Mitch's eyes were crazy, burning red. He was spitting damnation at me as I sat on Mitch's chest. There was little else for me to do but hit him, which I did, just as hard as I could, across his jaw. As I pushed myself off Mitch's unconscious hulk, I wondered if my hand was hurt more than Mitch's face. I hoped I hadn't broken a knuckle or two.

It was late, I was tired, I was hungry, I was feeling a little crazy, and my knuckles were swelling. But I had another call I had to make before the police caught me.

THIRTY-FOUR – The Lady Once Again

I parked the little Mustang at the front door of the Mark Estate after making sure there were no police cars around. By that time I was feeling so far beyond exhaustion, both physically and mentally, that I was close to saying "The hell with the cops, I don't care if they do see me". But I also knew that I wouldn't be able to do much for Sandy from a jail cell.

The guard at the door was the same one I had posted that first night. He bent over and looked into the car to see who had driven up the drive. When I got out he recognized me, stood stiffly, his hands behind his back, nodded to me and said, "The Police have been here. Looking for you."

"I haven't been here, have I?"

"Haven't seen you in days," he said and smiled.

The door was opened by Richard Bloome. His short, stocky physique shook uncomfortably as I took his out-stretched hand. I stepped inside and was struck by the remarkable change in the entryway. The long hallway was empty; the walls held only the discolored shadows of where the pictures had been. Our voices echoed in the tall, empty room.

"The Police have been here," he said.

"So I've been told. Are you planning on calling them?"

252

"Suppose I was? Would you try to stop me?"

"I would not only try . . . I would definitely stop you," I said.

He looked up at me and asked, "Did you kill anyone?"

"Not yet."

"Don't go any further," he said, holding his hand up and shaking his head firmly. "Don't tell me anything else. I hate to lie, especially to the police. Give me a dollar."

"What?"

"I said give me a dollar. I want you to hire me to represent you in the matter the police want to question you about. I know nothing of what you've done, except that you say you haven't killed anyone. Hire me and whatever we talk about will become privileged. If you have committed a felony I will advise you to turn yourself in. If you haven't, you have no reason to rush into the police station. In either case, if anyone asks, I can't tell them anything. I would be disbarred for breaking a privilege."

I reached into my pocket and peeled a five dollar bill from my shrinking supply of cash.

"I don't have a one. Will five do?"

"Fine, you hired me. Now, what do you want here?"

"I need to talk with Suzanne Mark, about her husband."

He rubbed his cheek again for a moment, thinking. "Is it important?" he asked.

"Very. I think I may know who killed her husband. I just need a connection that would put Mrs. Mark in the picture."

"Ask me. She shouldn't be put through all this."

Before I could say anything else, Suzanne Mark spoke from the far end of the entry way hall, at the foot of the stairs, her soft, gentle voice echoing in the empty channel of the hallway.

She stood almost majestically, her hand on the

banister, her hair flowing softy across her shoulders. She was dressed in a satin, pale purple nightgown covered by a loose lacey robe. For an instant, in the dim light of the far hallway, I imagined I was seeing a movie star of the forties. The armed Security Guard five steps behind her broke the illusion.

"No, Richard," she said. "If Mr. Crew can help me he should be allowed to ask me himself. I'm quite alright, you know."

In fact, her voice did sound stronger. And as she stood stiffly upright, her hair combed and her make-up simple but perfect, I saw that she was stronger.

She walked toward us, perhaps a little unsteady on her feet but with her head held high in an effort to exert what remaining pride was inside her. When she stopped she held out her hand to me, asked how I was, and what she could do for me. Her eyes were clear, surrounded by skin older and lined more than it should have been, but bright and clear all the same.

"I'd like to speak with you about your husband," I said. "Alone, if that's o.k. with your attorney."

Bloome said it certainly was not O.K. at the same time Suzanne said it would be fine.

"I need to step back into life, Richard. I need to face what is happening and when it is over I will be able to put it behind me. I understand your concern," she said and touched his hand in a very close and affectionate way. "But I need to do this on my own for the first time in a lifetime I need to do something on my own, to prove that I still can do something on my own."

He agreed reluctantly and Suzanne waived, slightly stiffly and uncomfortably but elegantly all the same, to the library. We stepped inside and I closed the doors behind us, leaving Lawyer Bloome standing alone in the empty hallway.

"Would you like coffee, Mr. Crew? Something to eat

perhaps. You look as bad as I must look."

"Coffee would be most welcomed," I said. "Thank you. It's been a long, hard day. A lot has happened. In fact, I hope I look half as good as you do. You look wonderful, I almost didn't recognize you."

"Thank you," she said, laughing lightly. "I'll take that as a compliment and I do feel better."

"Do you know the Police are after me?"

"I had heard. Is there anything I can do?" she asked as she sat in one of the tall wing chairs and rang a small silver bell that rested on the table next to her.

"Deny that I was here," I answered.

"Of course, that goes without saying. Please sit down."

I sat near her and ran my fingers through my hair to push it out of my eyes. I was feeling very tired and badly in need of a shower and shave, not to mention some food. I also felt a little embarrassed being in such shabby condition while in the company of such a lady.

"Please don't be concerned with your appearance, Mr. Crew," she said, anticipating my thoughts. "What you are trying to do, to help me I mean, must be very difficult. I understand. Be assured that you have a safe place here, to rest, to eat, whatever you need, whenever you need a safe place."

"Thank you. I'll keep that in mind. I need to speak with you about your husband and his business dealings."

"I'm afraid there is very little I know, but I will help if I can. Please ask."

The library doors slid open and a young olive skinned woman, a very pretty Mexican lady with silky jet hair tied tightly in a bun, took one step into the room.

"I insist that while we are talking I have some food prepared. You look like you need it," Mrs. Mark said to me and then nodded to the woman, who bowed ever so slightly and backed out of the room, quietly closing the mahogany doors behind her.

I admit I did need something to eat. I hadn't tasted food since breakfast and it was rapidly approaching half past ten at night. I waited a moment to collect my thoughts then said simply, "Parnell Rigsby."

"That loathsome man," she said immediately, spitting the words out. "Yes, I've had the displeasure of meeting him several times. I remember the first time, in New York at some political gathering, many years ago. My skin crawled when he took my hand and kissed my cheek. It felt like a snake was touching me."

"Your husband had business dealings with him?"

"You must understand that Frederick never discussed his business with me and he would always find an excuse to shoo me from the room if business matters came up. But, yes, I believe he was closely involved with Mr. Rigsby in many dealings."

"Was Frederick involved in Parnell's skipping town with all that money?" I asked.

"Frederick was seldom at home during that time. He was quite frightened and quite violent also. It was a particularly bad time for me and the children. Oh, please don't feel uncomfortable. I must be able to talk about it so that I can put it behind me.

"Yes," she straightened herself in the chair and went on. "I believe Frederick was involved in that whole matter. Quite closely involved as a matter of fact, although I have no evidence to give you. It's only my feeling that he was."

"How about drugs?" I asked.

"I've never seen Frederick use any drugs. He was quite a coward you know, afraid of everything and I believe he was afraid even of drugs. That they might have some detrimental effect on him."

She paused for a moment to think then continued,

"But, of course, you mean selling drugs. I am sorry. I've had my suspicions for many years that he might have been involved in many criminal matters. There have been some very strange people here at the house, not business people at all. Lots of outlandish gold chains and quite wild clothing."

"Have you ever been introduced to any of them?" I asked.

"Only a few of the more conservative ones. But their names . . . I'm afraid my memory isn't as good as it once was," she said with a slight waive of her hand as if trying to brush away her failing memory.

I handed her the list of names of local drug dealers Bob Sommers had given me, the list I had added Marc Springer's name to, and asked her to read through it. She held it for a long time, reading the names over and over again, trying very hard to clear the fog of time and alcohol.

"Yes," she said suddenly. "Yes, there is one name I seem to remember. This one, Marc Springer. I remember remarking that his first name was the same as my husband's last. It was about a year ago, perhaps less. Anyway," she said with another brush of her hand at the annoyance of poor memory. "It was early in the morning, I forget the day. I had just awoken and was on my way downstairs, I daresay headed for the nearest bottle to have breakfast.

"I was fairly sober but terribly hung-over as was usual after a night with only a few fretful hours of sleep. I stumbled right by my husband and a young man who were talking in the hallway. Frederick grabbed me by my arm, quite roughly," she said and rubbed her left arm at the ghost of the memory.

"He said I was being rude, that I should say hello to Mr. Marc Springer, which I did. I remember Mr. Springer as being well dressed in a very casual way. Expensive clothes although I couldn't begin to describe them to you now. He was a young man, very ruggedly handsome with lots of curly hair and one of those Tom Selleck mustaches.

"He was much younger than Frederick, but Frederick was treating him with some respect, deference if you will. There was some fear there also I believe, but then Frederick was afraid of everything and everybody.

"I didn't stay. I needed a drink very badly by that time. But now that I think back on it, I remember that Frederick was holding an attaché case. It wasn't his; he carried a very expensive elephant leather case always.   This one was much cheaper, vinyl I think.   Cheap black vinyl, if my ever so lacking memory holds true.   I've never seen it before or since.   Does that mean anything?   Could there have been drugs in that case?"

"More likely money. Cash," I answered.

"I see," she said thoughtfully. "Yes, that makes more sense."

"There are no other names on the list that you recognize?" I asked.

She read the list several times again and said, "I am sorry, but no. Perhaps pictures. I might remember faces better than names."

"Has anyone tried to contact you about any of Frederick's businesses since his death?"

"Only the attorneys. I let Richard handle all that. I don't know what I'd do without Richard." She said the name in a special way, with a great amount of caring as she examined the tips of her long, slender fingers.

The expression on her face right then, the delicate smile on her red lips, the dreamy cast across her eyes, were those of a young girl daydreaming of her love. But the expression vanished as quickly as it had arisen, and Suzanne looked at me once again, slightly embarrassed but rapidly composing herself.

I turned as the security guard posted outside the library door opened it to let the young maid bring in a wide silver tray holding a tall silver coffee pot and a large plate stacked high with sandwiches. She placed it carefully on the table between Suzanne Mark and me, poured steaming coffee into two delicate china cups, and left without saying a word.

"The last time you were here you connived me into eating. I must do the same for you," she said, smiling again. "Eat or I will refuse to answer any more of your questions." She smiled a very self-satisfied smile.

She needn't have said anything as the pangs of hunger were twisting my stomach, but I appreciated the thought, anyway. I wolfed down a delicious ham sandwich, trimmed of the bread's crust and cut into little triangular fourths, took a second one, and then said, "Tell me about Richard. Why is he so emotionally involved in this?"

"You are very direct, aren't you Mr. Crew? I suppose I should tell you."

She took a sip of coffee and placed the cup and saucer carefully on the tray, stirred the dark liquid with a small silver spoon, arranged her lace robe, folded her hands delicately on her lap, and began.

"Richard has been in love with me since I was a young girl. Like most young girls, I had dreamed of marrying a handsome prince. You know, tall, dark, good looking and rich. Richard hardly fills that bill. Had I known many years ago that beauty lies in one's heart and not on the surface of one's skin or in one's bank account; I would be happily married to Richard Bloome today.

"Not that I love him, you understand. Sometimes I hate myself for not being able to love the man. I care for him. I will be eternally grateful to him. But I will never love him, much to my personal shame and regret.

"Richard knows that, but he continues to take care of me and he tries in his own way to protect me. I know he loves me. He always has."

"Did he kill your husband?" I asked.

"My! Another very direct question. I do not know who was good enough to kill Frederick. I often wish I could have brought myself to kill him. I did want to, you know. I wanted to very badly. I even went so far as to plan ways I might kill him. I would often sit in this room all night . . . Drinking, of course . . . And dream of ways I might kill my husband. The many ways I came up with were usually very violent and would have caused Frederick no end of pain and suffering. But I was never able to do any of it."

She paused for a moment and reflected on her thoughts, then looked straight into my eyes and said, "I don't think Richard could kill anyone either, although I'm sure he wanted to kill Frederick many times. Richard is not the kind to hurt a fly, as they say. He simply is not a violent man.

"If Richard did kill Frederick that will be still another thing I will spend the rest of my life thanking him for. You must understand that Frederick had to be stopped. He was hurting too many people in what he called business. He would have eventually killed me and his daughters, I am sure of that.

"I suppose you must find out who killed Frederick if you are to find out who wants to kill me. You are wasting your time thinking that Richard may have done it, however. If he did kill Frederick, and if he wanted me dead also, he would have had several chances to do it. He has only been good to me."

"OK. I'll consider that. Now, why you? Why would anyone want you dead?" I asked, taking another sandwich as she filled my coffee cup once again.

"I have been thinking and thinking about that, Mr. Crew. I've hardly thought of anything else these past few days. Could I have seen something I wasn't supposed to see? A person perhaps, like Marc Springer? Do they think I was somehow involved in Frederick's dealings? Do they think I have a record or file of Frederick's of some sort?"

She paused to contemplate then continued. "There simply is no logical reason that I can think of for anyone to try to kill me. Please believe me; I am not withholding anything from you. I've told you all I know of Frederick's dealings and I find it hard to believe I know anything sufficient for anyone to wish to kill me."

"I agree, Mrs. Mark. And I do believe you. Revenge is the only thing I can come up with. Killing you as part of some deranged revenge against Frederick Mark. Where are your children?"

"My goodness! That never occurred to me. You mean a crazy person, don't you? Richard has sent the girls to my parents in New Hampshire. They left yesterday on a cruise across the Atlantic and through the Mediterranean. They will be gone three months. Do you think someone will try to hurt them?"

"I have the list of who may have killed Frederick narrowed down to a few people. I won't mention their names now because it would only frighten you. A few of those people could be dangerous anywhere in the world. I think you should cable your parents and warn them, right away."

"I will certainly do that. But revenge for what? What could Frederick have done?"

"I'm not really sure of the details," I answered. "I know enough of what happened to know that Frederick, Marc Springer, and some others were deeply involved in importing drugs into the United States through San Marcos.

"There have been a series of murders in the last few weeks, I believe all related to that drug trade. We're dealing with a sophisticated crime organization that is capable of doing anything, anywhere in the world. They are killers, vicious killers. Everyone involved in that organization, from the bosses to the lowest level of drug dealers in their employ.

"One of them is seeking revenge for something; it could be any one of several things that I know about. And the sick mind of this kind of killer somehow sees you as a target of that revenge. That's all I know right now. But I think I know a way to end it all. Until I do, please be careful. Don't put yourself at risk and don't trust anyone for right now, even Mr. Bloome."

THIRTY-FIVE - Bill Keilly

While Suzanne and I were eating our sandwiches, drinking our coffee, and talking about her dead husband, Attorney Bloome was across the hall. He was making a telephone call. It was the third time that day that Bloome had spoken with Bill Keilly. Each time it was Bloome who initiated the call.

Bill was on the City Council and one of his duties was that of Commissioner of Police. Bill and I were golfing buddies. Our friendship went back to High School when we both made believe we were football stars. I enjoyed playing golf with Bill. He was one of the very few Country Club members I really enjoyed being with. He was probably as close a friend as I had in those days.

"Hello, Mr. Keilly. This is Mr. Bloome again."

"Yes, Mr. Bloome. What can I do for you?" Bill said not making an attempt to hide his exasperation at being bothered again, this time so late in the day.

"Thank you for taking my call. I guess I've been quite a bother. But I wanted you to know that Morgan Crew has retained me as his lawyer."

There was silence on the line for a moment. Then Bill said, "When did that happen? You know the police want him for questioning."

"I know. I wanted to let you know that my client has not committed any felony. I have advised him to speak with the police, but he needs some rest first. He's been under a tremendous strain lately. I will try to have him at Police

Headquarters in the morning."

"I'd be surprised if the police go for that. They seem to want him now."

"I assure you we want to cooperate fully. But it is late now, and since my client has not committed a crime and there cannot be a warrant of arrest out for him, he will wait until the morning to talk with the police."

"I gather he's wherever you are right now. And I'd bet you're still at Suzanne Mark's. Look, I can send a dozen police cars out there right now. But I won't. Let me speak to him. I think I can reason with him."

Bloome did not answer but put the phone down and walked out into the empty hallway. As I left the library, Suzanne Mark took my arm and walked beside me as we slowly walked into the hallway.

As we walked she entwined her arms in mine and pressed her small, soft breasts against me. We spoke of inconsequential things, the weather and a collection of oriental vases in a glass case just inside the door of the library where we had sat. She told me the collection was one of the few things of hers in the house. It was obvious, even to my untrained eye, that the vases were quality and not just glitzy expensive.

As we stepped into the hallway Suzanne stumbled on the edge of a deep blue Oriental rug that covered the floor of the library. She held tightly to me, I held onto her, the Weedmarre Guard who had waited at the door reached for her, and from the doorway of the room across the hall, Richard Bloome ran to her also. Suzanne was embarrassed, her face colored and she tried to laugh it off, but tears burst the dam of her valiant attempt at composure.

Bloome took her from my arms and walked her back into the library, to a nearby, high back, elaborately carved dark wood chair. He sat her down, knelt at her feet, rubbed her hands gently and lovingly, and whispered to her.

Without leaving her, Bloome turned and told me that Bill Keilly was holding on the telephone for me. I didn't know whether I should run or stay. But if I ran where would I run to?

"I know Bill Keilly," Bloome said. "I think you can trust him. As your attorney, I strongly suggest you speak with him."

He was right of course. San Marcos was too small a town to hide in, and if I were going to continue digging into the dirt of all that had happened, to try to bring an end to it, and to somehow protect Sandy, I needed some freedom of movement. I hoped Bill Keilly would give me that semblance of freedom.

I started into the room across the hall, stopped, and asked Bloome as it occurred to me, "I'm curious. Did he phone you or did you phone him?"

"We've talked several times today," Bloome said.

"That's nice. But did you make contact with him or did he phone you?"

"I guess I phoned him. I know Bill. I thought he could help. You don't agree?"

"I was just curious," I said. "Who else have you spoken with in the last few days?"

"I resent that implication . . .," he began.

"Richard, please," Suzanne said. "Mr. Crew is just trying to help. Please be cooperative with him. For me, please."

"Alright, Suzanne," he said, stood, and motioned for me to walked into the hallway with him. I smiled my thanks at Suzanne and followed Bloome.

"I don't know what you're thinking, Mr. Crew," he began. "But if you must know, I've spoken with a Detective, Sommers I think his name was. He phoned me and asked where you were. I said I didn't know and at the time I didn't. When you leave here don't tell me where you're going and if he asks again I will tell him truthfully that I don't know.

"I phoned Bill Keilly," he went on. "I need to protect Suzanne above everything else. Even above protecting you. Bill promised he would not tell the police you were here; I promised you would speak with him on the phone. I've spoken to no one else," he said. He turned quickly and walked back to Suzanne in the library.

I walked across the hall to speak with Bill Keilly. "Bill? This is Morgan," I said cautiously.

"Morgan! Jesus, what the hell have you gotten into, buddy?"

"Some deep shit, apparently. Are you up to helping me out a little?" I asked.

"F'Christ sake, Morgan. You know I will. The cops are all over town looking for you."

"I know. Did you send them here yet?" I asked. I hoped I knew the answer.

He said only, "We need to talk."

"I guess I need someone I can trust, Bill. Can I trust you?"

"Do you really need to ask that? After all the times I let you beat me on the golf course? Let's meet somewhere. Just you and me."

"OK," I agreed and felt a little better. There wasn't much else I could do. I had the feeling I was in over my head. I had the San Marcos Police, probably the Feds, more than likely the local Mafia types, all after me.

"Where can we meet?" I asked Bill. "Some place where the police won't see me, at least for the time being."

"How about the Club?" Bill suggested. "The bar'll be open until two. We can talk there."

I said that would be a good place and agreed to meet him there in thirty minutes. I was comfortable meeting him there. I knew most of the members and a cop trying to play undercover inside the bar would be easy to spot. Besides, I could use just one more drink right about then.

I returned to the hallway and found a once again fully composed Suzanne Mark standing next to her attorney and friend.

"I am so sorry I lost control," she said. "Little things seem to affect me very badly."

"I understand," I said, taking her hand in mine. "I think you're doing fine and when all this is over I hope we can meet on a more social note. I don't get very many chances to meet a real lady."

"Why, thank you Mr. Crew," she said, smiling and blushing like a child. "I too hope we can meet under . . . Shall we say better circumstances?"

I listened as Bloome phoned in a very carefully worded wire to be sent to the ship Suzanne's parents were on, warning them to take special care of the children. No great detail was given; they would know enough of Frederick Mark to watch over them carefully.

When that was done Suzanne excused herself, saying she was very tired and needed to sleep. Bloome and I watched her walk up the stairs, the guard again behind her.

"That's a remarkable woman," I said.

"I know," he answered. "Was she able to help you?"

"Somewhat. She does care for you a great deal, you know," I said.

"I hope so. I care the world for her," he said. "Do you have any idea who is doing this to her?"

"I think so," I said. "But I don't want to make any hasty or rash judgments. I want you to know that I am beginning to get very personally involved in all this. I have someone very close to me who seems to be involved somehow." I started to leave then turned and asked, "What kind of juice do you have with the police?" I asked.

"Enough," he answered without hesitating. "What do you want?"

"I need to talk with someone called Marc Springer. He's a drug dealer. I need his address here in San Marcos. But the police can't know it's for me."

Bloome thought for a moment or two, and then said, "There is a rather young Deputy District Attorney who owes me several favors. I think I can trick her out of what you need. Wait here."

He walked to the library to make the phone call. In only a few moments he was back with a scrap of paper in his hand which he handed to me. "This is his address. Be careful not to get yourself killed," he said in a rather matter of fact voice. I told him I would try my best and laughed as I added that I wouldn't be able to make any promises. Bloome didn't see the joke, however.

"You look like you need some sleep," he said. "Will you stay the night here? After you speak with Mr. Keilly, that is. I'll have a room prepared for you." He started to turn to walk away before I could answer.

"No, wait, please," I said. "The police will be back here often, looking for me, if I can't work things out with Bill. It's best I don't stay here."

"Of course, you're right. Where will you stay?"

"I don't know. Some place," I said. I wasn't about to tell Bloome where I would be. I didn't trust him totally as yet, even if Suzanne did, and I needed a night's sleep without the worry of someone walking in and slitting my throat in my sleep.

THIRTY-SIX – Indian Falls

The San Marcos Country Club is nestled in a valley amongst groves of pine, juniper, oak, and tall redwood. It is beautifully landscaped, planned to look as natural as possible. Rhododendrons and azaleas are in bloom everywhere. The fairways are manicured to near perfection. Domesticated swans and flocks of wild ducks make their homes on the lakes and ponds. In the early mornings small herds of deer could be found enjoying breakfast. In winter months the club voted that money be spent to buy feed and salt for the deer. Each season of the years brought its own beauty to the club.

I turned the rented Mustang into the parking lot. I parked as far from the clubhouse as I could, in a corner of the lot away from the floodlights that lit most of the parking area, and waited. The Walther was tight and uncomfortable in my waistband. But I wouldn't need it to negotiate with Bill Keilly, I told myself, and there was no way I was going to shoot up the bar at the San Marcos Country Club. So I took it out and shoved it under the driver's seat.

Three minutes later Bill Keilly drove up, parked near the steps to the clubhouse, and got out of his car. He was alone, and hurried up the stone steps without looking around the lot for his friend. He wouldn't take notice of the red Mustang; he would be looking for my MGB.

I waited another minute to see if any cars would follow him into the lot. When none did I got out of the Mustang and began a slow walk to the club house steps myself.

From the foot of the stairs I saw Bill inside the glass doors, smoking one of the seven or eight cigars he consumed each day. Bill turned and saw me standing outside. He hesitated then walked out and down the steps.

"Thought you'd be inside waiting for me," he said.

"I'm sorry. I had to wait to make sure you were alone. It's not an insult. I just have to be careful. And besides, I probably don't look presentable enough to go inside."

"No problem," he said and slapped my shoulder in good buddy form. He didn't smile however. The cigar was clamped tightly in the corner of his mouth and he chewed on it nervously. An inch of ash fell from the red tip, unnoticed by Bill.

The parking lot wasn't very crowded; the bar would have several of the regulars in it, those who congregated at the bar almost every evening. We wouldn't have had a problem finding a quiet booth away from everyone. I suggested we go inside, despite what I looked like.

"Look," Bill said, searching around the lot. "Somebody inside might know the police want you. You never can tell. We better not take any chances. Let's get a cart and go for a ride. That way we can talk without anyone hearing us. And you're right. You do look like hell."

It was a warm night. The sky was clear and two days short of a full moon. Down an S-curved flagstone path, lined on either side with azaleas in full bloom, at the side of the clubhouse, is a parking area for the golf carts. I walked beside Bill and watched him out of the corner of my eye.

He twisted the cigar between his fingers, sucking smoke from it rapidly. I assumed Bill wasn't used to doing what we were doing. He may be Police Commissioner but he wasn't a cop and becoming involved with a major crime would scare him, I rationalized as usual. And he was probably thinking about what meeting with me like this would do to his political career, too.

We took the first cart we came to and drove off toward the first tee, down the hill, and along the edge of the 350-yard par four. Bill drove slowly and neither of us said anything until we got near the first green. The cart slowed as he took it around the sloping, downhill turn and started down the second fairway. The smell of night blooming jasmine was heavy in the cool night air.

"Morgan," he said finally after he had flipped the half-smoked cigar towards the stream that runs from Indian Falls along the left side of the fairway. Perhaps he was tired of waiting for me to say something. "Morgan, you've really got yourself in deep on this, I hope you know that."

"I kind of get that idea."

"Can you tell me what you're into?"

I wasn't quite ready to tell anyone everything I had found and everything I felt. I wasn't sure about Bill Keilly yet, either. After all he was the police commissioner and he stood to lose a lot by interfering in a criminal investigation on the side of a person who might well spend a few years in prison. And hadn't Brad Humphrey said that Springer owns everything, even the police? So I decided to tell him just enough to maybe make him feel sorry for me.

"I guess I'd better let somebody know what's happening," I began. "I'm taking a big chance telling you, considering your position."

"Forget my position. If I can help, I will."

"OK. I don't know that much, maybe I know too much. It seems two people I know, Franco and Jeremy Morelli were murdered. They were involved somehow in the local drug trade, it looks like they were using their boat to import drugs into San Marcos, although I have nothing but hunches to base that on. I get the impression that the people who did the killings are drug dealers; at least that's what Bob Sommers thinks. The Feds have been after these people and after somebody called Marc Springer, who Bob Sommers tells me is some kind of hotshot Mafia boss.

"There's been two other murders, Loretta Krueger. You know Mitch Krueger? We've played golf with him. And the tennis pro here, Dean Crosslund. I know who killed him. When this is all over I'll give the police a statement on that.

"You've met Sandy D'Angelo," I said.   "She's somehow involved with all this; I'm not sure how yet. The bottom line to all this is I want to protect her. If that means clearing up the murders, then I have to do that. I guess that's as far as I'm into it. What details I know, Bob Sommers knows. What I'm asking you for is time. Do what you can to keep the police off of me. When it's all over, if you need to charge me with obstruction or anything else, I'll cooperate fully and plead guilty. Just give me the time to try to help and protect Sandy."

"Who asked you to get involved in this, Morgan?" he asked.

"Nobody asked me. The Morelli's owned a fishing boat I used to like to go out on. Sommers and I found them dead and I guess I've been stumbling around, kind of freelance."

"You know, Morgan. I've told you a dozen times to stop being such a sucker. You need to stop sticking your nose into other people's business. Stop trying to help every nobody that comes down the pike. You're a soft touch. A guy like you ought to be in business some place. Using your money for some good. People are losing respect for you. You're becoming a laughing stock around the club. You're always out there trying to help people and all you do is screw things up."

"Well, I guess you're right, Bill," I said. I had to bend him around to helping me out of my jam and allowing me time to finish what I needed to do without the police chasing me.

"Is there anything else, Morgan?   Are you holding anything back?"

"Hell no, Bill," I said, trying to whine just a little. "I just don't want to wind up in jail and have to pay a fortune to attorneys while Sandy's out there somewhere, in trouble. If it were just the local police I wouldn't worry. But Sommers tells me the Feds are after me also. All I want is to be left alone. I mean, they were friends of mine and I love Sandy a lot. If by chance I come up with anything, I promise to let the police have it right away. Can you swing that for me, Bill?"

Bill Keilly didn't answer right away. I let him think about it as we drove slowly past the second green and along the tree side of the third and fourth fairways. In the still of the clear night I could begin to hear the sound of Indian Falls near the narrow seventh fairway. At that time of year the falls would be flowing fairly strong as a result of the frequent storms that came in from the sea.

The seventh fairway dog legs right about a hundred and fifty yards off the tee and is bisected by the stream that feeds off the waterfall, which crashes a mere twenty-five yards to the left of the fairway. The cart path crosses an old wooden bridge there, over the stream, at the foot of the falls.

Bill said nothing until we reached the bridge, where he stopped the cart and while gripping the wheel so tightly his knuckles turned white, he stared up at the water rushing over the falls. The sound of the water was as loud as a small jet engine there in the still night air.

"Morgan," he said finally, softly enough that I had to strain to hear him above the din of Indian Falls. "I have to ask you to get out of this. As a friend, I'm asking you to do that favor for me. Let the police and the Feds handle it. Come back with me and turn yourself in to Bob Sommers."

"Why?" I asked. "Why is everybody so interested in seeing me out of this? What can I do? Who would I hurt? Hell, you never can tell, I might actually be able to help the cops."

"Please Morgan, you don't understand. They want you out of it or in jail. You don't have a third option."

"Who wants me out of it, Bill?"

"It doesn't make any difference who wants you out. The damn police want you out . . . The damn Feds . . . What difference does it make? You're going to wind up dead and I don't want that to happen. Damn it! You're my friend, Morgan. Listen to me, will you!"

"Who will kill me, Bill? Who wants me dead?" I didn't like what I was hearing but I had nowhere to run.

"No one *wants* you dead, Morgan! For Christ sake! I'm afraid you'll get yourself killed if you keep in this thing! You don't know who you're dealing with!" He punched the cart's steering wheel, hard.

"Who am I dealing with, Bill?"

His hands grasped the top of the steering wheel and he laid his head on his hands. He had come to a decision. I was about to find out what that decision was. Bill pushed himself out of the cart and walked away a few yards, off the bridge and down the bank to the edge of the stream. The moonlight was bright enough for me to see him kicking at some pebbles, his hands sunk deep into his pants pockets. I followed him and stood on the edge of the wooden bridge, looking down at my friend. The bridge was wet; the ground around it was spongy, the air chilling. I shivered a bit and knew the cold, damp air didn't cause it.

"Bill, tell me what's going on. Trust me. Don't leave me hanging," I pleaded.

"You need time to think, Morgan. You need to reason with yourself. You need to convince yourself that you're better off out of this thing. I'm going to leave you here. It's a nice night and maybe the walk back will do you some good."

"Like hell you are . . ." I began but stopped as Bill turned to face me with a small .25 caliber semi-auto pistol in his hand. I had seen the gun before. Bill had kept it in his office and shown it to me several times. It was a shiny chrome, pearl handled pistol, so small that it almost vanished in Bill's hand.

"Don't be any more stupid than you have been already, Morgan," he said. "I'm going to go back to the cart and drive away. I'm sorry. There's nothing I can do for you."

Bill drove off and I sat on the bridge railing trying to decide what to do next. I thought again of what Brad Humphrey had told me. The old man was apparently right. Bill Keilly had to be involved in the drug business somehow, he had to be associated with Marc Springer, or been bought by him. There was no other reason to pull a gun on me and refuse all help. If he were not in their pockets, he would have either agreed to help his friend, or used the gun to bring me in.

And how about Bob Sommers? Had he been bought also? Did he have the cops after me to try to protect me or to kill me? Maybe shoot to kill a fleeing suspect?

What I had to do was decided for me by a shot that rang out from behind me. The bullet hit the wooden bridge less than a foot and a half in front of me and splintered it at my feet. I froze for a second or two, a rush of fear turning my reactions to mush. Then adrenaline took over and I managed to jump from the bridge, over the railing, and into the muddy stream bank as the second shot rang out.

The shots were from a rifle, not a .25 pistol. Someone had to have been waiting for me. Bill Keilly had set me up to be killed!

Three more shots rang out in quick succession and sent rocks and mud flying all around me. I pushed myself as far down the embankment as I could, into the icy water and mud near the foot of the waterfall. The shots were coming from the hillside, near the crest of Indian Falls, a couple of hundred feet above me. With the brightness of the moon, whoever it was had a clear chance of getting me eventually. The trees and their shadows would be my only protection.

Where I was lying, half in the stream and half in soft mud and weeds, was not only painfully cold but also left me open for the next well aimed shot. That thought plus the cold water got me to push myself up and make a run for the thickets behind me, across the stream.

I took three leaping steps across the stream and two more in soft, muddy ground, before I threw myself into a stand of heavy bushes. It was enough time for the shooter to get off two more shots, the second tore open my right leg just inches below the knee. I felt it and knew I had been shot, but the sudden burning pain meant little considering that if I had fallen before reaching cover, the next shot would have been the last thing I would have felt.

I pulled myself further into the bushes and took time to glance down at the blood staining my pants. I pulled up the pant leg and found a deep gash across the calf. Although it burned like hell, the bullet had done little more damage than to cut me deeply.

Behind me the trees and brush thinned out as the fairway curved. Across the fairway was open country and I was about as far from the club house as you could get without leaving the Country Club property. Making a run for it, even with two good legs, was out of the question.

I didn't know if the sound of the rifle shots would carry all the way to the clubhouse. I was in good cover, black shade and thick underbrush, but still nothing to stop a bullet. I guessed I could stay there until the shooter either got me or ran out of bullets.

I needed a weapon of some kind but the only things at hand were a few thin sticks and a few stones. It would have to do. I thought of the Walther under the seat of the Mustang. I took a stone that more than filled my hand and waited. Gently pushing a few branches aside I was able to get a view of the stream and part of the bridge. Moonlight cast weird shadows everywhere and a slowly rising breeze made everything move, causing ghostlike shadows to dance throughout the thickets.

****

On the top of the hill, near the crest of Indian Falls, a man stood next to an oak tree and peered through the darkness, down into the bushes and trees below. His rifle rested on a thin branch. He was ready to shoot at anything that moved. The trouble was that the damn wind was causing everything to move. It was so black down there that he couldn't make out what was a bush, what was a shadow, or what was the guy he was supposed to kill.

To make matters worse, the damn waterfall was making a lot of noise. No one told him it would be like that. He was told to just wait at the top of the hill and Keilly would bring the guy to the bridge. Once Keilly left, just kill the guy. Of course, he wouldn't be able to tell anybody he missed with the first shot. He had a certain reputation to maintain. So he would lie and say the guy didn't hang around the bridge, that he walked off before Keilly left. Who's to know?

But he had lost the guy in the dark. He wasn't even sure he was still there. He had to take a chance. He had to get closer. He had to go down there.

Starting down the hillside wasn't as easy as it looked. The ground was wet and soft. He began sliding, then his foot caught on something, and he began tumbling. The rifle slipped from his hand and fell away from him. He reached out and grabbed a bush and stopped himself. Rather than risk breaking a leg he started to carefully slide down the hill on his butt. His suit was ruined, his shoes were ruined, but he found the rifle below, knocked the mud off of it, and hoped it would fire.

He reached the bottom and stood up straight and listened. Nothing. There were no sounds but the damn waterfall crashing to his left. He began to walk, very slowly, bending over to take advantage of what cover there was, towards the last place he knew the guy was at.

****

My leg was aching and I was sweating out of pure fear in the cold night air. But then I saw a movement that had to be something other than a tree branch or bush moving in the breeze caused by the falling water. It was almost like something falling down the hillside.

Out of mottled shadows a figure, crouching low, moved. As he came near the stream's edge I saw the dark, long barreled rifle. Rather than use the bridge, the grey figure stepped carefully into the icy stream and across to the other bank. I adjusted the rock in my hand and as quietly as I could, I pulled my knees under me, trying as best I could to ignore the burning ache of my bleeding leg.

I waited until the figure was standing very near my covering bush. I waited until the figure had turned to look to his right, then I sprang up and in the same movement hit the man as hard as I could with the rock, in a broad sweeping motion of my arm. I caught him at the temple and the sickening crunch of bone told me immediately I had hit the man too hard.

He collapsed at my feet, like a limp, rag doll. Dark black blood streaked with thick grey slime poured from the crack in his skull. I felt for a pulse, first at his neck, then his wrist, then his neck again. Nothing. He was dead.

I had never killed before and had never been close to violent death. I buckled under my stomach's contortion and fell toward the stream as I emptied my stomach. I lay there for a few minutes, then splashed some of the icy water from the stream onto my face and drank deeply of it to wash the foul taste away. I pushed myself onto my feet, momentarily not noticing the pain of my leg.

The rifle was an AR-15, a civilian, semi-auto version of the .227 caliber military M-16, with a large scope attached. It lay next to the body. It was not the same rifle that had shot Frederick Mark and had shot at Suzanne Mark. My chief suspect was still out there. Somewhere.

I tied a handkerchief around my wounded leg and began the long walk back to the parking lot.

THIRTY-SEVEN – One Step At A Time

I drove over the hills once again, out of San Marcos. Pain was shooting up my leg and blood was pouring all over the car's floor mat. Near Highway One I stopped at an all night convenience store with a gas station out front. I filled the Mustang's tank and bought a disposable razor, a tube of toothpaste, a toothbrush and some bandages, gauze, and a bottle of peroxide for my leg. As an afterthought as I reached the cash register, I picked up a large bottle of aspirin, hoping they would dull the pain.

A half-mile further along the highway was "The Woodsman Motel", the very same place Loretta Krueger had been killed and found by the maid. I figured that was about as good a place as any to hide out for a night, get some rest, and bandage my leg.

The young lady at the desk looked questioningly at my dirty clothes and blood stained leg. But she just shrugged her shoulders and handed me a key hanging from a miniature, red plastic, woodsman's ax. She was used to all kinds of people checking in for the night, and many more for just an hour or two. I paid her in cash, in advance, $37.50 for the night.

In the room, I peeled my pants off and poured some of the peroxide across the cut. I winced in pain but poured a little more anyway and then bandaged my leg as best as I could. The leg needed stitches, that was obvious, but I couldn't risk going to a doctor or hospital. The pain had not eased any after the peroxide so I took two aspirin before I hit the shower.

I stood under the hot water for a long time, letting the heat do its job on my sore back, neck, and shoulders. After drying myself, I put some fresh gauze and tape on my leg and took two more aspirin, hoping they would do some good. The first two hadn't done anything. I wished I had had the foresight to stop at a liquor store.

I then took the three sheets of cheap stationary from the drawer in the room. I sat at a wobbly desk on a beat up chair and wrote as small as I could so that I could get everything I knew onto the sheets, using both sides. I wrote the whole story, everything I had done, everything I had found out.

I knew then exactly what had happened. I knew who had killed the Morelli's and I knew who had killed Frederick Mark and I knew who wanted to kill Suzanne Mark. I knew who had killed Loretta Krueger and who had killed Dean Crosslund. The details were still a little muddled but I thought I was pretty accurate in explaining the motives. The police could fill in whatever holes remained. I had one more thing to find out and when I knew that one more thing, the whole story would be clear.

I dropped the two bullets and the rifle shell into the envelope with the hand written pages, addressed the envelope to Harper, Harper, Jascro & Nettles, and walked it to the mailbox at the motel office. I bought two stamps from a machine there and dropped the bulky envelope into the mail slot. Back in the room I undressed once again, put a fresh bandage on my leg because the bleeding had not stopped, and fell onto the bed. I was asleep almost immediately.

In the morning I forced down a cup of the motel's instant, in-a-packet, in-room substitution for coffee, stood for a long time in the hot shower, shaved the night's stubble from my face, and once again changed the bandage on my leg. The bleeding resumed as soon as I took the brown stained bandage off. I put a wide patch of gauze on it and taped it as tightly as I could stand.

I drove slowly back to San Marcos without paying much attention to where I was, and found myself at Harborside. Parking the rental car at a busy intersection, I sat and waited. Turning off the engine, I switched on the jazz station and did some thinking. There were a couple of people I needed to see first. Then I fully intended to call on Marc Springer. If I could settle it, Sandy would at least be safe, even if I weren't.

I decided to take care of the easiest part of the puzzle first. Hector Morales. Although he was known to be a drug user and probably sold some, he was just too small to be a major player here. To settle that question, I drove back away from Harborside and pulled up to the curb in front of Mitch Krueger's home.

I had to ring the doorbell three times before the door opened. Barbara stood in the doorway, the runaway come home. She stared open mouth at the haggard looking man she knew as Morgan Crew. "My dad's not here," she said finally. "I don't think you should be here either."

"I need to know," I said, my voice gravely and tired. "Is Hector here with you?"

Before she could answer Mitch Krueger pushed himself between his daughter and me. "You were tol' to leave us 'lone," he said loudly, his voice slurred from drink at 9:30 AM. "You think just 'cause you got lots of money, you can stick your nose anywhere? Leave us 'lone."

"Is Hector Morales here?" I asked again.

"Yes, he is . . . an' he's gonna stay. Babs and Hector got married and that's all. So leave us 'lone, once an' f'all." He slammed the door in my face.

I drove away from Mitch's home slowly, my mind not focused on driving. The fact that Barbara and Hector got married and came home took Hector out of the picture for me. The police would be coming to see Mitch soon. There was enough trouble in that house. I didn't need any more of it.

I drove back to Harborside and found a place to park several streets away from the wharves and started walking. I stopped at a store that sold mainly fishing gear but also a carried small line of work clothes and jeans that the boat's crews would wear. I bought a pair of jeans and a tan work shirt and changed into them there. My bloody leg and filthy clothes were attracting too much attention, so the clothes were deposited in a nearby trash can.

On the wharf I stopped to talk to a few of the young men working on the boats. I found out more about Tony's new girl friend. She worked as a nude dancer at one of the bars in North Harbor, they told me. A few knew her as Angel, but no one knew her real name.

I then drove up to North Harbor and toured the beer bars that featured topless and nude dancing. They were dark, dirty, dank, and I didn't see one smiling face anywhere in any of them. Every bartender and bouncer I spoke with seemed to know Angel. It seems she had worked in nearly every bar in North Harbor as a nude or topless dancer, at one time or another. Again, no one had seen her in the last few days.

I had hoped to find someone who could lead me to Tony but that seemed unlikely now. Tony, I told myself finally, was probably dead. But Angel might not be. If she weren't, she was probably in hiding somewhere; she may even have left San Marcos. But there might still be someone who knew her.

I had one more call to make to find out if there was someone who in fact did know her and could tell me where

she was hiding.   I drove back to the piers fearing what I
would find out.

THIRTY-EIGHT – When The Cap'n Gets Angry

Walking slowly down the pier to Cap'n Nick's, I breathed in the clean, fresh sea air deeply. It helped to clear the cobwebs from my skull and made me feel a little stronger. The sun above me was warm, the sky clear and a deep blue. The sea beyond the harbor entrance looked calm. There were sounds of gulls calling as they circled above the harbor, looking for lunch.

I remember thinking that it would have been a good day for fishing on the Santa Maria. Then it occurred to me that it might be the last time I would smell the clean sea air, feel the warm sun, look out onto the Pacific, and hear the gulls overhead. In a few hours, I might be dead, but I had accepted that fact.

I glanced in the big front window of Cap'n Nick's first and then walked through the entry and quickly to the farthest corner table where I sat. I sat with my back to the wall and adjusted the gun that was tucked tightly and uncomfortably at my waist, under my shirt. The Captain saw me and joined me at the table, step-clacking across the sawdust covered floor.

"What's you been up to, boy? The police been here looking for you," he whispered conspiratorially, pulling a chair to the table and sitting.

"I know, they've been everywhere," I said. "I hope I can trust you not to phone them or tell them where I can be found?"

"F'Christ sake, Morgan! I ain't no friend a'cops, you should know that! You O.K. here! Cops never come here!"

"Look, I have to see a guy today by the name of Marc Springer and there's a good chance . . . Well let's say seeing this guy may not be the smartest thing I've ever done. Before I do, I want to know about Sandy. I want to know everything you know about her. You know her better than anybody. Tell me."

"I don't un'nerstand. You know Sandy. I know she loves you and she's a good girl. What else you gotta know?" he asked.

"I want to know where she was born. I want to know about her family. I want to know where she comes from. I want to know how she's involved with the Morelli's. And I want to know where she is now."

"You don't look so good, Morgan," he said. "You look tired and you look sick."

"Please Cap'n," I said. "Just tell me what you can and I'll get out of here."

Cap'n Nick leaned back in his chair, called for his waitress to bring two cups of coffee to the table, and began telling me a story about Sandy. He was speaking too quickly and without looking at me as he spoke. I knew almost immediately that he wasn't telling the truth, maybe parts of it were true, but it was not the whole truth.

Sandy, he said, had been born in 1982 in Chicago. The captain had known her grandfather during World War II when they both were Marines in the South Pacific. Sandy had been raised in what the Cap'n described as a good Catholic Italian home; Catholic schools, lots of praying at home, church a couple of times a week.

Her father died of a heart attack when she was just a young girl, about a year after Sandy's sister had been born. It had been hard on the family, a mother with two young daughters and not a penny in the bank. Sandy started working after school to help out. He said he visited them occasionally, often enough to see Sandy maturing into a bright young lady who did very well in school, and to see her younger sister, Claudia, doing as well.

As the years passed, he saw less and less of the family until not even Christmas cards were exchanged, he said. Then, eighteen months ago Sandy shows up at the bar and asks for a job, no explanation, no warning.

She told the Captain that her family was doing well. Her sister was in her last year of City College in Chicago. Her mother was working steadily and was happy.

"There's nothing else to tell," he said. I didn't believe him and that fact caused me to get angry once again.

"And how does Frederick Mark work into all this?" I asked.

"Frederick Mark?" The way he said it confirmed that I was right. He quickly looked away from me and a flash of redness colored his round face. "I don't know what you mean. Frederick Mark is a son of a bitch. But I don't know what you mean saying him and Sandy in the same breadth."

"I didn't mean Mark and Sandy had anything in common. I just asked how he worked into all of this. You just connected him and Sandy for me."

"The man's a bastard that don't care 'bout nothing. Money and women is all he cares 'bout. I spit on his grave. May he burn in hell."

"How do you know so much about Frederick Mark?" I asked.

He brushed aside my question with a wave of a thick arm in the air. "What you mean? I just heard 'bout him. Like ever'body else. Ever'body knows 'bout that man."

"Except that you've hated the man for years. You phoned Brad Humphrey to tell him about Mark and Springer partying with a young girl here on the pier, didn't you?"

"So what?" he said. "Yes, I don't like people like that. So what?"

"What brought Mark and Sandy together?" I asked.

"Don't be so stupid. She wouldn't look at that man. He's slime, that's all."

"Cap'n, please," I begged. I reached out and touched the Cap'n's bear-like arm. "I have to know the truth," I said. "Don't let me walk out of here not knowing the truth. There's a good chance I'll be dead before the day is out and I have to know."

He stared at me for a long time. A sad cloud darkened his face and he said, "What you mean, dead? How you gonna be dead?"

"Never mind that," I said. "Trust me that I have to risk that in order to help Sandy. I don't know any other way to protect her from what I know will happen   eventually. She's wrapped up in these killings somehow. And I need to know that she won't be a victim of the war that's going on. I can protect her, I know I can. But I have to have the answers first."

"Who gonna kill you?" he asked again. "Is somebody after you? This Marc Springer you gonna go see? Don't be stupid, Morgan. Sandy, she's ok. You go home and forget. Soon you see her again."

"God damn it!" I screamed and pounded my fist on the tabletop, the coffee mugs jumped and coffee spilled on the wooden tabletop. The few patrons in the bar, older fisherman, long retired, who were in the Cap'n's every day, turned to see what was going on. I ignored them and grabbed the old bear by his shirt collar. "You tell me! You tell me now you old son of a bitch!" I screamed.

The Cap'n carefully and slowly took hold of my hands and pulled them away from their grasp on his shirt. He continued twisting my hands until I was in a great deal of pain and unable to move. Without much effort, he held me motionless by the wrists. Then he breathed a deep sigh, his broad shoulders fell, and his vise-like grip on my arms loosened. The old man was dangerous despite his age.

"Alright," he said, resigned finally to telling me the truth. "Maybe you better know what's happen after all. I guess you got a right, I mean, considering you and Sandy . . Well, you know."

THIRTY-NINE – Angel

The true story of Sandy's past was finally unfolded before me. When Sandy arrived in San Marcos she was not alone. Her sister Claudia had come from Chicago with her. Claudia had been in trouble all her life in the tough section of Chicago where she and her sister had been raised. Gangs, drugs, prostitution, time in jail, they were all part of her past.

The Cap'n told me how much Claudia had hurt not just her mother and sister, but him, too. He had felt somewhat responsible for the two girls since their father's death, and he felt if he had done something more, been closer to her perhaps, done more than just send money, maybe she would have grown up differently. His guilt was tearing him apart, he would never be without it, he said.

Her mother and Sandy had all but given up on Claudia. In one last desperate attempt at doing something for her, at saving her life, Cap'n Nick had paid for airplane tickets for Sandy and Claudia to come to San Marcos. He and Claudia's mother hoped that by getting the girl away from the City where she had grown up, and the people whom she had been associating with, she might be straightened out.

Claudia, on the day she and Sandy left Chicago, was so badly strung out on heroin that she didn't even know they were leaving Chicago. The next day, at Cap'n Nick's home, she went crazy, breaking furniture and dishes, threatening to kill both the Cap'n and her sister. She was going into the first stages of withdrawal from her heroin addiction, and it would only get worse as the days dragged on.   Neither Sandy nor the Cap'n knew what to do.

Tony Morelli learned of the situation and brought her enough heroin to send the girl into a stupor of calm, half sleep.   No one asked where he had gotten the heroin.   But the Cap'n knew the sleep was only temporary.   She would wake soon and need another fix or go crazy with pain, sickness, and withdrawal again.

Tony brought more heroin, and then more, and still more.   Claudia was able to function well enough as long as Tony kept her supplied.   Over several months she and Tony started seeing each other regularly, more than regularly. Tony would supply her with drugs and Claudia would be gone for days.   Both Sandy and the Cap'n pleaded with her to no avail.   Eventually, the Cap'n's anger got the best of him and he began to threaten Tony, but Tony only laughed it off. Claudia was wasting away from not eating and word came to Cap'n Nick that she had started working at the bars in North Harbor.

That, of course, was the connection I had been looking for.   Claudia D'Angelo was Angel, Tony's girlfriend. And that was the connection that brought Sandy into danger.

The Cap'n went on, explaining that things only got worse for them.   One night Frederick Mark bought Claudia from Tony for a night of sex at his house.   He brought her to his home with the promise of drugs as well as money for herself.   Frederick had found out who she was, that her sister worked for Cap'n Nick, and where she had come from. Tony would have told him, of course.   The Cap'n didn't have to tell me that.   I knew by that time that Tony was capable of anything.

Shame is a deep-set emotion in Old World Italians like Sandy and Cap'n Nick.   Neither could bring themselves to tell me what was happening.   And asking for my help would be the last thing that would come to mind.

Then one day Sandy got a phone call from Frederick Mark demanding $25,000. If Sandy ever wanted to see her sister again, she would pay. Frederick had threatened to put Claudia to work in a brothel and keep her supplied with the drugs she needed. Sandy went to Cap'n Nick who phoned Mark and pleaded with him to no accord.

They had confronted Tony and he went insane, throwing chairs across the bar, shouting curses and threats. Yes, he admitted taking money from Mark, but not for this. Yes, he admitted Claudia was working as a prostitute and nude dancer to pay for her drugs, and he pleaded for them to forgive him for that. Yes, he admitted what had happened was his fault and he promised he would save her and things would change. Then he stormed out of the bar. That was the last time he was seen by the Cap'n or anyone else. That same night, Frederick Mark was murdered outside his office building.

Claudia showed up at the bar the next morning, with no explanation, with no remembrance of what had happened. And the newspaper that morning had the headline of Frederick Mark's murder.

"Did you kill Frederick Mark?" I asked.

"No," he answered, and I believed him. "If I had, it would'a been with my bare hands around his filthy neck. Close up, ya' know?"

I was able to make another piece of the puzzle fit perfectly. I was beginning to feel satisfied that what I had to do was the right thing to keep Sandy safe. With what Cap'n Nick told me, I was certain now that I knew who had killed Frederick Mark and now also why. I knew who had killed Franco and Jeremy and why. I knew who had tried to kill Suzanne Mark.

FORTY – Just Let Me Know I'm Not Stupid

I drove the little red Mustang slowly into Downtown and past the Greyhound Bus Station, stopping for a minute at the entrance to the back parking lot. My MGB was still there, unmoved and gathering dust. I realized I had forgotten to put the top up. If I went to the car now, I took a chance that someone watching it would see me. So my little car would have to suffer the weather for awhile. Besides, I had accepted the fact that I would probably be dead before the day was out. The next owner would have to worry about replacing the carpet and leather seats.

I stopped at the newly built strip mall on Flores Street, anchored by the Albertson's market. George Montgomery's company had built it less than a year before. There is a bank of pay phones near the front doors on the outside of the store. I dug into my pants pocket and pulled out some change and phoned George Montgomery at his office.

"Hi, George. Morgan Crew here."

There was a long silence on the line, and then George said, "Where the hell are you? Do you know what the hell's going on?"

"Never mind that, George. I just need to know a few things. How about just once being straight with me? You probably know there are people out here looking for me, and when they find me I'll be dead, anyway. There's nothing for you to lose."

"Morgan, cut that out, please. You're scaring me. Turn yourself in to the police. You'll get some protection there," he pleaded.

"Later. Right now, ease my mind. Let me know I'm not stupid. When I phoned you to open the Morelli house you took a long time getting there. It wasn't more than maybe a ten-minute drive. You told me you had to take an important call. The truth is you had to make a call, right? You had to call your boss and find out what to do.

"All those slum properties you own down at North Harbor, they're real money losers, aren't they?" I went on, getting it all out while not expecting George to answer.

"Costing you a bundle, I'll bet. Then you found a chance to turn a nice profit on them. Somebody, and I'll get to the name later, rented some or all of them from you. Turned them into drug processing labs and shooting galleries. Tons of drugs are coming into the U.S. and a lot of that is being processed, or cut, or whatever you call it, right here in San Marcos, then shipped to Frisco and L.A. probably. San Marcos is such a small, out-of-the-way kind of place, an operation like that would probably go unseen for a long time.

"All of a sudden your business is booming like when your father ran it. You started building new housing developments, and office buildings, and shopping centers. There's nowhere else the money to do all that could have come from.

"When I called you, you knew I couldn't go into the house and find a lab in the basement and evidence of drugs being moved in and out. So you had to phone Marc Springer, the guy who rented your properties, for instructions, to find out what you should do, how you should tell me 'no' without raising my suspicions. But your boss, Mr. Springer, said it was O.K. He told you they had cleaned out the Morelli house, moved the lab from the basement, and taken all the other boxes of stuff from upstairs.

"And so you rushed down to North Harbor, told me you were delayed by a business call, and opened the front door. Springer hadn't told you about the bodies inside, though. He wanted you to be surprised, and you were. You were expecting a clean house. Your reaction, tossing your cookies like that, couldn't have been faked. Now however, you're not just renting out slums to drug lords, you're also an accessory to murder.

"Don't worry, George. You know Springer has a large bounty on my head right now. There are more of his people than there are cops. They're bound to get me first, before the police do. And from what I hear, he owns most of the police, too. So it really doesn't matter who gets to me first, does it? Either way, your secret will die with me. Just let me know that I'm not stupid. Just say one word, say 'yes' if I'm right, and hang up the phone."

I waited. I could hear George breathing on the other end of the line. Then I heard the muffled, gagging words, "Yes . . . Jesus Christ, I'm sorry." The phone line went dead.

I dropped another quarter in the phone and dialed the Mark Estate. A guard answered. I asked for Suzanne Mark and waited. My stomach was growling for food, my head was spinning. I could feel warm trickles of blood oozing from beneath the bandage on my leg. I had still another thing that had to be done after speaking to Suzanne Mark and before walking into Marc Springer's web.

"Hello. Mr. Crew?" It was Suzanne Mark.

"Are you O.K.?" I asked.

"Yes. I was hoping you would contact me. Richard and I are leaving for Europe tonight. We are to meet my parents and the children. Do you think that's alright, I mean will I be endangering them?"

I had a feeling that the chubby little guy would be the best thing for Suzanne Mark right now. I had a feeling

Bloome would devote himself to her and to her children, because in his eyes he would be very lucky to have them.

"No, once you're out of the country you'll be safe. I know who killed your husband and who tried to kill you and I'm certain he's dead by this time. I'm fairly certain no one else wants to harm you, but if there is, you won't be found once you're gone. Make sure the guards stay with you until you are safely on the plane. I'm glad Mr. Bloome is going with you, by the way. I think he's a good man, and I think you can trust him."

"Yes", she said. "I'm glad also, and I do trust him. I owe him a lot. I think we will marry while we are in Europe. He hasn't really asked but I have a feeling he will. I don't know why he still wants me. But he does. And thinking about being with someone as kind and gentle as Richard, well, it makes me feel good for the first time in years."

"That's wonderful. I'm very glad for you."

There was a silence as we both were thinking how to say good-bye. Then she said softly, "Morgan. Will I ever see you again?"

"I hope so, Suzanne." I hung up the phone and felt good about her life finally changing for the better.

I fumbled in my pockets and found two dimes and a nickel among several pennies. Enough to make one last phone call. Bill Keilly answered his direct phone line at City Hall on the third ring. "Keilly here," he said quickly, annoyed at being disturbed by yet another phone call.

"Bill, this is Morgan." A slight hollow, electrical crackling was all the sound on the line for a long time. I broke the silence.

"You must know they didn't get me at the bridge last night. I hope I didn't get you in too much trouble with them," I said. I could hear him breathing steadily, but Bill said nothing.

"I'm making a few calls," I said. "Trying to make sure

I'm right, you know? I'd hate to die thinking I was stupid. There's a ton of drug money flowing through our quiet little town. A chunk of it has bought you and probably a few of the cops, too."

Again, silence filled the line except for Bill's breathing.

"Don't worry. I'm probably going to be dead in a few hours and there's nobody I can tell this to. I mean, I can't just get a cop to arrest you, now can I? All I want to know is am I right and if I am chances are I'll take it to the grave with me."

Still nothing.

"It's ok. I understand. I really do. Money can do a lot. I guess I should know that better than anybody. You've always been a friend, Bill. I can't really blame you for wanting what their money can buy. I know you tried to talk me out of this. I appreciate the fact that you at least tried. I know you had no real choice, if you did you wouldn't have let them try to kill me. I want you to know I understand and . . . I was about to say there's no hard feelings, but that wouldn't be true. I guess I can forgive but I'll never forget."

Bill's breathing became quicker, shorter, more labored.

"How about Bob Sommers? Is he dirty, too? I mean, he and I go back a long time. I'd like to think maybe he was more honest than you." I immediately regretted saying it the way I did. It was meant to hurt, I knew that, and I was sorry for having said it at all.

A childlike sobbing came over the line. It was muffled and soft but high pitched and uncontrolled. Suddenly the line went dead as Bill hung up on me. Friendship is a fleeting thing sometimes.

FORTY-ONE – The Sun Was Heading for the Pacific

Marc Springer's address was an exclusive and very expensive condominium on the top floor of a twelve-story building, three blocks west of Downtown. Springer had the entire floor as his home as well as the place he ran his businesses from. The building was one of George Montgomery's new developments.

I parked a block away. I looked around as I sat there, trying to build up enough courage and to find enough energy and strength to walk into Marc Springer's home. It's what I had decided I had to do. It was the last best hope I had of protecting Sandy. And if I was wrong, if I couldn't protect her, well then I assumed I would never walk out of the lion's den.

As I sat there I remembered playing as a child with Bill Keilly and sometimes George Montgomery. There had been empty fields were the condo stood. There hadn't been much traffic Downtown in those summer days. We could run in the streets and grow up safely and innocently. Even after dark we used to be able to stay outside, play ball and chase cute, silly, giggling little girls who wanted their pigtails pulled.

Those were long, hot days when the temperature dropped below 80 degrees only after nine PM. After dark now, the streets were no longer safe. Muggings and rapes, drugs and murders, had replaced the games we used to play.

I gave some thought to the time Sandy and I had been together. As hard as I tried, I could not remember how long it had been. It seemed I had met her only the day before. No matter how much time we had been together, it would not have been enough. I hoped she was safe. I hoped I would be able to insure her safety. I remember hoping I would be alive to see another day.

The sun was heading for the pacific. I was terribly thirsty, my mouth was dry, my stomach was knotted from hunger. George Benson was playing "This Masquerade" on the radio. The heat inside the car was relentless. Sweat ran in rivulets down my back. I swallowed hard, forcing bile back into my churning gut.

I waited another hour, sitting in the stifling car, watching the man who sat on the stone wall outside the condo entrance. He had been there when I arrived, he hadn't moved away yet. There would be a gun under the light tan windbreaker he wore in the heat of the afternoon.

Finally, the man who would take the next shift as guard at Marc Springer's home replaced him. The new man was shorter but broader and slightly older than the man he relieved. He wore a heavier jacket, dark blue with knitted cuffs and collar, in anticipation of the cool night air that would be coming in from the bay.

As I got out of the car my head spun from hunger and my rapidly growing fear. Quietly closing the car's door, I stood in the street, holding onto the roof of the car to keep from falling. I pulled the 9mm from under my shirt. I held it down between myself and the car, and pulled the slide back, sending a round into the chamber and cocking the hammer. The gun was heavy in my hand. I was feeling much weaker and sicker than I ever had. With the gun held at my side, I walked slowly towards the guard.

When I crossed the street the guard looked at me.

Realizing I was staggering, I pulled myself up and drew back my shoulders in an exaggerated and stiff motion. The guard, grinning and smoking another cigarette, leaned against the short stone wall surrounding the condo property. What he thought he saw was a drunk staggering down the street.

I was within six feet of the guard when he looked down and saw the automatic in my hand. Before he could drop the burning cigarette, and before his hand could get near his jacket, I leveled my gun at him and said, "I'll kill you here if you try that."

"It's you," he said. "I can't believe it's really you. You're crazy. You know that? I never figured you'd be stupid enough to come here."

"I'm hoping everyone else thought the same thing. Let's go inside. One mistake and I kill you dead." I told him to turn around. Reaching around him and inside his jacket I pulled a .357 magnum revolver from a shoulder holster and tucked it inside my beltless jeans. A slight push with the barrel of my gun and the guard walked up the five granite steps ahead of me. At the door to the building, in response to another jab of the gun, he touched numbers on the lock and the door swung open. We stepped inside, into the cool air of the building lobby.

We walked to an elevator and I said, "Push the call button for the elevator, when it gets here step in and face the back wall. Put your hands on the wall above your head. If anybody is in the elevator when the doors open let them out before you step in and don't say or do anything that might frighten me. I'm really messed up right now and it just wouldn't take much for me to pull this trigger."

He did as he was told. The elevator door opened revealing an empty car. We stepped in and I pressed number 12. Before the elevator stopped at the twelfth floor, I pulled the guard around by the collar and stood behind him, the automatic pressed into the small of his back while I held tight to the collar of his jacket.

When the doors opened I waited for a count of three. Then I pushed the guard out ahead of me, his hands still over his head. Another guard was standing outside the door to Springer's apartment. He began to pull a gun from under his suit jacket.

I had never shot anyone before I shot that man. I watched two soft nosed bullets from the 9mm hit the man's chest and open it up. He fell back, hard. Before he hit the ground the double mahogany doors swung inwards and another man, crouching low, looked out first at me, then at the other end of the hall. That gave me enough time to raise the heavy gun and fire again. My arm moved before I could think about it and my finger squeezed the trigger three times on its own. The man fell backwards, into the apartment, his head exploding as it was ripped apart by the bullets.

Pushing my human cover ahead of me, I moved quickly for the door. I pushed the man I was holding down on top of the one on the floor and picked up the gun the man had dropped. I quickly stepped over the two men and took three steps into the room. Inside the lavishly furnished condo, a thin, youngish looking man with lots of curly hair and a Tom Selleck moustache, as Suzanne Mark had described him, sat on a long, beige leather couch.

"WHAT THE HELL!" he yelled.

"Marc Springer?" I asked. "My name is Morgan Crew. I understand you've been looking for me."

FORTY-TWO - I Love It When It All Comes Together

I took Springer and the guard who had been my cover to a bedroom and through it to an outrageously big, black marble bathroom. I told the guard that if he wanted his boss, and more importantly himself, to come out of this alive, to just stay put inside. Springer nodded slightly and the man retreated meekly inside the bathroom.

I told Springer to sit on the bed and put his hands underneath him. I picked up the bedside phone and dialed Bob Sommers' direct number. Bob answered on the first ring. "By this time, you've gotten a dozen calls about a shooting at Marc Springer's place," I said. "I did the shooting. I hope I'll be able to explain later. Right now I want you to keep the cops away until I'm done here."

"No good. A couple of cars are on the way and I'm about to leave. There's a SWAT team van just pulling out right now." he said.

"Bob, I'm over the edge on this one. Springer will die the first time I see a cop. I mean it. I've got too much to lose here. Give me twenty minutes, maybe thirty at the outside. I swear, if I'm still alive I'll surrender to you. But not to any other cop in town."

Bob didn't answer but he didn't hang the phone up either.

"I've got to trust you, Bob. Just stay there and listen."

I laid the phone down on its side on the nightstand so that Bob could hear what was being said.

"Mr. Springer," I began. I had to pause and take a deep breath to try to keep my voice from quaking. My heart was pounding too fast. The room was spinning around me. I had to stay conscious and in control.

"I'm sorry to have burst in like this, Mr. Springer, but you left me no choice. I had a feeling you wouldn't receive me very well if I had called first for an appointment."

"I don't know what you're talking about and I don't know who the hell you are. If the police can hear me," he said towards the phone on the night stand, raising his voice, "Get the hell over here now and get this maniac before he kills somebody else!"

I pulled a chair away from the wall and sat a few feet in front of Springer. I leaned back and massaged the back of my stiff neck. "I have a very special friend," I said. "A person who has put herself in harm's way, trying to help her sister and a young man. I want to buy her protection."

A wondering look of curiosity flashed across his face. He said, now in a softer, calmer voice, "I still don't know what the hell you're talking about."

"O.K., we'll start at the beginning"

"Wait a minute. Hang up that phone first. Anything I say is not for the cops."

I stood, and picking up the phone I said, "Sorry, Bob. But I need to protect Sandy." I eased the phone onto its cradle without waiting for Bob to answer. I didn't want to give him an opportunity to say anything to try to dissuade me from doing what I had to do.

"Now, you correct me if I'm wrong," I said as sarcastically as I could manage, sitting in the chair again. "I don't think I'm that far off base, however. Parnell Rigsby. Let's start there.

"The hundred million he stole wasn't enough for him.

He started a drug smuggling operation. Maybe one of the biggest operations this Country has ever seen. After all, Parnell never did anything in a small way. And he had lots of juice and protection to keep the operation going, all the way into Washington, D.C. probably.

"Yes, there has to be hundreds of people on his payroll to run this operation. I mean, there's shipping and handling, lab people to refine and cut the stuff, distributors, mules, soldiers, the whole ten yards. Do I have the terminology right? All I know is what I see on TV.

"And of course, there's you here in San Marcos to oversee this particular import point. Maybe just one of dozens of import points, but certainly not the smallest."

Springer smiled when I said this. Pride cometh before a fall and it also told me I was on the right track.

"It was a beautiful operation, too. San Marcos is such a small, isolated place. Away from the mainstream, the last place the Feds might expect a major import - processing plant to be. My guess is Mr. Rigsby was looking for just such a spot, safe and clean. But how the hell could he have ever found it? I mean, he's an East Coast boy, probably never been to sunny California.

"But that leads us back to how this operation is set up. Rigsby needed a smart money man, a financial expert to handle the money, launder it clean. And that ain't you, sonny boy. You just aren't smart enough in that area. You're a boss maybe, but little more than an enforcer. That's where Frederick Mark enters. Smart man with money. Made a fortune. Mainly by screwing little old ladies out of their last dime. Just the kind of fellow to be admired by someone like Parnell Rigsby.

"Freddie had found San Marcos years ago and built that demented Disneyland of his he called home. He quickly discovered what a fine and dandy place this would be for Rigsby's operations. You were brought in from the East coast and probably through Mark, you found George Montgomery who was hurting for cash. Buying him, you had your labs set up in a couple of his North Harbor slums.

"What a perfect place. All the slime bags necessary to run your labs would blend in perfectly with their surroundings up there in North Harbor. Save for the two suits in the Caddy, that is. Bad mistake there. Too flashy, out of place, they stood out like a tuxedo at the beach. That's what first got my curiosity up about what was happening at North Harbor. Suits wouldn't be used solely as bagmen to collect numbers and vice profits. There are too many cheap hoods in North Harbor who could do that work. They were high salary soldiers, enforces, managers.

"Anyway, as I was saying. Processing the stuff and shipping it north and south was easy enough. Getting it into San Marcos presented another problem. But you solved that one quickly, too. Mr. Rigsby must have been proud of you. I hope you got a nice fat Christmas bonus.

"Tony Morelli was a wild kid, always looking for excitement and good times. Making a few hundred bucks by taking his father's boat out eight or nine miles off shore a couple of times a month and bringing back cocaine or whatever else was being moved in seemed easy enough to him. I mean, who would take special notice of another fishing boat leaving the harbor and coming back? He probably did it at night so his father and brother wouldn't find out. And I guess having a virtual supermarket of drugs around, being as wild as he was, he decided to try some and was hooked quickly.

"Now you had him working not for money but for drugs. As you cut back on the amount of drugs you paid him for each shipment, he had to start buying the stuff from you as well as work for you. Quite a deal you had going. He stole everything his old man ever had and drove him out of business just to get the drugs he needed.

"Franco had to start working for you, too, I imagine. He would probably have done anything to try and help his kid. Spoiled him rotten, I'm told. And having to help him like that probably drove Franco crazy. He had to all but give up his fishing business to be where you wanted him to be, when you wanted him to be there. They wound up living in one of the hovels you leased from Montgomery. You used it as a processing lab and Franco was probably paying you an arm and a leg to live there, too.

"But, you had a smooth operation that might have gone on for years. Except that people in your line of work aren't always the nicest folks to be found. Freddy Mark had his little quirks. He liked to bring whores home. His other little quirk was that no amount of money, no amount of things, no amount of power, was ever enough for him. When he found an opportunity to blackmail somebody out of a few thousand, like he really needed it, he jumped at the chance. Now it's going to get a little complicated here, Marc my boy. So pay attention.

"Freddie made the mistake of using as the subject of his little blackmail scheme, the sister of one of Tony Morelli's wet dreams. When young Tony saw how it was hurting the older sister, the girl of his dreams, he flew off the handle in a murderous rage. He took the rifle from his father's boat and shot Freddy Mark, using the explosive bullets I'd seen his father use on sharks a few times. Nasty damn things, made to explode inside the shark's head to make sure it's dead.

"Now, as you probably know, Tony Morelli isn't exactly the smartest guy downtown on a rainy Tuesday night. He got so pissed off because the woman he was chasing was hurt by Freddie, knowing that you and Freddy worked together, that he told you to stuff it, he wasn't going to work for you anymore. I mean, leaving the corporation without even two weeks' notice? You'd have no part in that. So you sent the two suits to take care of Tony and appropriate the Santa Maria. Anybody could steer her out and back, but nobody screws with the Rigsby organization, right?

"The suits came to the house in North Harbor, with shotguns, and wasted Franco and Jeremy. Before they could kill Tony, however, he headed for the back door. One of the suits shot at him with a 9mm, which is now in safe keeping by the way. The bullet hit the rotten wood of the door frame. I found it and it, too, is in safe keeping. The gun pointed at you is the 9mm from the other suit by the way.

"Tony wanted to get the sister back to his wet dream girlfriend, and using what little brains he had left after frying them on your drugs, he thought that Fred's wife had her. He went to the Mark Estate and saw the guards I had placed there to protect Suzanne Mark, so he tried to kill her and maybe then he could get the girl out of the house. I know it sounds crazy, but, like I said, Tony isn't any kind of genius. He didn't know the girl had gotten out of the house on her own the day Mark was killed and gotten back to her sister. Tony had been hiding out since killing Freddie and hadn't kept up on what was happening.

"He tried once to kill Suzanne Mark but he was too far away and missed. I haven't figured out what he planned on doing after killing her. My brain obviously doesn't work like his. You've been hunting Tony, and the girl, ever since. I suppose you thought, find one, you find them both. Too bad though. I understand the girl and her sister are somewhere safe. I don't think you've found Tony yet. Have you?"

I paused, seeing Springer smile a vicious smile.

"Just between you and me," Springer said. "Since you ain't gonna walk out of here alive anyway, he's about ten miles out . . . Face down, and in a couple dozen pieces stuffed into a half dozen lobster traps," he said, pointing out towards the ocean.

"That's too bad. He was bound to die young. But if

you hadn't killed the father and Jeremy, all this could have been avoided. But anyway, now we come to the part that's important to me. The subject of Tony's wet dream is important to me. She is somewhere with her sister, who you know as Angel. She's trying to protect her. I don't know if you want them dead or why. Again, there is a definite difference in brain operation between us. If you do want them dead, I want to make it profitable for you to leave them alone."

"Why would I want them dead?" he asked, smiling a sick, reptilian grin.

"Tony's obviously talked to them. They know about your operation. You think they may be angry and want some semblance of revenge. And as long as they are alive they might talk to someone else, like the police. Here's my offer. I will give you one million dollars in cash to leave them alone."

"You got that kind of money?" he asked incredulously.

"Yes."

He thought for a moment but I could see the wheels of greed spinning inside him, through eyes that were turning dollar bill green.

"You got a million . . . You must have two million. Up the ante."

"O.K. Two million. Do we have a deal?"

"If I take it, how you gonna know I won't kill them anyway and laugh all the way to the God damn bank?"

"Because I know about your operation and now my attorneys also know. It's all in writing and they are holding it. If anything happens to her, the police will know. As long as she lives, the police won't know."

"Suppose I kill you, too?"

"Right this second that looks unlikely," I said as I waved the gun at him. "However, sometime in the future you may try to kill me if you think that will gain you anything. But you'd also have to kill sixty, maybe seventy people in my attorney's firm, just to make sure no one is left to know. Are you up to that?"

"What about the cops who are probably waiting outside right now?" he asked.

"If we make a deal, we convince them I'm crazy. Hell, half the town believes that now anyway. I broke in here making wild accusations and I killed two business associates of yours. I may stand trial or I might be able to make a psychiatrist believe I really am sick. If I stand trial I can afford the best attorneys in the world. In any case, your operation is safe so long as Sandy D'Angelo and her sister remain alive and well."

"How do I get the two million bucks?" he asked.

"Three months from now, when all this cools down a little, two million dollars will be wire transferred to any overseas bank you name. If it isn't transferred, I've broken the deal and you can do whatever you want. Pick up where you left off. Kill the girl and me. She will be in hiding, afraid of you, but I'm certain with your connections you will eventually be able to find her. She won't say anything to anyone between now and then. She's too scared of you and all she wants to do is hide and protect her sister.

"After getting the money, if Sandy D'Angelo dies, if she is accidentally killed in an auto accident, if she falls and breaks her leg, if she passes away for any reason except extreme old age, your whole operation and the evidence of murder I hold goes to the FBI and the DEA."

Marc Springer's face began to crack into one of his snake-like smiles. He pulled his hands from under him, leaned forward on the edge of the bed, and then pushed himself to his feet lowly. I raised the heavy gun.

Then Springer said, "Mr. Morgan Crew. You got yourself a God damn deal." He held his hand out to shake on the deal. I ignored it.

FORTY-THREE – And The Shot Rang Out

I pulled the clip out of the automatic, jacked the round out of the chamber, and handed the empty gun into Springer's hand butt first. Springer wanted to let his man out of the bathroom where he waited.

"Mr. Springer," I said. "I may be tired and scared, but I'm not stupid. I still have your man's gun, and it's loaded, unlike the one I just gave you. Your guy stays where he is for the time being. You carry the unloaded gun, I carry the loaded one. Do anything but what we agreed to and I'll shoot you dead.

"You may now walk me outside, Mr. Springer," I said. "And you may hand me over to the proper authorities, as they used to say in the movies. Make yourself a hero. Tell them you captured the crazy bastard all by yourself, that you overpowered me. Cooperate fully with the police; a great many of whom I gather are on your extensive payroll anyway. Get your name in the newspapers. Be famous. You're about to become very rich."

We walked out into the hallway, stepping over the bodies lying at the door. I had pulled off my plan to save Sandy. I had proven to myself that I was not stupid, that despite everything, I had been able to figure out the details that tied all the murders together.

I was feeling sick. My head was spinning and I felt I might pass out before getting to the street. We had reached the middle of the hallway and I heard someone telling me to push the call button for the elevator, which I must have done, but can't remember doing. We waited. I turned and felt dizzy at the sudden movement.

"Hey," Springer said. "You ok or what?"

I said something to him although I don't know what I said. My sight was foggy, and things around me were only half there. Springer slapped me on the shoulder playfully, almost knocking me to the floor. He was giggling like a child at the way the deal had worked out.

I tried to concentrate on what I had to do, on what I would say to the police and to the judge. What the hell, the most I would get was a few years in prison. At least I hoped so. My lawyers would cut a deal for me. In prison or out, what was life without Sandy D'Angelo? At least she would be safe. But I had pulled it off, and I was still alive, and Sandy would stay alive, and Springer would wake up richer, greedy and stupid the next day.

The elevator door opened and we stepped in. The ride down was quick, the elevator purring away like a contented kitten. The floor numbers flashed across the board over the door. It slowed, the door opened, and we stepped out into the entryway lobby.

Outside, through the glass walls and doors of the lobby, in the dusty half daylight of early evening, we could see the street crowded with police cars, all with flashing red and blue lights. Barricades of the cars were semi circled in front of the building sheltering uniformed and plain-clothes cops. Pistols, rifles, and shotguns by the score all pointed at the door.

"I'd better put my hands over my head," I suggested.

"Yeah, good idea. And stay in front of me in case any of them pigs has ideas about taking both of us out."

I pushed open one of the doors and we stepped out into the still warm air of the late afternoon. The fresh air was once again a stimulant. The antiseptically clean air inside the building was too cold, too barren, and too artificial. The hint of sea salt in the air caused my head to clear a little and the fog in my eyes thinned enough for me to see almost clearly.

Springer shouted from behind me, the empty 9mm jammed into the small of my back, "I got him! It's O.K.! I got the gun away from him!   Must be some maniac or something!   Killed a couple friends of mine upstairs!   I wrestled the gun away from him! It's O.K.! Don't shoot!"

We started down the short walk to the steps that lead to the street. He stopped me at the top of the steps before the sidewalk. I glanced over my shoulder. Springer was sweating profusely, smiling nervously, and glancing rapidly around at the army of cops surrounding us. He wiped his hand across his forehead. I was not sure Springer knew what to do next, as we stood on the steps, waiting.

He pushed me slightly, towards the steps. I started down slowly, finding it still hard to feel my feet under me and hold my balance with my arms stretched above me. I was on the last of the four steps and about to step down onto the sidewalk. Springer was one step behind me, holding on tight to my shirt, when the shot rang out and Marc Springer's head exploded.

Although I wanted to move, to get away from the headless body, still standing and holding onto my shirt, I found my own body unable to move, even though I was telling myself to run. I heard a familiar voice screaming over a loud speaker, "Get down! Morgan! Get down!" I looked around and saw Bob Sommers running towards me, waiving a hand at me.

Everyone but Bob was looking down the street to my left, into the shade of some tall, old oak trees. I turned in the same direction the police were looking. I saw him a second after the police started firing. I yelled, "NO! NO! NO!

DON'T SHOOT HIM!", but it was too late. It sounded like a hundred guns were firing all at the same time. The noise was deafening and shook everything around me.

Old Cap'n Nick was hit too many times to count. The shark rifle that had once been part of the Santa Maria, the rifle he had just used to kill Marc Springer, and the same rifle Tony Morelli used to kill Frederick Mark and to try to kill Suzanne Mark, flew from his hands and spun slowly in the air above his head before it landed hard on the concrete. The wooden stock broke, the bolt twisted from the gun and bounced across the sidewalk.

The firing ended with the bloody hulk of Cap'n Nick lying across a hedge of rhododendrons, his wooden peg leg splintered. I stood frozen, with my hands still raised for what felt like an eternity. It all happened in a few seconds but it seemed like it took a lifetime.

Another two shots rang out, followed by a quick series of blasts, but I didn't see where any of them came from. The first hit me hard on the right side, under my still upraised arm. I felt myself spinning around into a dark, soft ocean of unconsciousness as I fell across Springer's blood soaked body. The second shot hit me in the back, at my left shoulder, as I fell. I found out later that Bob Sommers had fired the following rounds at the uniformed police officer who had shot me. The cop had been standing behind one of the police cars in the street. Bob filled the man's chest with seven bullets.

FORTY-FOUR – I'll Bet You My Last Million

Bob Sommers had threatened that he would come down on me like a ton of bricks, and he kept his promise very well. There were so many charges filed against me by the time I woke up in the hospital the next day, that I would have needed a second room in the hospital just to store all the paper work. I didn't take it personally, however. Bob was just doing his job, and doing it very well.

But my lawyers were good, better than good actually, and in the end all I got was an Attempted Obstruction of Justice charge and five weeks in a private hospital room, under guard, to which I moved as soon as I could be moved. And I was reprimanded by the court and placed on one year's probation. The bullets, fired by a police officer who had been on Marc Springer's payroll for years, did a lot of damage. But the doctors were as good as my attorneys, and I wound up with only two small scars as a remembrance of all that happened.

Bob Sommers proved that he was not on Marc Springer's payroll. He called in the California State Attorney General's Office to head the internal investigation of the San Marcos Police Department. The FBI and DEA massed several dozen agents each in my little town, doing their own thing and not making many friends locally while doing it.

Although the doctor's objected vehemently, and the

314

police and District Attorney did all they could to stop me, I was wheeled from the hospital and followed by four police officers, to Cap'n Nick's funeral. There was a mass in the morning; the small Catholic Church in North Harbor was packed with people.

Every commercial fisherman calling San Marcos home was there that cold, rainy Thursday morning. Every shop in Harborside was closed that day so that every owner and employee could squeeze into the wooden pews. Old men who shared a colorful and perhaps even a criminal past with Cap'n Nick flew in from around the Country to attend and honor the man.

The several hundred people who had squeezed into the church were joined by a hundred more at the cemetery. As they left the cars, and as I was carried across the wet grass in my wheelchair, the rain stopped suddenly, the wind died instantly, and the charcoal clouds above opened. Warming sun struck San Marcos as we watched the Cap'n being lowered into the open grave. The people filtered away. I was escorted back to my guarded hospital room. Life went on, but it would never be the same.

About three months after Cap'n Nick's funeral, in the middle of my trial and the arrests that seemed for a time destined to go on forever and to encompass everyone in San Marcos, my childhood friend, Bill Keilly, City Commissioner of Police, shot himself in the head in broad daylight, outside City Hall.

Bob Sommers was waiting for him at his office that morning with an arrest warrant. Bob was going to serve it himself in order to keep the newspapers out of it for a while. Someone on the police department, another one of Marc Springer's crooked cops, must have warned Bill.

I was later told that Bill had walked around outside the courthouse that morning for a long time rather than going right into his office. He said hello to people he knew, shaking their hands and slapping their shoulders jovially. He kissed babies like he was running for re-election. Then he started up the steps, turned on the third of the six marble steps, and breathed in deeply the fresh, salty air coming in from the bay. The sun was hot that morning, in a clear, deep blue, cloudless sky. Some sea birds circled overhead, cawing loudly on the soft breath of a breeze that blew in from the ocean.

He took the little .25 semi-auto he was so proud of out of his pocket, the one he had held on me that night on the golf course near Indian Falls. He drew it slowly into his mouth, smiled, and pulled the trigger in front of a handful of citizens who had voted for him over the many years that he had served the city.

Between the Attorney General and the FBI, a total of thirteen people, all wealthy and formerly upstanding San Marcos citizens, most of them Country Club Members, and eleven police officers were hauled before a Federal Grand Jury and indicted. Three full drug labs were raided, close to a million dollars of drugs seized, and dozens more arrests were made in North Harbor.

With Marc Springer gone, Frederick Mark gone, I began to feel comfortable that Sandy might be safe. Wherever she was.

Poor George Montgomery was found in a drunken stupor in a fifteen-dollar a day flophouse in South Los Angeles. He came home voluntarily and managed to work out a plea bargain of RICO charges of knowingly profiting from a criminal conspiracy. He paid a hefty fine, lost a few of his slums in North Harbor to the DEA, and went on with life.

Hector Morales left the Krueger home one afternoon to get some beer and never came back. Barbara Krueger went so far as to ask me to find him. I told her she was better off without him, which upset her, but a week later Barbara filed for divorce anyway.

Mitch Krueger was arrested for the murder of Dean Crosslund. I offered the services of Harper, Harper, Jascro and Nettles to my friend. Mitch refused, bluntly and angrily. He wrote a note to me from his jail cell. It was full of bitterness, resentment, rage, hatred, and fury at me for causing everything that had happened to him and his family. The words rambled and his handwriting deteriorated as the seven-page diatribe went on.

Mitch finally stood trial and received a twenty-five year sentence. He spent less than three months in prison when he was found huddled behind some washing machines in the prison laundry, his arms slashed in an unsuccessful and crude attempt to commit suicide. He was rambling and frothing at the mouth. Mitch was transferred to a State institution for the criminally insane, where he remains to this day.

Ten months into probation, I received a hand written letter from Suzanne Mark which she signed Suzanne Bloome. It was postmarked Athens, Greece. I could hear how happy she was. She thanked me again for what I had done and hoped that we would meet again. I hoped I would see her again, also. Suzanne, I was convinced, may very well be one of the last of a dying breed of genteel, Old World, refined ladies. I would not meet a lady like her again.

My year on probation was spent at home, watching the bay from the back deck and recouping my strength. San Marcos quickly returned to what she should be, a somewhat sleepy little town. Yet it was still growing too fast for its own good, and remained sharply divided between the rich in the hills and the poor below.

I had my beloved MGB back. The local police had impounded it and said it was evidence and it would be years before I would get it back. Bob Sommers asked what evidence it was supposed to be, exactly, and when no one could answer I got the car back. While having the interior replaced, I also had a fresh coat of paint sprayed on the body and, what the heck, while it was in the shop anyway, I had the engine overhauled.

It was at a little party that I had given to celebrate my final month on probation. I had invited a few friends who were good enough friends not to speak of what had happened. Bob was there, over-working the champagne bar. I made the bet with him after I thought Bob had enough booze in him to loosen up his wallet a little.

We were standing on the back deck of the house. A few of the guests stood around with drinks in their hands, talking of little meaningless things, as I carefully watched over the chicken that I was bar-b-queing, trying to keep the smoke down to a minimum.

"Come on, Morgan. Give it up," Bob said, just a little bit unsteady on his feet as he looked over the edge of the wooden rail, down the side of the hill. "You've been convicted of a felony. I made sure of that. You screw up again and they will throw you in prison, no matter how many lawyers you got. Hell, you can't even vote no more."

"I'll bet you my last million that I'm not a convicted felon," I bragged loudly.

"Knowing you and that wolf pack of relatives you've got, I wouldn't want to bet even on a sure thing. Not even the lousy buck and a half I can just about afford to lose," he said.

I walked into the house, and came back with an envelope in my hand. I gave it to Bob and went back to my chicken, which by that time was burnt, but still barely edible. Bob pulled the single sheet of paper from the open envelope. It had the seal of the Governor on it, and in a few short paragraphs granted me a full pardon from all crimes I had committed and/or been convicted of, effective the day after my probation ended.

Some weeks later, I sat alone on the back deck of my

house, in the beautiful San Marcos sunshine, enjoying the warm afternoon and sipping at a bottle of Pepsi. The beer was all gone but I wouldn't need to restock the fridge.

It was the last day of my probation. On the table next to me were a first class airplane ticket to Chicago and a scrap of paper with Sandy's mother's address on it.

THE END

www.ingramcontent.com/pod-product-compliance
Lightning Source LLC
Chambersburg PA
CBHW020907200626
46814CB00001BA/217